D0403146

Midnight in Berlin

Also by James MacManus

Ocean Devil

The Language of the Sea

Black Venus

Sleep in Peace Tonight

MIDNIGHT *in* BERLIN

James MacManus

Thomas Dunne Books
St. Martin's Press New York

This is a work of fiction. All of the characters, organizations, and events portrayed in this novel are either products of the author's imagination or are used fictitiously.

THOMAS DUNNE BOOKS.
An imprint of St. Martin's Press.

www.thomasdunnebooks.com
www.stmartins.com

Library of Congress Cataloging-in-Publication Data

Names: MacManus, James, author.
Title: Midnight in Berlin : a novel / James MacManus.
Description: First edition. | New York : Thomas Dunne Books/St. Martin's Press, 2016.
Identifiers: LCCN 2015045464 | ISBN 9781250079404 (hardcover) | ISBN 9781466892132 (e-book)
Subjects: LCSH: World War, 1939–1945—Germany—Fiction. | Man-woman relationships—Fiction. | BISAC: FICTION / Historical. | FICTION / Literary. | GSAFD: Historical fiction. | War stories. | Love stories.
Classification: LCC PR6113.A267 M53 2016 | DDC 823/.92—dc23
LC record available at http://lccn.loc.gov/2015045464

First published in the United Kingdom by Duckworth Overlook

First U.S. Edition: April 2016

10 9 8 7 6 5 4 3 2 1

Dedicated to the memory of
Colonel Noel Mason MacFarlane
British military attaché, Berlin, 1938–39

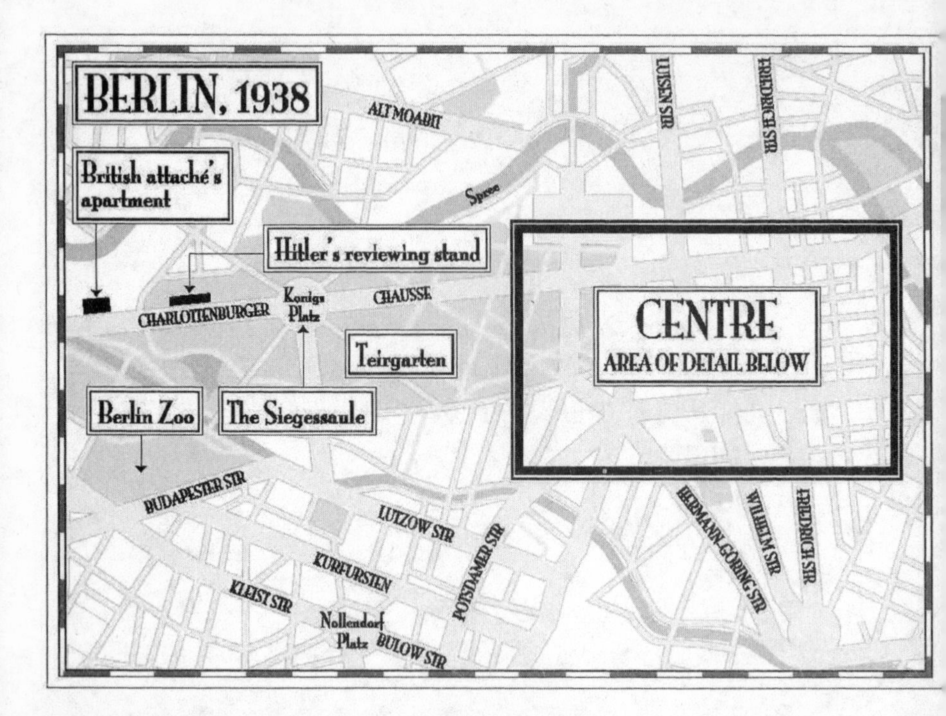
BERLIN, 1938
ALT MOABIT
LUISEN STR
FRIEDRICH STR
British attaché's apartment
Spree
Hitler's reviewing stand
Konigs Platz
CHAUSSE
CHARLOTTENBURGER
CENTRE
AREA OF DETAIL BELOW
Teirgarten
Berlin Zoo
The Siegessaule
BUDAPESTER STR
LUTZOW STR
POTSDAMER STR
HERMANN-GÖRING STR
WILHELM STR
FRIEDRICH STR
KURFURSTEN
KLEIST STR
Nollendorf Platz
BULOW STR

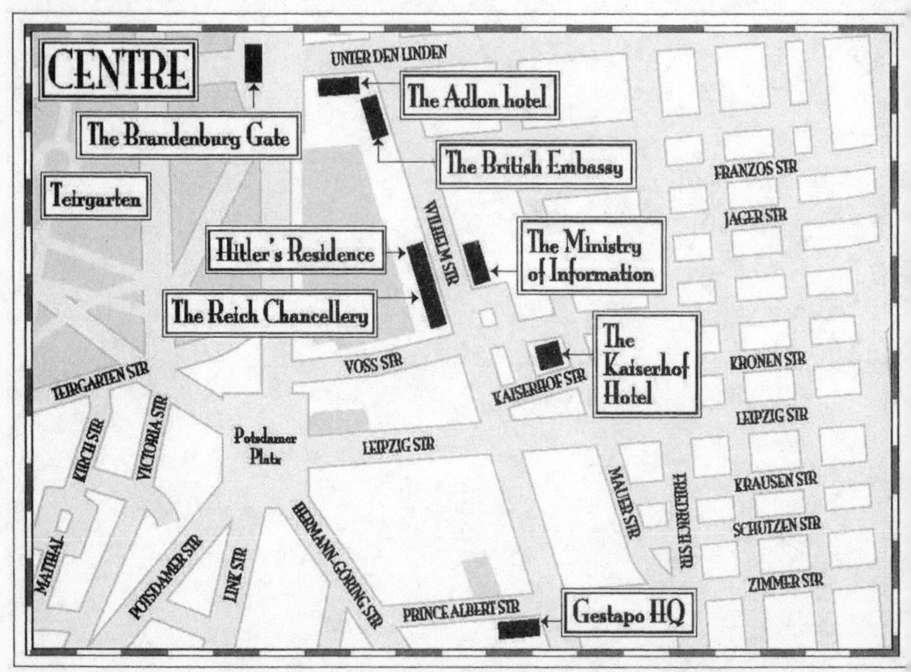
CENTRE
UNTER DEN LINDEN
The Adlon hotel
The Brandenburg Gate
The British Embassy
FRANZOS STR
Teirgarten
JAGER STR
WILHELM STR
Hitler's Residence
The Ministry of Information
The Reich Chancellery
The Kaiserhof Hotel
VOSS STR
KRONEN STR
TEIRGARTEN STR
KAISERHOF STR
LEIPZIG STR
Potsdamer Platz
LEIPZIG STR
KIRCH STR
VICTORIA STR
MAUER STR
FRIEDRICH STR
KRAUSEN STR
HERMANN-GÖRING STR
SCHUTZEN STR
MATTHAI
POTSDAMER STR
LINK STR
ZIMMER STR
PRINCE ALBERT STR
Gestapo HQ

Midnight in Berlin

Prologue

She reached across the table and placed a hand on his arm. Frown lines creased her forehead. The dark eyes looked at him imploringly. She was breathing heavily – hyperventilating, thought Macrae. He saw the swell of her breast against the red dress. She's going to faint, he thought. He looked around for a waitress.

"Look at me," she whispered.

He looked at her properly for the first time, swirling the dregs of brandy in the tulip-shaped glass, badly wanting another one. Her eyes were dark and deep beneath long lashes heavy with mascara. Her small oval face, pale and powdered, looked fragile and pretty, like a fine china doll. Claret-red lipstick traced a perfect bow over her mouth. There was a beauty spot on one cheek and faint beads of perspiration along her upper lip.

She would have looked childish but for the long ringlets of dark hair that dropped to her shoulders. Her sleeveless dress rose from ankle to neck. It was tight, designed to emphasise her figure, and he could see the faint rise in the fabric made by her nipples. The image of a china doll dissolved, to be replaced by that of an actress. That's what she was, he thought, a beautiful actress, with the powdered face and imploring eyes of a silent-movie heroine.

"I'm not asking much, just news of my brother."

"Joseph Sternschein?" he said.

"Yes. I'd give anything to know that he is at least alive." She shifted slightly in her chair, taking her hand from his arm, sitting up, her shoulders back. "Anything," she said again.

He shook his head, finished his brandy and got to his feet.

"If I asked, they would want to know why. The Gestapo would be curious. I am a diplomat, after all."

"And he's just a kid in one of their camps, right? Just another number on a file?"

He sighed and looked across the room at the door. "We have to deal with these people every day; it's not nice and it's not easy."

"And you don't want to upset them – is that it?"

Her eyes had lost their soft appeal. She was angry. "You know, I hear things back there . . . She jerked her head towards the fanlight door.

"What sort of things?"

"You'd be surprised what some very important people tell me. It's all part of the power thing, isn't it? Men want to impress me with their little secrets."

"I must go," he said. "I don't know what you're doing here, but . . ."

She reached across and took his arm, this time gripping it tightly. She stabbed her forefinger at the table, the varnished nail beating out an urgent tattoo. "I've told you what I'm doing here. I'm doing it with some of the most powerful men in this country. I'm good at it. They like me. And I don't have any choice – do you understand?"

She got up and walked back to the bar. Almost immediately, a man sat beside her.

I

The train arrived at Berlin's Anhalter Station shortly before noon, hissing a cloud of steam into the freezing air. They had left Vienna only a few hours earlier on a sunlit winter morning. Looking back, they could see from their carriage window the tower of St Stephen's Cathedral receding over the rooftops of a city that had lost, but not forgotten, the imperial splendour of an empire that had once ruled eastern Europe.

Berlin that Sunday morning was cold and empty, a monochrome city whose spires and steeples were lost in low cloud that vented occasional flurries of snow onto silent streets. Windows were shuttered as if those inside could not bear to look on such a desolate scene. Even the swastika bunting strung from lampposts along the route of a recent parade seemed about to wither and fall.

The embassy car crossed the River Spree before driving through the Brandenburg Gate and west along Charlottenburger Chaussee. They passed the gilded Victory Column that celebrated the Prussian triumph over France in 1871 and minutes later reached their destination – a four-storey house on a side street just off the avenue.

The driver opened the front door and began to unload the luggage. Colonel Macrae got out and held the door of the car for his wife. She did not acknowledge the courtesy and walked into the house, her pale, powdered face set in a frown. She had accepted the sudden upheaval as the lot of a diplomat's wife. This was to be their new home, and he watched as she marched up the stairs to begin a tour of inspection. He had told her only six days ago that he had been posted to Berlin and was expected to be at his desk in the embassy the following week. Surely she could follow on later, she had asked, say goodbye properly to their friends in Austria, have one last dinner party at the old house?

No. The orders from the War Office were specific: the military attaché and his wife were to be in their new residence within the week. The duties of both would start immediately, she to carry on the usual round of entertaining and he to continue the excellent work of his predecessor. Colonel Eveleigh Watson's heart attack had shocked the embassy and drawn unusual tributes from senior German officers.

Macrae went to the bottom of the stairs and raised his voice. "We have a lunch, dear – you remember, I told you?" He knew she would be somewhere on the upper floors pulling back bed covers, opening the curtains, turning on taps, running a finger over the furniture to check for dust. In fact, the house was spotless and the kitchen equipped with that most modern of conveniences, a refrigerator, which had been well stocked with perishable provisions.

There was no reply. He walked up the broad staircase to the second floor. A door on the landing gave onto a large L-shaped drawing room. Three sofas were placed around a fireplace. A large mirror stood above the mantel. The floor was polished wood. At one end, French windows and a small balcony overlooked the avenue.

He opened the windows and stepped out. Much of the Tiergarten park was heavily wooded, but on this stretch of the road the trees had been felled to make way for a row of houses, a police station and a kindergarten. To his right, he could see the Siegessäule, the Victory Column they had passed, a grandiose martial memorial rising 220 feet into the air.

He had read in a guidebook that the Nazis had somehow added thirty feet to the column when they moved it, stone by stone, from its original position in front of the Reichstag parliament building half a mile away. They said it was done to create space for Albert Speer's plans for the new Berlin.

A voice floated down, saying something about lunch. He looked at his watch. It was twelve forty-five. They were due at the ambassador's residence in a neighbouring suburb at 1 p.m. for what had been described as a small welcome lunch. They would be late.

"I'll wait in the hall," he said loudly, and walked downstairs.

By the front door he caught his reflection in the gilded hall mirror: a rakish hat pulled down over an angular face whose long nose pointed over thin lips to a jutting chin. At school they had called him Nosey, but he was tall for his age and a handy forward in the rugger first XV. Nobody had ever tried to bully him. He pulled the belt of his overcoat tight and looked at his watch. He had been told that the ambassador disapproved of guests arriving late, especially if they were on his staff.

Sir Nevile Henderson was well known on the diplomatic circuit in Berlin. He was always elegantly dressed in the old-fashioned style of an Edwardian gentleman: wing-tip collar, dark tie, waistcoat and watch chain. His one concession to colour was the red carnation he invariably wore in his button-hole. He was unmarried and often invited a middle-aged lady on his staff, Daisy Wellesley, to act as his hostess. This somewhat unusual arrangement was the subject of quite unfounded gossip. It was also said, quite truthfully as it happened, that Sir Nevile provided only fine German wines, whether at lunch or dinner, for fear that French vintages might upset his official guests.

On this Sunday, Noel and Primrose Macrae were offered a light white Bavarian wine while standing around a log fire at the far end of the dining room. The table had been laid for seven, Macrae noticed. There were three other guests: the political attaché, David Buckland, and his wife Amanda, and a stout, middle-aged man with the veined nose of an habitual drinker, who clearly did not wish to be there.

He was introduced as Roger Halliday, "a senior member of the team". He certainly did not dress like a diplomat. His clothes looked as if they had been acquired at a flea market and flung on in the dark. The shirt collar was frayed, the cuffs protruded from an old hunting jacket that had lost its buttons. The jacket had deep baggy pockets, presumably once used for stowing the odd game bird. His hair was a mop of uncombed white, curling in lank waves over his collar. He looked like a poacher, thought Macrae. He guessed he was a member of the Secret Intelligence Service.

Macrae watched as his wife thawed out under the charm of the ambassador and the effect of the wine. Her face, which had been set in a frosty mask since they left Vienna, had relaxed.

Sir Nevile said he was terribly sorry about the abrupt move, which must have been very awkward. He hoped their new home had been made as welcoming as possible. Had they, by any chance, noticed the champagne in the fridge?

Primrose said she had not, but thanked him for being so generous and thoughtful. Yes, she said, the move had been a bit of a struggle. They had not really had time to say goodbye properly to their friends, but when His Majesty's Government calls . . .

She gave a tinkling laugh.

The ambassador smiled and gestured to the table, where plates of soup had been served. He tucked a napkin into his shirt collar and turned to Macrae.

"How long were you in Vienna, Colonel?" he asked.

"Three years, Sir Nevile," said Macrae. The ambassador liked his title to be used, even by his own staff.

"Good listening post, Austria," said the ambassador.

"Indeed, one probably learns more about what the German High Command is thinking in Vienna than here in Berlin."

Sir Nevile found the remark irritating. The British ambassador in Berlin did not need his new military attaché to tell him what was in the mind of the German High Command.

"Really," he said drily.

"German generals spend a lot of time there on military cooperation meetings, holidays, socialising, that sort of thing; they talk more freely there, in a way they can't here."

"So perhaps you would enlighten us and tell us what the High Command is thinking?"

Daisy Wellesley glanced at the ambassador. She knew that tone all too well. The lunch had taken a wrong turn. Other guests had fallen silent. This was not the cosy Sunday lunch she had been told to arrange for the new arrivals. The ambassador leant back. His sarcasm was as evident as his instant dislike of the new military attaché.

Macrae slowly raised a spoon of soup to his mouth and wiped his lips with the napkin. He looked at the ambassador, noting the club tie and the carnation, fresh that morning. All the man needed was a monocle to become the cartoon caricature of an English gentleman that featured in satirical continental magazines. I have three years working with this man, he thought. Dear God.

"The German army does not want war," he said.

"And who said there is going to be a war?" said the ambassador, allowing himself a slight smile.

"I thought British policy was predicated on the belief that we are dealing with a highly aggressive, militaristic regime and that we must use diplomacy to prevent German overreach? Which is the diplomatic term for war, I think."

"This is frightfully dull," interrupted Miss Wellesley. "Can't you men save this boring talk for the office? I want to tell Primrose about the new winter coat in Wertheim's. Do you know that department store, dear? It is absolutely wonderful. Bigger than Harrods. The weather is icy here and I am sure you are going to need a new coat, aren't you?"

The guests gratefully turned to the one subject on which everyone was happy to express an opinion, Berlin's long and bitter winters.

"We're on the central European plateau and there is not so much as a hill between us and Moscow," said David Buckland. "Frankfurt has the Main river and Hamburg the sea to keep them warm, but here we just have to buy ourselves new winter coats."

Macrae looked at the political attaché. He hadn't said a word until then and was obviously hoping to be helpful. He was young, probably late twenties, and almost certainly with a background at Eton and Balliol College, Oxford, but a possible ally nonetheless.

Daisy Wellesley guided the conversation from the weather to the latest rumour that Marlene Dietrich had been offered a huge sum to return from California to make another film in the Berlin studios. She had apparently agreed on condition that she bring with her a fellow exile, the director Josef von Sternberg.

"That put an end to it, I'm told," said Miss Wellesley.

"Why?" asked Primrose.

"Sternberg is Jewish," said Daisy Wellesley, regretting that she had mentioned the story. "Anyone for coffee?"

Sir Nevile suggested that he and Macrae leave the other guests and take coffee in his study. The two men settled before an unlit fire in a book-lined room.

Macrae declined the offer of a brandy but accepted a slim cigar. He knew Primrose would be keen to get back to the house and start unpacking. There were fires to be lit, clothes to be aired and books to be placed on shelves. Their new home was waiting for them and he was about to be given a lecture by his ambassador.

"I think I will have that brandy after all," Macrae said.

Sir Nevile looked pleased and poured a generous measure. He lit his cigar, puffed and leant back in the armchair.

"The German problem is not easy," he said.

"I could not agree more," said Macrae, glancing discreetly at his watch. Agree with everything the ambassador says and he could be out of there in twenty minutes. By then Primrose would have been bored to distraction by talk of new winter coats in Wertheim's department store.

"But I believe that we are on the right track," said the ambassador.

It was a question rather than a statement. The ambassador knew little about the new man or his views on official policy.

"That's good news," said Macrae.

Sir Nevile looked at his military attaché through cigar smoke, searching for a hint of irony in the remark.

"Herr Hitler is ill-educated, indeed hardly educated at all, but he knows his history."

"So I have heard," said Macrae, waiting for the history lesson that he knew was coming. That was the point of the talk. It was going to be an account of the rationale for British policy towards the Third German Reich. The ambassador drew deeply on his cigar, exhaled and began talking.

"I have had many meetings with the chancellor, and every time he rambles back to the way Frederick the Great in the eighteenth century created an empire here in central Europe. Then Napoleon came along in the nineteenth century and broke it up. Bismarck created a unified German state towards the end of the last century, which was once again broken up after the last war. The Treaty of Versailles – some people call it a peace treaty, I can't think why – gave France Alsace and Lorraine on Germany's western border and lopped off a chunk of the eastern territory and gave it to Poland. Then the Allies occupied the Rhineland."

The ambassador paused, eyebrows raised, waiting for a comment. Macrae said nothing.

"That's pretty crude history," the ambassador said, "but it's the way the chancellor sees it, and that's what matters. He calls all those territories the 'lost lands' and he wants them back. That is our problem."

"Well, he's got the Rhineland back, hasn't he? He just walked into it."

The ambassador shifted in his chair. That was the sort of facile comment one would expect from a reader of the *Manchester Guardian*, not a British military attaché.

"And what do you suppose we should have done about that?" he asked.

"He only had three divisions. A little show of strength from the French might have stopped him."

"The French weren't up for it and nor were we. Frankly, HMG didn't see much of a problem in the Rhineland – he was just walking into his own back yard."

"He seems to see most of eastern Europe as his own back yard."

The ambassador eyed Macrae. His first impression had been right; the man was going to be a problem.

"As I said, it is not an easy situation."

"So we are looking at another German Empire with Hitler as a new Bismarck or Frederick the Great?"

Sir Nevile was silent for a while, a theatrical trick he had learnt early on in the Foreign Service. Make the other chap wait for an answer – it adds weight when it finally comes, and gives time for thought.

"He greatly admires Frederick the Great," he said finally.

Two can play the history game, thought Macrae, who had abandoned the tactic of deferential agreement.

"That's the problem, isn't it? Frederick the Great loved war and Bismarck said you could do anything with bayonets but sit on them."

"We and the French lost over a million men in the last war. We cannot afford another one."

"But not peace at any price, Sir Nevile?"

"There is always a price to pay for peace," said the ambassador. "Now, let's rejoin the others, shall we?"

The two men stood up. Macrae finished his brandy. The ambassador paused at the door.

"One more thing. Just a bit of advice I give all new staff."

Macrae waited while Sir Nevile weighed his words. Finally, he turned and looked him straight in the eyes.

"Stay away from the Adlon."

"The hotel?"

"Yes."

"Why? It's the best in Berlin, isn't it?"

"It was once. Now it's full of journalists and racketeers."

"Racketeers?"

"Arms salesmen, conmen of every stripe. The journalists are the worst, though. The Gestapo bug the place. Hardly surprising, really. Best avoided."

"I'll bear that in mind," said Macrae.

They tried to celebrate their first night in their new home. Macrae lit the fire in the dining room and opened a bottle of champagne. Primrose found some tinned pâté and prosciutto in the fridge and served it on crispbread. The house remained chilly despite the fire. She wore a thick jersey over her dress.

"I am sorry," he said.

"It's not your fault. Ghastly lunches come with the job, don't they?"

"No, I mean I'm sorry we had to come here. I know you didn't want to."

"We must play the cards we have in our hand, mustn't we – that's what father used to say."

She got up, brushed crumbs from her dress and walked through to the kitchen. They had met at a summer ball in Surrey while he was on leave from France during the war. It was 1917 and almost every friend he had made at school had been killed or wounded. Primrose had lost her brother too, near Mons, in the final horrific day of that battle.

They had slipped out of the ballroom, walked into the welcoming semi-darkness of the garden and sat on a bench, sipping champagne and smoking. She was just twenty and was wearing a long white dress with a silver headband and a black armband. Most of the girls wore similar armbands, all mourning brothers, fathers, uncles lost in the carnage of the trenches.

"I feel the world is coming to an end," she said.

"I know. I hardly have a friend from school left."

They smoked in silence, watching the dancers move like marionettes in the well-lit ballroom. The band was playing waltz after waltz and the music drifted into the garden through open French windows.

"Come on," she said suddenly.

She got up, took his hand and led him into the darkness at the end of the garden.

She threw away her cigarette. "Hold this," she said, and handed him the fluted glass.

She knelt down and unbuttoned his trousers. He was so surprised that he did nothing but gawp down at her, watching the silver headband move rhythmically back and forth. No girl had ever done this to him before, although he was not a virgin. There had been that girl, a cousin, when he visited an aunt in Maidenhead. He looked back at the blaze of light from the house and saw dancers in the ballroom still moving to the same music. He felt he must be one of them and that there was someone else here in the darkness, that this must be a dream.

She paused, breathing hard.

"Give me my glass," she said.

She gulped the champagne, tossed the glass to one side and resumed. He came quickly, with a gasp, and felt his legs buckle. She stood up, walked to the bushes and spat noisily.

"Let's go back," she said.

He caught her arm.

"Primrose, have you had boyfriends before?"

"Why do you ask?"

"Forgive me, but – "

"But girls like me are not supposed to do things like that?"

"Well, yes."

"I wanted to try it – the taste of a man."

She bent down and picked up her glass.

"Do yourself up," she said. "I need a drink."

He had proposed to her two weeks later at the end of his leave. He was twenty-eight years old, a second lieutenant in the Seaforth Highlanders, a regiment that was moving to the front line near Arras. She had refused, saying she was not going to become a war widow.

Three months later, he was posted to the staff college at Quetta in India. Lieutenant Noel Macrae had been marked out as a man with a future. He had twice been mentioned in dispatches, not for his skill as a sniper, but because he had gone into no man's land at night under fire to guide a patrol back to safety through a minefield.

His brother officers liked him and, unusually, so did the men, although he never led them over the top. That was the beauty of being a sniper. You did your killing from a distance. Most of the officers in his regiment were dead now or had been shipped home with wounds that would never heal and memories that left them screaming in the night.

He had survived because of his skill with the Lee–Enfield rifle. He had not asked to be a sniper; in fact, it was an army rule that you could not volunteer. He had been selected after a series of high scores at the rifle range in Aldershot.

A sniper's life was lonely and dangerous. But he proved a natural hunter of men, with a high kill record that brought him praise and promotion from lieutenant to captain.

He worked with an observer who used a telescope, but usually he found his own targets: an officer shaving in a rear trench, a pair of binoculars quickly raised for a view over no man's land. These were his chances and he took them. As a sniper, you learn that humans are creatures of habit. The same officer will take his binoculars to peer over the trench line at the same place and at the same time every morning. He will be wearing a peaked cap with the emblem of his regiment. The insignia will be shiny enough to catch the eye and make a perfect target.

He had seen those heads fall backwards or sometimes simply explode, scattering blood and skull fragments. Usually the range was too long for a certain hit. At eight hundred yards, the sniper version of the Lee–Enfield was at its outside range. Then the sniper needed to calculate the strength and direction of the wind; even a strong breeze could make a difference over half a mile of open ground. And all the time the sniper knew he too was being stalked by enemy marksmen. You fired a single shot, then ducked down to seek a new camouflaged position.

He had enjoyed the job. The killing was easy, and his reports were praised for their meticulous attention to detail. He recorded long-range shots at periscopes raised in second-line trenches, because he had a theory that the shattered glass would be driven into the eyes of those peering into the bottom half. That report had been well received and circulated to other units on the Western Front. It was ghoulish, unfair and not at all sportsmanlike, but, as Macrae told himself, there was nothing fair or sportsmanlike about life in the trenches. He also knew that he would never become a prisoner of war. If the Germans captured a sniper, they shot him out of hand.

Primrose's family had reluctantly assented to the match. They were wealthy landowners in Somerset and she was their only daughter. He was a doctor's son from St Andrews in Scotland. But there were few eligible bachelors after the slaughter in France, and in any case Primrose quietly told her parents she would never speak to them again if they withheld their consent. The wedding took place in London early in

1918. The honeymoon was spent on the ship to India, sailing via the Suez Canal and Aden. This was his new posting and, as he told his bride, a miraculous chance to escape the slaughter in Flanders and start a new life.

That was twenty years ago, since when he had returned from India to command a field battery unit at Aldershot. He had been promoted to major and then again to lieutenant colonel when he was made a military attaché, a hybrid role reporting to both the ambassador and his military masters in London.

His first posting had been to Budapest, then Vienna. Primrose had put up with the rigours of life as a soldier's wife. But the further they travelled, the more distant she became. She grew tired of the circle of wives in India and even more so back home in the regimental world of Aldershot. The impetuous sexual adventurer Macrae had met in the darkness of a Surrey garden became a bored housewife whose indifference to her marriage slowly turned into resentment.

Macrae had finally suggested they sit down and discuss their problems. He had just come out of the bathroom into the bedroom and was towelling himself dry. She was sitting in front of the dressing table wearing a black petticoat. Black was her favourite colour. The portrait of her brother by her side of the bed was framed in black. Her dog, a Labrador, had been chosen for its colour. They were going that night to what she called another BBDP – bloody boring dinner party. It was always the same people, the same gossip, the same under-the-table grope from some senior officer, and the same food, she used to say. The Foreign Office must issue their diplomatic wives with a menu card limited to smoked salmon and lamb chops.

"I want you to have an affair," she had said without looking round from the dressing table.

He sat on the bed in shock.

"What on earth are you talking about?"

"Don't look so surprised. I'm going to, so you might as well too. It could improve things, don't you think?"

"And who exactly are you going to have an affair with?"

She stood up and turned to face him. "I don't know. Does it matter?" She went into the bathroom.

He had briefly wondered if his wife was going mad. It happened a lot to Foreign Service wives when they got back from India, it was said. They were given a lot of strange pills and quietly sent to rest homes in the Home Counties.

"Do you want a divorce?" he had said when she reappeared.

"Don't be silly. What would be the point? Men are all the same. You're a bit hopeless but you're still my husband – and always will be." Then she had kissed him, a full-throated, passionate kiss.

The memory made him smile. There was a clatter of plates from the kitchen, a crash and a muffled curse.

"I'm going for a walk," he said. "Do you want to come?" It was half past four and dark outside. The temperature in Berlin would be falling below zero soon.

She popped her head out of the kitchen.

"It's bloody freezing out there. I'm going to unpack."

Macrae walked up the Charlottenburger Chaussee under the glare of street lamps and the lights from a stream of traffic. On the far side of the Brandenburg Gate he could see the illuminated outline of the Hotel Adlon.

He had been to Berlin just once before and then only for a day-long meeting at the embassy for military attachés in the region, those from Vienna, Budapest, Prague and Warsaw.

To save money, he had arrived from Vienna that morning by train and returned on the last train at night. He had learnt nothing at the meeting he did not know and seen nothing of the city. He had tried to return, but Colonel Watson was possessive about what he called his patch and had declined to arrange a meeting. Now Macrae was going to explore the secrets of a city that had surrendered the chaotically creative pleasures of the Weimar Republic to the joyless diktat of the National Socialist Party. A cocktail at the Adlon would be a good start.

Two doormen in dove-grey uniforms and top hats stood by the red-carpeted steps to the entrance of the hotel. Two sets of doors opened onto a large lobby flanked on one side by a gleaming mahogany reception counter and concierge desk. Three heads came up to observe Macrae as he looked around for the way to the bar.

"The bar is through here, sir," said the concierge in perfect English.

He hurried forward to usher Macrae into a richly carpeted room, framed by four marble pillars, that stretched the entire width of the hotel. Elegant palms rose from large urns at the foot of each pillar. A long bar stretched down one side of the room, with leather-topped bar stools. At one end, a large spray of pink and white long-stemmed flowers added a splash of colour to the room.

Macrae seated himself at the bar and looked at a long menu of drinks handed him by one of three barmen.

"Evening, sir. What will it be?"

The barman had an American accent. Macrae wondered if all the hotel staff spoke English. Maybe it was a requirement of the job.

"A gimlet, bitte."

"Gordon's or Plymouth?"

"Plymouth."

"Coming up."

Hollywood B movies were very popular in Germany and every barman in Berlin seemed to have studied the dialogue in the inevitable bar scenes.

The barman mixed the drink, made a theatrical gesture of polishing the bar in front of Macrae, placed a small drink mat down and set the glass upon it. Macrae put a twenty-mark note on the counter, which was accepted with a nod.

He sipped the drink and looked around the room.

"New in town?" said the barman.

"Yes."

"Business?"

"Sort of."

The barman laughed.

"If you are a journalist, they're all over there," he said, nodding to a group of men on the far side of the room.

Macrae looked over at half a dozen middle-aged men, their heads bent forward over a coffee table, talking quietly and nodding to each other as if to prevent anyone hearing their conversation. Occasionally they sat back, laughed, raised their glasses, drank, lit cigarettes and then leant forward again. They looked like a flock of birds feeding in a field.

"Who are they?" said Macrae.

"Americans, British, all the big names. They're here every evening."

"You know them?"

"Sure, I know them, and I know what they like to drink."

He began to recite a list of names and cocktails.

"Shirer likes a whisky sour; he's CBS. Then there's the *Times* man from London; he's straight whisky on the rocks."

"And who's that group over there?" said Macrae, cutting in.

The barman leant forward confidentially, taking a quick look at either end of the bar.

"Arms dealers. From all over."

"And there?" said Macrae, nodding to a third group who had drawn two tables together and sat in a circle, looking serious.

"Businessmen. There's a lot of business in this city, if you know the right people."

"You said Shirer, didn't you?"

"Yes."

"Which one is he?"

"That's Shirer in the middle," said the barman.

"A small favour," said Macrae, taking his card from his wallet and putting it on the counter. "Send this over to him, would you?"

"Sure," said the barman. "Any message?"

"No."

The barman frowned, looked at the engraved card, glanced up at Macrae as if to confirm his identity and walked over to the journalists' table.

Shirer was round-faced, balding, with a moustache. He looked up at the barman, took the card, listened for a moment as the barman whispered in his ear, then looked across the room and nodded in the direction of the bar.

Macrae ordered another drink. The gimlet had worked but he would need a second for the walk home.

She was asleep when he got back but had left his bedside light on. There was a tumble of fair hair over her face. In sleep she looked younger than her forty years, a face unlined, the skin shiny with night cream. She had miscarried late in pregnancy while in India and had insisted on seeing the foetus of a baby boy almost fully formed. The authorities would not allow a burial in the cemetery, so she had servants dig a grave in the garden and placed a small cross over it. She had called her baby Richard. They had never tried again.

The portrait of her brother stood on her bedside table. He was sure she talked to him every night before sleeping. Good-looking boy, aged just nineteen when he was killed. He had been in a shell hole, stranded for two days between the lines while an artillery duel raged. Two of his own men died trying to reach him. Then they gave up.

Macrae went to sleep wondering whether he should have sent his card to Shirer. His broadcasts from Berlin had become famous in America and he was said to be very well informed. The Germans were keen to promote their version of events in Europe to an American audience and they were greatly helped by the support of such celebrities as Henry Ford and Charles Lindbergh.

Shirer might be useful. Joseph Goebbels himself was said to feed him stories. The American correspondent was adept at sifting the truth from the propaganda and if you listened carefully to his broadcasts you could detect his own views on the rise of the Third Reich.

Shirer was smart and well connected, but if all went well, Macrae wouldn't need him. He had his own man well placed to know what was going on, a source nurtured over the years he had spent in Budapest and Vienna. It would be risky making contact again. He'd have to be careful. Berlin was a dangerous city.

Beside him Primrose turned, talking to herself in her sleep, long muttered conversations he had often heard but could never understand.

2

Berlin got to work early on winter mornings. From around seven, office workers streamed in from the suburbs by tram, overground and underground trains to staff commercial and government offices, cafés, shops and the big department stores. The biggest of all, Wertheim's in Leipziger Platz, had a brilliantly lit quarter-mile frontage and employed a thousand people. At the other end of the square another huge store, Tietz, had sought to trump its rival by offering free breakfast to the first fifty customers to enter.

Berliners were constantly reminded that the efficient transport network was the creation of the National Socialist government. The days of the Weimar Republic, when overcrowding and strikes made public transport both uncomfortable and unreliable, had gone. Not only could workers get into the city on time, but those employed in the industrial belt further out could rely on trains and buses to take them to huge factories such as I. G. Farben, the chemical plant that alone employed three thousand people.

The tented cities for the homeless and unemployed around Berlin's lakes had been swept away to beautify the city for the 1936 Olympic Games. There were to be no homeless or unemployed in the new Germany. The rearmament programme had created jobs for all – at least for men – and cheap housing developments meant a home for every worker.

This was part of the National Socialist government's economic miracle, and those who did not choose to contribute to its success found the government had thoughtfully provided another option – incarceration in a labour camp.

The throng of commuters of all ages who poured out of the train stations and bus terminals were almost all male. The few women to be seen were working on the food stalls selling bratwurst, coffee and warm pastries. The most prominent of the many government posters on walls, pillars and the sides of buses proclaimed that a woman's place was at home with her children. Those women who did work were reminded in similar fashion that trousers were not to be worn and that skirts must fall to at least an inch below the knee.

One exception to the all-male morning rush hour could be seen on the corner of Wilhelmstrasse and Prinz-Albrechtstrasse, where a long queue of men and women formed outside a graceful five-storey building that had once been the School of Arts and Crafts. Here, in the decadent decade of the 1920s, painters, sculptors, weavers and potters had learnt their craft and exhibited their creations. Now it was the headquarters of the Geheime Staatspolizei, better known by its widely feared abbreviation, Gestapo.

There was no signage to announce the identity of the building, and the men and women waiting to enter for the day's work looked no different from any other government employees. A casual observer might have noticed there were rather more women among them than was usual. The observer would not have been able to see that within the building the regime and the rules were very different from that of a normal government office.

There were strict identity checks. All staff were required to sign in and out in a large ledger placed on a desk in the hall. No one was allowed to leave during working hours. Two separate cafeterias provided morning coffee, lunch and afternoon tea for carefully timed staff breaks. All staff had to wear swastika armbands within the office but were forbidden to do so outside.

Around the corner, in Joseph Goebbels's Ministry of Public Enlightenment and Propaganda, the doors opened at eight and everyone was expected to be at their desks fifteen minutes later.

All those who depended on, or worked with, the government – foreign businessmen, diplomats and journalists – were also at their desks early. The National Socialist government ceaselessly proclaimed itself to be a model of early-to-work efficiency and it demanded the same from everyone with whom it did business. On this particular January morning a group of Western correspondents had gathered grumbling at the Hotel Adlon, waiting for buses to take them to a Luftwaffe airbase for a demonstration of the new Messerschmitt 109 fighter plane.

The one exception to this early-morning activity was the German chancellor. The man who was head of the National Socialist Party, the government and the German state never got to his desk at a regular hour and sometimes didn't appear in his office until the early afternoon. Only when he did so were his three secretaries able to confirm his diary for the day. Usually the chancellor rose at ten o'clock, took breakfast of toast and his favourite brand of German marmalade at eleven, and only then walked through from his living quarters to the office.

Those who worked most closely with Adolf Hitler felt that he enjoyed the element of surprise that his refusal to conform to an arranged timetable gave him. He was a creature of habit, they said, especially when it came to his vegetarian diet, but not when it concerned the management of state affairs. In such matters he was deliberately unpredictable.

Hitler lived where he worked, in the Reich Chancellery on Wilhelmstrasse. From his office on the second floor he could look across the street to the Hotel Kaiserhof, preferred by senior Nazis to the Adlon. Here the chancellor would often take tea at four o'clock with his inner circle of advisers and such favoured foreign visitors as the British socialite Unity Mitford. For an hour or more, he would indulge his passion for cakes and regale his audience with long monologues about foreign affairs. The hotel made sure that the chancellor was presented with a different choice of cakes every day – all baked with care in their own kitchen.

The hotel was flanked by government ministries, which Hitler had personally sited on the street. Wilhelmstrasse was Hitler's powerbase in Berlin. Across the road from the Chancellery, he could almost look into Goebbels's office, while at a corner on the crossroads a few hundred yards away stood the Gestapo headquarters. This was important. Above all, the chancellor wanted Heinrich Himmler, head of state security, and Reinhard Heydrich, head of the Gestapo, the rising man he admired so much, close at hand. If there was a flaw in the urban geography of power, it was the presence of the British embassy a mere three hundred yards up the street. It was far too easy for the ambassador to visit him.

Sir Nevile Henderson called the twice-weekly meeting of senior staff his morning prayers. Shortly after nine o'clock this

January morning they gathered in the conference room next to his office, gratefully pouring coffee or tea from Thermos flasks placed on a side table. The first secretary, Kirkpatrick, sat to his left and the political attaché, David Buckland, to his right. Very much feeling like the new boy at school, Macrae took a seat at the far end of the table. The commercial, naval, air and military attachés made up the meeting.

Roger Halliday was there that morning, but he only attended when he felt like it – a fact that irritated the ambassador. Halliday reported directly to the Secret Intelligence Service HQ in London. The ambassador had no control over the man – or his drinking, for that matter. He distrusted Halliday's information and disliked the methods by which it was obtained – bribery and blackmail, as far as Sir Nevile could gather. There was something else about Halliday the ambassador deeply disliked. The man was unmarried and made little secret of the reason why he never would marry. Henderson was surprised that the Secret Service employed such people. Apart from anything else, it left them wide open to blackmail.

The meeting began with the ambassador welcoming Colonel Noel Macrae to the embassy team. Heads turned and smiled and Macrae nodded back. Each member of staff then described their plans for the days ahead and reported any information of interest. At the end, Sir Nevile summed up with the same short address they had all heard before, although at every meeting he tried to deliver it with a different angle. The message was simple. They were all working to ensure that diplomacy would triumph, that the German question could be settled peacefully and war avoided. The German government, he said – and abruptly stopped.

Someone at the table had muttered, loud enough for everyone to hear, "Nazi regime." The ambassador looked around to identify the miscreant.

The German government, he continued, was both brutal in its treatment of opponents and highly aggressive in its pursuit of lost territory. Neither fact needed to lead to a wider war if the Western powers, principally Britain and France, pursued their diplomacy of containment. Hitler was many things, but not stupid. He did not want a European war, he was not ready for a European war and there would be no reason for a European war once negotiations had satisfied his demands.

The ambassador looked round, seeking the usual nods of agreement, and prepared to end the meeting. Some people were staring at the ceiling, some down at the table. No one was looking at him. He closed his folder and got to his feet.

"Thank you, gentlemen," he said.

"There is one thing you should know," said Roger Halliday.

He was sitting at the back and, as usual on a Monday morning, he looked hung-over.

Sir Nevile sighed and sat down again.

"I hear reliably that Field Marshal Blomberg has married. The wedding took place at the War Ministry on Saturday. It was in secret."

Halliday had the attention of the room. He rarely spoke at these meetings, indeed he hardly concealed his contempt for them, but when he did say something it was usually important.

"Well, we must congratulate him. Blomberg is a fine general and, as head of the army, I, of course, know him well," said the ambassador.

"Hitler and Göring were witnesses. There was no one else present except the general's five children."

Sir Nevile picked up his folder and prepared to rise again. He would send a minute to London about Halliday. The man had been in Berlin too long.

"Really?" he said. "That just shows how important he is to us."

"There is a problem, however," said Halliday. "His bride is twenty-seven – thirty-two years younger than him."

"The old goat," said Buckland. "Jolly good for him."

"Unfortunately, photographs of the woman of a pornographic nature have surfaced. They were taken when she was much younger. Worse still, the police have established that ten years ago she was working as a registered prostitute in Munich."

There was a silence while the meeting digested this news.

"Are you sure?" said the ambassador. He was furious but determined to remain calm. This was typical of the man, waiting until the last minute to throw some scandalous piece of information into the meeting, as if it had any relevance.

"The Gestapo have the information and they are sure."

"How do *you* know this?"

Halliday sighed, shook his head and fished a pack of cigarettes from his pocket. Smoking was forbidden in the ambassador's meeting. He tapped a cigarette from the pack, put it in his mouth and said nothing.

The ambassador turned to Macrae.

"Did you know about this?"

"No. But Blomberg is Hitler's favourite general."

"I know that. Can you check – find out what it means?"

"It means," said Halliday, getting to his feet, "that Hitler is going to get rid of Blomberg and what follows will not be good news for the army – or for us."

He left the room. Sir Nevile turned to Macrae again.

"I don't think we need to get too worried about this. Find out what you can and report to me later today."

Like all military attachés, Noel Macrae had been reminded at the start of every posting that his role was not that of a spy.

The Foreign Office spelt out this policy in unmistakable detail with a note that read:

> *You should take the greatest care to avoid any action liable to create suspicion that you are attempting to acquire secret information by illicit means. You must have no relations or communications with persons acting, or professing to act, as spies or secret agents . . .*

The note went on to state that information of interest to His Majesty's Government should be gathered through contact, either formally or socially, with military personnel of the host country or by observation: "Your status is the same as those of diplomats working within the embassy and you are expected to behave accordingly."

Those were the rules laid down in a little book drawn up by the Foreign Office in London called *Practice and Etiquette for Service Attachés*. The trouble was that such gentlemanly behaviour did not work in the Berlin of 1938. The year was hardly a fortnight old and Macrae could see the beginnings of a crisis that might finally shake the complacency of those in London who thought the best way to deal with a ravening wolf was to keep feeding him.

He made one phone call from the embassy, took a taxi down the Unter den Linden avenue and got out at a bridge across the Spree. It was mid-morning and the streets were quiet. He walked over the river, turned left and marvelled as a magnificently domed renaissance building came into view through the leafless trees of the Lustgarten. The Berliner Dom called itself a cathedral but in fact lacked a resident bishop and thus had no claim on that title. It was simply a religious building designed to celebrate the Protestant faith in Germany. It was half past eleven. There would be a short prayer service at noon, as there was every day.

He killed time by climbing the 267 steps up to the gallery that ran round the interior of the domed roof. The view onto the nave below was dizzying. A lavish marble and onyx altar dominated one end of the church. The polished bronze pipes of a large organ rose over the choir stalls like the masts of a stately galleon at the other end. Gilded statues and royal sarcophagi gave the interior the extravagant appearance of an Egyptian temple rather than a German church.

He retraced his steps and went into the shop by the entrance. Amid books, reliquaries, candles and tourist guides he saw a large pile of prominently displayed copies of *Mein Kampf*. He picked one up. It was the same edition he had bought in Vienna four years earlier. An incoherent, badly written book dismissed as the ravings of a lunatic when it first appeared in 1926. Twelve years later it remained a bestseller, or so the publishers in Berlin reported.

"You want to buy it?"

He turned to see an elderly woman with strands of grey hair falling over the folds of a face that had once been very beautiful. She had spoken in accented English. It had been silly of him to wear his cavalry twill overcoat and lace-up brogues.

"No. It seems strange to find such a book here in the church."

The woman gave a low chuckle.

"Ah, you English. You think you know everything, don't you?" She took the book from him and replaced it on the stand. "Not for sale," she said.

"Why do you display it?"

"Protection, young man. You want a candle?"

The service began promptly at noon with a full congregation of several hundred people. There were prayers, the choir sang the twenty-fourth psalm, the priest gave a brief address extolling Christian powers of endurance and fortitude in times of stress. Twenty minutes later he was walking down the steps of the cathedral when a young officer in the uniform of a lieutenant and wearing a swastika armband detached himself from the worshippers and walked over.

"*Heil Hitler!*" said the officer loudly, and saluted with outraised arm and a click of his heels. Macrae saluted in return, his right hand rising to his head with palm facing outwards in a sharp gesture. It was against army rules to salute in civilian clothing and without military headgear, but Macrae was damned if he was going to offer a handshake to a young man who had just bellowed the Führer's name at him.

The Hitlergruss was the required social and professional greeting at all levels of society in Germany, and although at first the practice was widely ignored, it was now commonplace. Just another form of protection, political camouflage, as the lady in the bookshop had said.

"Since tomorrow is a public holiday, the colonel will be taking his children to the zoo."

The young man saluted again and rejoined the departing worshippers.

Berlin's zoo was the largest in Europe, sprawling over thirty acres in the Tiergarten, west of the Brandenburg Gate. The city made much of the number of species on display and the way in which their cages and enclosures were carefully designed to recreate their natural habitat. The zoo was high on the list of Berlin's most popular tourist attractions, and visitors were urged to take at least half a day to explore it and advised to include on their itinerary lunch at the excellent restaurant adjacent to the penguin pool.

Macrae paid the entrance fee and stood inside the gates. Crowds milled around him, old people shuffling into groups, parents marshalling children, all eager to begin the adventure of a visit to the zoo. A public holiday in midwinter Berlin was a good time to escape the new rules and regulations that governed everyday life and above all the watchful eyes of neighbours. Macrae wondered how he would find Florian Koenig and his family. The German was tall, well over six foot, but the zoo was crowded. He stamped his feet and blew into his hands. The biting cold seem to cut through his cavalry overcoat and the layers underneath. He thrust his hands into his coat pockets, making a mental note to buy a pair of thick woollen gloves, and examined a large map of the zoo.

He wondered how the Big Four from Africa – elephant, rhino, lion and giraffe – were faring in the weather. The penguins, seals and polar bears would be thriving. But the species from warmer climes would have heated indoor areas. He would visit the elephants first, he decided, less in the hope of finding Koenig than because it would be warm.

"*Das Reptilienhaus ist sehr gut*," piped a small voice beside him.

Macrae looked round to see a boy aged about ten, his face barely visibly beneath hat and scarf. The boy backed away, gave a little wave, then ran off.

Macrae turned to the map. The reptiles were kept on the far side of the zoo between a children's play area and the bear enclosure. He pushed through the crowd and began to walk.

It was dark and warm in the reptile house. A large sign in English and German asked visitors to be silent and not to disturb the creatures by tapping on the glass. At first he could not see properly, then he became aware of a row of dimly lit plate-glass windows stretching either side of a long gallery.

He walked to the first and peered around the heads of a family, mother, father and three children.

They were all looking into an Amazonian jungle setting, hoping to see a yellow anaconda. The jungle had been cleverly brought to life with a pond fed by a small stream and a painted backdrop of a tree canopy, through which flitted parrots and parakeets. In the centre was a log, around which was draped the anaconda. The reptile was motionless, its yellow and black markings creating such effective camouflage that it was hard to tell what was log and what was snake. The eldest boy tapped on the glass and was immediately restrained by his mother, who hissed something in his ear.

Macrae walked on, hoping to find a window that might afford him a better view. He was feeling warmer. He had almost forgotten what he had come for. A large crowd had gathered around one of the bigger enclosures. Macrae peered over their heads. Two snakes were moving slowly over a tangle of branches and logs. They were identified on a sign as Burmese pythons, the world's longest snake, which could grow up to six metres in length and normally ate small mammals such as rabbits but would on occasion take a deer or an unwary human being.

There was a murmur from the observers and they began pressing forward, jostling for a better look. A thin pole had appeared at the top of the cage, from which dangled a rat on a short length of twine. The rat was alive and it struggled as it was slowly lowered into the cage. It was fastened to the pole with a loop. Both snakes began to raise themselves, their hoods opening. With a shake of the pole, the rat was released and dropped onto the vegetation below. The crowd gave a loud "Ahhh!"

The rat vanished from view towards the back of the enclosure. As if by agreement, one snake remained still while the other moved fast, its silvery skin slithering swiftly through the undergrowth. The snake reappeared within seconds. The rat was struggling in its jaws. Mothers began to move their children away but they tugged back, determined to witness the final scene in the drama.

"Feeding time at the zoo is very popular," said a voice.

Macrae turned to see Koenig behind him, smiling. They shook hands. It was the first time he had seen the German out of military uniform. He was dressed smartly in country clothes: a brown herringbone overcoat on top of a tweed jacket, thick corduroy trousers and boots.

"I didn't know you were allowed to feed live animals to these snakes."

"Not quite the same as the London zoo, I am sure," said Koenig. "But this is Berlin. Shall we have coffee, and maybe something with it?"

He reached into his pocket and drew out the top half of a silver hip flask.

"Where are your children?"

"They have gone off to see the lions. It's their feeding time, too. Very efficient. If you have them at the same time, you halve the crowds."

They sat in a corner of the cafeteria with two cups of coffee liberally laced with cognac.

"You wanted to see me?" said Koenig.

"It's been a couple of years and I thought it might be good to renew our friendship."

Koenig laughed. "Of course. I knew you were here, but it is difficult to get in touch. These are, how shall I say this . . .?"

"Interesting times?"

"Let's just say times when it pays to be cautious. Anyway, good to see you. How is Primrose?"

They talked for a while of Primrose, his children and his new job. Koenig had risen to be a full colonel on the general staff. He was proud of the promotion and it reminded Macrae of the time they had first met in Vienna four years earlier.

It was Macrae's first week in post in the Austrian capital as military attaché. His predecessor had left him a list of English-speaking German officers of sufficient rank and prospects to merit a good dinner at Maxim's. The restaurant was one of the oldest in Vienna, frequented by those rich enough to afford the extravagant cost of a meal or lucky enough to work for an organisation that conferred a liberal expense account upon its executives.

His predecessor's list included senior officers of known conservative views in infantry or armoured regiments who were excelling at the staff college in Berlin. Such officers regularly visited the Austrian capital for staff talks. And in Vienna it was easier to approach them than in Berlin. In turn, they were more free with their views. Lieutenant Florian Koenig's name had been top of the list. He had accepted the invitation by return post.

It had been a memorable evening for all the wrong reasons. They had drunk cocktails at the bar and sat down at a table on which stood a bottle of Krug champagne in an ice bucket. It was a gesture of friendship, Koenig said, a gift from one fellow officer to another.

Two tables away a scion of Austrian nobility, with monocle and scar and wearing evening dress, sat with a woman in a black low-cut dress who looked remarkably like Marlene Dietrich. Macrae found himself casting long sideways glances at her, trying to work out if she really was the famous film star.

"You find her attractive?" said Koenig.

"No, not my type."

"Yes you do, you were staring at her."

"Half the room's staring at her. She looks like Marlene Dietrich, that's why."

"You English are all the same, you never tell the truth. Admit it, you'd take her to bed if you could."

Macrae noticed that the champagne bottle was already half empty. Lieutenant Koenig was drunk.

"But I can't. I'm married. Let's order."

"See what I mean? Hypocrisy. You know the trouble with the English? Corrupted by class and empire. You lord it over all those dusky peasants around the world and think you're better than everybody else."

"Unlike the Germans, of course? Anyway, I'm not English; I'm Scottish. Shall we order?"

It was not a good start to the evening.

Koenig had close-cut iron-grey hair, making him look older than his thirty-nine years. He had been too young to serve in the Great War. As the only surviving son of an old Prussian family with a long tradition of military service, he had joined the shattered remnants of the German army in 1920 out of family duty and as a tribute to his two brothers who had been killed in the trenches. He regarded the army less as a career than as an obligation.

A family estate in Mecklenburg in the north of the country provided the comforts of home life with his wife and three children while he moved from his infantry brigade based in Bavaria to the staff college in Berlin to pursue promotion. Family connections and a series of impressive exam results enabled him to attend an exchange training course at the military college of Sandhurst in England, where he learnt excellent English.

They were on the second bottle of champagne and the main course had not arrived. The German lieutenant had become morose and Macrae wondered whether he could find an excuse to leave early.

"You know both my brothers died in the trenches?" Koenig said this casually, as if remarking on the passing of a long-forgotten relative.

"Yes, I did know that. I'm sorry."

"Second battle of the Somme. I blame the English entirely for the war."

"Really? I thought you Germans started it."

"We did. But you should have stopped us."

"Easier said than done."

"Not if you consider the power of your navy, the fact that the royal families of both countries were all kissing cousins and that the French were fast asleep as usual. If you had woken them up and made a joint diplomatic démarche there would have been no war."

"That would have been asking a lot."

"What, waking the French up?"

They both laughed. They got drunk over dinner and afterwards Macrae allowed himself to be taken to a night-club, where the entertainment was provided by young women who paraded around in diaphanous knickers with silver hearts on the front and the words *Küss Mich* stitched to the back.

"You can touch them, you know," said Koenig. "It's part of the show." He slapped a passing waitress on the backside and ordered more drinks.

"I think it's time for me to go home," said Macrae, yawning.

Koenig was too drunk to reply. He was slumped over the table, seemingly asleep, a handsome young man who would probably do well in the army but was of no use now or later to Macrae. He left.

The next day a handwritten letter of apology was delivered to the embassy.

Dear Colonel Macrae,

My behaviour last night was unforgiveable. I hope you will accept my deepest apologies. I assure you that in vino there was no veritas last night. It produced rude and unacceptable remarks that were totally out of character from someone who should have known better. I trust you will allow me to take you to dinner when you are next in Berlin or I am next in Vienna.

And that it was how it had started. Macrae tried to remember exactly when it was: eight, nine years ago? It didn't matter. A few months later they dined again, this time in Budapest. Koenig had changed. He was quiet, reserved and very careful with his drink. He was endlessly curious about the military preparations in Britain, or rather the lack of them.

"It is strange to me – indeed to my colleagues – that at a time like this you appear to be disarming. Is that true, or is Perfidious Albion playing one of its tricks?"

He had laughed. It was 1935 and the government of Stanley Baldwin in London had announced a cut in the defence budget and once again refused to countenance conscription. Meanwhile, Hitler had defied the advice of his own generals and sent three divisions into the demilitarised Rhineland, breaking the terms of the Versailles treaty.

"You know you could have stopped us? All the French had to do was move a brigade near the border while the British sent a naval task force into the North Sea with the threat of a blockade. Hitler would have backed down."

"You think we made a mistake?"

Koenig laughed. They were in a café by the river. Koenig said he preferred meeting in Budapest rather than Vienna. There were too many spies in Austria and they were all Nazis, he said.

"Ah, you English and your sense of humour. Mistake? The mistake is that you think you know Hitler. You don't. We do. That is our problem."

"We're not alone, you know. The French have the biggest army in Europe."

"The French!" Koenig had almost fallen off his chair laughing.

Primrose wanted to meet the man she called "your debauched German lieutenant". Having heard about their first evening, she was curious to meet someone who could behave so badly and apologise so sweetly. Primrose thought she understood something of Koenig's behaviour. He had lost two brothers in the war, just as she had lost her Richard. Grief did strange things to a person, she said.

When Koenig was next in Vienna it was arranged they would lunch at a new fish restaurant called Esterhazy several miles out of town on the Danube. The lunch began promptly at one o'clock, but it was not until early evening, as the waiters were laying tables for dinner, that they finally left.

Macrae had sat back and watched and listened as his wife and the German officer explored the deaths of their siblings, talking as if they were part of the same family. He had never heard Primrose talk in that way. The millions of dead in the Great War had created a bond between those who had lost loved ones in the slaughter that transcended all barriers. Denied the intimacy of shared grief, Macrae felt like a stranger at the table. At one stage, Koenig had comforted Primrose as she was recalling the last time she had seen her brother.

"I never said goodbye properly – that's the awful part. I never told him good luck or that I loved him or anything," she said.

She had begun to cry, which is when Koenig had put his arms around her. They were drinking a light Austrian wine and Macrae noticed that by four clock they had each had a bottle.

As the lunch stretched into early evening, Macrae felt more and more like an intruder on private grief. Primrose and Koenig shared memory after memory of their lost siblings. Macrae knew that if he were to get up and silently walk away, they would hardly notice. Their conversation flowed like a river emerging from dark subterranean caves where guilt and grief were etched in crude images on rock walls. Alcohol, memories of the dead and the thin thread of desire were creating a catharsis for these two people, his wife and the German lieutenant.

Macrae got to his feet. "I think it's time to go home, darling," he said.

They were both drunk when they got back. Primrose poured more drinks, threw her arms around him and danced a slow waltz in the drawing room. He tried gently to break away but she would not let him go. She pressed herself against him. For the first time in months she wanted him to make love to her and flung herself naked on the bed, arms and legs spread wide, urging him to take her with a string of profanities that shocked and excited him. He came quickly, then fell asleep, waking later to hear her deep gasping breaths from the far side of the bed, and then silence.

After that, Macrae and Koenig had kept in touch discreetly. The information exchanged was always political rather than tactical. Koenig helped Macrae track the manoeuvring between the German High Command and the Nazi leadership. The extent to which the Nazis and their policies were despised at a senior level was surprising. Koenig never revealed such details as the development of new weaponry. That would transgress his oath of loyalty, he said. He was not a traitor. He was a Prussian officer and a German patriot. Yet he was prepared to take elaborate precautions to arrange a meeting at the Berlin zoo that morning. He must have his reasons as well, thought Macrae.

"I don't really deserve my promotion," said Koenig. "I am good at what I do and I like it, but it was my family background, the record of my brothers in the war, that really got me to full colonel."

"I heard. Congratulations."

"But you didn't get in touch."

"I thought it best not to – anyway we have only just arrived."

"And now?"

"I need your advice."

Koenig smiled. "'Advice'?"

"Blomberg has just got married, we hear."

Koenig stopped smiling. He drained his coffee and poured more cognac into the cup.

"You're well informed. But what advice could you want about that?"

"Apparently the bride has a history."

Koenig finished the cognac, coughed, patted his chest and stood up.

"Feeding time for the lions has finished, I think."

Macrae got to his feet.

"I need to wake people up in London."

Koenig picked up the bill, placed some coins on the table.

"Follow me," he said.

They went back into the reptile house and walked through the first gallery into a second, a smaller room. This was the insectarium, and behind glassed windows an array of beetles, spiders, cockroaches, ants, millipedes, scorpions and other arthropods were to be seen, if you looked carefully enough. The two men peered through the glass windows as if really interested in the bug life on display. Finally, Koenig turned and leant against a window. He took a zoo guide from his pocket and began to study it.

"Don't look round and don't try to take notes," he said. "Do you have a guidebook?"

Macrae nodded and took the leaflet from his pocket.

"Read it."

Macrae studied the leaflet.

"This is what he has been waiting for," said Koenig. "There is going to be a purge. Blomberg and Fritsch will be fired. The Führer will take their positions and become supreme commander and war minister."

"The army will stand for that?"

"He's going to remove a dozen or so generals and transfer all the senior field commanders to new posts."

"A reverse coup?"

"Exactly. He's going to get them before they get him. He is going to set up a new armed forces high command, with Keitel as his deputy. Keitel is a loyalist and his younger brother Bodewin will be made head of army personnel. That means Hitler will control the appointment and promotion of all officers."

"Surely he won't get away with that?"

"You're dealing with a man who wants to make history. He's clever and he has the devil's luck. Make sure your people in London understand what this means."

Koenig flipped the leaflet back into his pocket, patted Macrae on the shoulder and walked away. From the next-door room Macrae heard a child's voice say, "Daddy, where have you been?"

Back at the embassy, Macrae found several messages from the ambassador asking for a meeting. He ignored them and took out the files on senior German military personnel.

The notes on Wilhelm Keitel were lengthy, well documented. He began reading and soon realised why Hitler trusted him so much.

There was a knock on his office door. Macrae looked at his watch. It was five thirty. He had been reading the file for forty minutes.

Daisy Wellesley peered round the door. "Sir Nevile wonders whether you have received his messages?"

"Please make my apologies and say that I would be happy to join him at six."

Daisy made a face. "All right," she said.

Sir Nevile Henderson was displeased. He had been waiting for his military attaché for almost two hours and had received what he felt were less-than-polite brush-offs. Now the man was coming to see him at a time of day when it would be difficult not to offer him a whisky. The trouble was military attachés reported to the War Office and not the Foreign Office. It was a damned nuisance.

The two men settled down with their whiskies – a blended Scotch, Macrae noted, not the twenty-year-old Glenlivet malt he knew the ambassador kept in his drinks cabinet.

Macrae talked quietly for ten minutes. Sir Nevile did not like what he heard.

"When is this going to happen?" he said.

"By the end of the month. The arrangements are under way."

"And no one in the army knows?"

"Blomberg's misfortune to have married a woman who was once a prostitute is widely known. How Hitler plans to take advantage of this is not."

"Is it not a little strange that you know something as important as this and they don't?"

"I trust my source."

"Disinformation, perhaps?"

"What would be the point? It would quickly be disproved and burn the source as far as we were concerned."

Sir Nevile moved from his chair and poured them both more whisky.

"Let me sum up. Hitler is going to remove his two most senior army officers and then unleash a purge of most of his generals. He is going to transfer field commanders and declare himself supreme commander and war minister. This man Wilhelm Keitel will be the number two, in day-to-day control of the army."

"That's it."

"What do we know about Keitel?"

"Loyalist, brilliant war record, which means a lot to Hitler, and heavily engaged in the secret rearmament programme."

"Ah yes, that . . .," murmured the ambassador.

There was a silence. This was not what the ambassador wanted to hear. The German question was the major diplomatic issue for the government in London. Reaction to the alarming speed of events in Berlin had been based on the carefully calibrated diplomacy of reason and persuasion. The one unalterable fact that coloured the thinking of every politician in Britain and France, and indeed elsewhere in Europe, was that a return to the carnage of 1914–18 must at all costs be avoided.

It was widely known that public opinion in Germany and that of the business community were of the same frame of mind. The wounds of the war were still fresh in a country that had suffered a disproportionate number of casualties. The German High Command was also known to be against any military adventures.

Given these facts, it was beyond belief or rational construction to suppose that the German Führer would actually want a new war. He himself had served in the trenches and lost many friends there, whom he still publicly alluded to as heroes.

And yet now the ambassador's new military attaché, a man he hardly knew, was telling him that Hitler was about to unleash a sweeping purge of the army command and take control of the army himself, thus removing any threat from the one power base that could check his military ambition.

"If this happens," said Sir Nevile, "and you will forgive me for saying that I have my doubts, but let's assume you are right, if this happens, what are we to make of it?"

"The army is being placed on a war footing. Hitler intends to go to war sooner rather than later. There will be nothing to stop him if he gets away with this."

"We lost almost a million men in the last war. Germany and France lost over three million between them. Go onto the streets of London, Berlin or Paris and ask people whether they want another war."

"Is that the point, Sir Nevile?"

The ambassador rotated his glass, staring at the swirl of peat-brown whisky. It was precisely the point, he thought.

"Thank you. I will consider this information," he said.

Macrae leant forward. "I suggest we urge the foreign secretary to make the case in cabinet for the strongest possible message to be sent to the chancellor."

"And what would that be?"

"The prime minister must agree to conscription and we must accelerate our rearmament programme. We must arrange joint manoeuvres with the French: show Hitler the mailed fist."

Sir Nevile Henderson got to his feet, putting his glass down hard on the table.

"You arrived in this country a matter of days ago, Colonel. With respect, you know nothing of the psychology of the man we are dealing with, nor the thinking of his inner circle. The German chancellor can be susceptible to reason and logic. He can also become irrational, over-excited and prone to lash out, if threatened. Trust me: the mailed fist will just make matters worse. I know the man."

3

Joachim Bonner placed the cup of coffee on his desk, sat down, lit a cigarette, looked at his watch and picked up the top file from his in-tray. It was 8.38 a.m. His day always started like this. A stack of files, each with a small note attached. The notes were all signed in tiny script with just two initials and the date written in roman numerals. He squinted at the first file: "RH IX.I.VIII." Typical arrogance from a man who had been brought up as a pious Catholic and educated at the finest private school in Bavaria. And Reinhard Heydrich never let his staff forget it, thought Joachim. Why couldn't he just write "09/01/1938" like everyone else?

He examined the file: William L. Shirer of the Columbia Broadcasting System. He glanced at the next one: Ian Colvin of the *News Chronicle*, London. He flipped through the others. All were new arrivals in the foreign press corps, mostly English-speaking, but there were Spanish, Portuguese and Italian journalists as well.

Bonner lit another cigarette. It was a complete waste of time using surveillance on the foreign press. They were always to be found at the Adlon bar; if not, there were one or two restaurants where they gathered like sheep, ate, drank and then argued over who would pay what share of the bill. Their rooms were bugged anyway, so what was the point, except perhaps to marvel at how they managed to get up in the morning, given the money they spent at the bar the night before.

He was about to replace the pile when he caught sight of the final file: Colonel Noel Macrae, military attaché at the British embassy. A Christmas baby, thought Bonner, and he opened the file to check the date. That's right: born 25 December 1890, Inverkeithing, Scotland.

Macrae had just arrived in the Berlin diplomatic corps and would already be under the usual surveillance. That, thought Bonner, is what my job amounts to. At the age of forty-four, after twenty years' hard work in the police, he was in charge of surveillance, occasional bribery and, more rarely still, entrapment, of members of the foreign community in Berlin: bankers, arms dealers, the occasional church dignitary and, incredibly, tourists, who came to enjoy the dark allure of the Third Reich. Not much reward for a brilliant war service and the Iron Cross 1st Class that went with it. After the humiliation of Versailles, Bonner had been an early member of paramilitary groups such as the Freikorps, which sprouted like mushrooms from the dank earth of shame and betrayal. That was a lot more than you could say for Reinhard Heydrich.

He lit another cigarette and indulged in a favourite pastime, reminding himself of how the official account of his superior's career differed somewhat from the actual version. Reinhard Heydrich headed the Sicherheitspolizei and Sicherheitsdienst, two agencies combined to form the Gestapo. Heydrich, who had been too young to fight in the war and who had spurned the chance to join any of the revolutionary movements against an imposed peace deal and the corrupt Weimar Republic that followed. Heydrich, who hadn't been able to hold down a job until he went into the navy, and guess what happened then.

Bonner smiled and lit another cigarette. He enjoyed recalling this moment in Heydrich's now sanitised past. The man who currently controlled the political, criminal and border police in Germany had been kicked out of the navy because of his betrayal of a woman to whom he had been engaged. And he would have got away with it if he had not been so arrogant at the court martial.

Then, through marriage to that ghastly woman Lina, Heydrich had somehow engineered an introduction to Himmler, who had given him the job of creating a security police force. That was six years ago, and now Heydrich was one of the most important and feared men in the Reich. And I, Joachim Bonner, work for him. Unofficially I am his number two, but Heydrich refuses to create such a title and instead demeans me with oversight of surveillance duties.

Bonner knew what the files meant. Entrapment was the method used to discredit those diplomats deemed to be irrationally hostile to the Reich. One did not expect foreigners to kneel down and embrace the creed of National Socialism, but one looked for respect and professionalism. Thus diplomats and members of the wider foreign community who were considered to be actively critical were given the special attention of his department.

He pressed the intercom buzzer and called his secretary, a broad-beamed lump of a girl from the farmland of Bavaria. She came in, leaving the door open as usual. Hilde may not have been much of a looker but she had the one attribute required of every man and woman who worked in the building. She was a true believer, loyal and trustworthy. Her family were all party members from a village outside Munich. Like everyone else in the building, her personal file carried the names and addresses of her immediate family and those of her uncles, aunts and even cousins. Everyone knew why that information was so carefully recorded.

Hilde was not just loyal; she was ambitious. Behind those thick-lensed glasses lay a sharp mind. She wanted promotion into a real executive role. Joachim appreciated that.

"Yes, sir?"

"Call Frau Schmidt at the Salon and tell her I will be coming over at noon."

"Yes, sir."

He picked up the file on Macrae.

"Send this downstairs and say I want a decent photo, full face."

A sudden scream rent the air, a terrible sound of pain and anguish, followed by a second almost more terrible strangulated gargling of someone trying to shout "*No!*" but dragging the word out as if in recognition not just of imminent death but of a wider horror that would be visited on family and friends.

Bonner got up and closed the door. That was the trouble with having an office on the fourth floor. The view across the tree-lined Prinz-Albrechtstrasse was pleasant, especially in spring, but extra interrogation rooms had been built in the attic to complement those in the basement. Those rooms were directly above them and sometimes the interrogation teams did not close the soundproof doors properly. He would have to speak to someone about it.

Hilde picked up his cup.

"Of course," she said. "More coffee?"

The Salon occupied a house on the corner of a block of shops and businesses in the residential area of Charlottenburg, a quiet upper-class district that housed many foreign diplomats and their families. The ground floor had been altered to suggest a smart bar or restaurant, although there was no name above the entrance and the windows were heavily curtained.

Visitors were received at the door by a middle-aged woman wearing a tight-fitting full-length grey woollen coat, buttoned at the neck. The woman greeted Bonner with a nod of recognition and opened the door, showing him into a vestibule. Once the outer door had been closed, the curtains of the vestibule were pulled back by unseen hands to reveal a large room laid out as a restaurant dining room. A marble-topped counter ran the length of the back wall. There was a mirror behind the bar, above which fairy lights had been strung in swooping beads of light. Otherwise, the room was lit only by the red-shaded lamps on each table. A fanlight above a door at one end revealed a pink ceiling in the adjoining room.

Kitty Schmidt was waiting for Bonner at the bar, smoking and drinking coffee. She had aged in the two years since he had first met her. He had thought her quite glamorous then, in a dyed-blonde, big-bosomed sort of way. She had the commanding charm of a woman who had run the most famous brothel in Berlin in the late twenties. Kitty Schmidt certainly had secrets, and they interested the newly formed Gestapo in 1934. They had made her what Bonner thought was a very reasonable offer: cooperate with us and continue to run the brothel – and keep the money, or most of it anyway. The cooperation meant closure for a month while cameras and tape recorders were concealed in all the rooms.

This was a genuine offer, but Kitty Schmidt had not seen it that way. She had closed the Salon, paid off the girls and tried to escape. They had picked her up at the Dutch border six months later and brought her back to Berlin. Bonner had personally conducted the interrogation in the basement. He'd stripped her and slapped her around a bit – to remind her where she was – and then made a rather different offer. Schmidt would reopen the Salon, but she would be given new girls hand-picked for the work. She would hand the profits over and be paid a weekly wage.

Kitty Schmidt had no choice but to agree. They had found her mother living in Hanover and a brother working in the Krupp armaments factory in Essen. It was a reserved occupation, but they conscripted him anyway just to make the point. And so the Salon started back in business. Bonner had personally chosen the girls, mostly from Munich, and to his irritation but not his surprise, Reinhard Heydrich had taken a keen interest in the procedure.

That is where Bonner had to admit his boss showed a flair for creative risk that amounted to genius. He despised Heydrich, and not just because he was an arriviste who had joined the party only when it had become successful. Like all such people, he had had to prove himself more Nazi than anyone else. Heydrich was cold, calculating, with the high intelligence of a well-educated man. He did not try to conceal his ambition, which seemed to gnaw away at him like cancer. He had a talent for spotting and exploiting the weakness in others, especially his colleagues in the Nazi Party.

What Bonner despised was the *way* in which Heydrich operated. There was a political calculation to his cruelty. It was almost as if the man had decided to promote himself in the party hierarchy by becoming more monstrous, more violently sadistic, than those around him. He had certainly succeeded. He was feared as much by those in power as by the Reich's many enemies. Even Himmler, the overall director of the Gestapo, was said to be wary of the protégé whom he had done so much to promote since they were introduced in 1932.

Above all, Bonner despised his superior officer because Heydrich had allowed personal ambition to corrupt the working practice of a secret policeman. It was not enough to trap the insects, as Heydrich termed his enemies; he had to pull their legs off as well. He was a psychopath whose pleasure in savagery was counterproductive and also ran against the grain of good secret-police practice. The most valuable weapon in the Gestapo's armoury, the priceless commodity that underpinned every secret operation, was solid, irrefutable information. As Bonner well knew, you don't get reliable information from those you torture to death.

He paused in front of Schmidt, raised his right arm and said, "*Heil Hitler.*"

She smiled, raised the palm of her hand to him by way of reply and said, "*Guten Morgen.*"

Bonner sat down and scowled. He had never been able to make this woman respond properly to the Hitlergruss. She did so, of course, when Heydrich came, because he terrified everyone. But somehow Bonner did not inspire the same fear.

"Coffee?" said Schmidt.

Bonner yawned. "Yes. Is Sara in?"

Schmidt nodded and reached over the bar and under the counter, pressing a hidden button. Seconds later, the door at the far end opened and a tall, dark-haired young woman walked in. She was wearing a tight-fitting, low-cut dress, different in style and colour from that of the woman on the door. She looked tired. He face was pale, the pallor accentuated by black lipstick and nail varnish. Her eyes were dark pools under long lashes. She had been working there for over a year and must be about twenty-three years old by now, thought Bonner.

"Tea?" he said to her.

The woman nodded, lit a cigarette, sat on a bar stool and stared ahead into the mirror. Bonner looked at her profile next to him and then at her reflection in the mirror. She had the moody look of a woman with secret sorrows, yet her eyes were lit with silent laughter. Her face held you, so that if you turned away for fear of being caught staring, you immediately wanted to turn back again.

She was Heydrich's masterstroke, an act so brazen that Bonner could still scarcely credit his boss with the nerve to take such a risk.

Sara was Jewish. Her real name was Ruth Sternschein, but the Nazis forced all Jews to take first names that denoted their racial origin. The women were all made to take the first name "Sara" and the men "Israel". The names were stamped on their identity papers. So Ruth became Sara. She was the eldest child of a family of doctors in Hamburg. She'd been well educated and was studying law at university when her life ended. That was how she described it. She was twenty-two years old and her life didn't just change, it ended.

The reason was simple. The head of the Gestapo had decided that a Jewish girl would become the lead attraction in his Berlin brothel. Here, senior party members, army officers and foreign visitors dallied by night. Here, their every intimate move was photographed and recorded. Every one of the rooms, including the small swimming pool in the basement, had been wired for sound and film. These men were not just caught indulging in sexual excesses that defied imagination – they were in many cases caught doing so with a Jewish woman.

At a time when the mere suggestion of Jewish ancestry would bring shame and expulsion on any member of the Nazi

Party or senior member of the military, such illicit liaisons gave Reinhard Heydrich extraordinary power over those caught in the web. Heydrich himself would bring senior colleagues to the Salon for an evening's amusement. Those he wished to entrap and blackmail would be introduced to Sara. Sometimes no more than drink and some exceptionally good food were served, but on most occasions the guests slipped through the fanlight door and found a comfortable sitting room, where the girls on duty that night would be sipping tea, smoking and reading magazines.

A large crystal vase in a round centre table was filled with carnations. The rules were strict. The girls must all wear smart grey dresses as if about to go out for an evening drink or afternoon coffee. They were to have polite conversation with their guests, nothing political but usually harmless chat about the latest film, the weather or the birth of a polar bear cub at the zoo – anything but politics.

It had been Kitty Schmidt's idea that her Salon should create the illusion of a small social gathering at which two people who find each other attractive may discreetly, and immediately, indulge their desire. When the establishment had originally opened, sometime around 1927, the police were paid off and the major hotels informed that their wealthier guests would find discretion and entertainment behind the big door at 11 Giesebrechtstrasse. The word spread and soon senior military officers began to knock on the door, then foreign diplomats. As the Salon became well known, the prices went up and Schmidt developed a restaurant to sustain the illusion of a social rather than sexual ambience. When Heydrich took over, he liked the idea and improved it by supplying champagne in what became known as the Pink Room. He hired chefs to make sure the food was the best in Berlin and insisted that the wine and champagne be of the most expensive vintages.

The Salon's guests – they were always referred to as guests, never as customers or clients – made their choice by taking a carnation from the vase in the centre table and offering it to whoever had caught their eye. He would then follow the girl down a corridor along which heavy, soundproofed doors gave onto luxurious bedrooms.

If Sara was in the party room, she almost always became the first choice. She was sometimes allowed to wear a more daring dress than the other girls, usually a red dress in the oriental style with a long side slit. Her dark sultry looks, a full figure with a tight waist and the laughter in those eyes were enough to attract any man. No one suspected her racial origins, because who would expect such a place to employ a Jewess?

Sara usually only appeared in the Salon when Heydrich had special guests he wished to impress – or rather entrap. It was how he had got Fritsch just before Christmas. The army commander had been in with two fellow officers. They were drunk. Heydrich was not there. The army hated him, and with good reason. Sara had her orders. She made a play for the general at the bar. It had worked. The two were laughing and joking until well after midnight, when Sara had suggested a swim in the private pool; just us, she had said.

Fritsch was cautious, even if drunk.

"Just us – really?" he had asked.

"Of course."

She had smiled sweetly and let one hand rest on his thigh. A few minutes later he was naked, moving his scarred body along the pool with a clumsy breaststroke as Sara swam beside him. And the cameras never stopped.

Sara had settled her account with life the moment they picked her up and drove her to Berlin. She knew her life was over and merely wished to find a swift way to end it. It was Joseph who had kept her alive.

Her twin brother had been a member of the underground communist party and, worse still, had joined a small resistance group in Hamburg. They did nothing too drastic, circulating underground leaflets attacking the party and especially the Führer, defacing party posters. Such offences merited execution, but when he was caught they sent him to a new concentration camp in the east instead and began to watch his family more closely.

As a well-known Jewish family, the Sternscheins were in any case already under the watchful eyes of the Gestapo. It was when Heydrich saw a surveillance photo of Sara smoking at a café that the idea came to him.

Bonner took Sara aside and briefed her. She had heard it all before. The target had to be charmed, seduced and compromised. The photographs must show him in acts of sufficient depravity to place his reputation and career beyond redemption. The target was an enemy of the Reich and thus must be destroyed. She listened, looked at two photographs, nodded and said nothing. What irritated Bonner about Sara was that she showed no gratitude. Her brother would have been executed by now, and she and her family would have been in a camp, but for Heydrich's intervention. Here she was, living a comfortable life in Berlin in a rented room next to the Salon, with all bills paid, and with little more to do than satisfy the lust of a few perverted middle-aged men.

In return, she received monthly letters from her brother, in his handwriting, assuring her of his survival in a camp called Buchenwald. Every three months, she was handed a photograph of her mother reading a current copy of Hamburg's evening newspaper in the front room of their home. Most Jews, thought Bonner, would have regarded that as an act of mercy. Sara and her brother were at least safe. After all, things were going to get much worse for the rest of her tribe in Germany. The forced emigration programme had not had the required result, despite the terror tactics used against the community. There were simply too many left, maybe as many as six hundred thousand. Heydrich was said to be working on other solutions to the problem.

Bonner had never subscribed to the fiction that Jews were somehow responsible for the defeat in the last war. It was a central plank in the party ideology and it was important to support it vocally and publicly, and he did so. Privately, he had never had a problem with them. Jews always seemed to be bumping into history, or maybe history bumped into them, but frankly so what? He wasn't religious and didn't give a damn who had nailed Christ to the Cross.

The real battle lay with the communists. Those bastards had undermined the country after the war, seeking to subvert it in the name of Marxist tyranny. That was what he was fighting for. He had fought in the street battles against the reds in the early twenties in Munich, Frankfurt and Berlin. The republic had been sliding towards anarchy then, and the communists were well organised and using weapons imported from the new Marxist regime in Moscow.

Bonner got up and put out his cigarette. Sara stood up beside him.

"Understood?" he said.

"Yes," she said.

He stepped towards her, put his arm around her waist and let his hand slide over the curve of her backside. The dark eyes looked straight at him. He held her gaze and squeezed softly. She didn't smile, merely nodded in the direction of the fanlight door.

"You want to come in?"

You had to admire the nerve of the girl. She knew he could not follow her into the Pink Room. Sara was reserved for special visitors, and Bonner suspected Heydrich included himself in that category. Heydrich controlled the film and recording room at the top of the building. There were times when the operators were told to turn their machines off and leave for the evening.

Any other member of the service, even one so senior as himself, would risk dismissal at best if they were caught on film with this woman. She knew that, which is why she was tempting him. And she was tempting. There was something about her that seemed distant, unobtainable, as if the real Sara Sternschein was somewhere else and this was a cipher she had created to perform in the Salon.

"No, I want you to follow my orders."

"You know I always obey orders," she said.

There was laughter in her eyes when she looked at him. She turned and walked away through the fanlight door.

4

On the evening of 5 February, just three weeks after Macrae and Primrose had arrived in Berlin, they were playing a game of backgammon at home before supper when they received the first of a series of telephone calls.

The first caller was Halliday, who was clearly in a hurry.

"No time to talk. Just listen to the radio at seven."

He rang off. Macrae turned the radio on and refreshed his whisky and soda. Primrose looked up from the backgammon set.

"What's happening?"

"I don't know. It must be serious if Halliday is in a flap."

Instead of the hourly news bulletin, the announcer said an important communiqué had been issued by the Reich Chancellery, which he would read in full.

The head of the armed forces and war minister, General Werner von Blomberg, had resigned with immediate effect on health grounds. The commander of the army, General Werner von Fritsch, had also resigned.

The announcer then read out the names of sixteen generals who had been relieved of their commands and placed on the reserve list. Forty-four other senior officers, including a number of field commanders, were said to have been transferred to other units. There was a rustle of paper as the announcer paused, as if unable to grasp the text that followed.

The chancellor, Adolf Hitler, would become supreme commander of the armed forces and minister for war. The minister of foreign affairs, Neurath, had resigned, to be replaced by Joachim von Ribbentrop.

The ambassadors in Vienna, Rome and Tokyo had also been replaced.

Macrae placed a bottle of whisky and a soda siphon by the phone. It was midnight when he finished the last call. Sir Nevile was the first to contact him after the radio announcement, insisting on an early meeting the next morning. Then the political attaché David Buckland rang to ask what the hell was going on. The War Office called from London with requests for a lengthy analysis, to be ready for an emergency cabinet meeting the following morning. And then journalists from every British newspaper represented in Berlin rang for quotes and comment, anything to make sense of what most were describing as a Nazi purge of the army.

Macrae realised they had his home number through long acquaintance with his predecessor. The final call was from William Shirer.

"We haven't met. My fault. Thanks for your card. Shall we have a drink at the Adlon tomorrow evening?"

"Anywhere but there," said Macrae.

"OK, make it the Drei Schwestern at seven. Small place off Gendarmenmarkt. General Staff use it, but no harm in that."

Macrae was drunk by the time he staggered into the bedroom. Primrose was reading a magazine in bed, with curlers in her hair.

"You poor thing," she said. "What a night."

"This is just the start," he replied.

The next morning, the German newspapers gave the news front-page treatment with sensational headlines. The more informed correspondents pointed out that Blomberg had not been popular with his fellow senior officers, owing to his closeness to Hitler. That was what made his dismissal all the more surprising. None of the reports even hinted at the remarriage of the general, although all noted his recent divorce. Fritsch was a different matter. He was popular, highly regarded, and there was even speculation in the controlled press about an army backlash against what officers were said to see as a political takeover. And that was the point the German papers conveniently ignored but which the western correspondents fully understood: in making himself head of the army and minister for war the German chancellor had placed his country on the path to inevitable conflict with the European powers.

Macrae leafed through the daily papers at breakfast the next morning while forking pieces of grapefruit into his mouth. Primrose had not dissected the fruit properly, so that the segments clung together as he lifted them. First one, then a second fell onto the papers.

Primrose looked up from the previous day's edition of the London *Times* as he grunted in irritation.

"I thought we had a grapefruit knife," he said. "You know, the one with the curved blade."

"It got lost in the move, like a lot of other things."

She reached over and used her knife to cut the remaining grapefruit into separate pieces.

"I don't suppose I'll be seeing much of you for a few days," she said.

"Yes, I'm sorry. It's going to be busy."

"I'll be going out tonight. The cook will leave something for you in the oven."

Macrae looked up in surprise. "Where are you going?"

"Some of the wives are having a night out."

"Really? Where?"

"I don't know, a drink at the Adlon maybe and then dinner somewhere."

Sir Nevile was smoking a cigarette when his staff assembled for the morning briefing. This was highly unusual and against his own strict orders. He looked as if he had slept little and they noted that he had cut himself shaving that morning. Before him lay a pile of German newspapers and to one side a file of cables that had come in overnight from the Foreign Office.

They took their coffees and found seats around the long polished mahogany table, which had been a focal point of the British diplomatic day in Berlin since the embassy was first established in 1872. That had been in Bismarck's time of the Second Reich. Now they were to hear how His Majesty's Government intended to deal with a crisis in its successor.

Sir Nevile thanked everyone for coming at such short notice. It was important, he said, to set the current developments in German politics in context.

The door opened and Halliday came in, looking less like a poacher and more like a sheepdog that had lost its flock. Shaggy and shambolic were adjectives that inevitably came to mind when the SIS agent appeared. Macrae noted Sir Nevile's obvious irritation. The ambassador had paused midsentence and waited while Halliday poured a cup of coffee and sat down.

"Sorry I'm late," he said.

"I was just saying that it is important to place the current developments in context. There is a great deal of sensational reporting in the German press this morning and, from what I hear, the British press are no better."

Sir Nevile picked up a sheaf of documents and waved them at those around the table. He was the head of one of Britain's biggest missions abroad, with a complement of over a hundred, if you counted the commercial and consular staff, and they all needed to know and understand the government's reaction to what an irresponsible press in both countries was describing as a political coup and a Nazi purge.

The *Daily Express* in London had a screaming headline above a crude cartoon showing a jackboot kicking open a door marked "War". It was utterly irresponsible. A free press was all very well, but there had to be limits. The papers had no right to whip up war hysteria at a time when calm diplomacy was required.

The eyes of the world were on Berlin. The staff around the table and the wider British diplomatic community had to understand what had been discussed well into the early hours of the morning. He had talked on a secure telephone line with both the PM and Sir Anthony Eden, the foreign secretary. The question that had been tossed back and forth was how to respond to Hitler's sudden seizure of military power – indeed, how would the German army respond?

"I wish to share a view that was agreed in London last night and that will be put to cabinet this morning," he said. "You all know that the cause of this current crisis is the marriage of General Blomberg to a young woman who turns out to . . . have had a past."

He can't even use the word "prostitute", thought Macrae. A late-nineteenth-century mind shaped by the Victorian values of womanly virtue and gentlemanly conduct is seated at the head of this table trying to explain how to deal with a group of gangsters.

"HMG thinks Hitler has succeeded in manoeuvring himself out of a difficult position with remarkable adroitness," the ambassador continued. "He has taken the opportunity to remove the conservative elements of the army who posed a threat to his legitimacy, while at the same time showing the wilder element of the National Socialist Party that he is in charge and that his will is supreme."

David Buckland was the first to break the silence.

"This can't be a good thing, sir, can it? The one check on Hitler's power has gone."

"Not at all," replied the ambassador smoothly. "If I can quote you the very words the prime minister said to me only . . ." He raised his left arm, looking at his watch in an exaggerated gesture designed to give emphasis to his remark. "Only a few hours ago: 'It will be much easier to deal with a man who is not continually looking over his shoulder fearing a military coup. The Reich chancellor is both head of state and head of the army, and effectively minister for war, and thus someone with whom we can negotiate in confidence.'"

There was a further silence around the table, finally broken by the noise of a door closing quietly. Halliday had left the room.

The Drei Schwestern restaurant was designed to resemble a hunting lodge. Stuffed game birds were placed in each of the mullioned windows looking out onto the street. Two large sets of antlers locked horns over the studded wooden door on which there was a knocker fashioned from an old rifle butt. Inside, mounted heads of stag, boar and what looked to

Macrae like wolves lined the walls. A leaping log fire at one end of the room and candles set on tables spread with red patterned cloths provided the only light.

On one side, alcoves had been created to give diners more privacy. A large menu by the door written in old-fashioned curling script announced a series of middle-European dishes, most of which featured dumplings of one kind or another. In January, the hunting season was at its height and the menu made much of the hare, venison, pheasant and partridge on offer.

Shirer was already there when Macrae arrived, sitting in an alcove in front of a large tankard of beer.

"You like it?" asked the American.

"It's like a Hollywood version of what a German tavern should look like – without the lighting."

"It's a bit dark, I agree. The army loves this place – senior officers, that is. It's not cheap. They like the atmosphere and they don't mind those either." Shirer pointed to three young waitresses dressed in lederhosen with white cotton blouses.

The restaurant was already almost full. There were several officers in uniform among the guests, the firelight glinting off medals, brass buttons and shiny straps. Swastika armbands were visible at every table, catching the eye as glasses were raised in frequent toasts.

They ordered venison soup with dumplings and Macrae chose a Wiener schnitzel to follow, while Shirer opted for roast duck.

"Thank you for coming," said Shirer. "I know you're very busy."

"I am, but one of my more pleasant duties is reading transcripts of your broadcasts."

Shirer laughed and drank his beer, leaving white froth on his moustache.

"They can't get enough of it in the States. To a lot of people Hitler is some kind of messiah."

"'Messiah'?"

"Sure, giving the bolshies a good kicking. Bringing order and discipline back, putting people to work. You should hear Henry Ford on the subject."

"They quote him a lot in the press here."

"Sure they do. They love him. He's done a lot of deals here."

"They appreciate his views on the Jews, I suppose."

Shirer paused as the soup was placed deftly on the table by a waitress. Macrae noticed that the pendant around her neck was a small swastika set in a circle of faux diamonds.

"They quote him on Jews all the time. Man's a raging anti-Semite. But you know what? Your government and my government don't give a damn about the Jews."

Macrae murmured his assent. In all the briefings he had been given in the embassy and in conversation with his fellow attachés, the treatment of Jews was hardy mentioned. Never once had Sir Nevile Henderson commented on the forced immigration, seizure of property, street beatings and compulsory wearing of the yellow star. When Macrae had asked why no stronger protest had been made, the ambassador had treated the question with the condescension of a teacher addressing a new pupil in class.

"This is a brutal regime; we never doubt nor deny it. Our job is to stop that regime starting a conflict that will drag Britain and France into a second great war. The treatment of Jews, Gypsies and what the government deem social misfits is regrettable, but it is none of our business."

Macrae wanted to ask what Queen Victoria's favourite prime minister, the great Benjamin Disraeli, would have made of such a policy. But he didn't, and no one else in the meeting seemed to find anything untoward in the ambassador's statement.

Shirer was waving a hand in front of his face.

"Hey, come back. I've lost you."

Macrae smiled and apologised. He wondered briefly if Shirer had ever heard of Disraeli, the first Jewish prime minister of Britain and indeed of any supposedly civilised country. He thought not. They turned to the army purge. Macrae quickly realised that Shirer had not invited him in the hope of eliciting useful information. He wanted to make sure Macrae was aware of his views. And Macrae wanted to hear them. Like most western diplomats he steered clear of the press corps in Berlin, but Shirer was an exception. He was well informed.

"I knew your predecessor," he said. "Watson. Nice guy, but hopeless. They wined and dined him and he swallowed everything they told him. He even believed the bullshit about the creation of a greater Germany being in accord with Woodrow Wilson's doctrine of self-determination for all peoples."

Shirer paused, allowing Macrae the opportunity to defend his predecessor. Macrae said nothing.

"You know the trouble with you Brits?"

"No, but I have a feeling you're going to tell me."

"You left your balls in the trenches."

"We lost almost a million young men," said Macrae softly.

"I know, but it's not the issue, is it? If you don't wake up, he's going to walk all over you – and the rest of Europe."

Across the room, a group of officers were settling in around a table. One seemed familiar. Macrae recognised Koenig in his colonel's uniform. He was looking serious, as were his companions.

"Know someone over there?" asked Shirer.

Dining with a journalist was exhausting, thought Macrae. When they weren't asking for information, they were giving you their world views, and in between they watched every move you made.

"No, thought I recognised someone."

The main course arrived and, as the waitress bent over the table, Macrae glanced at Koenig. He was raising his glass in a toast to his fellow officers, all of whom were of the rank of colonel or above.

"So you guys have worked out what this is all about?" Shirer was speaking through a mouthful of duck.

"If you mean the army purge, yes I think so."

"So what do you make of it?"

"How do you mean?"

"Well, Hitler takes over the army, becomes his own war minister, fires all those ambassadors that had got too close to the guest governments. It means war, doesn't it?"

"This is off the record, right?"

"Sure," said Shirer. He grunted in pain, sat back suddenly, fished in his mouth with a finger and brought out a sizeable pellet of shot.

"Would you believe it? They used number two shot on a duck. Must have been hoping for a goose."

Macrae wasn't listening. Across the room, on a table adjacent to Koenig's party, a party of well-dressed ladies were taking their seats. Primrose was among them, looking pretty in a dark blue dress with a silver bow that caught the light. He recognised other wives from the embassy. He could just hear their English voices, a pitch higher than the guttural German accents around him. Shirer had summoned the waitress and was discussing the size of the shot he had found.

Macrae waited for what he knew would happen next. Colonel Florian Koenig rose from his seat, bowed before

Primrose and extended his arm in the Nazi salute. The ladies at the table giggled. Primrose rose, offering her hand, which Koenig took and raised lightly to his lips, holding it there for a second while his eyes held hers. Primrose turned and said something to the ladies and then appeared to introduce them, since each raised a hand in greeting. Koenig clicked his heels and bowed at every name. He gestured Primrose to sit down and pulled her chair back, moving it gently forward as she did so.

"Hey! You've gone again!"

Macrae turned back to Shirer, who was looking across the restaurant, trying to see what had attracted his attention. Shirer leant forward confidentially.

"Look, if you like those waitresses, I can take you to a place where the girls are much prettier and very, very discreet."

"No thanks," said Macrae. He felt like a voyeur. He could not go over to Primrose. It would be awkward with Koenig at the next table, and especially now they had exchanged such a greeting. It would be embarrassing. Shirer was talking again in a low urgent voice.

"I am going to give you a jump on my next broadcast. It's Austria next. They are going to go in with troops, tanks, the lot, and take the place. Annex it. Soon, very soon."

Macrae turned his attention back to the American correspondent. Shirer was well sourced and often given high-level information. Austria next, he had said – annexation with troops and tanks. Another violation of the Versailles peace treaty signed by President Woodrow Wilson, among others. Another big step on the road to a wider European war. Was that what Goebbels wanted the American people to hear?

"They say a majority of the Austrian population will support them. Question is, what will HMG do when the tanks roll across the border?"

Macrae put a slice of the breaded veal into his mouth, playing for time. He knew exactly what HMG would do: nothing. The government would say very little beyond trying to persuade parliament and the press that Hitler had merely moved once again into his own back yard and reunited territory that had historically belonged to Germany anyway. If that would salve the German wounds over Versailles, then so be it.

Macrae put his napkin on the table.

"We have not fully evaluated the meaning behind the army purges. As for Austria . . ."

"You have not fully evaluated that possibility either . . .?"

Shirer laughed and Macrae joined him.

"I'm sorry, I'm not much use to you," Macrae said. "And I have to go."

"You need to find your balls – that's the message you should take back to that ambassador of yours."

The resignation two weeks later of the British foreign secretary, Sir Anthony Eden, was greeted with jubilation by the German press. Goebbels's ministry summoned correspondents to Wilhelmstrasse to brief them that not just an enemy of Germany but an enemy of peace had been rightly removed by the prime minister.

Neville Chamberlain was praised for having come to his senses, although the praise was tempered by a stern warning that Germany would not tolerate third-party interference in central European affairs. That evening, Hitler himself drummed home the point with an aggressive speech to the Reichstag parliament, now sitting in an old theatre, declaring that the separation from Germany of ten million Germans now living in Austria and Czechoslovakia because of an unfairly imposed peace treaty was unbearable.

The next day, Macrae met Halliday in the corridor on the way to the staff meeting and was beckoned into his office. Halliday carefully closed the door.

"What are you hearing?" he asked.

"Same as you," Macrae said. "He's got away with it. Now he's winding himself up for a move into Austria. The new generals quite like the idea. You don't have to be a Nazi in the army to appreciate the chance to test your new tanks."

"The Austrians won't fight – they'll just walk in."

"And we'll do nothing?"

"Nothing we can do, old boy," said Halliday. "Now that Eden's gone, that's the end of it. But I want to ask a small favour."

"Which is?"

"If you have any good contacts in the army, ask them what they will do if Czechoslovakia really is next after Austria. I hear the army may not be up for that."

"What are you suggesting?"

"I'm not suggesting anything. I'm just asking for a little help. Now, let's go and hear what the oracle has for us."

Sir Nevile spoke for thirty minutes and never once mentioned the resignation of the foreign secretary. His greater concern was a meeting he was to have with Herr Hitler the following week. He would make it clear, in a conventionally diplomatic and thus discreet way, that any move into Austria would not meet with an aggressive diplomatic response from Britain.

David Buckland raised his hand. "Could we not at least prepare a very strong condemnation and ask for an emergency meeting of the League of Nations? After all, it's not as if Austrians have been asked if they want to be annexed."

Sir Nevile cast a cold eye on his political attaché. Buckland had obviously been spending too much time with those troublemakers Halliday and Macrae.

"It is part of my job to understand the thinking of the National Socialist government and to represent that thinking to HMG. One can hardly argue with an ambition to unify German-speaking people into one nation from which they were separated by an unequal treaty. The question HMG poses is: will Herr Hitler stop there? The answer is, I do not know, but I do know I would not be doing my job if I believed the worst of Hitler, because that can only lead to the worst happening."

Macrae had asked William Shirer and his wife, Theresa, to dinner at home. It was Primrose's idea. She had heard much about the famed American correspondent and wanted to meet his Austrian wife, who worked as a fashion photographer in Vienna.

The Shirers arrived promptly at six thirty. Theresa was well wrapped up in a long black fur coat, from which a pretty face emerged below a woollen bonnet. Macrae helped her out of the coat. She seemed shy and shook hands without looking at him. She was much younger than her husband; Macrae guessed she was about thirty.

It was hard to tell how old Shirer was. He was one of those men who achieve middle age early in life. His hair had receded to reveal a gleaming bald pate. The moustache was carefully trimmed into a thin line above the lip and the waistline was that of a man who preferred to take a cab a couple of blocks for breakfast of a coffee and a Danish rather than walk.

Theresa appeared relieved to be invited to accompany Primrose into the kitchen.

"I am going to make you an Old-Fashioned cocktail. We'll join the men again when they have stopped being so boring," Primrose said, taking her by the arm.

Shirer opened the window and stepped onto the balcony. The evening sky had lightened in the first days of March and the sun had yet to set. Green buds on the branches of the trees in the Tiergarten promised the coming of spring.

"Nice view you've got. You're lucky," he said.

"Where are you staying?" asked Macrae, guiding his guest back inside and closing the window against the cold.

"We're renting a serviced apartment. Can't complain. CBS pays, but . . . ermm."

"You have a third person in your life there?"

Shirer laughed. "Yeah, it's all bugged. Comes with the territory, I guess."

Macrae poured both of them generous whiskies. They sat down and Shirer began to ask about the abdication of King Edward VIII two years previously. Every American Macrae had ever met wanted to talk about the affair between Wallis Simpson and King Edward, as if it was of any importance. The monarch had abdicated and in his place the nervous, stuttering, chain-smoking George VI had ascended the throne. No American could ever understand why the king had felt the need to step down just because he was denied the right to marry his mistress. It had cheated them of an American First Lady living in Buckingham Palace.

"Folks back where I come from sure would have liked to see Mrs Simpson on the throne," said Shirer.

"It happened two years ago. It's history."

"That's not history," said Shirer. "That's just nice fat juicy gossip, and we love it. Out there is history." He pointed to the window. "You Brits are going to have to put your tin hats on soon. That's history."

"And you Americans?"

Shirer laughed, choked on his drink and laughed some more. Macrae faintly heard Primrose from the kitchen urging Theresa to have another cocktail and telling her it stopped the men being boring.

"We are going to sit this one out. You're on your own this time. Isn't that right, honey?"

The ladies had returned holding drinks. Theresa looked a little flushed.

"What are you laughing about?" she said.

"He's just told me a war is coming and the Americans are going to stay on their side of the Atlantic," said Macrae.

"War, war, war – that's all you talk about," said Theresa.

She seemed irritated and sat down heavily next to her husband, spilling some of her drink.

"What do you want to talk about, sweetheart?" he said, putting his arm around her.

"I want to know if I should join the Nazi Party."

They all laughed.

"It's not funny," she said. "If you're Austrian, it might be a good idea."

Shirer suddenly looked at Primrose and slapped his knee.

"Hey! It's just come to me! Weren't you in the Drei Schwestern the other night?"

"Yes, we were," said Primrose, looking surprised. "Don't tell me you were there?"

"Yes, we were both there, in one of the alcoves."

"*You* were there?" said Primrose, looking at her husband.

"I didn't want to break up your hen party. Besides, we were being very boring, talking shop. Did you have a nice time?"

"We had a lovely time. And guess who I met – Florian."

"Oh! That was who was bowing and scraping around you, was it?"

Primrose flashed him a glance, then turned to Theresa.

"Florian is a friend of ours, a colonel in something or other. German colonels are frightfully smart, with all those medals and shiny boots. You've got to hand it to the Nazis, they do know how to dress up."

"I'm Austrian, not German, so we don't quite see it that way," said Theresa, her voice slightly slurred. She raised her glass and drank.

"Oh, be fair. They do have a certain chic, don't they?"

"That's what frightens me," said Theresa. "It's what that bitch Riefenstahl did at the Olympics. She glamorised them, and now you talk as if they've suddenly become fashionable."

Her voice had risen. She drained the rest of her drink and stood up, looking for the door.

"Darling, calm down and come and sit," said Shirer, holding out his arms.

"I can't calm down. My country is next, isn't it? That's what you talk about all day! Yesterday the Rhineland, tomorrow Austria, then Czechoslovakia. You talk about it as if it were a bloody tourist itinerary."

Theresa fished in her bag, lit a cigarette with shaking hands and sat down. She began to cry.

Shirer put his arm around her. "Darling, I'm sorry. I'll take you home."

"I don't want to go home. I'm sorry. It's just that you people don't live here and I do." She smiled at Primrose through her tears and raised her empty glass. "That was lovely; can I have another one?"

Later that night, Primrose and Macrae lay in bed. They were both smoking.

"Did you really see us in the restaurant?" she said.

"Yes. You seemed to be having a good time. I was going to come over and then I saw Florian."

"You should have. He would have loved to see you."

"I doubt it. Not with his fellow officers there."

"He's asked us to go and spend a weekend at his hunting lodge, somewhere in the north. I thought you might like that. You could do a bit of shooting."

She stubbed her cigarette out. He blew a smoke ring at the ceiling, put the cigarette out and was about to reply when he saw she had gone to sleep.

The second rendezvous at the reptile house had been arranged by an unsigned note posted through the embassy letter box. Macrae arrived first and was admiring a cobra from Malaysia when a tap on the shoulder made him turn.

Koenig was in uniform and even in the semi-darkness Macrae could see he must have been on parade that morning. The cap badge, medals, leather boots and even his swagger stick gleamed in the low light.

"You will be interested to know that I am doing research for a lecture," Koenig said, not looking at Macrae but staring at the cobra. "And this charming creature is how I am going to hold the attention of thirty young staff officers whose only thoughts are how to satiate their thirst for beer and their appetite for those plump young ladies that one used to be able to pick up on the Kurfürstendamm priced at a hundred reichsmarks for half an hour."

He tapped on the glass and the snake swung a lazy head around, trying to identify the noise.

"This chap is clever. It can move fast and kill quickly with powerful jaws. Its prey is small animals, mostly rabbits. But it chooses to use not speed but charm. The snake makes friends with its prey. It sways back and forth, mesmerising the victim, drawing it closer until it can strike without effort."

Macrae had been wondering when to bring up the invitation to a shooting weekend at the colonel's lodge.

"You follow me?" said Koenig.

"Not really."

"It is a question of tactics, isn't it? In the cobra's case, the tactics are charm and guile."

"Meaning?"

"Austria. It will all be over in a day."

He wheeled and walked away in the darkness.

"But when?" said Macrae softly, his voice trailing after the departing figure.

Koenig turned. "It's time we drank some more good whisky. You are coming to spend the weekend soon, I think."

"But Austria – when?"

Koenig had disappeared.

5

"The bastard was crying! I saw him, tears streaming down his face, in the main square of Linz, and everyone was cheering and the bells were ringing, and there he was blubbing like a baby . . .!"

The ambassador sighed and snapped his pen down on the table.

"You know perfectly well that that is not the way we refer to the head of state."

"What would you rather I called him?"

"That's enough!" The ambassador had risen from his chair, white-faced. "Make your report and then go and clean yourself up."

Macrae had arrived at the embassy only minutes earlier after an eleven-hour ride on a motorcycle from the Austrian border. Sir Nevile had called a meeting of senior staff to hear his first-hand account of the long-awaited German invasion of her smaller neighbour. All phone links between Austria and the outside world had been cut and the staff of the British embassy in Vienna had even found radio communications with London mysteriously jammed.

Macrae was handed a cup of coffee by a secretary. He placed his briefcase on the table, sending a small cloud of dust into the air. His suit was smeared with mud and his face caked in dirt. His eyes looked out from the circular imprints of the goggles, giving him an unworldly appearance. He looked round the table. All the usual faces were there except Halliday. Macrae sat down, drew out a notebook from his briefcase and began his report.

In the early hours of the day before, 12 March, columns of German infantry and armour crossed the Austrian border on the Munich – Salzburg road, while at daybreak paratroops landed at Vienna airport. There was no opposition. The troops were garlanded with flowers by cheering crowds. Tank crews were given free fuel at roadside garages. Church bells rang in every village and town across Austria.

Hitler flew to Munich that morning, then drove in a motorcade across the frontier at his birthplace, Braunau, and spent the day in Linz, the town where he had grown up. As he walked through a throng of admirers in the main square that afternoon, hands reached out to touch him, grasping and pulling at his long grey overcoat. Small boys thrust autograph books at him, while schoolgirls curtsied and bobbed. Suddenly he began to cry, tears streaming down his face. The crowd drew back, surprised at such a display of emotion.

Later that day, Hitler had driven to a neighbouring village to lay flowers on his parents' grave. In a speech that evening from the balcony of the Linz town hall, he declared that he had decided to return his beloved native country to the German Reich. Austria was to become part of Germany. The declaration was met with thunderous cheers.

• • •

Macrae paused and looked up from his notes.

"That all took place yesterday," he said. "Having received the ambassador's permission, I followed the invasion force by car. There were broken-down tanks and military vehicles all along the road. Once in Austria, the main problem was the crowds along the route. They would not let one pass. They thought I was German and kept giving me flowers and fruit."

"No sign of any opposition?"

It was Halliday, who had slipped into the meeting late.

"Not where I got to," said Macrae, "quite the opposite. But I hear it's very different in Vienna."

"That's pretty clear, then," said the ambassador. "A country that emerged from the wreckage of the war has thrown itself into the arms of its larger and more powerful neighbour. There was nothing we could have done about it and nothing we should do now but accept the situation. And may I say, this might make Hitler much easier to deal with. He's got what he wanted, and if it's the wish of the Austrian people, then who are we to argue?"

"A point of information," said Halliday. "I hear the railway and bus stations in Vienna are jammed with people desperate to leave. Cars are pouring out of the city towards the Czech border. Worse still, there are mobs of Nazi thugs hunting down anyone deemed to be an enemy: Jews, Gypsies, the usual suspects. You're not safe on the streets of Vienna unless you're wearing a swastika armband."

There was a silence. David Buckland raised his hand, looking enquiringly at the ambassador, who nodded.

"Can I ask whether HMG received any communication from the Austrian government during these events?"

Sir Nevile Henderson closed his eyes, rested his elbows on the table and placed his hands together as if in prayer.

"The Foreign Office received a cable from President Schuschnigg asking for assistance the night before the Germans moved. Lord Halifax replied that there was nothing we could do to guarantee Austria's security."

"Do we know what's happened to the president?"

The ambassador was about to reply when Halliday cut in.

"He and his entire government are under house arrest. I hear they are all going to be sent to the Sachsenhausen camp."

The ambassador looked around the room, the pallor of his face betraying irritation. Only Halliday and Macrae of those present had fought in the last war. And Halliday had paid the price. The man was an alcoholic wreck. The rest of them had no idea of the horror that had consumed the lives of so many hundreds and thousands of young men from every corner of the United Kingdom – English, Scots, Irish and Welsh.

And here were his staff, sitting around the table, doubt about HMG's proclaimed and popular policy of appeasement written on their faces. They hadn't talked to the widows and orphans left adrift by the slaughter, had they? Had they any idea of the numbers of maimed still hobbling around the streets holding out tin cans for charity? Had they ever visited the mentally scarred still lingering in squalid institutions far from the public gaze? No, of course not. Well, he, Sir Nevile Meyrick Henderson, *had* visited such institutions and seen the madness inflicted by war. And he would do everything in his power to prevent it happening again. He stood up and closed the meeting.

Macrae went home to change his clothes, have a quick bath and eat some breakfast. Anger trumped his exhaustion. He had not slept for the best part of twenty-four hours, but he knew that if he put his head down for even a few minutes he would be asleep all day. Primrose told her circle of friends among the diplomatic wives that she had never seen him so angry. He had come into the house looking like a ghost, drunk the best part of a jug of coffee, gulped his way through a bowl of cornflakes, gnawed at an apple and departed, giving her a brief peck on the cheek.

"He said it was the saddest day of his professional life," she told her friends. "He can't stand Henderson, and the feeling is mutual. I fear for his job – just as I was getting to know you all too."

Back in the embassy, Macrae told his startled secretary to take a long walk in the Tiergarten for at least an hour, then locked his office door, took the phone off the hook and sat at her desk in front of an Olivetti typewriter. He fed a sheet of paper into the machine and began pounding the keys like an enraged pianist.

Memorandum to the Secretary of State for War, The Hon. Leslie Hore-Belisha.
Copy: The Right Honourable Sir Nevile Henderson.

Macrae paused, lit a cigarette and rolled the paper out of the typewriter. He searched the side drawers of the desk until he found one containing carbon paper, then started again. He was going to need a copy.

Following the German takeover of Austria, I have drawn up first thoughts on the military consequences for HMG. The facts speak for themselves. I place them before you without comment.

The incorporation of Austria has given Germany an extra seven million people. Thus their population now totals 75 million versus 50 million in Great Britain.

The Austrian Army has sworn personal allegiance to Hitler, giving him an extra twelve infantry divisions.

Germany now has free access to large quantities of iron, steel and magnesite, all key raw materials for its rearmament programme.

That programme is proceeding at a rapid rate. The German Wehrmacht currently comprises 40 divisions at full strength, four of which are armoured. This does not include the recent addition of the Austrian divisions. By the autumn, at current rate of production, that will increase to 60 divisions, 72 including the Austrian army.

This compares to United Kingdom's five front-line divisions. In case you doubt that fact, it comes from the Ministry of War in London. Our disarmament programme has also reduced our territorial reserves to eight divisions.

The Luftwaffe has 1,500 warplanes, ranging from fighters to heavy bombers.

The UK has 960 combat aircraft, none of which are a match for the Messerschmitt, Heinkel, Junkers and Focke-Wulf aircraft in the Luftwaffe.

The main German manufacturer of German weaponry, Alfred Krupp, has developed a new long-barrelled 88 mm anti-aircraft gun which has a wheeled undercarriage, giving the weapon great mobility. Six batteries have been sent to Spain for testing during the civil war there. The guns have proved surprisingly effective when used against tanks or infantry. Hitler has ordered their mass production and Krupp is already working on more advanced designs. The British army does not possess any comparable weapon. Our only anti-tank gun, the Vickers QF 2-pounder, cannot penetrate the front armour of the latest German tanks. Our anti-aircraft guns have been criticised as hopelessly inadequate by a parliamentary subcommittee on defence affairs.

German U-boat production has tripled . . .

He stopped. There was a loud knocking at the door. Macrae heard Halliday's voice. He let him in.

"I hear the furious sound of a typewriter," said Halliday, setting a cup of coffee on the desk. "I thought you might need this."

"Thanks," said Macrae.

Halliday looked over Macrae's shoulder.

"Interesting," he said.

"It's a military force comparison – now that they've got their hands on Austria."

"I am sure they will be most interested in London," said Halliday. "But there may well be an Anschluss closer to home. The ambassador, I hear, is making a formal complaint about you to the Foreign Office. He says the German authorities believe you are an obstacle to our policy of appeasement, and the ambassador agrees. He wants you withdrawn."

Macrae picked up the coffee, drank it in one gulp and put the cup down.

"You know this for sure?"

"The Germans monitor our cable traffic to London, but they don't have the codebook used for the ambassador's communications."

"And you do?"

"Let's just say my own masters are very interested in the private views of the ambassador," he said, smiling.

"I see. What do you suggest I do?"

"Nothing. Keep on doing exactly what you're doing. And I wouldn't mind a copy of that memo when you've finished."

He closed the door quietly. A second later the door opened again and his head reappeared.

"When you've finished trying to change British foreign policy, may I suggest a prelunch drink at the Adlon?"

Macrae looked at his watch. It was eleven thirty.

"Give me an hour," he said.

The Adlon bar was busy when Macrae arrived. He perched on a stool and placed his coat on the one next to him to reserve it. At the far end of the bar a middle-aged man was deep in conversation with a dark-haired woman whose face was obscured. The journalists were in their usual place. Businessmen were scanning menus over glasses of what looked to Macrae like gin and tonic.

He could do with one of those. He ordered a large measure for himself and asked the barman to pour the tonic to the brim of a long glass. He began to relax for the first time in almost two days. He had completed the memorandum, noting disparities of equipment right down to the marked difference between British and German shortwave radio sets and the quantity of ammunition held in reserves.

It probably wouldn't do any good, because he was only telling his own government what they secretly knew but refused to admit publicly. The one encouraging thought was that he had sent the memo directly to the secretary of state for war. Leslie Hore-Belisha was an unusual choice for the post. He was Jewish and as such subject to the anti-Semitism so prevalent among the English upper classes – or so Macrae had heard. Hore-Belisha was a believer in rearmament, but the prime minister had already rebuffed his plans for the introduction of conscription and turned down a proposal to increase weapons manufacture.

The cable had been sent in code to the secretary of state, copied to Sir Nevile. There had been a little difficulty with the cable clerk, because all such communications to London were supposed to be signed off by the ambassador. Luckily, Sir Nevile was out of town and Macrae was able to plead the urgency of the information.

There would be a hell of a row. Macrae realised he might well prove to be the most short-lived military attaché in the history of the diplomatic service. He didn't care. He turned as Halliday slipped onto the stool beside him, pointed to his glass and said to the barman, "Same again for him and likewise for me."

The barman placed the drinks in front of them and began polishing the counter. Halliday barked something at him in German that Macrae didn't understand. To make the point, he banged his fist on the bar. The barman sulkily moved away.

"That was a bit rough," said Macrae.

"He's Gestapo. They all are here. So, have you calmed down yet?"

At the far end of the bar, the man and woman had left their seats and seemed to be about to leave.

Macrae nodded. "I'm going to sit here all afternoon and quietly get very drunk."

"You're right about what's going on in Vienna. Worse than anything here. Nazis have been going to the railway stations and pushing those trying to leave onto the tracks. Especially the women. It drives the men mad, and then there's a fight and out come the truncheons. Up on the Czech border they're abandoning cars and trying to cross through the woods at night. It's freezing up there and they're dying, whole families together."

"We won't give them visas, I suppose?"

"Nope. Our embassy has closed all its consular offices there. Orders from London. They're like rats in a trap."

"I see you've come here to cheer me up."

Macrae noticed that the man had persuaded the woman to have another drink. They had moved up the bar, closer to where he was sitting. The man was smartly dressed in an expensive striped suit with a white handkerchief peeping from the breast pocket and a golden clasp across a purple tie. A businessman maybe, thought Macrae. The woman was dressed in a fashionable red-and-white-striped skirt that broke into pleats and dropped to her ankles. Around her neck she wore a thin silk scarf that matched her skirt and spilled over a flowing white blouse. She might have been a minor member of the aristocracy, except that her dark sultry looks and the clothes suggested a fashion model.

"I have come to congratulate you on a good job," said Halliday. "Don't so anything silly like resigning. No one is going to fire you. There are people in London – especially my people – who know we need someone like you here right now."

"Trouble is, I don't want to be here. I can't stand the place. It's evil."

"I'll drink to that," said Halliday. "You have to hand it to the Nazis. The quality of evil here is exceptional. It's pure, unadulterated, and clear and cold as a mountain stream. You won't find evil like this anywhere else in the world. Genghis Khan, Nero, Caligula, they've got nothing on these fellows. They specialise in evil in this town and they're very creative, they turn it into theatre, so count yourself lucky – you're getting a front-row seat."

He finished his gin and tonic and slid from the stool.

"I wouldn't go back to the office today if I were you," he said. He gave Macrae a pat on the back and walked off. The barman moved in the moment Halliday left.

"Another one?" he said.

"Please, and a glass of water on the side."

Macrae lit a cigarette and turned to look at the room. The corner where the journalists camped out was empty. He looked at his watch. It was lunchtime. He didn't feel like eating. He felt like getting drunk, and that was exactly what he was going to do.

"Has your friend left?" said a voice.

He looked at the woman in the red-and-white-striped skirt, who was now two bar stools away.

"Yes," he said. "He's gone back to the office. Which is where I should be."

"My friend too," she said.

He tried to place the accent. It sounded north German. It would be good to talk to someone normal for a change.

"What does he do, your friend?" he asked.

"He runs a restaurant here in Berlin. The food is French. He hires his chefs in Paris. And you – what do you do?" She asked the question with a smile and moved a seat closer. "Do you mind if I join you?"

"Please do. Would you like a drink?"

"I would love another of these." She held up a wineglass. "Dry white from the Tyrol. You should try it."

"I think I'll stick to gin."

He ordered drinks. The barman placed them on the bar and began polishing the counter. Macrae tried to remember what it was that Halliday had said to him. He was feeling hazy and waved the man away, before turning back to the woman.

"Cheers," he said.

"Bottoms up," she said, speaking this time in accented English.

"Ah! You speak English?"

"I try."

"So what do you do?" he asked.

"I asked first," she said.

Macrae drank his gin, enjoying the intoxicating taste of juniper and cane spirit mingled with the knowledge that a strange and very attractive woman had suddenly started talking to him. Was she a prostitute? Unlikely, dressed like that, and in the Adlon, where the Gestapo had eyes everywhere. A businesswoman? Possibly, but more likely a journalist. The German press had been neutered by the Nazis, but the reporters were still on the prowl for stories that might suit the regime.

"Import and export," he said. He had no wish to reveal his business in Berlin to a stranger.

"How interesting. What line?"

"'Line'?"

"Yes – what do you import and export?"

"You haven't answered my question yet."

She laughed, sipped her drink, looking at him over the rim of the glass, and said, "I manage a restaurant and bar here. That man is the owner. He takes me out for a special lunch every so often, then makes the usual suggestion. I say no and he goes off in a temper. He'll probably fire me tomorrow."

He laughed. "I think I'm going to be fired tomorrow as well."

"What? Your company is going to fire you?"

Macrae realised his mistake.

"No, my wife is going to fire me. Let's have another drink."

They drank and talked, and every now and then Macrae shooed the barman away. She said her name was Ruth and she came from Hamburg. She talked in a dreamy way of her summer holidays in England in a seaside village called West

Wittering, and how her parents had made her and her brother speak English. Then she looked at her watch and said she must go.

"I should get back too," he said, and checked his watch. It was four in the afternoon. He slid unsteadily from the stool.

"Nice to meet you," he said.

She opened her bag, took out a business card and gave it to him.

"Drop in some time. The food is excellent."

He looked at the card.

Der Salon
11, Giesebrechtstrasse
Charlottenburg, Berlin

They shook hands and he watched her leave. He sensed she was lying and wondered if she felt the same about him. The double deception made the conversation bizarre, thought Macrae. But he was drunk enough not to care.

He walked unsteadily along the Charlottenburger Chaussee. The intense cold tightened its grip as he passed the Brandenburg Gate and headed into the long avenue through the Tiergarten. The cold cleared his head. He had not eaten any lunch and had drunk, well, how much exactly? Six or seven large gins and then a couple more with that woman, maybe half a bottle, maybe more.

Headlights from passing cars swept over the trees, creating a ghostly throng of monsters that watched his unsteady progress and reached out misshapen arms as he passed. He admired their courage, standing stripped bare of all elements of life with only a cloak of bark against the bitter cold. The ground was frozen to a depth of three feet or so, yet somehow these creatures – and trees were definitely creatures, thought Macrae – somehow they tapped long tubular roots deep into the earth below the crust of frost and ice, drawing moisture and nutrients during the winter months.

It was almost six o'clock when he reached the house and fumbled in his coat pockets for the key. The door swung open. Primrose stood there wearing a fur coat over an evening dress. He noticed the gold teardrop earrings he had given her as a wedding-anniversary present.

"Where on earth have you been?"

"Had a difficult day," he said, slowly raising an arm to the door jamb to steady himself.

"You're drunk."

"Possibly," he said simply. "It's been a . . ."

"A difficult day?"

Her eyebrows arched with displeasure. Behind him a vehicle drew up and he turned to see a taxi.

"Do you realise we've been looking for you all afternoon?" she said. "The office called. No one had any idea where you were."

"Adlon," he said, and lurched into the house.

"I'm going out. There's some soup in the kitchen."

"Where?" he said, but the door had closed. He heard the clackety-clack of her shoes on the steps as she hurried to the taxi.

6

Behind the fanlight and lion-headed door-knocker of 10 Downing Street a long corridor led through a red baize-covered door to the Cabinet Room. The narrow, high-ceilinged meeting place of the British head of government and his ministers was dominated by a table some twenty-five feet in length surrounded by leather upholstered chairs. Black leather blotters worn with age and a carafe of water and a glass lay in front of every chair. A portrait of Sir Robert Walpole, the first and longest-serving prime minister, hung over a marble fireplace, in front of which the prime minister's chair marked the centre of the table.

Two clocks stood on the mantelpiece on either side of the portrait. Tall windows looked out over the garden wall of Number 10 through plane trees onto Horse Guards Parade and St James's Park.

There were in all twenty-one ministers of cabinet rank in the government of Neville Chamberlain and on Monday, 14 March, nineteen of them trooped into Number 10 and walked the long corridor to the Cabinet Room, taking their seats in carefully arranged order of seniority – of the post not the person. On either side of the prime minister sat Sir John Simon, the chancellor of the exchequer, and Sir Samuel Hoare, the home secretary, while Lord Halifax, the new foreign secretary, took his place opposite him.

This was an unusual gathering, in that such meetings were normally held on Tuesdays, but the prime minister had summoned his ministers to decide what might usefully be done about the German annexation of Austria two days earlier. Those were his very words in telephone conversations with his ministers over the weekend and they carried the unspoken codicil that the most useful thing to do would be nothing at all. The ministers understood that the response of elegant inaction would be high on the agenda, even if it did not appear as a written item on the briefing papers that lay on their blotters – and most were disposed to agree.

Chamberlain led the discussion by suggesting strongly that the government should not condemn the action that Hitler had undertaken but merely the methods he had used to achieve complete control of the Austrian government. The brutal suppression of dissent and the mob violence that had been unleashed in Vienna against opponents of the Nazis had been widely reported in the British press that morning, especially in the *Daily Telegraph*. This was to be condemned in a statement issued by the Foreign Office. The Anschluss itself was to go unremarked by the government.

There was a pause while the cabinet considered this view. Lord Halifax immediately agreed, allowing the prime minister to declare to his ministers: "No statement should be issued that would lead the public or the European powers to suppose that events are heading towards a general war. Nor must we mindlessly antagonise the German leader at the very moment we intend to negotiate a settlement of all his outstanding territorial claims."

There was a ripple of unease in the room signalled by several ministers reaching for their carafes and pouring themselves a glass of water. This had gone further than most had expected. Chamberlain and Halifax had clearly agreed this approach beforehand.

Leslie Hore-Belisha raised his hand and the prime minister nodded. The minister for war was a difficult but useful member of his team. When he was transport minister he had caused a storm of controversy by suggesting that motorists might not in future be able to park their cars where they pleased on the streets of major cities. He had also introduced orange beacons to mark crossing points for pedestrians, which had made him very popular with the general public but less so with the motoring classes. Hore-Belisha was a man of ambition and energy, and was not afraid to speak his mind. He knew his colleagues described him as "one of our Hebrew friends" behind his back, and while he despised such casual anti-Semitism, he did not let it trouble him.

The prime minister had promoted him to the War Office because he believed Hore-Belisha was more concerned with reform of the army's top-heavy command structure than with rearmament. However his minister had of late been showing grave concern about the violent and degrading treatment of Jews in Germany and had written a number of newspaper articles on the subject. This troubled Chamberlain.

"I don't quite see the logic of condemning mob violence in Vienna while not addressing the cause, namely the Nazi aggression that has wiped Austria off the map," Hore-Belisha said.

Chamberlain sighed. He looked at Halifax, who said, "Leslie, we have been here before. We knew that Hitler was intent on entering Austria and around this table we accepted the fact that the majority of German-speaking Austrians were in favour. Don't forget Hitler has announced a plebiscite."

Hore-Belisha was about to reply when a voice from across the table cut in.

"In any case, what does my ministerial colleague propose we do about it? Why condemn an action that we are in no position to alter or challenge? It just makes dealing with Hitler so much more difficult."

It was Sir John Simon, the guardian of the nation's finances and as such a man determined not to allow any expenditure on rearmament to unbalance a fragile economic recovery. Hore-Belisha had expected little else from the Treasury.

"Firstly," Hore-Belisha said, "the idea of a Nazi plebiscite is a mockery, and we all know it; so let us not use that as a fig leaf for inaction. Secondly, I recognise that we are in no position to use military force to influence events in central Europe. We do not have that force to deploy anywhere in Europe, for that matter. The policy of appeasement is one thing, and I support it – up to a point. The reduction of our military capacity, which has been going on as a matter of policy for some years, is quite another."

There was a further pause. Chamberlain looked at his watch. He was due to leave for Buckingham Palace to lunch with the King at twelve thirty. It was now just after noon. Damn. Hore-Belisha had obviously been talking to the arch troublemaker Winston Churchill, a thorn in the government's side and obsessive about rearmament. The problem with Winston was that he was still fighting the last war.

"And before anyone accuses me of taking a brief from Mr Churchill . . ."

Hore-Belisha left the sentence trailing and looked around the table. There was a general stir of unease, as if a rat had been spotted scuttling along the wainscoting. Every man in the room except one regarded Churchill as a warmonger, a man who could hardly wait to fight the next war, having made such a mess of the last one with his ill-judged Gallipoli campaign.

"I would like to draw your attention to a confidential document I have received from our embassy in Berlin," Hore-Belisha went on.

"May we know the author?"

It was Lord Halifax, looking affronted. Confidential cables from the embassy in Berlin should have crossed his desk before going on to any other department.

"Our military attaché in Berlin."

"What's his name?" asked Chamberlain sharply.

"His name is Colonel Noel Macrae and this is his information on the disparity between the forces of HMG and those of Germany."

Hore-Belisha read out a précis of the document. When he came to the current size of the army and the number of active divisions, there was an intake of breath around the room. Surely, Hore-Belisha thought, they must have known about the figures. Or did such information evaporate in the warmth of their clubs, where lunch was followed by a gentle rest in an old leather armchair, usually by a decent fire at this time of the year? He didn't belong to a London club, for the simple reason that while a prominent Jew might find a proposer and a seconder, somehow such candidates never found favour with the membership committees.

Chamberlain sat stony-faced while the figures were read out.

"My conclusion," said Hore-Belisha, "is that we need from this day forward to launch a rearmament programme that will equip our ground and air forces with the minimum required to meet the German military machine. We do not have much time."

Chamberlain looked at his watch.

"Thank you. That is most interesting, but it does not tell us anything new."

"With respect, Prime Minister, it tells us that we need to introduce conscription immediately," said Hore-Belisha.

"And what would Hitler make of that?" snapped Chamberlain. "It would give him the perfect excuse to call off all negotiations with us."

The prime minister stood up, placing clenched hands on the table, and looked around, as if defying anyone to disagree with him. The cabinet knew that Hore-Belisha had touched on a raw nerve. The one strand of the appeasement policy about which Chamberlain was least sure, and thus most sensitive, was his adamant refusal to contemplate any form of conscription for men of military age.

The repeated proposal from senior generals in the army and civil servants in the War Office was for the compulsory enlistment of men aged between eighteen and thirty for one year's training. France had instituted such a policy and was urging Britain to follow suit. Chamberlain had consistently refused.

"Now, if you will excuse me, I have lunch with the King," he said, and left the room.

Sara had gone straight from the Adlon to the Salon. She had drunk too much with that Englishman and she was hungry. It was only seven o'clock and there was a scattering of guests in the room. She sat at a table reserved for staff and ordered a steak and frites. The table was deliberately placed in the shadows at one end of the bar. The Salon did not stint the girls when it came to food. Guests ate well and the girls did likewise. Kitty Schmidt made sure of that.

Sara drank mineral water and looked around. There were three Italians at one table, all from the embassy. They were supposed to be allies and friends of the Reich, but Bonner trusted nobody. The moment they got into the rooms with the girls, the cameras started turning.

On another table she recognised two executives from the Krupp steelworks in Essen. They would have come to Berlin to negotiate an arms contract and decided to celebrate with a night at the Salon. It was where everyone with the money and the contacts came. There was nowhere else like it in Berlin, or indeed Europe.

She knew the Krupp executives well. They were regulars. The elder of the two was a sadist who liked to bring his own riding crop and left the girls badly marked and unable to work for a day or two. Kitty Schmidt had taken him aside and said that he would be charged five thousand marks for every day the girls were off work as a result.

The strange things men wanted, thought Sara, and she smiled at the idea of that Englishman. What would he like? There was always something they wanted. Perhaps a fantasy with the girls dressed up as nuns or schoolteachers – they were the most common. It didn't matter, but Kitty Schmidt made sure the men paid for their pleasures. Everything from sodomy to lesbian shows was added to the drinks or dinner bill in the form of charges for fine wines and champagne. That was how the Salon did business. Elaborate receipts were given. It was all part of the pretence that the discreet house in a classy Berlin suburb was merely a restaurant and bar that stayed open later than most in Berlin and provided an occasional cabaret show for its customers.

The only thing Kitty Schmidt would not accept was a request, however delicately phrased, for male homosexual encounters. Any such suggestion and the client would be thrown out and reported to the Gestapo. Bonner had insisted on that.

A group of officers in uniform walked in, all very senior, judging from the insignia. Sara saw Bonner fussing around them, pulling out chairs, snapping at the waitresses. That could only mean one thing. Sara shifted her chair back into the shadows and watched as several girls descended on the group, taking their coats and hats. In the centre, as she had expected, sat Reinhard Heydrich in the all-black uniform of the Obergruppenführer of the SS.

The uniform told the story of the man and his organisation. The Totenkopf death's-head symbol was placed just below the swastika and stretched eagle symbol of the Nazi Party on the peaked cap. Oakleaf insignia on both collars were picked out in silver, matching the colour of the four diamonds stitched to the lower left sleeve. Boots, trousers, shirt jacket and tie were all of the deepest black. It was said that Heinrich Himmler had personally designed the uniforms. He had told a German radio station: "I know there are many people who fall ill when they see this uniform. We understand that and don't expect to be loved."

Sara had seen Heydrich several times in the Salon. Every time he came in, the ceiling dropped, the walls drew in, the room seemed smaller, colder, darker. People looked at the new arrival and then quickly turned away. No one wanted to catch his eye. Voices dropped to whispers as guests shuffled their chairs forward and hunched over their tables.

None of them had heard of the English poet T. S. Eliot, still less read his poetry, but they would all have recognised the force of that most famous line from *The Waste Land*: "I will show you fear in a handful of dust." That was Reinhard Heydrich, a man who could create fear with the flick of a finger.

He looked innocent enough, much younger than his thirty-four years. The receding hair was combed back and flattened with brilliantine, which emphasised the line of the parting on the left side. A large forehead broke into a long aquiline nose running to a small, thin-lipped mouth. The nose looked as if it had been stamped on his face as an afterthought. It was too big for the rest of his features, which suggested both feminine delicacy and cruelty. The delicacy lay in the mouth, the cruelty in the eyes. Sara wondered whether the face looked so cruel because she had heard so many stories of his personal savagery, or whether those frozen features really were shaped by evil.

The girls in the Salon knew a lot about Heydrich. He was said to be obsessive about personal hygiene, taking a shower two or three times a day. He took fencing lessons twice a week and after those sessions he would personally clean and oil his sabre, wrapping it in greaseproof paper until the next lesson. His fencing clothes would also be washed, dried and ironed. Everything about the man was clinical, tidy and neat. The nails were manicured, the eyebrows trimmed. The black uniform was well fitted to his athletic body. There was method in the way Heydrich presented himself to the world: the uniform, the slim muscular build, the carefully groomed hair, the pale blue eyes and the cold hawklike features projected power and instilled fear.

Sara was tempted to leave quietly. Heydrich was drinking and laughing with Bonner and two other colleagues. They were raising fluted crystal glasses of champagne in a series of toasts. They'd probably come straight from headquarters and were celebrating the success of an operation. But departure meant leaving the shadows and walking close to Heydrich's table on the way to the fanlight door. He would see her, because he saw everything. He would call her over, offer her champagne, ask silly questions about how she was and whether she was enjoying her work. There would always be a question about her mother and her brother, as if they were old friends whose welfare concerned him. Heydrich's attention to detail was well known. He remembered everything.

He would place a hand on her knee and slide it up under her skirt, all the time talking to the others and laughing and drinking. He would turn and look at her as his fingers tightened on her thigh, squeezing hard, and she would smile. And then he would loosen his grip, remove his hand and turn to the others, allowing her to slip away.

But even Heydrich had to be careful with Sara, in case whispers got back to Heinrich Himmler. Sara smiled at the irony; the man who had unleashed a wave of terror to force Jews to leave their country, the man who was said to be working on more sinister means to solve "the Jewish Problem", could do no more than grope her under the table. She was Jewish and supposedly forbidden even to one of the most powerful men in the Reich. When Heydrich was drunk, such rules did not apply, of course. He would stagger back to one of the rooms with her, while his bodyguards waited at the bar. An hour or so later he would leave hurriedly, the peaked cap pulled well down over his face.

The greatest irony of all was that Reinhard Heydrich was said to be Jewish too. At least, that is what Bonner had told her one night when drunk. It had been late, well past midnight, and they were sitting at a corner table. Bonner was trying to please her. He wanted to be friends with his star attraction at the Salon. He wanted her to understand that he was doing his job, just as she was doing hers. In a slurred speech that kept repeating itself, he told her how much he admired and appreciated her work, and he knew she felt the same way about him.

"I'm going to tell you a secret," he had said.

"I don't want your secrets," she replied. She didn't want to talk to him; she didn't want him near her. She didn't even want to have to look at him. But Bonner was both her captor and saviour. He kept her alive, and that meant survival for Joseph.

He had bent towards her, pulling her head so as to whisper in her ear. His breath reeked of an evening drinking schnapps.

"Heydrich is Jewish."

He had looked at her triumphantly through glazed eyes.

"I don't think so," she had said.

"Exactly. He can't be, can he? It wouldn't make sense, would it? But think about it; maybe it does make sense. Maybe it explains a lot. There are important people who say his grandfather married a Jewish woman, name of Süss. That would be back in the late 1870s. And that would make him a Jew. And you know what? The bodyguards have heard his wife, during their rows, screaming at him 'You filthy Jew!' And then he goes mad and threatens to kill her!"

Sara said nothing. It was always best to allow Bonner to ramble on to the end of these occasional monologues. He had no one to talk to, because he trusted no one and no one trusted him. He usually complained about his wife, the long hours of the job and the fact that no one trusted anyone else in the closed world of the Gestapo.

"Strange thing is, the party had an investigation and cleared him of racial impurity. Himmler made sure of that. I don't think Himmler gave a damn who his grandfather married. Heydrich was too useful, too clever and, above all, too ruthless to be thrown out of the party. He knew too much."

Bonner was talking to himself more than to her. He had drifted off into an alcoholic dreamland where he could denounce his boss as a Jew and have him drummed out of the party. Then Heydrich would disappear in a "Nacht und Nebel" operation, one of those dark foggy nights when murder squads tracked down enemies of the Reich. And he, Joachim Bonner, would become SS Obergruppenführer, chief of the most powerful and feared secret police force in the world.

Normally, Sara quickly forgot whatever Bonner was complaining about. But that time she tucked the information away. It might just be useful. Heydrich seemed to be able to get away with anything. His treatment of women was known to all senior members of the party and security services. It was true that his bodyguards occasionally gossiped about the rows they had witnessed between Heydrich and his wife, with flying Meissen crockery and insults of the most personal nature flung back and forth.

It was after these rows that he would cruise the bars of Berlin at night with his guards. He would never wear uniform, preferring a long black leather coat over a suit with a fashionable trilby pulled well down over his face. He liked to go into the poorer suburbs seeking out girls behind the bars in working men's clubs or in cheap restaurants. Whenever he saw a girl he liked, she would be drawn aside by his guards and offered a chauffeur-driven car to one of several apartments Heydrich used. If the offer was refused, Heydrich would move on to find another woman. But the bodyguards always went back later in full SS uniform and the woman who had been foolish enough to say no to the Obergruppenführer would be dragged out and beaten up in a nearby back street. If the guards went too far, and they usually did, the woman would be raped and thrown into the river. Everyone knew about it. No one dared make a complaint.

If Heydrich was Jewish, it might explain what she was doing in the Salon, Sara thought. Maybe deep down in whatever dark soul was possessed by that tormented psychopath, there was a flicker of guilt or shame. Maybe his self-loathing made it easier for him to use a Jewish woman to trap his enemies.

Sara stood up. Heydrich had gone to the bar. He was talking to Kitty Schmidt and beckoned his group to follow him. This would be one of the inspection nights when he would go to the control room on the top floor and view recent film of the activities in the rooms. Usually after such sessions the cameras and recording equipment would be switched off and Heydrich and friends would go to what was euphemistically called the Group Room. The girls from the Pink Room would all assemble there and their other guests would simply be told that they would be busy for an hour or so.

Heydrich and his party had gone. The Salon was filling up with customers. She walked through the fanlight door to the Pink Room. In an hour or so, when the film show had finished upstairs, there would be no girls in this room. For now, they were accepting a few carnations. Sara sat down and lit a cigarette. She had to get out of this place. She had to escape. What could they do to her brother in that camp that they were not already doing? What would he say if he saw the life she was leading in Berlin? It was all she ever thought about.

7

Noel Macrae began to squeeze the trigger gently, holding the stag in the telescopic sights, moving the cross-hairs from the magnificent antlers to the heart of the beast just above the shoulder. The animal was about seven hundred and fifty yards away, hobbling slowly through thick heather.

Lying beside him, Koenig peered through a short telescope and whispered, "No. He's too far. We'll walk up on him."

The stag swung its head towards them and began to move. Macrae tightened his finger on the trigger. It was a long shot, at the outside range of the gun, but there was no wind and the target was moving slowly. He was a large beast, but for a clean kill the shot would have to be through the heart. He had done this many times before at the same range. In the trenches you could kill a man at eight hundred yards with good sights – if your target gave you time. They rarely did, of course. Their heads bobbed up and down like those moving targets at a fairground, and then you had to chance a quick shot without time to aim properly.

For a snap shot, the maximum range was two hundred and fifty yards, and then there was only a split second to aim and fire. More often than not, you missed or wounded the target. The disadvantage was that you gave away a carefully camouflaged position and had to start all over again elsewhere on the line. The advantage was that a traumatised soldier, with his shoulder or arm blown away by a high-velocity .303 bullet, would have to be taken back through lines of trenches to a field station and then to a rear hospital. This required first manpower, then the attention of nurses, then transfusions, bandages and finally further transport to a hospital well away from the war zone. All the time the target would be screaming in pain and begging people around him not to let him die. In purely military terms, it was a better result than a clean shot, which would see the enemy swiftly dumped into a common grave.

Macrae pulled the trigger, felt the recoil kick into his shoulder and saw the stag sway for a second, then crumple to the ground.

"Nice shot!" said Koenig admiringly, getting to his feet again. He helped Macrae up and said, "Can I see the gun?"

Macrae handed him the rifle. Koenig examined it.

"This is an old Lee–Enfield," he said. "My brother brought one home on leave once. Picked it up after they had taken one of your trenches. This should be in a museum."

"It's the sights that count, not the gun," said Macrae, holding out his hand for the gun.

Koenig swung the rifle up to his shoulder, assumed firing position and squinted through the sights. He gave Macrae an odd look.

"This is a sniper's rifle," he said, handing the gun back.

"Which is why I am standing here today."

"And why a lot of other men are not?"

"It was a long time ago," said Macrae. "Let's look at the stag. A sixteen-pointer, I think."

They walked over the hill, down across a small stream and up the far side of the valley, to where the stag's antlers protruded from the heather. Its eyes were open and its flanks still heaving. Blood was pumping from a small hole in its side. The bullet had missed the heart. Koenig knelt down, pulled a pistol from a holster on his belt and fired one shot through the head. The animal jerked convulsively and lay still.

That night, they dined at what Koenig called his hunting lodge in the low hills of the Mecklenburg lake district, about 250 miles north of Berlin. Primrose said the three-storey mansion, designed in Gothic style with turrets and battlements, looked more like a Scottish ancestral home than a German hunting lodge. Macrae had taken the wheel of a pool car from the embassy, a Daimler with diplomatic plates displayed front and rear. Primrose had sat beside him on the four-hour drive from Berlin. It was a crisp day in late March and she seemed pleased to be leaving the city for a weekend with strangers in the deep countryside. The autobahn speeded them past small towns that were footprints in time for anyone who knew the rich history of north-west Germany. From Roman times, the rolling flatlands had been a battleground between invaders from the frozen north and the powers that held the warm, rich southern states.

At a little town called Oranienburg, Macrae pointed out a distant group of buildings surrounded by watch towers that would leave their own mark on history. Sachsenhausen concentration camp, he said, recently built for political detainees arrested in Berlin.

Primrose turned her head and looked briefly at the white-painted towers and the wire-topped walls. She looked back at the smooth ribbon of tarmac unspooling before them between filmic images of churches, farms, herds of cattle and well-timbered houses all planted on the dark earth of the north German plain.

"Say what you like about the Nazis, but they build wonderful roads," she said. She was far from Berlin, where she had friends and things to do. But she liked the idea of this weekend and laid a hand on her husband's arm.

Good tank country, thought Macrae as he glanced across the plain to a ridge of distant hills covered in green gorse and purple heather. They had arrived in Berlin in the middle of a bitter winter and now spring was bringing colour to the countryside. Soon the gorse would flower and turn the hills a buttery yellow. That's where the infantry would be dug in, along those hills, he thought, while the tanks raced across the plain. Battle would one day come to this quiet corner of the country as an invading army closed in on Berlin. They would come, whoever and whenever. He knew that.

For the last few miles they had driven on a private road through a dark pine forest. Now the trees parted and the Humber crunched over carefully swept gravel to stop before a large wooden front door.

Koenig's wife received them politely but without enthusiasm and took them upstairs and down a long corridor to their room. A servant followed with the luggage, including Macrae's leather rifle case. Koenig had told him to bring it, although there seemed no reason, since the hunting season had long ended. Koenig's wife introduced herself as Gertrude and, facially at least, reminded Macrae of an actress in an early silent film. She was pale and looked undernourished, with a thin body that lacked shape and suggested a recent serious illness. Like her husband, she spoke perfect English. He wondered where she had learnt it.

"Come down when you're ready and we'll have drinks," she said. "Florian will be back soon."

• • •

Primrose looked around the room. It was much more modern and pleasing to the eye than the exterior of the house had suggested. There was a proper bathroom, with a shower and bidet. The sheets had been turned down on a big four-poster bed. Carafes of water, glass tumblers and hot-water bottles lay on side tables. She put a hand on the radiator and found it warm. She threw open the window and took a deep breath.

The country air was different, less smoky and sweeter than in Berlin. She wondered about their pale, disapproving hostess. She could hardly imagine such a woman as the wife of the sociable Colonel Florian Koenig. He was charming and undeniably handsome, with that close-cropped greying hair making him look older than his years, and that smiling face, faintly pockmarked from a childhood attack of chicken pox, she imagined. There were no greater secrets than those held in a marriage, as one of the Berlin wives had remarked the other day. Perhaps the spectral figure of Mrs Koenig turned into a vampire at night and danced in the moonlight wearing a scarlet robe. Primrose sighed, knowing that she would be seeing a lot of Gertrude Koenig that weekend. They had been invited so that the men could talk freely, far from the prying eyes and ears in Berlin.

"I'm going to have a bath," she said.

A few minutes later, there was a shout from downstairs and a thunder of feet on the stairs and then a loud knocking on the door. Macrae opened it and Koenig stood smiling in the doorway, dressed in a brown checked hunting jacket, corduroy trousers and leather boots.

"Sorry I wasn't here to welcome you. How was the drive?"

"Fine," said Macrae.

"Where's Primrose?"

"In the bath."

"I'll bet she didn't want to come. I'll bet she said she was going to be in for a boring weekend in the country."

"Not at all," said Macrae, forced to deny what had certainly been true when he first mentioned the visit to Primrose. Now she seemed happy to be there.

"Come down when you are ready, and please tell your wife we have our amusements in the country."

They drank sparkling wine before dinner and sat down at an elaborately laid table to a meal of venison soup and roast pheasant as the main course. The birds had been kept in the ice house since the end of the shooting season eight weeks earlier. A servant appeared at regular intervals to serve wine.

Koenig talked of his family history, of growing up in a house into which his father, grandfather and great grandfather had been born. The money came from farming, he said, and whenever one generation broke away from the soil to make money in commerce or industry, the next generation always lost it.

"Families are like empires," he said, "their fortunes rise and fall, but in our case we have always had three thousand acres here in the lake district of Germany to fall back on. And in a hundred and fifty years we have not sold an acre. We are Prussians, you see. We love the land and the army. Bismarck was our god and the army was our life, but we always kept one son back to run the land."

Gertrude said suddenly, "Do our English guests really want to hear about your family's love of Bismarck and the army?"

"Quite right, dear," said Koenig. He began talking of the ties that had once bound Germany to England, the shared bloodlines of their royal families, the parallel rise of great writers such as Goethe and Dickens, and a common passion for sports, especially, among the upper classes, hunting and shooting.

"We don't hunt now the season is over, but there is an old stag on the far side of the lake in a valley. He's caught himself in barbed wire and has a nasty gash, which has become infected. We will go after him tomorrow," he said, and turned to Primrose. "And tomorrow night, Mrs Macrae, to make sure you will not be bored so far from Berlin, some guests are coming to join us for a little dance."

"A dance? Where?" she said.

"Here. There is a small ballroom at the back."

"And who will come?" asked Macrae.

"I have asked some neighbours. Just a few of us."

Primrose clapped her hands. "How exciting. Isn't that exciting, Mrs Koenig?"

Gertrude Koenig gave a wan smile by way of reply.

"Usually we ask local musicians to play, but they are so old-fashioned, they do nothing but the waltz, wouldn't you agree, darling?" said Koenig.

His wife looked at Primrose and Macrae in turn, as if reminding herself who these strangers were at her table.

"I like the waltz," she said. "It reminds me of when I was young."

"And what dance music do you like, Mrs Macrae?" Koenig asked Primrose.

"Primrose, please," she said. "Oh, jazz, swing, something with a bit of life in it."

"Now, that is my kind of music," said Koenig.

The two of them began to talk about music for the dance. Primrose named her favourite American bands, Duke Ellington, Benny Goodman and Fletcher Henderson. Koenig knew them all and had a collection of their records and what he called a squeaky-creaky gramophone. Primrose laughed. She loved the term "squeaky-creaky". She and Koenig began to plan the order of the numbers they wished to play.

Macrae once again felt he was eavesdropping on a private conversation. He tried to talk to Gertrude about the gardens around the house and the estate beyond, but she had nothing to say on either subject and restricted herself to monosyllabic answers and the offer of more wine.

"I am sorry," said Koenig. "We are being very rude. Gertrude dear, shall we have coffee next door?"

The next morning, Macrae and Koenig followed a gillie up into a line of hills to the north of the estate where the wounded stag had last been seen. With great pride, Koenig had shown his guest his Mauser rifle, a sporting version of the new gun that had only recently been issued to the army, he said. He loaded the magazine and snapped the bolt forward to chamber the first round, as if ready for an ambush.

Macrae kept his gun sheathed in its case slung over his shoulder. He had only brought it at Koenig's insistence and had no intention of using it. It was his old army rifle, a Lee–Enfield 1914 model issued at the outbreak of war to front-line infantry. His weapon had been specially adapted, with telescopic sights and a customised stock to fit his shoulder. That was why he had been allowed to keep it when he left France. His specialised role meant he would remain on the reserves, even when promoted to become a military attaché within the Diplomatic Service.

They had found the stag easily enough in mid-morning and later that day they took twelve-bore shotguns and walked around the state on a vermin hunt, shooting hawk, crows and rabbit. A gamekeeper struggled behind with a bag of the fallen prey.

As they kicked off their boots at the rear of the house, Koenig said, "One of our neighbours will be coming to dinner tonight – Herman Schiller, a colonel like me, armoured division – I want you to meet him. You'll like him. Old school."

Before dinner that night, the three men met for a drink in Koenig's study. He offered whisky or vodka, taking old crystal decanters from a small table and pouring generous measures into matching crystal tumblers. Primrose and Gertrude were upstairs. Colonel Schiller was wearing evening dress, which surprised Macrae. Koenig had told him this was to be an informal weekend.

The colonel was the image of a German officer, ramrod stiff, with a moustache that turned down at the corners of his mouth, and round rimless spectacles perched high on his nose. Macrae guessed he was in his early fifties, old enough to have fought in the war. He was an infantry officer and would have been in his twenties and very much in the front line.

"I wanted you to meet Colonel Schiller because he is of a like mind, and there are many more like him at all levels of the army," said Koenig. "Less so in the Luftwaffe, because Göring has purged those he considers disloyal, then bribed the rest with new planes and given them the chance to try them out in Spain."

He sipped his whisky.

"Herman, do you want to begin?" said Koenig.

"I think first we need some reassurance that this will be a private conversation," said the colonel, staring hard at Macrae.

"You have my reassurance," said Macrae.

"Ah, but do I?" The colonel raised his glass and drank, all the while keeping his eyes fixed firmly on Macrae. He seemed angry. He pointed at the curtained windows.

"Somewhere out there, miles away, Göring has his schloss. The Reichsmarschall loves hunting and likes showing off to his friends, especially his foreign friends. Do you know one of the people he invites to shoot with him? Your ambassador, Henderson. He is a frequent visitor, and not a bad shot, I am told."

Macrae was well aware that Sir Nevile Henderson not only spent shooting weekends with Göring, but also accepted invitations to the opera and music evenings. The British ambassador had been photographed recently with Göring at a Mozart festival in Munich. The two had been pictured side by side laughing. Halliday tracked those meetings carefully. Macrae had no doubt that Stewart Menzies, the head of the Secret Intelligence Service in London, was aware of the close relationship between the British ambassador and the man who had assumed the role, if not the title, of Hitler's deputy.

"I'm sure that is just part of an ambassador's duties."

"Duty be damned," said the colonel, and he stood up, his face flushed with anger. "Henderson thinks Göring is a 'jolly good chap', a gentleman who can be trusted."

"I think you have made your point," said Koenig.

"And what exactly is the point?" asked Macrae.

"Can we trust you not to repeat to the ambassador what we are going to discuss? Because I have a feeling that Sir Nevile Henderson would go to great lengths to ingratiate himself with Göring and that gang."

Fair enough, thought Macrae. The ambassador placed the avoidance of war above all other considerations. He saw that as not just an official duty but almost a religious calling.

Henderson was a fervent churchgoer, so much so that junior members of staff were expected to join him at Sunday-morning service in the Berliner Dom. It was very likely that Henderson *would* pass on reports of unease among the senior military to his good friend Göring.

"I quite understand," said Macrae, and he raised his glass slightly, prompting Koenig to refill. He paused, searching for the right words. He was a soldier, not a diplomat, and those words were hard to find, words that would encourage the confidences that he was sure were forthcoming, without making him party to a betrayal of his own ambassador.

The two men were watching as he sipped his whisky. Finally Macrae said, "I believe we have a shared view of the dangers facing Europe and the wider world if the German leadership continues its current course. And I do not believe those dangers can be averted if the British government continues its current policy of appeasement. I will do nothing to aid that policy – quite the reverse."

He stopped and reached over for the whisky bottle. The colonel stared at the ceiling for a minute, then nodded at him.

"Very well," he said. "Let me pose a question: when and where will the British draw the line? When will you make a stand? Hitler pushes forward and you step back; he moves again and you retreat. If this was a chess game, you would be off the board by now."

"HMG's view is clear," said Macrae. "The British government wants to negotiate a territorial arrangement that will satisfy Hitler without leading to war."

"That is our point," said Colonel Schiller. "War is coming whatever you do." He sat forward and stared at Macrae. "Do you realise that plans are being drawn up now, at this very minute, for the invasion of Russia?"

"You surprise me," said Macrae. "What about Poland?"

"Don't be naive. Poland is a foregone conclusion." He paused. "I am sorry. I did not mean to be rude."

Macrae was cautious. "And after Russia?"

"Oh, you stupid British! Sorry, forgive me, but really! You think you can sit in the mist and rain of that little island and do a deal with Hitler. You think he is going to let you keep your navy and empire while he turns Europe into a racially pure Aryan state. After Russia, he intends to conquer the world! And why not? Who is to stop him?"

"That is surely a gross simplification," said Macrae.

"Really? Are you sure of that?" said the colonel.

"There are many people in the United Kingdom who are warning of German intentions. Winston Churchill makes the point all the time."

"Churchill!" snorted the colonel.

Koenig got up, opened the door as if to check whether anyone was listening, closed it and returned to his seat.

"Gentlemen, let us get to the point and not argue about the details," he said. "The point is if, and I repeat if, there were to be a move against the regime, where would the United Kingdom stand?"

"'A move'?" said Macrae.

"You want me to spell it out?" said Koenig.

There was a silence.

"If the army removed him," said the colonel.

"I can hardly speak for the government," said Macrae, "but I think they would be relieved, as would the rest of Europe."

"Ah, 'relieved'. Yes, I am sure. But would you *act*?" said the colonel.

"In what way?"

"Recognise a military government until we had time to organise elections. That might take a year or two. It would be messy. The Nazis would fight."

"Are you talking of a civil war?" Macrae could hardly believe he had asked the question.

"No, it would be faster than that," said Koenig.

"Bloody but quick," said the colonel. "But very bloody."

An army coup against Hitler. Halliday had told him there were rumblings in the elite Prussian officers corps and that the men would follow them. But he had not heard anything so specific.

But Halliday had also told him something else: Himmler was a master of entrapment and would seek to embarrass any envoy deemed hostile. There were many ways, but involvement in an armed resistance to Hitler was most certainly one of them. These two men, Koenig and Schiller, had asked for reassurance. Perhaps he should do the same. Was this conversation being recorded?

He looked around the room and then at his host. Florian Koenig, with his two brothers dead in the war, holding the family estate together while his cadaverous wife clearly sickened for something. No, Koenig could never be part of any Nazi machinations.

"Do you have support for your plans?" Macrae asked.

"We would hardly be having this conversation if we didn't."

"And the timing?"

"That is up to you," said Koenig.

Koenig paced the study, describing the plan, while the colonel kept his eyes fixed on Macrae. Hitler's next move would be against Czechoslovakia, he said. The Führer would argue for the return of Sudetenland on the grounds that the German-speaking population were being mistreated, a familiar propaganda trick. But the Nazis had a problem. Czechoslovakia had a good standing army and big armament-manufacturing capacity. If Britain drew the line at Czechoslovakia and made clear it would join France in military action to support the Czechs, Hitler would probably try to call their bluff. He would have to. Since assuming power, he had been driven by the political imperative of seizing territory in the name of *Lebensraum*, the code name for the creation of a new German empire. He had deliberately created the impetus for war and could not now draw back.

The crucial question was whether Britain would make an invasion of Czechoslovakia the red line. Would such an action, in defiance yet again of the Versailles treaty, finally persuade the government in London to abandon its appeasement policy and join France in meeting the threat of further aggression with a pledge to respond with full force of arms? If that happened, Hitler was finished.

It had been a long speech, delivered with passion. When Koenig finished, he and the colonel looked at Macrae. There was nothing meaningful he could say. He was mumbling a few words about the difficulty of responding to such views when Koenig knelt before him and gently took his hand. Such an intimate gesture after the stirring speech left Macrae almost speechless.

"Tell us the truth. It is better we know," said Koenig.

"The truth is, I don't know. But I can promise you that what I have heard tonight will be relayed to those in London best placed to make use of the information you have given me."

"Who are *they*?" snarled the colonel. He was half drunk and angry.

Koenig put a finger to his lips.

"Gentlemen. Enough. The ladies are waiting."

There were just six of them for dinner that night. Two other neighbours had cancelled with apologies owing to illness.

The colonel's wife was almost exactly the opposite of Gertrude. She was called Henna, a large florid-faced lady with a loud laugh and two plaited pigtails that fell over a revealing black dress. Her English was not good but she insisted on speaking it, thus slowing the conversation as everyone tried to understand what she was saying or explain to her what they had just said.

Finally Koenig took them through the house to the ballroom at the rear. The semicircular room with glass walls and dome had been built onto the back of the house by his father at the turn of the century, he explained. The death of Queen Victoria at that time had liberated England from the oppressive social conformism of her reign and dancing parties suddenly became fashionable in London. Paris and Berlin quickly followed the new fashion. The stately waltz and foxtrot were swept away to be replaced by fast-moving ragtime dances with risqué names like the Black Bottom. Even more daringly, the tango arrived from Argentina, creating the shocking sight of couples dancing not just cheek to cheek, but thigh to thigh. Dancing schools sprang up in major cities, and across Europe ballrooms were added to stately homes, country houses and hunting lodges. Such additions merely required a well-sprung and polished wooden floor and a small stage for the musicians, although the invention of the gramophone had rendered the latter unnecessary for an evening's entertainment.

The guests looked around the ballroom in wonder. Curved glass windows encircled the room. Pillars painted in red and white stripes rose to support the domed roof. Hollows had been carved into the pillars to hold candles, which in this case were red in colour and threw a shimmering light up to the glass roof. White candles had been placed at intervals behind the cushioned seating that ran around the room beneath the windows. Where the ballroom abutted the straight line of the house, white panelling had been laid and from this a white tasselled canopy hung over a small circular dais.

The room looked to Primrose less like a ballroom and more like a cross between a fish tank and a gigantic greenhouse that had been decorated for a children's party.

A waiter appeared with glasses of champagne. Koenig proposed a toast.

"To friendship between our two great countries," he said.

They clinked glasses and drank. Koenig mounted the stage and raised the lid of a large wooden box. A gramophone was revealed inside. He pulled out a wooden drawer beneath the instrument and took out a handle, which he inserted into the machine and began turning vigorously.

"He's very proud of that instrument," said Colonel Schiller, who was swaying back and forth as if on a ship's deck.

Primrose resisted the temptation to giggle. Their host was trying to operate a gramophone that must have been in use during the last war. His neighbour the colonel was clearly incapable of dancing and would probably fall flat on his face if he tried. The colonel's wife was beaming at everyone with a demented smile, while Gertrude lay limply on the seating by the window, looking as if she had recently been raised from the grave and wished for nothing more than a swift return to that state.

As for her husband, Primrose looked around and saw him on the far side of the room. He was smiling that thoughtful, interior smile, a smile made for no one but himself. Something had made him happy, thought Primrose. They had been away a long time before dinner, those men, and had joined them all rather drunk. More talk about a bloody war, she supposed.

Koenig finally turned to his guests.

"Sorry about that. This machine belonged to my brother Angelus. He took it with him to the trenches. Very important family treasure. Plays wonderfully well."

He turned, put the stylus on a record and stepped down to join his guests. The music of Glenn Miller filled the room with a surprisingly rich sound, emanating as it did from a small wooden box. Koenig offered an arm to his wife with a bow. She stood up and he led her gently onto the floor. She was smiling as she stepped into his arms, her feet matching his as they moved in a fast version of the waltz.

He led her into quick turns, whirling around in time to the steady beat of a bass drum behind the rise and fall of the band's brass section, pausing to hold her, so that both were momentarily frozen in one as if they had stepped into each other; then they broke apart and swirled away. Primrose and the others watched in amazed admiration the acrobatic grace with which they moved. Gertrude had suddenly come to life in her husband's arms. Their bodies and limbs merged in sinuous flowing movements to the seductive tempo of big-band swing. They moved in a sensuous embrace that suggested an unlikely depth of passion between them.

Gertrude wore an expression of total concentration as she took the lead from Koenig, pressing into him, moving and swaying with him, so that the dance became something more than mere motion to music. He was utterly rapt in her arms, watching her intently as her mouth opened, and even above the music Primrose heard her gasp as he turned her in a tight pirouette.

Macrae glanced at his wife. Primrose was following the dancers' every move, clearly impressed at the grace and passion that flowed across the floor, and perhaps a little jealous.

Encouraged to believe they could do the same, the remainder of the party rose to their feet. Primrose felt a tap on her shoulder. Colonel Schiller was standing behind her. He bowed and clicked his heels. She glanced appealingly at Macrae but saw he was being held in a close embrace by the colonel's wife, who was moving him around the floor as if propelling a wheeled piece of furniture across the room. Schiller slid his arm around her waist and took her hand. She felt hot whisky-and-wine breath on her cheek. His eyes were glazed. He gripped her waist tightly and tried to guide her in a series of fast turns, with steps that had little relation to the music. His legs became tangled with hers and she felt him gripping her ever more tightly as he lost his balance. She struggled to hold him up while trying to find some form of movement that bore a relationship to the music.

The music suddenly stopped. Everyone paused. Breathing hard, Macrae stepped back from the colonel's wife and began to thank her. She immediately stepped forward and took his arm, waiting for the music to begin again. Primrose released herself from the colonel and steadied him. Koenig leapt onto the dais, wound the gramophone furiously and selected a new shiny black record.

A waiter appeared with fresh glasses of champagne. Primrose drank her glass gratefully. She was hot, thirsty and desperate to get away from the colonel. He watched her drink.

"You dance very well," he said. "I'm afraid I really cannot match the music."

"Oh, you do awfully well," she said, wondering why people have to lie on such occasions. The music had begun again, an up-tempo jazz version of a popular standard. Koenig shouted above the music.

"Tommy Dorsey band with something jazzy! Something to get us all in the mood."

"I would rather sit this one out," said Primrose.

Colonel Schiller was insistent. He liked jazz and wanted to dance. She was swept back onto the floor. Across the room, Primrose saw Macrae being wheeled furiously into a series of turns by the colonel's wife. She was clasping him close to her and seemed to be trying a cheek-to-cheek version of the tango. He looked desperate.

Gertrude had gone. Koenig was dancing by himself, circling the floor with an imaginary partner in his arms. He seemed utterly absorbed. Schiller suddenly fell with a thump onto the floor. Encouraged by Koenig's solo performance, he had broken away to perform a series of twirls and had tottered across the room until his feet slipped from under him. His wife had left Macrae to help him. They sat down heavily by the window while she mopped his brow. Koenig came off the floor to pour them all a glass of champagne.

"Where's Gertrude?" asked Primrose.

"She's gone to bed. She's not well and dancing always tires her. She sends her apologies for neglecting her social duties."

"Oh, I am sorry," said Primrose. "She dances beautifully. You both do."

"Thank you. Perhaps you would have the next dance?"

Primrose was about to reply that it was late and they had to leave in the morning when Colonel Schiller and his wife joined them. Primrose noticed that Macrae had left the room.

"All too much for me," said the colonel. "I never could dance."

"Well, I enjoyed myself," said his wife, "but I think, how do you say it in English? I mismangled your husband a little."

"Yes, he did look a bit mismangled," said Primrose. "What have you done with him?"

"Come on, we're having one more dance," said Koenig, and he put another record on.

The colonel and his wife edged to the door, making good-night noises. Koenig paid no attention and took Primrose onto the floor. They began to dance to a slow melody called "The Way You Look Tonight".

"Fred Astaire and Ginger Rogers," he whispered. "They're good, aren't they?"

Macrae had searched the ground floor for what seemed like a long time looking for a lavatory. He finally found an oak-panelled room by the back door filled with boots, shoes, brushes, hunting clothes and an assortment of umbrellas and riding crops. He leant forward, his head resting on an arm against the wall, and tried to calculate the alcoholic content of the stream that flowed into the bowl.

He had as usual broken his rule to match every glass of wine or whisky with one of water. He looked into the mirror. The face that stared back seemed grey and crumpled. He had learnt something that could be of real importance that night. The journey had been worthwhile. Why would Koenig have gone to the trouble of inviting him for the weekend if they had not meant what they said?

He returned to the ballroom. Colonel Schiller and his wife had gone. Many of the candles had guttered, leaving the room in semi-darkness. He picked up his old glass. Primrose and Koenig were dancing slowly, closely entwined, to the music of a song with which he was faintly familiar.

He tried to make sense of the information. Senior officers in the Wehrmacht would lead a coup against Hitler if they were asked to use force against their Czech neighbour. Their men would follow orders. That piece of information was certainly true; you could bet on that. The German soldier was by instinct and training loyal to his unit and commanders.

There was no question that if senior officers gave orders, they would follow.

They would need a general to lead them, of course. Who would that be? Not Keitel, for sure. Maybe Halder or Beck. But this would only happen if Britain precipitated the crisis by making a stand against Hitler. If the Führer backed down, his war strategy would be shown for what it was – bluff. Then the army would move. But what was Macrae going to do with the information?

Koenig left the dance floor to put on a new record. A light rain was tapping on the dome roof. He looked up briefly. He did not seem to notice Macrae in the darkened room. One thing was for certain: Macrae could not tell the ambassador. The colonel was right. Henderson would take the information to Göring, and Göring would pass it straight to Hitler and the Gestapo. Stalin had just purged his entire officer class, ordering the execution of tens of thousands of entirely innocent men, on the grounds that they posed a possible threat. Hitler would not dare contemplate such barbarity, but there would be a purge all the same; arrests, show trials, executions.

Koenig and Primrose began to dance again, this time at a slower tempo, to a long-drawn-out solo by a saxophone player whose notes floated from the gramophone and coiled around the dancers in a melodic embrace. Primrose lacked the skill and grace of Gertrude, but she danced with desire. It was evident in every step she took; in the way she held him, her fingers locked through his; in the way she rested her head on his shoulder, with her cheek against his; in the way she pressed herself against him. Koenig's dance with his wife had been an act of remembrance, a recital of past pleasures recalled in dance, a long-married couple finding release rather than lust on the ballroom floor. With Primrose it was different, as was obvious to anyone watching from the shadows that night.

Halliday was lounging against the wall by his office door when Macrae returned the next morning.

"Decent weekend, was it?" he said.

Macrae unlocked his office. There was ten minutes before the morning meeting and he needed a coffee. The secretary he shared with the others had not turned up on time. He put the kettle on to boil and reached for the jar of instant coffee below the telex machine. Halliday followed him into the room. He would want coffee too. He was known as the embassy scrounger.

"Get any shooting in?" asked Halliday.

"It's not the season." Macrae was tired, the tone abrupt. There were times when a little of Halliday went a very long way.

"Oh, I know, but still plenty of pigeon, rabbit, hares, that sort of thing?"

Macrae thrust a cup of coffee at him.

"I thought you were supposed to spy on the other side."

"Take it easy," said Halliday. "I just thought it might be useful to see if you are hearing what I'm hearing."

"Which is?" snapped Macrae.

"Dear me, but you're in a bad mood. We can discuss this later."

"No, go on."

"Czechoslovakia, Sudetenland, and the army is . . ."

"Not happy?"

"Exactly, but how many units at what level, do we suppose?"

"We suppose nothing. Let's have a drink later."

• • •

At lunchtime Macrae walked back from the embassy towards home. He had eaten a sandwich in the canteen and needed time to think. It was the first warm day of spring and he wanted to see if the park had finally thrown off winter. He passed by the Brandenburg Gate, dodged the traffic and crossed the road to Charlottenburger Chaussee. It was lunchtime and people were hurrying to meet friends, maybe lovers, or just heading home. The trees of the Tiergarten were breaking into leaf and a large flock of starlings darkened the sky as they swooped overhead as if to celebrate the fact.

Ahead in the crowds a taxi stopped on the avenue. Under new traffic rules it was illegal to park anywhere near national monuments. A woman got out and the cab drove off rapidly. The woman began walking away from him, about a hundred yards ahead. She was hatless and her long dark hair fell in ringlets over a light fawn overcoat. She seemed to be looking for somewhere to sit down. She looked too glamorous for a secretary or an office worker but might be the wife of a wealthy businessman, thought Macrae. Even from behind, there was something familiar about her. He quickened his stride until he was a few paces behind. Now he was sure. The woman sat down on a bench.

"The lady from the Adlon bar," he said, catching up with her.

She turned, looked startled and then smiled.

"Hello. The businessman – import and export, wasn't it?"

Macrae had forgotten his clumsy subterfuge. "Er, yes . . . so where are you going?"

"I am going to sit here in the sun, enjoy the warmth and eat an apple."

"May I join you?"

He sat down. She dug into her bag and produced a green and red apple. Immediately, several starlings appeared and began strutting back and forth in front of the seat.

"I think you told me a little fib when we met in the Adlon the other day," she said, and bit into her apple.

"What makes you think that?"

He waited while she finished the first bite.

"Because you're a British diplomat, aren't you?" she said, taking another bite.

"Why on earth would you say that?"

She munched the apple, swallowed, laughed. "The trilby, that suit, those shoes. You all look the same, and there aren't many other British people in Berlin these days."

"And you?"

"I've told you, I am a manager of a restaurant."

"Perhaps we have both been fibbing."

She suddenly looked serious and threw the apple core on the ground. By now the starlings had been joined by several others, who fought over the core. A larger bird than the others bore it away, with the rest of the flock in noisy pursuit. She leant forward, her elbows on her knees, and began talking, head down, in a low voice, very quickly.

"I would like a small favour. My brother is in a concentration camp. It's Buchenwald; you may have heard of it. He's my twin. I need to know if he is alive. That's all. Just if he is still alive."

Macrae looked around, trying to see if they were being watched. Impossible to tell, given the lunchtime crowds. He shifted away.

"There are many such people, I am afraid. I have no means of finding out. Have you tried the Red Cross?"

"They are useless; no access. Please help me. It's not much to ask. You're a diplomat; you could find out."

"They are arresting people all the time, holding them for interrogation and then releasing them. Unless he's done something, he'll be all right."

"Not my brother. He's my twin. We're Jewish." She scrabbled in her handbag, then thrust a piece of paper at him. There were tears in her eyes. "Please," she said.

Macrae shifted back. This was an old trick. An agent provocateur, a document passed over in a public place and a hidden camera somewhere. He didn't know why he had followed her and joined her on the bench. It had definitely been a mistake. She had planned this meeting. He had been followed. He was being set up.

"Put the paper away," he said, getting to his feet.

"Joseph. Joseph Sternschein. Buchenwald," she said.

He turned and walked away. He did not look back, but he knew she was watching him. It had been a mistake to talk to her. Ruth, she had said her name was. Whoever she was, she wasn't a restaurant manager.

8

Bonner looked with dismay at his desk. Two fresh stacks of different-coloured folders had been placed there while he had been at what Heydrich chose to call his "planning-and-action" meeting. Heydrich loved planning, especially large-scale arrest operations. He would interest himself in every detail, questioning his subordinates about the number of trucks or cars to be used, the condition of their spare wheels, fuel consumption, back-up vehicles and so forth.

Sometimes there would be Nacht und Nebel operations when prominent people, occasionally police officers deemed disloyal or Jewish community leaders judged guilty of nothing at all except their racial identity, would be spirited away after a late-night knock on the door, never to be seen again.

Heydrich spent hours going over these cases before signing them off. More often, the operations were conducted in daylight, because Heydrich never ceased telling them that the violent arrest of one or two people and the physical abuse of their family, especially children, when witnessed by neighbours helped break the communal resolve to resist. To make people truly believe in us, you must first break them, he would say.

Bonner noticed that he always looked happier after such decisions had been taken. Then he would leave in an excellent mood for fencing lessons or to take his violin to play with his own quartet. In fact, he was always in a good mood on those afternoons when he left early to play the violin. He would bring the instrument to the office, place it on a table behind his desk and open the case. If he noticed you looking at it, he would allow you to inspect it, proudly announcing that it had been made by the Italian master craftsman Giovanni Battista Guadagnini in the eighteenth century. He would hold and stroke the instrument as if he had a baby in his arms. Then he would tell you he was playing this or that concerto, usually Mozart or Beethoven, with musicians who met at his home.

Heydrich clearly meant what he said when he demanded that his senior staff work without pause until the mission was complete. "Sleep in the office, don't leave the building, I want those files back here in twenty-four hours," he had said at the close of the meeting. He did not shout. He spoke quietly, unlike Himmler, who occasionally conducted the senior staff meetings and ranted and raved at them, so that his spittle flew across the table, landing in shiny droplets on the polished mahogany.

There had been twelve people in the room and there was not a man among them who did not know that Heydrich would have them arrested if they questioned the logic or purpose of what they were told to do.

The mission lay in those files on his desk. There were more, no doubt, waiting for his attention in the secretary's office. Bonner picked one up. The name on the cover was "Case Green", code name for the invasion of the Sudetenland province of Czechoslovakia in the summer. The files contained names of people who were to be arrested and organisations that were to be eliminated once the German army had crossed the border. It would do so in overwhelming force, although combat was not expected.

The military planning for Case Green was based on the fact that there would be a spontaneous uprising in the majority German-speaking province to welcome the invading troops. And guess what, Bonner thought, who is going to organise that spontaneous uprising? We are, of course. Gestapo gold had already been paid and weapons secretly distributed to paramilitary groups in the Sudetenland.

Further information was required about those enemies of the German Reich in the Sudetenland that had already been identified. Their homes and work addresses had to be cross-checked and added to the file, along with addresses of relatives and close friends. The lists contained the obvious targets: communists, social democrats, Jews, political priests, saboteurs, known homosexuals and general antisocial scum.

There were many more suspects deemed possible enemies of the Reich. You didn't have to do much to fall into the grey area of suspicion. Those who had written to newspapers condemning paramilitary violence in Czechoslovakia or who had demanded international intervention to prevent precisely what was about to happen – they were on the list. People overheard by neighbours complaining about how national radio had been subverted to broadcast Nazi propaganda – they were very high on the list.

The SS, effectively the military arm of the Gestapo, and very much under Heydrich's control, would move in after the military and arrest them all. There would be initial interrogations. A few, very few, who were obviously innocent of harmful intent towards the Reich would be sent home. The rest would be put on trains to concentration camps in Germany, mostly to Dachau. Rough estimates placed the number of those in the first wave of arrests at ten thousand. Dachau would be the clearing centre, Heydrich had told the morning conference. It had recently been enlarged for that very purpose. At the end of the meeting, he had looked around and asked quietly if there were any questions. There never were. Reinhard Heydrich always made his plans perfectly clear.

Bonner drank his coffee and took a savage bite from a sandwich. This is what his life had come to: lists and files of people and places, endless reams of paper produced with lethal intent. At least he would not be involved in the laborious cross-checking of information. That was clerical work. Down below, the machinery of the Gestapo had been working on those files all morning. Teams of mostly women had been checking telephone directories, police files, local government records and witness statements for days, collating information that would pluck a person from his house, office or the street and within twenty-four hours place him, bloody and bleeding, in a sealed railway truck on the way to Dachau. Heydrich always said that women did the cross-checking much better than men. They were more patient, more thorough. That was why the Gestapo had the highest proportion of female staff in the whole government.

Bonner's job was more delicate and, as Heydrich had put it, suitable only for someone of his talent and experience. Heydrich knew the power of flattery and praise. He never overlooked the opportunity to thank one of his senior staff for an operation well done or for an idea that he liked. He was good on birthdays too. His secretary made sure he knew when to offer a little cake and a greeting card to a senior colleague.

Bonner's job was to select those deemed sufficiently subversive to be spared the journey to Dachau. They would be brutally beaten for information, maybe for a day or two, and then executed, usually in the basement of the building where they had been detained. These people were a real danger, mostly communists receiving pay from Moscow and bent on subversion and even assassination. Communists were the real enemy; they always had been. Ask anyone in the army and they would just shrug when you talked of the Jews. As Bonner well knew, many Jews had risen to rank in the last war and fought well. The army did not have a problem with them. Communists were different. They deserved everything that was coming to them.

At exactly the same time every morning, Sir Nevile Henderson walked from his residence to the embassy next door through a connecting corridor. This morning, however, he cancelled his early appointments and decided to spend the first hour of his day on a walk. It was when he did his best thinking, free from the distraction of his office and far from the household chatter around him in the residence. He was a bachelor, but there always seemed to be a relative or friend staying.

It was May and there was no better time for a long and thoughtful stroll in the Tiergarten. The park was in its spring beauty, with buds breaking into pink and white flowers on every branch and the freshly mown grass in the picnic areas looking like an emerald-green carpet.

He had a lot to think about. As a good Christian, he knew that doubt was an essential element of his faith. You had to doubt the existence of God, the Father, the Son and the Holy Ghost, because only by overcoming that doubt and accepting the truth of divinity could you find real belief in the god you served. And Sir Nevile Henderson believed he served his god, just as he served his country, with faith and humility.

The doubt that troubled him that morning had been forming in his mind for several weeks. It was like an uninvited guest at a party who would not leave when politely asked to do so. It approached him at inconvenient moments of the day, when shaving in the morning or during that quiet moment after lunch when he would do the *Times* crossword.

Try as he might, Sir Nevile could not dismiss the small cloud that had formed in an otherwise clear blue sky of rational policy and logical diplomacy. Was the British government right about Hitler? Was it sensible to treat the German leader as a sane and rational politician who wanted merely to redeem the national shame of an unjust peace treaty and create a nation embracing all German-speaking peoples in central Europe? Or was there a deeper and more menacing ambition hidden behind that cowlick hairstyle and silly moustache? Was the man bent on a return to war, of which he had had personal experience in the trenches of Flanders Fields?

Nevile Henderson disliked the term “appeasement”. It smacked too much of deference, even surrender. They were, after all, dealing with a man who had come to power through the tactical use of violence and intimidation. And it *was* tactical, was it not? The murderous coup against Röhm and the old SS had left hundreds dead and thousands more in prison camps. That had happened one blood-letting night back in 1934. But this was a young country finding its feet in a Europe hostile to its history and culture. Hitler had been forced to consolidate his power with brutal means that would have been familiar to the Tudors in England.

Sir Nevile took a seat in the sunshine and looked along the avenue to the Brandenburg Gate. Napoleon had walked through that triumphal arch as a hero, and he remained so in France to this day. Yet look at the record and one will find many a dark deed on his path to power. Was Hitler any different?

The Frenchman had launched his coup d'état against the ruling Directoire in Paris with a band of musketeers. Hitler had crept up on power like a tiger, flattening himself in the long grass while he stalked his prey, always waiting for the right moment to pounce. If anything, the new leader of Germany was the better tactician, using genuine anger over the Versailles treaty terms to mask his real ambitions. You had to admire that, thought Sir Nevile. Hitler had taken his party from two per cent of the national vote in the parliamentary election of 1928 to a majority and supreme power in 1933. That was little short of political genius.

A certain respect was due a leader of such calibre. There was a thuggish aspect to the Nazis' rise to power, of course; one had to admit that. Then there was the Jewish thing, which seemed to obsess Hitler and his inner circle, although Sir Nevile had been told that ordinary members of the Nazi Party, especially women, were not inclined to racial hatred, despite the propaganda of Goebbels and his crew.

Anti-Semitism was not pretty and although the ambassador was privately appalled by the excesses that followed the Anschluss in Austria, it was clear to him that Hitler had not known, still less approved, of the errant behaviour of the SS in Vienna that spring. In any case, Sir Nevile had made it a personal and political priority not to let the problems of the Jews get in the way of his diplomatic mission. He was comforted in this thought by the fact that the prime minister entirely agreed with him. Both men knew that the key to the future of Europe lay in the character of a man they believed to have been widely misunderstood and thus misjudged.

Sir Nevile had learnt to appreciate the personal qualities in Hitler that few others saw. He felt it gave him an important advantage over other heads of mission in Berlin. Hitler could be both charming and very persuasive, especially when he expressed what the ambassador felt was a genuine desire to forge a relationship with Britain that would benefit both countries.

He knew there were those on his staff who saw nothing but evil in the man, disliked the appeasement policy and favoured the more aggressive diplomacy preached by Winston Churchill. But Churchill was an egoistical old bore who was often inebriated after lunch in the Commons and was always indisposed after dinner. Frankly, it flattered the old man to call him, as some did, an old elephant trumpeting past glories from the fringe of the herd. He was more like a war veteran warming himself by a winter fire on memories of distant battles and cheap brandy.

Sir Nevile turned away from the Brandenburg Gate and walked quickly back to the embassy. The world was suddenly a better place. His doubts had been banished. He raised his hat occasionally to ladies as he passed, leaving them in his wake looking surprised at such old-fashioned gallantry. His confidence had been restored. He walked with vigour and looked forward to the day ahead. He told himself that he had, like Christ in the Garden of Gethsemane, conquered his doubts. Had not Christ fallen to his knees as his attackers closed in and pleaded with his father, saying, "If it is possible, may this cup be taken from me?" Then he had risen and faced the men who would crucify him.

The ambassador summoned his senior staff to the delayed morning meeting the moment he returned. He watched them take their places. This would be a quick meeting to make up lost time, a canter around the course to familiarise everyone with the jumps, as he liked to say. That was the one thing he really disliked about his job in Berlin. There was never time to ride his horse. Sir Nevile looked at the agenda and saw that as usual David Buckland was to give a summary.

Buckland spoke briefly. He said that behind the drumbeat of propaganda and hysteria one hard political fact had emerged. The German leadership had collectively decided to invade Czechoslovakia in six weeks. The German army had been given orders to move into the Sudetenland region in July.

"I am sorry to say that it seems the time for talking is over. Supremely confident after the lack of any international condemnation of his Austrian Anschluss, Hitler will now move against his eastern neighbour."

Buckland sat down. Sir Nevile sighed. The day was not going to go quite as planned. He had been rebuked by inference by a senior member of his own staff. Of course neither he nor the government had condemned the Austrian takeover. In fact, the foreign secretary, Lord Halifax, had virtually congratulated Hitler on the move. But what was the point of an empty condemnation when one had no military force within five hundred miles to back it up? He looked up. Halliday had raised his hand at the far end of the table.

"Just to confirm, Ambassador. The code name for the assault on Czechoslovakia is Case Green. Hitler has personally signed the operational document issued to his commanders using the following words as a preamble. I quote this verbatim: 'It is my unalterable decision to smash Czechoslovakia by military action in the foreseeable future.'"

"Do the Czechs know this?" It was all Sir Nevile could do. Keep calm, ask a question, persuade those anxious faces around the table that he was in control, that he had known this was coming and that he had already weighed the diplomatic response.

"Yes," said Halliday. "They are mobilising their army as we speak."

"Macrae?" snapped the ambassador.

"I can confirm what we have just heard," said Macrae.

"And the German High Command is going along with this?"

"It rather depends whether the aim of the operation is annexation of the Sudetenland region or a wider assault to take the whole country," said Macrae.

"Well, which is it, man – you are supposed to be the military attaché, aren't you?"

Macrae picked up a sheaf of papers and flipped through them as if trying to find the answer to the question. He was enjoying the ambassador's anger. The frightening reality of the apocalypse that was about to descend on Europe might just be brought home to a man convinced by class and privilege that he knew best.

"I am not privy to the secret strategy behind Case Green, and I suspect the generals are not either. The one man who knows the answer is the Führer himself, and may I suggest that on your next meeting with Herr Hitler you demand an answer to the question."

There was silence as those around the table awaited the ambassador's response. He had never been challenged in such a manner before; indeed, every minute of the brief meeting so far had been quite extraordinary.

Sir Nevile Henderson had been staring at the table, his face pale and creased with lines. He raised his head.

"I will thank you not to tell me how to do my job, Colonel Macrae. Yours is to find out the true German intentions towards Czechoslovakia and report back."

He had risen halfway through his retort and was at the door when he stopped and looked at Macrae.

"We have no time to lose, do you hear?"

• • •

When he got back to his office, Macrae saw a folded note on his desk. Written in the school handwriting of his secretary, it said that a William Shirer had called three times that morning asking for "a private word".

Halliday popped his head round the door, grinning.

"I have a feeling you've just dropped off the ambassador's Christmas card list," he said.

"I don't think you'll be getting one either. Come in."

Halliday perched on his desk.

"It won't make any difference," he said. "It will only increase their desire to do a deal." He picked up the note from the desk. "So Shirer has been calling you too, has he?"

Macrae took the note from him.

"Mind your own business, Roger."

He scrunched the note into a ball and flicked it into the wastepaper basket.

"Don't get touchy. I only asked because he wants to meet up with me at some smart restaurant tonight. Why not come along – one bird with two stones?"

"Where?"

"Smart place, very exclusive. Sort of club. Bit different. You'll like it. I'll pick you up at eight."

The Salon was full when Halliday and Macrae walked in. The woman on the door had seemed to know Halliday and waved them in. Through the smoky haze they had trouble finding Shirer. The woman maître d' did not recognise his name on her reservation list. Finally they saw him tucked away at a corner table next to the small bandstand. There was a bottle of champagne in an ice bucket and three glasses.

The American correspondent rose to greet them.

"Welcome," he said. "You know this place, Colonel Macrae?"

"No," said Macrae, looking around at the mirrored décor in what appeared to be a restaurant, nightclub and bar combined. "What's it called?"

"The Salon," said Shirer. "Good observation post, wouldn't you say, Mr Halliday?"

Macrae tried to remember where he had come across the name before. Halliday laughed, raised a glass of champagne and looked around the room. The Italian journalists were in again and he recognised a senior commander in the Luftwaffe in civilian clothes dining with three young men in evening dress. Halliday guessed them to be part of Göring's Reich Air Ministry, which controlled all Luftwaffe operations. On the far side the French chargé d'affaires was hosting dinner for what looked like a group of French businessmen. At the bar every seat was taken by suited drinkers. Everywhere the waitresses wearing the usual grey close-cut dresses threaded their way through tables with trays of drinks and food.

From a purely operational point of view, Halliday took his hat off to Reinhard Heydrich. He had developed the Gestapo into an efficient machine for creating terror, thus suppressing dissent, and gathering intelligence. And he had turned a broken-down Berlin brothel into a small but lethal reflection of the wider strategy.

The Salon was a keyhole through which you could catch a glimpse of privileged Berliners at play in a city where pleasure had been publicly forbidden, and entertainment only licensed if it promoted the goals of the National Socialist government. The cinema and theatre had not entirely been suborned to the demands of Goebbels and his Propaganda Ministry. Harmless vaudeville entertainment and imported

American films were allowed, as long as they did not transgress the censorship rules.

Here in the Salon the rules were different. Under the watchful eye of Kitty, the Nazi elite and those who did business with them could eat sumptuous food, drink fine wines and indulge in the carnal delights to be found behind the fanlight door.

And it gave Heydrich and his goons both power and intelligence. They listened to and watched everything that was said and done in the Salon. What they did not realise was that the Salon also provided very useful information to those like himself who did not share the interests of the National Socialist Party. Halliday tried to work out who in the club that night had come for those pleasures that were not on the menu. The Italian journalists, for sure. They were always here.

"This is rather expensive, isn't it?" said Macrae, looking at the menu, wondering who was going to pay for the dinner, if dinner was what they were here for. He wasn't entirely sure. Primrose was out again that night but had said she would not be home late. He wanted to talk to her, hear her news, tell her something of the job he was trying to do. He had hardly seen his wife for days now. She seemed to spend endless evenings with other embassy wives. They passed like distant ships at sea, semaphoring the occasional signal as a courtesy rather than to communicate anything of importance.

"It's a very exclusive place; that's why," said Shirer. "Look around. You'll see senior members of the Nazi hierarchy, the civil service, foreign diplomats, big names in entertainment circles. They're all here."

"You had better explain a little further," said Halliday with a smile, and Macrae realised they had a secret and that he had been brought to the Salon that night to share it.

"Fine food, best in Berlin, incomparable wines, and you get some very decent songs, not just all the old German lieder they sing in the beer halls."

Shirer was smiling as he gestured around the club. Macrae was becoming irritated with the game the two men were playing.

"I've never heard of the place," he said.

"Of course not; it keeps itself to itself, never advertises, and there is a strict door policy."

"You're making it sound very secretive."

"It has to be. It's exclusive. So are the waitresses . . ."

Shirer gestured at a young woman passing with a tureen of soup.

"They're very pretty," agreed Macrae.

Shirer leant forward, pouring more champagne into their glasses. "That's the whole point," he said.

"What is?" said Macrae, feeling even more irritated.

"Because this is a brothel," whispered Shirer. He sat back, laughed and slapped the table to make the point.

"Welcome to the Salon, Colonel."

Macrae looked around the room. He was sitting in an exclusive and very expensive Berlin restaurant, not a brothel. Shirer was kidding him. The American was making a strange and rather tasteless joke, a further reminder that, whatever else crossed the Atlantic with the good ship *Mayflower*, it certainly wasn't an English sense of humour.

"What, all these waitresses . . .?"

"Well, not these," said Halliday, "because they have to work tonight, but behind that fanlight door there are plenty more."

Macrae looked around the room. "These women are all . . .?"

"Available? Yes," said Halliday, getting to his feet. "I have to go; you two have things to talk about. But remember: 'look don't touch' is our rule here. And watch that door and see who goes through it – could be useful."

For the next half hour Macrae and Shirer jousted as they ate their steaks, using nuggets of information to tempt the other into indiscretion.

"What I want to know is what we all want to know," said Shirer finally.

"Who's 'we'?"

"Every hack and dip in this city."

"What do we all want to know?" said Macrae.

"Cards on the table: I want information from you and you from me. Deal? OK. You know about Case Green?"

"Possibly."

"And you have heard that Hitler has actually put in writing – writing, mind you – his order to his generals to smash Czechoslovakia, those very words."

"You are very well informed," admitted Macrae.

"And you would like to know the reaction in the High Command to that order?"

"That would be interesting."

"In which case, you might like to know what I want to know," said Shirer.

Macrae slid a cuff back trying to take a discreet look at his watch. Shirer reached over the table and placed a hand on his wrist.

"We have time," he said. "This is important."

"I can't stay too late. What do you want to know?"

"Simple. What will HMG do when it learns that Case Green is about invading Czechoslovakia, all of it, and opening the way for further aggression against Poland? What will that do to the appeasement policy?"

"A very good question," said Macrae, and he looked across the room, hoping to see someone he knew, so that he could end the conversation. He wished Halliday had not left so early.

And there she was at the bar, smoking a cigarette in a holder. Ruth the restaurant manager. Except she wasn't the restaurant manager. And her name probably wasn't Ruth. She was wearing a red dress rather than the dove-grey uniform of the Salon's waitresses.

"Well?" said Shirer.

Macrae turned back.

"It's impossible to say, but if you want my private and candid opinion, only if the government falls in a confidence vote in the House of Commons will there be a change in the current policy towards Germany. The prime minister has staked his career and his future reputation on the belief that Hitler will listen to reason, that a deal can be done, that in the final analysis the Führer will not provoke a wider war. Chamberlain has his party and the country behind him on this."

"What I thought," said Shirer. "OK, fair enough. All right, my turn."

Macrae turned to scan the room again. Ruth, or whatever her name was, was talking to a man at the bar. She seemed bored and blew a smoke ring into the air. The man offered her a drink, snapping his fingers at the woman behind the bar. She shook her head.

"All the girls here are the same, are they?" asked Macrae.

"Yes," said Shirer. "It's the oldest story in the world, isn't it? Love for sale. Now, are you listening?"

Macrae nodded and bent his head while the correspondent launched into a long explanation of how the army dealt with the former corporal who had become its commander-in-chief.

The Führer would issue an order, usually of an urgent and highly impractical nature, Shirer said. The generals would pass the order on to the planning staff and they would in turn send it to technical teams. Within days, a complex document would be laid before Hitler, who would characteristically launch into a tirade about the incompetence of the military. Then he would issue a revised directive, and so the process went on until the army got a plan that was feasible and very roughly to their liking.

Macrae was listening while keeping an eye on the bar. The man had left her and she was looking over the room. She was looking straight at him. She frowned, then smiled and slid off the stool. Macrae faced Shirer.

"Are you telling me that the generals are going to turn Hitler down?"

"They don't want a wider invasion, that's for sure."

"Doesn't answer the question."

"Put it this way. There's going to be a big kick-back in the army if the Führer decides to smash Czechoslovakia and take the whole kit and caboodle." Shirer raised his hand, signalling for the bill. "Let's just keep in touch. If you hear anything from the London end I would be grateful, strictly between us, of course."

A waitress brought the bill It wasn't Ruth, and Macrae couldn't see her anywhere. Shirer glanced at the bill, laid a large number of reichsmarks on the platter and struggled into his coat. He reached for the bill, leaving the money on the table.

"You coming?" he said.

"I think I'll stay for a nightcap," said Macrae.

"Really?" said Shirer, surprised and smiling. "Well, well, well. And I thought butter wouldn't melt in your mouth. Take care." And he was gone.

Macrae sat down and picked up the menu.

"Coffee?" she said, standing there, having materialised, so it seemed to Macrae, out of thin air.

"Thanks – and maybe a brandy."

"And may I join you?"

"Are you allowed to?"

"That's the whole point of this place," she said, and sat down. She looked over at the bar, nodding twice, and, by a process that Macrae could not understand, a tray with coffee and two glasses of brandy was swiftly delivered to the table.

"What a surprise," he said, raising the glass, "to find that nice young woman I met at the Adlon, the woman called Ruth who said she was a restaurant manager, the woman who suddenly appeared by my side in the park, to find out she works here in . . ."

"Did you find out about Joseph?"

"Why would I bother? Everything you told me was a lie."

"I told you I worked here. I told you my brother was in a camp. Those aren't lies. And my name here is Sara, by the way."

"Ruth yesterday, Sara today – what will it be tomorrow?"

"Who are you to talk? You lied to me, didn't you? You think this is what I want to do? I do it because I am safe here. They can't touch me."

"What do you mean?"

"I mean I'm a Jewish whore in a Nazi bordello."

She sighed and lit another cigarette. Macrae wanted another drink. He also wanted a cigarette. He had tried to give up two years earlier but occasionally yielded to temptation.

"I thought you might come in one day," she said. "Most of the attachés do."

"And they sleep with the girls, do they?"

She shrugged. "Not necessarily. But a lot of them do. This is where power comes to play. There's danger in the air here. Men like that; they like the taste of adrenalin, don't they?"

"I think I'd better leave," he said, pushing back his chair.

"Please don't go."

Once outside, he leant back against the wall of the club, breathing in cool night air. He badly needed that cigarette. She was beautiful, she was in trouble and she was Jewish. Everything about her told him she was telling the truth. And her brother Joseph Sternschein was in a camp – was that true too? It would not be easy to find out.

The Gestapo kept meticulous records of certain categories of those who fell into their clutches: communists, saboteurs, sexual deviants and political opponents were all documented by name and address and usually with a headshot photograph, but the sheer number of Jews being arrested at any one time and sent to camps meant that names were often superseded as a means of identification by a file number and the date and place of arrest.

He walked quickly away from the Salon, turned off the well-lit main avenue and took a footpath into the darkness of the Tiergarten. It was nearing midnight, but he did not feel tired. The brandy had invigorated him, although he knew there would be a price to pay in the morning. If Primrose was home she would be asleep. He needed a walk to clear his head and think. The headlights of cars driving around the Siegessäule roundabout threw a Catherine wheel of lights into the woods. He could just see the path and walked slowly.

Above the faint hum of traffic he heard the sound of hurrying footsteps. He stopped and listened. The clip-clop of steps was coming down the path he had just walked. He reached for the door key in his pocket, a heavy old-fashioned object whose jagged teeth would make a useful weapon.

The footsteps were getting closer and louder, light, fast-moving steps that spoke of urgency, or perhaps hostility. He leant back against the trunk of a tree and peered down the path. A figure took shape in the darkness wearing a flowing cape with the hood pulled over the head. He took the key from his pocket. The Nazis had a tight grip on almost every aspect of life in Berlin but they had not eliminated street crime, especially in the darkness of the Tiergarten at night.

The figure stopped in front him, breathing heavily. Macrae raised the key to show the stranger he had a means of defence.

The figure pushed back the hood, showing a tumble of dark hair. "I am sorry. I didn't mean to alarm you," she said.

He put the key back in his pocket.

"What are you doing here? Why are you following me?"

She fished a cigarette from her bag and offered one to him. He took it gratefully. She snapped open a lighter and in the light of the flame her face seemed different. The young actress in the Salon was now a woman who looked tired, anxious and older than her years.

"I wanted to talk to you."

"Maybe I don't want to talk to you."

"You don't trust me? You're right. These days no one trusts anyone. Especially in there." She nodded in the direction of the Salon.

He drew on the cigarette, wondering how he had ever even thought of giving up. She stepped off the path and joined him under the tree.

"I've told you: I can help you," she said.

"I doubt it," he said, wondering why he didn't just say goodnight and walk away.

"I have information."

"What sort of information?"

"You would be amazed what goes on in those rooms. They film and tape everything."

"What's the point?"

"Blomberg and Fritsch, remember? That's the point."

He inhaled deeply, almost his first cigarette in two years. He knew it would not be his last. Blomberg had fallen from grace through a stupid marriage. General Fritsch was different. He was a tough career officer, known to have stood up to Hitler, especially at one long meeting in the Reich Chancellery back in November 1937 when the Führer had revealed plans to take the Reich to war. Fritsch had argued back very convincingly and Hitler had grudgingly retreated.

But from then on Fritsch was a marked man. Now he was gone, supposedly through some sexual scandal arranged by Heydrich. Maybe Fritsch had been compromised in the Salon. Maybe Sara had been the bait. Maybe everything she had told him had been a lie.

"Why was your brother arrested?" he asked.

"Silly stuff, just leaflets."

"For the Communist Party?"

"No, just leaflets denouncing the Nazis, calling for justice for those detained, asking Western powers to intervene."

"How did they catch him?"

"Usual thing. An informer, someone he trusted. They tortured her, of course."

"'Her'?"

"It was his girlfriend."

"Oh," he said.

She had moved closer. The glowing ends of their cigarettes made twin tracks of light in the darkness. He could smell her perfume, a scent of citrus, something he had not noticed in the club.

"Do you think you can do it?" she said.

"Find out about your brother?"

"Yes."

"I'm a diplomat. It would be beyond my duties and in breach of protocol – interference in the internal affairs of a sovereign state."

She suddenly laughed. "You think I'm wearing a microphone, don't you? You think this is a trap."

"I didn't say that."

"Let me show you."

He watched bemused as she let her cape fall to the ground. She unzipped her dress and stepped out of it, the action taking no more than a moment. She was wearing a black brassiere and panties.

"Get dressed," he said. "This is not necessary."

"It *is* necessary," she hissed. "Because this is exactly what they would do. I have told you – they film and tape everything in that club. Why wouldn't they send me here to do the same to you? They don't like you, did you know that? They have you on a file."

Macrae stiffened. She was probably right.

"How do you know that?" he said.

"I've told you, I hear a lot in that place. You need proof that I'm not working for them tonight?"

She unhooked her brassiere and let it drop to her feet. The occasional flash of headlights in the darkness revealed her breasts, full and pale like misty moons in the darkness. She was wearing only a suspender belt and black stockings.

"That's enough," he said. "Get dressed."

"Don't be stupid," she said, and slipped out of her panties.

"This is where we hide the mikes – here," she placed her hand on a triangular tangle of thick pubic hair. "They have not invented one yet that works inside – sorry, am I shocking you?"

She stood there in the darkness, naked but for her stockings, and pirouetted slowly, hands raised above her head. All the time distant headlights sliced through the darkness, throwing spears of light onto the contours of pale skin and strands of dark hair.

"You see. I'm clean," she said.

"Put your clothes back on," he said again.

"First tell me you believe me."

"I don't believe you've been sent here to trap me, if that's what you're asking."

She got dressed much more slowly than she had undressed. He felt his heart beating faster. His mouth was dry. He needed another drink. She pulled her dress over a full-figured body that had been naked before him only a minute ago, turning her back in false modesty.

This had been planned; it was deliberate; he was being set up. He looked into the shadowy outline of the surrounding trees, half expecting a lurking figure to explode from the darkness with a camera and flashbulb.

Once dressed, she turned, smoothed her dress and ran fingers through her hair.

"It's not much to ask, is it? Will you try?"

He sighed. He was tired, he was drunk and he would try to make sense of this midnight melodrama later, much later.

"All right," he said.

"Thank you," she said, and stepped forward to kiss him. He turned his head, feeling the feathery brush of her lips on his cheek. He turned his head towards her. Suddenly their lips met lightly, a soft touch in the darkness. She stepped back, fished in her bag, taking out a pack of cigarettes. She lit one and inhaled deeply. Then she put it between his lips, a gesture so unexpected that he opened his mouth and drew on the cigarette without thinking. She lit her own and rested against the tree beside him. He felt her hand take his and squeeze it.

They stayed there for a moment, a minute, an hour, he couldn't tell; then he saw her cigarette end flying into the night.

"I must go," she said, and turned and walked away into the darkness without another word.

He watched the cloaked figure vanish into the night. He looked at his watch. It was midnight. He levered himself away from the tree unsteadily and walked back to the house.

Primrose was asleep when he got back, curled up on her side of the bed, one hand still holding an open book. He took it from her and glanced at the title. *Goodbye to Berlin* by Christopher Isherwood. He laid it on the bedside table, went to the bathroom and washed his face. In the kitchen he filled a tumbler of water from the tap and drank thirstily. The kitchen was spotless and exactly as the maid had left it that morning. There were no dishes drying in the rack by the sink. No one had cooked in there that night. Primrose had been out to dinner again.

The next morning, the ambassador's meeting was an ill-tempered affair. For the first time that anyone present could recall, an open discussion on policy verged on disagreement about the stated aims of the government in London. Sir Nevile had begun with a poorly judged metaphor about the weather. It was only May, he said, but outside summer had arrived and the temperature was rising to an unbearable degree.

His staff looked at him blankly. The weather outside was normal. It was a warm day in late spring. The ambassador tried to explain. "I am talking about the political temperature," he said.

"Oh, I see," said Buckland, scarcely trying to conceal his sarcasm. "Well, you are quite right, Ambassador. Have you heard the announcement from Prague this morning?"

"No," said the ambassador, wondering why no one had warned him of what was clearly going to be more bad news.

"It's a news agency flash, just come in," said Buckland, waving a copy of a cable. "Prague claims that five German divisions are on the move close to the border and an invasion is imminent."

"Macrae?" said the ambassador.

"German spring manoeuvres always take place at this time of year. The Czechs are understandably very jumpy right now. I will check further."

"I thought your job was to warn us of these things in advance." Sir Nevile was determined not to let this meeting slide away from him like the last.

"My job is to keep you as informed as possible, consistent with the willingness of my informant to take risks to provide the information."

"Exactly who is this informant?" said the ambassador, knowing immediately that the stupidity of the question would be obvious to everyone. "I mean, not his name, obviously, but an idea of rank and status would be helpful," he added.

"Not to him I fear, Ambassador. I have given my word that his identity will never be revealed, even to that extent."

"Very well. You had better go to the border region and report back."

"I've already made the arrangements. I'm leaving after conference with a driver."

And you have not asked my permission, thought the ambassador. The man was intolerable. He had received no answer to his request for Macrae to be transferred. He would send another cable to the Foreign Office. In the meantime, the man was better off out of the office swanning around the Czech border. It was obvious that Hitler was only rattling his weaponry to get his way, as usual. The issue of the three million or so ethnic Germans in the Sudetenland region was simple. They should be incorporated into Germany under the terms of the Versailles treaty, which allowed for self-determination of such ethnic groups. That would satisfy Hitler. *Si vis pacem, para bellum*, as the old saying went. Macrae wouldn't understand that. If you want peace, prepare for war. He wouldn't understand that either.

Macrae slipped a note to Halliday as the ambassador turned to the subject of an international hunting expedition organised by Göring for sportsmen around the world.

The note said, *Joseph Sternschein interned camp called Buchenwald. Can confirm status – alive or dead?*

Halliday raised an eyebrow. Macrae put a finger to his lips and rose to leave the room.

For the next week, Macrae travelled through what the international press called Sudetenland but what was in fact an area made up of the old territories of Bohemia, Moravia and Silesia. These had once been principalities within the Holy Roman Empire, which Macrae, along with every schoolboy of his generation, had been taught was not Holy nor Roman nor an empire. These were Hitler's "lost lands", which abutted the mountainous region along the central border between Germany and Czechoslovakia.

Where the mountains folded into valleys, the soil was rich and farming prosperous. The abundance of fast-flowing water powered hydroelectric plants, which turned the wheels of important industry in the area, especially chemical plants, fertiliser factories and glass and china works.

No foreign visitor to the Reich Chancellery in Berlin escaped without a lengthy harangue about the crime that had placed the area in the hands of the Czechs. These brainstorms, as they were described by many shaken ambassadors, did not concern the riches of the Sudetenland, although the Germany military had long cast covetous eyes on the chemical plants. What drove the chancellor to such rages was that the vast majority of the inhabitants were German-speaking and could trace family roots back to medieval times. And they were now living under the control of Slavonic peoples of the east, a race Hitler viewed with almost as much disgust as the Jews.

For the first three days, Macrae toured the German side of the border and found no evidence of troop movements or any military build-up. He was driven by a locally employed driver who had been on the embassy staff for over twenty years and was judged to be both discreet and loyal.

They stayed in small inns, where Macrae ate dinner alone, reading a detective novel and drinking the occasional glass of wine, which always seemed to amount to a full bottle by the end of the meal. He found reading difficult. His mind kept wandering from the page back to Berlin. He had said a brief goodbye to Primrose and received a peck on the cheek and a "Good luck, darling." He could not say she was pleased to see him go, but then she didn't evince any enthusiasm for his presence when he was there.

She seemed to have become his wife in name only, leaving him with a marriage that lacked any meaning or emotion. It was hardly a new state of affairs, but as he sat in a remote inn in Saxony eating yet more venison stew and drinking deeply of the local red wine, the bleak state of his marriage assumed the proportions of a breakdown.

His wife was leading a secret life. She was having an affair. Almost certainly her lover was Koenig. No wonder he had been so difficult to get hold of recently. Macrae gloomily concluded that he had lost both his wife and his main contact in the army.

Then there was Sara in the Salon. The memory of that strange night in the Tiergarten had not receded. A carousel of images went round in his mind: the way she had placed the cigarette in his mouth, the two glowing fireflies in the dark as they smoked, the soft touch of her lips, the sight of her naked, the rounded breasts, the curve and cleft of her buttocks, the flat stomach falling to the dark triangle . . .

"More wine, sir?"

Macrae looked up. A young waitress was standing beside him holding a carafe of wine. His driver had long gone to bed, as had most of the drinkers and diners. There was the usual blowsy barmaid and a few old men muttering into their beer and blowing smoke at the ceiling. His wineglass was empty.

"Why not?" he said.

He raised the glass, drank and considered the questions that came at him every night demanding answers: had Halliday found any information about her brother? What would she do if he had died in the camp? The boy would be young and fit, but those were the ones the guards were ordered to break. They beat them mercilessly. She would try to escape if she found he had died. They would catch her and kill her. That was as certain as an invasion of the damned Sudetenland. Hitler was going to take it and then move on to the whole Czech nation. That was blindingly obvious to everyone except the ambassador and the mandarins in London.

What was it that some Frenchman had said in the eighteenth century after visiting Berlin? "Prussia is not a country with an army, it is an army with a country."

And Prussia, the heart and soul of the German state, had captured Berlin. Bismarck, that towering military genius and empire-builder of the last century, had been replaced by a corporal with a silly moustache. But both were driven by a psychological urge to wage war. Bismarck had done so repeatedly. Hitler would surely do the same. Macrae would go back to Berlin first thing in the morning.

9

Miss Daisy Wellesley was the scion of a famous British family that had used its influence to secure her a senior secretarial post in the Foreign Office after an unfortunate affair with a married Member of Parliament. The resulting abortion had been bungled and she had spent several days close to death in a London hospital. Her survival had given her good reason to rejoice in whatever life provided, and at the age of forty-six she was, if not the youngest, certainly the most cheerful of the ambassador's staff.

Her formal position placed her above that of the secretarial assistant to the three defence attachés in the Berlin embassy, but she looked after them all the same, just as she did the ambassador.

Miss Wellesley, who could trace her ancestry to the great Duke of Wellington, felt it only fitting that she had become a social aide to Sir Nevile, attending the various lunches, dinners and cocktail parties he hosted. The organisation of such events was time-consuming and required a delicacy of touch that only a member of a good British family could provide.

Daisy seemed to know exactly where to seat people at lunch or dinner and flitted around cocktail parties making sure that the right people were introduced to each other. It was further remarked that despite the obvious favouritism bestowed on Daisy by the ambassador, she remained popular with other members of staff. Above all, Daisy wore her grand lineage lightly. She was not, in the words of one of the three cipher clerks, at all "stuck up". She joined them for beer in a local inn after work on Fridays almost every week, providing the ambassador had no social duties that night.

When Macrae returned to the office, Daisy greeted him with a smile, hung up his coat and put the coffee percolator on a small gas ring. He looked tired and worried, she thought. If she had a favourite among the staff, it would be the figure that now sat wearily at his desk, running a hand through his greasy locks. He had not had a bath for days, she thought. He needed to look after himself, or rather his wife did.

"I have two messages for you," she said. "And an anonymous note came in yesterday. Which do you want first?"

"The note, please."

"Shall I read it?"

"Please do."

"'A pair of rare Siberian tigers have arrived at the Berlin zoo – a male and female.' That's all. Does that make any sense?"

"Was there a date or time in the message?"

"No, but I have checked and they are going to present the beasts at a private viewing tomorrow at noon. There will be a light buffet afterwards."

"And you've got me an invitation?"

She smiled and nodded. That was Daisy. Bloody efficient, thought Macrae.

She gave him his coffee and waited while he tasted it.

"Very good," he said.

"Sir . . .?" she said hesitatingly.

Macrae had given up trying to get her to call him Noel.

"Yes, Daisy?"

She sat down in front of his desk and leant forward.

"I do not wish to be disloyal or break confidences," she said, "but, having thought carefully, I think you should know this."

She told him that it was gossip among the cipher clerks that the ambassador had twice asked for Macrae's recall from Berlin in telegrams to the Foreign Office. On both occasions, the reply had been couched in classic Civil Service jargon to the effect that his request had been noted and the matter would be considered by the appropriate authorities at the appropriate time.

"I thought it best that you knew," she said again.

"Thank you, Daisy. You said there were two messages."

"Oh yes, I forgot, sorry. Mr Halliday will be away for a few days. He said to tell you 'He's dead.' Said you would know what he meant."

She watched him sit back in his chair and take a deep breath.

"Someone you knew, sir?"

"No, no, not at all. Thank you, Daisy."

The lions and tigers at the zoo were housed in a covered enclosure that allowed the animals to move from internal cages, where they slept and were fed, into large open-air cages, where they were viewed by an admiring public. About two hundred people had gathered under a large awning opposite one of the outdoor cages to observe the new arrivals. White sheeting had been draped over the cage, to shield the occupants from view. A microphone had been set up on a dais for speeches. Macrae noted an unusually heavy police presence at the entrance to the zoo and around the carnivore enclosure.

Judging by the number of armbands and bemedalled uniforms, there were several senior Nazis present. Macrae scanned the crowd, looking for Koenig. With his height he would have stood out, but there was no sign of him. He thought of Sara and how he was going to break the news of the death of her brother. He would wait until Halliday returned and ask for details, not that such information would help the girl. Her brother would have met a miserable end, tortured, beaten and starved to death.

Around Macrae, well-dressed ladies with fashionable hats and their husbands in smart suits or uniforms talked and gossiped carelessly, arranging dinner that night or a visit to the opera later in the week. And in camps such as Buchenwald men like Joseph Sternschein were choking on their own blood in the last minutes of their young lives. Macrae suddenly wished he had brought his hip flask with him. Or a grenade. A decent Mills bomb would wipe out a good half of those present. Then they could lie screaming in agony on the ground, blood seeping into their smart clothes, life ebbing away. Macrae rebuked himself. It was too easy to let emotion master the mind. It was too easy to feel pity and sheer rage. That was the trouble with Berlin in 1938. It was hard not to succumb to such emotions.

The crowd fell silent and parted to allow the official guests to take their seats behind the dais. To Macrae's surprise, the bulky figure of Field Marshal Hermann Göring strode through the crowd and onto the dais. He wore a peaked cap and a cream suit, from which hung a veritable constellation of medals. It was a standing joke in Berlin that if there was a power cut the city would be illuminated by the sparkle from

Göring's many decorations. The man looked like a music hall comedian from the 1920s. He had acquired almost as many titles and responsibilities as the ribbons and medals that crowded his chest.

He was commander-in-chief of the Luftwaffe, prime minister of the state of Prussia, chairman of the State Opera House and every important museum in the country. As supreme head of the Ministry of Economy, he had appointed himself commissioner for the four-year plan designed to make Germany economically independent of other countries. He owed his indisputable but unofficial position as second in command to Hitler not only to his unswerving loyalty but also to his talents as an administrator.

Beyond that, there was one outstanding feature about the clownish figure that now stood on the dais. As Macrae had recorded in his reports to the War Office in London, Göring was the only senior figure in the Nazi hierarchy who was personally popular with the public. Hitler was regarded with awe and fear, Himmler and Goebbels were hated, but somehow Göring, with his childish vanity and love of display, struck a chord with the German people.

The field marshal pulled a small piece of paper from his pocket and talked for ten minutes about the need for animal conservation and the importance of giving endangered species such as the Siberian tiger a safe environment in which to breed. Shortly, he said, they would be privileged to see the latest arrivals, a magnificent pair of tigers that he had personally arranged to be imported from a zoo in Vladivostok.

There was a gasp as the crowd registered surprise. Russia was the declared enemy of the Third Reich. A state of cold war existed between the two countries. Why had Joseph Stalin gifted two tigers to Adolf Hitler? It was a surreal moment in a city where every day life moved closer to the grotesque.

Macrae had often thought that of the many writers he admired, only Edgar Allan Poe could do justice to the Gothic absurdity of Berlin in 1938. It was as if someone had taken the mythical land of the vampires and placed it in the heart of Europe.

Göring finished his speech and pulled a cord with a flourish. There was a sigh of admiration from the crowd as the sheeting dropped, revealing the tigers. The female lounged languidly on a platform at the back of the cage while the male paced restlessly along the bars, the black-striped rusty red coat rippling with menace, the tail swishing back and forth. There was an outbreak of applause as the crowd moved closer to the cage. Göring was talking again to those around him, pointing to the animals.

Macrae suddenly realised where Koenig would be. In the darkness of the reptile house, it was difficult to see at first, but then Macrae spotted him peering into the window of the python cage. He stood beside him for a moment while the tall, stooped figure inspected two pythons, rare species imported, a notice said, from the Amazon region of Brazil. Macrae wondered whether Göring's interest in conservation extended to snakes. Since they hardly moved and rendered themselves almost invisible, thanks to their ability to camouflage themselves, he thought not.

Without looking round, Koenig said, "They can take a crocodile, you know."

"I'll remember that," said Macrae.

"It's been seen. The struggle goes on for several hours and eventually the python squeezes the life out of the croc – even a big one."

"I didn't know you were interested in snakes."

Koenig straightened up and laughed. "How did you like the tigers?" he said.

"Splendid animals. I'm amazed Göring finds the time."

"He's a busy man."

He was in full colonel's uniform, which surprised Macrae, until he realised that there were so many senior Wehrmacht officers in the zoo that day that uniform was his camouflage. Koenig began walking slowly, peering into the glass windows as if inspecting the reptiles within. He talked in a low and urgent tone.

"It's Beck. Chief of the General Staff. He will lead. Halder, a very high-ranking general, is with us. There is significant support from within the High Command of the army. The air force and navy are not involved; they don't matter because they don't have guns and boots on the ground."

"When?"

"That depends on you British and the French. If you confront Hitler over Czechoslovakia, we will move."

"Meaning?"

"Hitler will be arrested along with the top five: Göring, Himmler, Goebbels, Hess and Heydrich. A provisional government will be formed, headed by a civilian; elections will be announced."

There was a clatter of feet and a babble of conversation from the entrance. Macrae saw that some guests from the tiger event had come to look at the reptiles. There were several officers with their wives and officials from the zoo moving down the row of reptile cages. Macrae turned to warn Koenig, but the colonel had gone.

Walking back to the embassy through the Tiergarten, Macrae considered the extraordinary information he had been given. Senior generals in the Wehrmacht were prepared to arrest their own leader, the chancellor of the Third German Reich, an emperor in all but name, and install a civilian government. He took a seat on a bench and asked himself questions that had to find answers if he was to pass on the information with any hope of being believed.

First, was Colonel Koenig telling the truth, or was this a provocation designed to entrap and expel an unpopular military attaché? The answer had to be yes to the first question and no to the second. Koenig was a Prussian officer with a long family history of military service. He had every reason to betray a Nazi regime that threatened the very future of the army he served.

Secondly, was there a good reason why the army should take such high-risk action? Again the answer was yes. Macrae had ample evidence that the generals feared a two-front war against east and west. And, of course, those Prussians loathed the little upstart from Austria.

Thirdly, was Hitler seriously planning such campaigns, taking on Russia on one front and Britain and France on the other? He must know of the army's misgivings. Why would he gamble on such a risky strategy? This was a more difficult question. Macrae felt the answer to be credible, but he knew it would never stand up to cross-examination by Sir Nevile Henderson.

Hitler had become supremely confident after five years in power, during which he had acquired the aura and trappings of divinity in the eyes of most Germans. The Führer's self-belief was such that in recent speeches he had talked not just of the expulsion of Jews from Germany but the racial cleansing of the inferior Slav peoples of the east. And by east, Hitler meant every nation that lay between Berlin and the Ural mountains, including Russia. In short, the man had become a megalomaniac bent on the domination of an entire continent.

And now to the question to which every diplomat, every service attaché, every intelligence officer and most intelligent Berliners wanted to know the answer. Who would come out on top in the struggle between the Nazi Party and the army?

Hitler and members of his immediate senior circle, Himmler and Goebbels especially, had never trusted the army. After the enforced retirement of Blomberg and Fritsch, their distrust deepened. Hitler was now commander-in-chief, but he was aware that the hard core of the High Command of the Wehrmacht, the old Prussian elite, resented what they regarded as a political coup.

He knew they would never truly accept a one-time corporal, and what is more an Austrian, in the most senior position of power. In their eyes, Hitler lacked class, character and pedigree. Where had he come from? A hick town in Austria. As for his service in the Great War, he had been a mere messenger boy running errands in communication trenches.

Macrae looked at a group of sparrows on the path before him, cheeky little birds that he had seen everywhere he went in the world. Somehow, those tiny bodies had crossed oceans and deserts to colonise cities from Cape Town to Delhi, from London to Singapore. No other small bird was such an opportunistic adventurer.

For all the snobbery that coloured their view of the chancellor, the officers were all too aware of the raw power that Hitler had gathered into his hands. The Nazi leadership ruled through the efficiency of a brutally effective secret police, backed by an extensive and well-armed paramilitary network.

The military were also aware that the major industrialists were doing very nicely under the Nazi regime. Krupp, I. G. Farben and the others were not complaining. As the malcontents in the messes would also admit, the rearmament programme had given all three services, but most notably the army and air force, vast quantities of new equipment, especially tanks and field guns, but also right down to modern radio sets and medical kits. These supplies were flowing into the quartermasters' stores all over Germany.

If Colonel Florian Koenig was correct, Beck and all those other generals knew what the supplies were for. They knew the Austrian Anschluss was the beginning and not the end. And at that moment in the early summer of 1938, they were apparently planning to do something about it.

The sun rolled behind a cloud. It was chilly and Macrae rose from the bench to continue his walk. The sparrows scattered, wheeling behind him to perch on the bench and inspect the seat for crumbs that might have dropped from a sandwich.

If all this was true, what was Hitler doing about it? The Gestapo must surely have warned him that elements of the senior command might turn to conspiracy as his plans for war became clearer. Hitler would not ignore such warnings. He had survived a number of assassination attempts through extraordinary good luck. He had Fate on his side and the remarkable figure of a man he trusted to root out all traitors, Reinhard Heydrich. Hitler called him "the man with the iron heart", and Heydrich had once boasted at a Nazi gala that "a man's mark of success is to have made powerful enemies".

The remark had been overheard by a French journalist. By the time he had been appointed Obergruppenführer of the Gestapo, Heydrich had indeed assembled a remarkable collection of enemies: the aristocratic officer class of the army, the liberal intelligentsia of the decadent West, Jews, communists, Gypsies, homosexuals. He hated them all and pursued them with a savage efficiency driven by desire for vengeance.

Revenge was writ large across everything Heydrich did. He had never forgotten the humiliation of his dismissal in disgrace from the navy over some trifling affair with a woman.

If anyone was going to put a stop to a military coup, it would be Heydrich, thought Macrae. All roads in the Nazi Party led to him in the end.

Macrae passed by the Brandenburg Gate and turned into Wilhelmstrasse, noting the flag above the embassy entrance. The Union Jack had flown there for over fifty years, but the mere sight of it so infuriated Hitler that he had asked Göring to demand that it be flown only on ceremonial occasions.

Sir Nevile had refused to lower the flag. Macrae marvelled at the mystery of a man who would insist on serving German wine for fear of upsetting his official guests but somehow had the mettle to run up the Union Jack in defiance of the Führer.

Bonner was also thinking of Heydrich as he entered the Salon that same day. Heydrich had told him that Noel Macrae, Percy Black of the US embassy and the French attaché Pierre Moutet had been identified as personally hostile to the regime. They were therefore likely conduits for messages from disloyal military officers to their respective governments.

"I don't just want them dismissed, I want them disgraced," he had told Bonner.

Bonner noted with satisfaction that Kitty herself was behind the bar. She had seen him at the door and prepared his favourite cocktail. He sipped the vodka martini. The restaurant was half full. It was nearly nine o'clock, midway through the evening. Bonner looked around but could see no one of interest or importance at the tables.

"Where's Sara?" he asked.

Kitty jerked her head towards the fanlight door.

"Who?" said Bonner.

Kitty smiled and leant over the bar. "Italian diplomat, number two in the mission."

"First time?"

"No, he's been before, I think. Difficult to tell. They all look alike when they're drunk."

"Men or Italians?"

"Men," she said, and laughed.

Bonner frowned and ordered another drink. Sara should not be wasting her time with Italians. There was no point.

He was halfway through the drink when she seated herself in the chair beside him. She was wearing a short black dress and looked so fresh and well groomed that she might have come straight from the hairdresser.

"How was your Italian friend?" he said.

"They are all the same," she said, "boring."

Bonner pointed to the ceiling with a finger and raised an eyebrow.

"I told them not to bother. No point," she said.

She should not have done that, thought Bonner. Sometimes she behaved as if she ran the club. The trouble was that the recording team upstairs really liked her. Everyone did. He would talk to Kitty.

"Have you seen the Englishman?" he said.

"Which one?"

Bonner slammed his fist onto the counter. "You know bloody well which one!"

"The attaché?"

"Yes."

"Oh, him. He was in the other night with the American correspondent."

"And?"

"And nothing. I had a drink with him, that's all."

"Don't tell me your famous charms have failed you at last?"

She moved her face close to his and whispered in his ear. "Sarcasm doesn't suit a secret policeman. He's not interested."

He brushed her off. "Make him interested."

"He's English; they don't do that," she said, nodding to the fanlight.

"Of course they do. The English are the most repressed people in Europe. Get him drunk and show him a few tricks."

"I told you, he's not like that."

"Well, put something in his drink. I want him done and soon."

"I want something from you first."

"You don't make conditions here, Sara."

"Why have I had no letter from my brother for a month?"

Bonner sipped his martini. It was a good question. The boy was in Buchenwald camp and there had been orders to keep him alive. That was all he knew.

"I don't know. He's fine."

"I want a letter in his handwriting, understand? He's got to mention the weather. Got that? The weather. Before I do anything."

Bonner was being dictated to by a Jewish whore in a bordello run by the Gestapo, of which he was a senior officer. He smiled at the absurdity.

"Your brother is a convicted terrorist," he said. "You're lucky he is being kept alive and going through re-education. So, you do as you are bloody well told or you'll join him."

She sat back, nostrils flaring, dark eyes glowing.

He didn't want to make her angry; what was the point? He softened.

"Join me in a drink," he said. "Let's have some smoked salmon and sausage – yes?"

She nodded, said nothing, accepted the drink and sat beside him, staring ahead.

"I wish no harm to come to you," he said. "We get caught up in things, don't we? All of us. We lose control. You have your brother; I have my family. We do things to protect them – is that so wrong?"

"No," she whispered. "That's not wrong."

"I need results. I need that Englishman. He is no different from any one of them. He'll have a dark little secret – they all do. Something he'll want you to do."

Bonner waved an arm at the diners and in doing so almost fell off the bar stool.

"They want you, all of them, because, you know what?, you have something beyond beauty and they want it."

He put a hand to her cheek, lifting the hair away and pushing it around the back of her neck. She didn't flinch. One more man touching her hardly mattered.

"Maybe it's the way you look."

"Maybe it's because I'm a Jewish whore," she said, shaking her head away.

"Exactly! So bloody well do the job." He was angry again now. The drink was talking. "Kitty! Get her some of the pills."

Kitty reached behind the bar and produced a small bottle.

"Put one in his drink. Get him into a room."

"Where's my letter?" she hissed at him.

"Do what you are told or you will never hear from him again – or your mother – understood?"

She rose from her chair, shaking, it seemed to him. For a second he thought she was going to slap him.

"I'm sick and tired of it all," she said. "You, your little games and all those maggots out there." She waved an arm at the room and left.

10

As spring gave way to summer, journalists from newspapers and radio stations around the world descended on Berlin to cover what was called "the Czech crisis". In daily broadcasts and in print, the propaganda machine in Berlin insisted that the three million members of the German-speaking population of the Sudetenland were being persecuted by the majority Czech population in the region. Cavalcades of correspondents could find no evidence of this. If anything, it was the Czech speakers who were suffering at the hands of pro-Nazi thugs in the disputed territory.

In meetings with the French, American and British ambassadors, Hitler launched ferocious assaults on what he called the Jewish-owned press of those countries and their vile attempts to smear the German people and its government. In London, the government refused to join France in pledging to come to the aid of Czechoslovakia, should that nation be attacked. As a result, the French government collapsed, the eighth administration to do so in three years.

In Washington, President Roosevelt suggested a conference of all European leaders, to include the Russian government, in order to negotiate an end to the crisis. Deeply engaged in the New Deal programmes that were slowly turning the US economy around, the White House was not disappointed when the initiative was dismissed out of hand by the German foreign minister.

Halliday had vanished from Berlin for almost a month and no one in the embassy knew where he had gone or when he would return. When asked at the weekly meeting, the ambassador muttered something about official duties in other countries and left it at that. The senior staff in the embassy concluded that he knew no more of the whereabouts of the intelligence officer than anyone else.

Macrae had little time to worry about his missing colleague. A heat wave in June continued into the following month. There was no air conditioning in the embassy as he worked through daily requests from the War Office in London for information on the Czech frontier fortifications, manpower of the country's front-line units and the likely order of battle against an invading German army.

After a flying visit to London, Sir Nevile Henderson grandly announced that he had urged the cabinet not to give Hitler a final warning. This would only provoke him and make an invasion more likely. He was happy to report, he told his staff, that the prime minister had followed his advice. Chamberlain had decided that a face-to-face meeting with Hitler was the only way to resolve the crisis. There was no question of Hitler being invited to England. The meeting would take place in Germany, probably Munich, sometime in September.

• • •

Long hours in the embassy and exhausting trips through the Czech border regions meant that Macrae had seen little of Primrose that summer. He spent the best part of July in the Sudetenland. He now knew exactly what was meant by the old saying, a "wild-goose chase". All that month, journalists had thundered around the hills in expensive cars, searching for signs of military activity, of which there was no evidence beyond that supplied by helpful local innkeepers and hoteliers.

They were only too happy to assure the press that there had recently been tank movements in the area and sightings of new artillery emplacements in the hills. But such activity always seemed to take place just before the press arrived. The hills kept their secrets beneath the thick foliage of their forests. By the end of July, the press, military attachés and curious tourists had all given up the chase and returned to Berlin.

On his first evening back at the embassy, Macrae was told that the ambassador was spending a few days at Göring's estate in Saxony, David Buckland was in hospital with appendicitis, and Halliday was still missing. After relaying this news, Daisy Wellesley remarked that he looked tired and should rest. She had left a bottle of champagne on his desk – won in the raffle, she said – and suggested Macrae take it home to celebrate his return.

"I've phoned your wife – she knows you're back," she said.

Macrae left the embassy early with the bottle of champagne. He was going to have a quiet dinner that evening with Primrose. He needed some time with his wife and she with him. He would surprise her with a champagne cocktail. Whether they dined in or out depended on what was in the fridge.

She was somewhere upstairs when he arrived. He opened the champagne in the kitchen and mixed the cocktails: a sugar lump, splash of cognac and a shake of bitters in each glass, topped with champagne. He placed the glasses and the bottle on a tray and walked carefully up the stairs to the bedroom. Primrose was sitting on a cushioned stool in front of the dressing-table mirror in a white bathrobe. She was brushing her hair and turned as he came into the room.

"What a nice surprise," she said, getting up and taking the tray. "What are we celebrating?"

Macrae untied his laces and kicked off the shoes, so that they clattered into the wardrobe door. He loosened his tie and sat down on the bed with a thump, lying back at full stretch against the pillows.

"My return. Us. Anything," he said.

Primrose hadn't seen her husband for months, or so it seemed. The man lying on her bed – or rather their bed, she reminded herself – looked like a stranger. The lines on his face had deepened, the skin looked grey with fatigue, and there were dark pouches under his eyes.

"You look exhausted," she said. "Poor thing. Have a drink."

Macrae sat up against the bedhead and accepted a cocktail. She kissed him gently on the forehead and sat down on the dressing-table stool again. She began to rub cream into her forearms.

"Are you all right?" she said.

"A bit tired."

"You're working too hard, travelling too much."

"I know." He watched as she sprayed eau de cologne under each arm.

"I suppose it is all very exciting, isn't it? History on the march, and all that."

"The trouble is, it's marching the wrong way," he said.

"I don't know what the fuss is about. Why shouldn't Hitler have the Sudetenland? They are only bloody Germans there, aren't they?"

"It's not his to take. Europe is not a sweet shop where you just grab what you want."

"Don't patronise me, Noel." She got up and walked to the wardrobe.

"I'm not patronising you. But do you really think he is going to stop at the Sudetenland?"

"Oh, dear God! Have I heard this a thousand times? Next it will be all of Czechoslovakia, then Poland and then Russia, then the whole bloody world. Let Hitler run the world, I say. He might make a better job of it than the lot we have now."

She pulled open the doors of the wardrobe and looked over a rack of dresses.

"Where are you going?"

"I had no idea you would be home tonight. I have a drinks do and then the opera."

"I thought Daisy told you I was back."

"She just said you were back in the office. I thought it would be another late night with all those cables."

"Well, I'll come with you."

"I think you'd better stay here. You wouldn't enjoy it. Have a bath and finish the champagne. You need a rest."

He watched her take off the bathrobe and reach into the wardrobe, pulling out first one dress, then another. Her skin was pale, almost milk-white. She had put on weight, he noticed. There was an attractive plumpness to her figure, the breasts heavier but still firm. Primrose used to complain about what she called her derriere, and say it was too big, but it looked fine to Macrae. He noticed that she had trimmed her pubic hair so that the dark matted tangle had become a glossy lawn. There you have it, he thought: my wife fresh from her bath, powdered, perfumed and creamed, choosing a nice dress before going to meet her lover.

"Where is the drinks party?" he asked.

She had pulled on a dark red dress and walked to the bed so that he could zip up the back.

"At the opera house. Boring really. An American touring company is putting on a short opera. I don't know what. There's drinks beforehand."

It was too obvious a reply to be a lie, he thought. The deceit lay in whom she would meet there. He sat up and sipped the cocktail. It had a kick and he felt better.

"Are you having an affair?" he said.

"Are you going to be very boring?" She was twisting to pull up the zip of a light blue satin dress. She had decided against the red one.

"No, I'm just asking if you're having an affair."

"I might well ask you the same question. You're never home before midnight when you are in town, and that's not often. Are *you* having an affair? It wouldn't bother me if you were, frankly. Probably do you some good, cheer you up a bit."

"Well, are you?"

"I'm not going to discuss it. This is childish. We're adults. Anyway, we agreed that as far as that department is concerned, you go your way and I go mine."

"We didn't agree any such thing."

"We did. We talked about it – remember?"

"We did *not* agree that you should take a lover."

"For God's sake, Noel! Stop behaving like an idiot. Don't you have enough on your plate trying to stop the next war without worrying whether I'm having an affair?"

He flung the champagne flute across the room, where it shattered against the wall, leaving shards of glass on the floor and dregs of the cocktail trickling slowly down the wallpaper.

"Why shouldn't I? I'm your husband, aren't I?"

"Yes. And I'm your wife. And a bloody good wife too."

She sat down in front of the dressing table and began applying lipstick. She was talking quite normally, as if they were having a discussion about the menu for a dinner party.

Macrae got off the bed, picked up the bottle and raised it to his lips. The champagne fizzed over his face.

"Go and find a pretty girl. You're still quite attractive."

"You haven't answered my question."

"What about Daisy? She likes you. I've seen her looking at you at those embassy parties. She'd like a fling, I'm sure."

"Don't be absurd."

"I'm not being absurd! I'm being serious. Go and enjoy yourself. Joy. J-O-Y. It's not a word you understand, is it?"

She put on her shoes, picked up a handbag, looked briefly at the shattered glass, shook her head and left, closing the door quietly behind her.

Macrae lay back, gazing at the ceiling. Tiredness stole over him and he fell asleep.

The phone woke him. He looked at his watch. It was eight o'clock. He rarely got calls at home. Diplomats were told to use the phone as little as possible, on the assumption that all lines were bugged. It was Daisy from the embassy.

"I thought you should know he's back."

"Who?" said Macrae groggily.

"Our mutual friend. He's in a bar in Mauerstrasse."

Macrae found Halliday looking more dishevelled than ever, sitting alone at a table studying a wine list with a glass of beer in his hand. The veins on his nose had spread to his upper cheeks and gave his face a florid glow. His hair hung well below the collar of a linen jacket, the same one that Macrae had seen him wearing at his first morning meeting. Sweat stains coloured the armpits. He wondered if Halliday actually slept in his clothes. It certainly looked like it.

They settled for a light Austrian wine with a plate of cold meats. Halliday had not been seen at the embassy for six weeks, but Macrae knew better than to ask where he had been. He got straight to the point.

"Thank you for letting me know about the boy."

"He tried to escape. He almost got over the wire. They beat him badly and then put him up against a wall."

"Is that how he died?"

"Yeah, they shot him. Unusual. They don't usually waste bullets."

"Are you sure?"

"Well, I wasn't there, was I? But the informant is reliable."

"Damn!" said Macrae.

"This is a bit out of your territory, isn't it?"

"Yes, but it's useful info."

"As in . . .?"

Macrae shook his head. He rather enjoyed his colleague's curiosity. "As in useful info."

"Come on," said Halliday. "Fair exchange; what's this kid to you? There are thousands like him in the camps and they're dying every week."

"I'd rather not say. Sorry."

"Your choice – but you owe me, right?"

"Right."

Without prompting, Halliday began talking about Stalin's purge of his army. Tens of thousands of officers had been arrested and shot after summary trials lasting only a few minutes.

"So that's where you've been – Moscow?"

"Maybe."

"Why?"

Halliday laughed. He slapped Macrae on the back and refilled their glasses.

"You were a cat in your last life. Too damn curious. Anyway, for your ears only: Heydrich set the whole thing up. He was contacted by a couple of Russian generals who wanted to stage a coup and asked for German help. Big mistake. Heydrich betrayed them to Stalin, exaggerated their support and, bang!, that's the end of the Soviet officer class. Thirty thousand at the last count."

"I don't get it. Why were you involved?"

"Tried to tell them it was a set-up, a German trap. We need a strong Russian army. They wouldn't listen."

They finished their drinks and Halliday shambled to the door, claiming the need for an early night.

"By the way, they're beautiful creatures, aren't they?"

"Who? What?"

"Those Siberian tigers. G'night."

Macrae watched him go. He was glad Halliday was on their side. It was ten o'clock. He should also go home, but what to? An empty house and a cold bed. Joy, she had said, and that is what she would be doing tonight, this very minute, enjoying herself. Perhaps even now she was . . . He let the thought burn briefly in his mind, then extinguished it. He would go to the Salon and tell Sara tonight. Get it over with. Commiserate with her, help her through the pain.

This time the woman on the door seemed to recognise him and pressed the bell without saying a word. The door swung open and Macrae stepped inside. A violinist and a pianist were playing. He saw Sara immediately, sitting at the far end of the bar. She smiled and watched him as he was led to a table for two at the back of the room.

Service in the Salon was always efficient. His coat was taken and a menu placed in his hands before he had sat down. He glanced at it. He had hardly eaten. He would have a steak, perhaps a decent glass of claret.

"May I join you?" she said.

He looked up and gestured to the empty chair with the menu. "Of course."

"You've been away," she said.

She was quite calm, her face expressionless beneath the same pale powdered make-up.

He ordered a bottle of red wine and a steak, rare, with a green salad on the side. She turned her head and looked around the room, and he followed suit. The restaurant was full, the bar stools and tables all taken with drinkers and diners. He knew nobody. She would know almost everybody, of course, and could tell who were the businessmen, the party officials and the occasional foreign dignitaries. Some, the important ones, she would have taken through the fanlight door to one of the rooms. Maybe even that night she had been playing her role, acting out her part under the camera eyes of the Gestapo. They would watch every turn and twist of her body, just as they would be watching him in the club right now. There were always Gestapo in the club.

She turned back to him. "Do you remember what we talked about in the Tiergarten?"

A waitress arrived with the wine and poured two glasses. Macrae had been trying to find the right words to answer the question he knew was coming.

"About your brother?"

"Joseph. Yes."

Macrae took a deep breath, drank a little wine and was about to speak when she said, "He's dead, isn't he?"

"I'm afraid so."

The muscles of her face flexed in a ripple of pain. It was like watching a sudden wind ruffle calm water. She put her glass down, bent her head and clenched her fists on the white tablecloth.

"Are you sure?"

"Yes."

"Can you tell me what happened?"

He told her what little he knew. She finished the wine and he refilled her glass. His steak arrived but he sent it back to the kitchen to be kept warm. She repeated questions he could answer only in vague terms, the where and when and how of her brother's death. He told her he had been put up against a wall and shot after a second escape attempt. It would have been a quick death, if that was any comfort, he said.

He reached for her hand across the table and took it gently. "I'm sorry."

For several minutes they said nothing. The waitress reappeared with his steak and he accepted it. He wanted to eat as quickly as possible. He wanted to leave, get away from the pain printed on the face of the young woman opposite him. She watched him eat. When he finished, he sat back, dabbing his mouth with a napkin.

"They want me to take you to a room," she said.

He gave a snorting laugh. "They, whoever they are, must know I am not that stupid."

"They've given me something to put in your drink."

She took a small bottle of pills from her handbag, held it concealed in her fist and put her hand on the table. She opened and closed her hand quickly. Macrae could see the bottle. It might have been aspirin, for all he knew. Macrae looked around and reached for his glass. He was about to drink when he put the glass down.

"Don't worry," she said. "The wine is fine. But you should be careful. They're watching you."

"No more than I would expect. I'm really sorry to have brought such bad news. I must go."

"I need help."

She spoke the words without looking at him in a low monotone as if to ask for another glass of wine.

"I've done all I can."

"You don't understand. I'm free now."

"What?"

"He's set me free – Joseph." She leant across the table. "Don't you see? I can get out of here now. Will you help me?"

"I've told you, I've done all I can. I'm sorry about your brother, but . . ."

She wasn't listening to him. She was looking at him with eyes that sparkled with anger. She had aged in the short time they had been together at the table.

"I need papers, travel papers," she said. "And remember, I have information."

It was midnight when they met at the same place in the Tiergarten. He could hear a church clock strike the hour, the chimes ringing loud and clear on a summer night that clung to the warmth of the day. He heard the footsteps and saw the shadowy figure emerge from the darkness, led by the glowing end of a cigarette, a firefly in the night.

He wanted a cigarette badly and knew she would give him hers, allow him a few deep breaths, then take it back, smoke herself and jettison the stub in the darkness. Then he knew she would kiss him, pushing him back against the tree, and he knew that was what he wanted, what he desired most of all, Sara Sternschein, her body leaning against his, her hands lifting his shirt and sliding fingers up his back, her crotch pressing into his, hardening him, and all the while kissing him.

He knew too that somehow – against the tree, on the bench or maybe lying on the dry hard earth beneath the bushes, with his raincoat beneath them – they would make love, and he would clamp a hand over her mouth as she cried out, because there would be other lovers in the Tiergarten that night. They would not be alone. He knew, too, that he would help her.

They lay together afterwards, her head resting on the crook of his arm, her clothes clumped beside her, both breathing hard, feeling their hearts beating fast and the sweat cooling on their skin. She lit a cigarette and passed it to him.

"Will you?" she said.

"Yes, I will."

II

The plane seemed to skim the line of hills south of London, the houses and gardens rising beneath the silver wings of the twin-engined aircraft and then falling away again as they cleared the ridge and began the descent into Croydon airport. Below, the fields and gardens were burnt sere by a long drought. It was early August and there was still no sign of rain.

Macrae was excited and nervous, a curious feeling that clenched his stomach. He'd wanted a drink on the plane, but it had been a bumpy flight from Berlin and even the stewardesses had remained strapped to their seats. Anyway, it would not do to spill drink on the full dress uniform of a lieutenant colonel in the British army. And it was hardly the occasion for a drink. He would be met at the airport by an official car and driven straight to the War Office in Whitehall. There, he was to brief the chiefs of staff on the likelihood of a military coup in Germany should Hitler invade Czechoslovakia. Later he would repeat his briefing for the prime minister and at a full meeting of the cabinet, where he would be cross-examined by ministers.

He could hardly believe that the government had finally woken up to the fact that an army-led coup against the Nazi regime was a real possibility. Over the last three months his coded reports to the War Office had been carefully phrased so as not to allow the accusation of exaggeration or wishful thinking.

Initially, the ambassador had been copied in on the cables, but his attempts to change the emphasis of their message and cast doubt on their meaning had led to a short and unpleasant exchange, during which Macrae announced that the minister himself would be informed of any further attempt to censor the reports of his military attaché. Sir Nevile Henderson had not spoken to him since. Macrae was sure that it wouldn't be long before Daisy Wellesley let him know that a further attempt had been made to have him posted away from Berlin.

The relationship between the two men became even worse when Sir Nevile was told that his military attaché had been invited to brief both the prime minister and cabinet on the accelerating German rearmament programme and the disaffection within the German army.

Sir Nevile Henderson had summoned him for a briefing.

"I don't know how this has come about, and I want you to know I am not happy. However, if this is what Number 10 and the War Office want, so be it. But I insist that we at least agree on what you will say."

Macrae had wearily repeated the outline of a conspiracy he had already reported, but without mentioning names. The ambassador dismissed the reports as at best the work of a few isolated provocateurs and at worst a Gestapo attempt at entrapment.

"I want names," said the ambassador. "You can't take woolly conspiracy theories to London without hard facts, and that means names."

The ambassador was glaring at him. The cloak of diplomatic courtesy and ambiguously crafted language had dropped, revealing the naked fury of a man in high office who had been defied by an insolent subordinate.

Macrae needed to remain in post in Berlin. He needed to retain at least the semblance of a formal relationship with this difficult, narrow-minded man. The ambassador could not dismiss him, but he could make life very difficult. It was within his power to exclude him from all meetings and the reports of the political and commercial officers.

"General Beck is leading," he said.

Sir Nevile Henderson sat down, his face registering not anger but shock. "Beck? The chief of the General Staff?"

"Yes."

"Are you sure?"

"Yes."

"And how far have things got?"

"As I will tell the prime minister, Ambassador, if we, that is Britain and France, stand up to Hitler, draw a line at Czechoslovakia and threaten armed intervention, the army will move against their Führer."

"Suppose Hitler takes fright and backs down – has anyone thought of that?"

"Hitler will call what he thinks is the West's bluff – his pattern of behaviour until now tells us that, as I am sure you will agree. But even if not, he has marched his soldiers up the hill. He has told his generals he is going to smash Czechoslovakia – there are four armoured divisions within thirty minutes of the border, ready and waiting. If he backed down now, the humiliation would be so great, the army would move anyway."

"Well, I hope you know what you're talking about," said the ambassador, "because I am not sure I do."

He glanced at his watch. It was lunchtime, time for a civilised conversation with his American counterpart. Enough of this nonsense. Macrae would make a fool of himself in London with this talk. The prime minister would not believe a word of it. It might even help to get Macrae removed and sent elsewhere. The ambassador allowed himself the pleasure of deciding where in the world he would send his errant military attaché if it lay within his power to do so. A dominion posting, South Africa maybe? No, far too comfortable. Gibraltar, that was it. The bloody boring Rock, with all those ghastly fish-and-chip shops and people with that hideous lower-class way of talking, all serviettes, toilets and having dinner at lunchtime. Macrae and that frosty wife of his would enjoy a few years there. Much cheered by this fantasy, Sir Nevile Henderson got into his car, to be driven to the American embassy for lunch.

Primrose, for once, had been impressed by news of his mission and had wanted to come too.

"I could do some shopping while you get on with all your frightfully important briefings with the ministers, and then in the evening we could have dinner somewhere really nice – Sheekey's – why not?"

It wasn't possible, as Macrae kept explaining. It was to be a very quick and secret trip. He would be returning the next day.

That night, Primrose had sent the cook home and made him supper, lamb shanks with peas and carrots. She had found a bottle of very good burgundy from somewhere, which was unusual, because she didn't care for red wine. She had become flirtatious and very funny as the dinner progressed, teasing him about how he would lecture the cabinet on the error of their ways, Superman in a Savile Row suit flying in to save the world from war, she said.

There stirred in Macrae the memory of the wife he had once known; the outrageous young woman deep in mourning for her lost brother who had been mad enough to take him into the darkened garden within minutes of their first meeting and bad enough to pleasure him briefly before spitting him out into the bushes.

She was that sort of woman, wild, shocking, bewitching, and with a rich throaty laugh that made everyone who heard it want to laugh too.

After dinner that night she had tried to make love to him, but he was tired, a little drunk and not looking forward to the early departure the next morning. It had not worked.

The plane landed with a thump on the grass landing strip and rolled to a stop before an impressive collection of whitewashed terminal buildings. Croydon was London's second airport, and a longer drive from the centre of town than Heston in the west, so it was not until mid-morning that the car drew up before the War Office in Whitehall.

Macrae was taken in a creaky lift to the top floor and shown into a corner office. Large windows in two walls overlooked the Thames Embankment and the river in one direction and the Gothic architecture of the New Scotland Yard police headquarters in another. Sir Leslie Hore-Belisha sat behind a desk, smoking a cigarette, looking through documents presented by an elderly woman secretary.

Macrae had only seen newspaper photographs of the minister, and there had been plenty of those in recent years. He had stamped his mark on the nation's streets with his orange flashing beacons at pedestrian crossings and a number of other measures designed to cut the death toll on the roads. Needless to say, the motoring lobby had risen in fury at this intrusion on an Englishman's liberty. In person, the minister was smaller than his photographs suggested and with a dark, almost Levantine countenance.

The appointment of a secretary of state for war who had no military background, and was a Jew as well, had angered military commanders. The army, especially, saw this as the prime minister's move to make further cuts in manpower and investment, in line with the official policy of appeasement towards Germany.

As Neville Chamberlain repeatedly told colleagues, nothing would persuade Hitler more of Britain's sincerity in its dealings with the German Reich than a continuing reduction in the defence budget. And Hore-Belisha was just the man to do this, a proven administrator with a track record of good fiscal management in the various government departments he had run.

After a few months, to the delight of the armed services, it was clear that the prime minister had misjudged his man. The new minister for war argued in cabinet forcefully not just for increased defence expenditure but also for the introduction of conscription. Privately, Chamberlain and his colleagues felt that such arguments were motivated by the sympathy that one eminent Jew naturally felt for the plight of his co-religionists in Germany, but they dared not say so.

Macrae was ushered to one of several chairs around a low coffee table, which had been laid for tea. The minister immediately joined him, shook his hand, enquired briefly about the flight and then said, "Tell me everything about this conspiracy within the German army."

Macrae relayed almost the exact words that Koenig had told him a few days earlier. Hore-Belisha listened carefully while his secretary took notes.

"You say they will arrest Hitler and put him on trial?"

"Yes."

"Wouldn't that be risky? The man is the legally recognised head of state and quite popular, is he not?"

"The army will make it clear that they are acting to prevent another European war. That will trump any feeling of loyalty to the Führer. People are worried sick about a new war. Every Sunday, the cemeteries of all major German cities are full of people laying flowers on the graves of relatives fallen in the last war. They do not want another one – and neither does the army. On this issue, the Nazis are isolated, and people like Göring and Goebbels know it."

"You think there will be a trial?"

"No. They'll have to kill him. It'll be the usual story – shot while resisting arrest, something like that. They know his powers of oratory. They will never give him a public platform."

The minister looked at Macrae and smiled. "It might be wiser to omit that last point from your briefing to the cabinet. An army coup that removes a dictator and places him on trial is one thing; assassination is a rather different matter."

"Thank you," said Macrae.

The minister looked at his watch and nodded to his secretary. A waitress came in with a tray of tea and biscuits.

"You are certain of your sources?"

"Absolutely."

"And they won't act unless we do?"

"No. They want to see Britain and France take a firm stand, backed with the threat of military action."

"That is going to be very difficult for the prime minister to swallow. He simply won't believe you."

"I know, but I'd appreciate the chance to try."

"You haven't heard this from me, but he didn't want to see you. You've got a reputation as a troublemaker – did you know that?"

"The ambassador and I have had our differences."

Hore-Belisha gave such a broad smile at this remark that Macrae thought he was about to break into laughter. He got up, indicating the interview was over.

"There is one thing," said Macrae.

The minister looked at him and waited.

"I have a good contact there, a young German woman I believe to be in danger. I would like to get travel documents for her, if possible."

"Doesn't she have a passport?"

"The Gestapo has it."

The minister looked directly at Macrae for the first time.

"This woman is . . .?"

"Jewish? Yes."

"And you say she is a contact."

"Yes."

"Can't the embassy do something?"

"There is no quota as such, but the embassy doesn't make it easy for . . . certain people to get the necessary visa."

"You mean Jews?"

"Yes. We are not alone. No one wants them. Even the Australians have turned them down, and God knows they have enough room."

Hore-Belisha sat down and spoke softly.

"I have tried to bring this home to the cabinet. How I've tried. But they are terrified of upsetting Hitler, and then, of course . . ."

The minister walked to the window and gazed out over the Thames. He held his hands behind his back and Macrae could see the nails digging into the flesh of the palms. When he spoke, it was with a voice that seemed to come from elsewhere in the room, as if an invisible presence had suddenly joined their conversation.

"The truth is, Colonel Macrae, that large-scale immigration of Jews into this country from Germany presents the government with political difficulties, if you know what I mean. We, that is the government, do not wish to encourage emigration to Palestine because that creates problems in the region, but at the same time, and unofficially of course, His Majesty's Government is not encouraging Jews from Germany to find refuge in large numbers here."

Hore-Belisha swung round. His face had coloured but his voice was calm. He must have had this conversation many times over with Jewish leaders in Britain.

"And that is a disgrace, a craven attitude born of cowardice and prejudice," he said. He walked over to Macrae and shook his hand. "I hope the prime minister and my colleagues in cabinet listen as carefully as I have to your information. I will be in cabinet, but we may not meet again. I wish you a safe journey back to Berlin."

The minister walked back to his desk, pressed a buzzer on a console and picked up a set of papers. His secretary walked in and held the door open for Macrae.

"Oh," said Hore-Belisha. "Leave the details of that woman with my secretary, would you?"

The first meeting of Neville Chamberlain's day at 10 Downing Street was always with his diary secretary. The prime minister encouraged his staff to arrange an orderly series of meetings that had a certain logic in their progression through the day.

There was no point, he remarked, in having a discussion about agricultural subsidies for Welsh hill farmers sandwiched between a confidential brief from the chief whip about the sexual transgression of a junior minister and a plea from the head of the Secret Service for unbudgeted exceptional expenditure. It was also particularity important that the prime minister should have fifteen minutes before the weekly cabinet meeting every Tuesday at eleven, to examine the agenda and consider the required tactics to achieve a consensus on the increasingly difficult issues of foreign policy.

Thus it was with irritation that Neville Chamberlain found on the Tuesday in that first week of exceptionally hot weather in August that a meeting with the British military attaché in Berlin had been inserted in the diary immediately before the cabinet session.

When he queried the diary entry, his secretary told him that the minister for war had personally requested the meeting but would not be attending himself. Furthermore, the secretary said the minister had arranged for the attaché to address the full cabinet.

"I don't have time for this," said Chamberlain. "When was it agreed?"

"When you were in Birmingham last week, sir. The foreign secretary approved."

Chamberlain at once saw the trap. If Hore-Belisha and Lord Halifax both wanted him to see this man, he would have to go along with it. And he would have to agree to the fellow addressing cabinet. He did not wish to be accused of refusing to listen to voices and views that disagreed with his own. And from what he had heard of this attaché, that is exactly what he was going to do.

"Very well," he said, "but all these military men smoke like chimneys. Make sure he knows that it is not permitted in my office or cabinet."

The prime minister was seated at his desk when Macrae was ushered into his office about an hour later, and he rose to greet his visitor with a handshake. Neville Chamberlain looked older than his photographs, with short grey hair fading to white at the sides, a neat moustache and steel-rimmed spectacles. He was wearing a dark suit with a stiff wing collar and a gold watch chain across his waistcoat. Macrae felt like an errant customer who had come to see his bank manager to explain an unapproved overdraft.

A stenographer took her seat at the back of the room while the cabinet secretary, who had been introduced as Sir Maurice Hankey, sat on a chair positioned to the left of the prime minister's desk. Macrae took a chair facing the desk. He noticed that Hankey had folded his arms and was looking at the ceiling. Macrae now felt less like a bank customer and more like a schoolboy facing his headmaster. Chamberlain pulled his watch from a waistcoat pocket, looked at it and said, "Don't think me impolite, Colonel, but we have only fifteen minutes, so may I suggest that you begin."

The prime minister grasped his chin between forefinger and thumb and gazed at his blotting pad while the attaché repeated what he had told the minister for war that morning.

"What exactly do you mean by 'stand with Czechoslovakia'?" said the prime minister.

"We must threaten hostilities. Hitler won't fight. Call his bluff."

"No democratic state can make a threat of war unless it is ready and prepared to carry it out. Wouldn't you agree, Maurice?"

The cabinet secretary lowered his gaze from the ceiling and nodded his agreement.

"Then, Prime Minister, with respect, I think we should be ready to follow up our threat. The whole point is that if the Nazi regime truly believes we will act, Hitler will be forced into a humiliating climb-down or a reckless act of folly, either of which will trigger the military coup."

The prime minister leant forward on the desk, clasped his hands and said, "Surely this talk of a coup is just that, is it not? Talk, rumours. Walk around the pubs of Westminster and you will find plenty of people who want to get rid of me, but it's all talk, isn't it? What do you say, Maurice?"

"I don't think you are in any danger of a coup, Prime Minister."

The two men laughed at their little joke, nodding to each other.

"I think it would be useful to hear more about Colonel Macrae's sources," said the cabinet secretary. Chamberlain raised an expectant eyebrow at his visitor.

Macrae told them in greater detail than he had vouchsafed to the ambassador that, well beyond the army, there were cells in the Abwehr whose military intelligence operations were controlled by Admiral Canaris, all of whom were prepared to cooperate in the high-risk venture of a coup. Furthermore, the Catholic Church would give moral support, with announcements from pulpits across the country, once the operation had begun. The plan was to arrest Hitler in Berlin by . . .

The prime minister raised a hand to halt the briefing. The door had opened and a uniformed messenger entered and without a word handed a note to Sir Maurice Hankey. The cabinet secretary read the note and silently left the room. A whispered conversation was heard outside, then Hankey returned and whispered something in the prime minister's ear.

"We have just received an urgent cable from the embassy in Berlin. I had better study it before cabinet, so if you will excuse me."

Chamberlain rose and extended his hand. Macrae shook hands and turned to the door.

"Oh, Colonel," said Chamberlain. "That was most interesting. I hear what you say."

Macrae knew exactly what those words meant. His journey had been wasted.

A secretary handed him a cup of coffee while he waited in a corridor. The coffee was thin and bitter, but Macrae reflected that anything he drank at that moment would probably have tasted the same.

He waited twenty minutes before his name was called and he was ushered into the Cabinet Room, where seventeen ministers were sitting around the long oval table. The room seemed too warm to be comfortable but no one had taken off his jacket. Macrae was introduced by the prime minister, who asked him to make an opening statement.

The ministers looked curiously at the colonel standing at the head of the table. They had mostly been called from holidays on the salmon rivers or grouse moors of Scotland or in country houses in the fashionable counties of Gloucestershire, Oxfordshire, Somerset and Devon. None resented their recall, because the crisis in European affairs was obvious to all. But they were surprised that they were to be given a briefing by a military attaché from the Berlin embassy. The ambassador had already made his views known and had supplied sufficient information to justify the retention of the current policy.

Macrae cleared his throat and looked at his text. He knew fears of another war ran deep among these decent, intelligent and utterly complacent men. He knew most had served in the last conflict, in which many had lost friends or relatives.

He knew too that clubby, consensual cabinet discussions among men who had been to similar schools and universities, married similar women and wined and dined in similar clubs rarely strayed from the path carefully laid down by the prime minister and his immediate advisers.

Neville Chamberlain proudly called his policy towards the Third German Reich one of appeasement, and he defied anyone to explain how else one was supposed to deal with a man who was merely behaving as a patriotic nationalist, a man who did not want war with Britain and expressed nothing but admiration for her history and empire.

"Let me tell you exactly what is happening on the ground in Germany – at this very moment," Macrae said. "All military leave has been cancelled, the army has bolstered fuel reserves through large purchases on the international market, labour has been conscripted to improve the fortifications facing France, airspace along the left bank of the Rhine has been closed and several armoured divisions are on the move at key points on the border with Czechoslovakia."

He waited while the cabinet mulled over this new and unwelcome news.

"Furthermore, the planning staff of the High Command in Berlin has been instructed by the Führer in person to update plans for the invasion of Russia."

Silence descended on the cabinet. Ministers frowned and looked hard at their blotters.

"I thought we were talking about Czechoslovakia," said the foreign secretary.

"We are," said Macrae, "but I wish to alert you to the extent of Nazi ambitions in the east. Hitler will not stop at Prague or Warsaw; he is intent on domination of everything up to the Urals. His aim is a race war, to drive the Slav peoples back into the far reaches of the Eurasian continent."

The ensuing shocked silence was finally broken by Duff Cooper, first lord of the admiralty, whom Macrae knew to be the only opponent of the appeasement policy in the government.

"What do you suggest we do about it?"

"There is strong evidence, of which your colleague the secretary of state for war is aware" – Macrae turned to the prime minister, who was sitting with a face as hard and grey as granite – "and of which I have just informed the prime minister, namely that significant numbers of senior officers within the German High Command are conspiring to remove Herr Hitler from power."

"Unsubstantiated rumours," said Chamberlain.

"Let him finish," said Hore-Belisha.

"And let the conspirators finish Hitler – good luck to them," said another voice.

Macrae looked down the table and recognised Duff Cooper again.

"They will only move if Britain issues an unambiguous warning that any German attack on Czechoslovakia will be met with force. That is the precondition for the coup."

The prime minister rose.

"Forgive the interruption, Colonel. Colleagues, I think I should share with you this cable from our ambassador in Berlin, which has just been decoded."

Macrae stepped back from the table. He had wondered when the long oar of the ambassador would be poked into his meetings in London.

"'I am aware that cabinet is discussing a response to the increasingly provocative nature of German statements and actions in relation to Czechoslovakia,'" the prime minister read. "'Ministers should be aware that last night I was given an audience by a senior member of the government, a minister close to the Führer, who affirmed that the door to negotiation remained wide open but who warned me that any bellicose statements from London would precipitate the very action we seek to avoid.'"

Chamberlain turned to Macrae with a slight smile.

"I do not wish to embarrass you, Colonel, by reading further, but I think it right to let colleagues in this room know that the ambassador goes on to dismiss reports of a military coup against Hitler as, and I quote, 'not based on a realistic assessment of the opinions and operation capabilities of disaffected members of the German High Command'. I know you do not share these views, but I think it is right that the cabinet should hear the latest report from our ambassador."

"This is outrageous." Duff Cooper had risen from his chair and was leaning on his fists on the table. "Colonel Macrae has not even finished his report to cabinet, and you have interrupted with a contradictory report from Berlin. Frankly, Prime Minister, I am shocked."

Hore-Belisha had also risen.

"May I echo those sentiments and express my disappointment. Our ambassador in Berlin is known to be more enthusiastic about the policy of appeasing Hitler than most of us in this room, and thus it is only natural he would dismiss reports of military disaffection. Personally, I think we should do all we can to encourage such treachery."

The rest of the cabinet shifted uneasily in their seats, uncertain how to respond to these remarks, looking to their prime minister for guidance. Chamberlain rose, gripping the lapels of his jacket.

"May I remind you that Herr Hitler is both the legal head of government and head of state, thus occupying a position analogous to that of our own king and myself as prime minister. There will be no talk of regicide in this room. Thank you, gentlemen."

He turned to Macrae.

"Now, Colonel Macrae, we all thank you, but if you will forgive us, we will move to the next item on the agenda. On behalf of us all, I bid you a safe journey back to Berlin."

Macrae just had time for a large gin and tonic before his plane left Croydon airport late that afternoon. The weather was fine and as the plane cleared the South Downs, the pilot announced that seat belts could be unfastened, which was the signal for stewardesses to start serving drinks.

Macrae ordered another large gin. His rage had subsided. He had been treated with contempt by the prime minister and betrayed by his own ambassador. Hore-Belisha had said nothing after the cabinet meeting but merely bade him farewell with a limp handshake. Macrae drank deeply of his gin and looked through the large porthole windows of the aircraft at the green fields and woods below. Romans had carved roads through the soft chalk down there, planted vineyards, built elegant villas, tended livestock and raised families. The conquerors had pushed their empire north to the borders of his own country, Scotland, then less a nation and more a collection of warring clans. There the Romans had stopped and built a wall that survived to this day. But Hitler would not stop, nor would his conquest bring light and learning to the land below, as the Romans had done. A Nazi conquest would unleash terror and mass murder on the country basking in the summer heat beneath him, ignorant of the tyranny that threatened them only a few hundred miles across the Channel.

England lay asleep like an old hunting dog by the fire, dreaming of past triumphs and occasionally twitching as it remembered the excitement of a famous chase and a fallen prey.

He was Scottish, but the Scots were just as much prisoners of their romantic past as the English, in fact more so. The Celtic delight in myth, magic and illusion cast an even greater spell over Caledonia than its martial history did over England. But what did it matter whether English, Irish, Scottish or Welsh, rich man, poor man, beggar man or thief? Where was the will to throw down the gauntlet to a regime of unimaginable evil? Who down there, in Shakespeare's sceptred isle, was going to fight Hitler?

He replayed that morning's conversation. It was very easy to dismiss the planned coup as mere rumours – how could plans for such treachery be proved to the satisfaction of a British cabinet? It was easy to understand the fear that gripped the government and its people, fear that another war would bring devastating civilian casualties as bombers flattened major cities, fear that a terrified population, traumatised by air raids, would force their political leaders to surrender and accept ignominious defeat. Those were real fears, fears that had been allowed to loom so large that they now conditioned every act of British foreign policy.

On the other hand, what if Chamberlain were right? Were Koenig and Colonel Schiller indulging in dangerous fantasies when they talked that night in the hunting lodge? Was Koenig dreaming when he said that Halder and his armoured divisions were ready to move? If that were the case, why had the Gestapo not got wind of such dangerous disaffection? Above all, Macrae forced himself to consider the fear he had buried away at the back of his mind, the suspicion that he was being set up in a counterfeit coup designed to expose him as a diplomat bent on subversion and thus to be expelled in disgrace. Was that possible?

He closed his eyes and thought again of Florian Koenig, handsome, charming, intelligent, a man educated in the wider world. He would surely never fall for the Nazi mystique, the fake glamour of those torchlight parades, with their swastika banners, polished jackboots, arms raised in salutes, and on a distant floodlit platform, the small figure with his Iron Cross 2nd Class pinned to his uniform, bellowing the web of lies that had ensnared an entire people.

There was something in this demonic man that tapped deep roots within the German psyche, stirring an atavistic urge to relive the savagery of those days when the German tribes rose against Rome to murder and plunder their way into the heart of a stricken empire.

Koenig couldn't have been seduced by this potent brew of twisted psychology and crude racial patriotism, could he? He was surely not the man to fall for the Nazi fantasy of creating an Aryan super-race to rule Europe – and one day the world. Because that was what Hitler was selling, what the German people were buying and what the British government was choosing to ignore. No, that was not Koenig. In any case, if he were playing a double game as an agent of the Gestapo, he would hardly be having an affair with Primrose. The thought consoled him and made him smile. It was strange indeed that he should find reassurance in his wife's infidelity.

The stewardess came round with last drinks as the plane began the descent to Tempelhof airport. Macrae accepted another large gin.

He was going to make a plan. He would arrange to see Koenig as soon as possible. He would ignore the affair and persuade him to provide more information. He would ask Halliday to chase the travel documents for Sara. He doubted Hore-Belisha would do anything. He would take Shirer to lunch and probe the American response to the threat of war in Europe. Roosevelt was deeply engaged in the New Deal and was said to have little regard for Chamberlain. But then the US president was said to dislike Churchill equally.

The plane bumped down hard at Tempelhof airport and then flung itself back into the air before putting both wheels firmly on the ground and rolling to a stop in front of the terminal.

The afterglow of the gin had lifted his spirits and created a euphoric sense of confidence: an adulterous wife, a deceitful ambassador, pusillanimous politicians – they would all bend to his will, accept the path ahead that he would lay out. He was sure of that because, as he walked across the baking tarmac of the airport, he knew he possessed what they did not, the absolute certainty of what had to be done.

He was glad to be back in Berlin.

The newspapers at the airport kiosks all carried similar headlines. The Führer was to make a major speech to delegates at a party rally in Nuremberg, where he would announce the fate of Czechoslovakia. The rally had been the talk of Berlin's diplomatic circles for weeks, but now a date had been set, 12 September. The editorial comment in the Nazi-controlled press was unanimous. Hitler would use the Nuremberg rally to announce his terms. Either the Czechoslovakian government in Prague would agree to the return of millions of ethnic Germans in Sudetenland to the Fatherland and thus cede the territory to Germany – or there would be war. Macrae had a large black coffee while waiting for his car and driver. It was Friday, 31 August. He had two weeks.

Primrose opened the door and gave him a brief hug. She was wearing a new dark blue dress with a single rope of pearls. Dressed for an evening out, thought Macrae wearily.

"Hallo, darling," she said. "Have you had a wonderful time? You lucky old thing, being in London. Everyone here has been talking about nothing but bloody Czechoslovakia." She looked at him. "You're looking tired, dear, would you like a bath before supper?"

He had only been away for a day and a night and yet he felt like an explorer who had spent several years in a remote part of the world. She ran a bath and handed him a gin and tonic as he lay soaking in the steamy warmth.

They had a light supper that she said she had cooked specially, turbot with a creamy lemon sauce, accompanied by a very good wine.

"We're not going out tonight, are we?" he asked.

"Of course not. I just wanted to look nice for you. And you're going straight to bed after supper. You need a good night's sleep."

Later she climbed into the bed beside him as he dozed off and said, "Oh, I forgot: good news. I have tickets to the opera, *La bohème*. It's a gala performance by that new American company."

Macrae stirred. "When?"

"Tomorrow night. Would you like to come?"

"You know I hate opera."

She leant over and pushed him gently back against the pillow and kissed his forehead.

"I know. You put your feet up for a change. I'll take one of the girls from the embassy."

12

When Macrae got to his desk at the embassy the next morning he was told Sir Nevile Henderson was out of town. Halliday supplied this information with a cup of coffee. He had knocked on the door, walked into Macrae's office without waiting for an answer and sat down in a chair. The laces of his shoes were undone as usual, Macrae noticed, and he had slipped his feet half out of them. It eased the gout, he had once explained.

"Where's he gone?" asked Macrae.

"Went to London this morning. RAF plane."

"Strange. I've just got back."

"I know. How was it?"

Macrae jerked his head to where the ambassador's office lay down the corridor. "He ambushed me. Now he's probably gone over to make doubly sure they don't believe a word I said."

"And did they?"

"What?"

"Believe a word you said?"

"No. The PM doesn't think there is any chance that the army will move against their anointed leader, however much they may distrust him. Germans are not like us, he said; they're disciplined and loyal to their commanders. And he kept saying where's the evidence, where's the proof? And do you know something? If I had presented him with sworn statements signed in Prussian blood as evidence, he still wouldn't have believed it. They just don't want to know."

"There are some very senior people – my people – who believe that what you have heard is true. Number 10 has been made aware of their views."

"And?"

Halliday shook his head and poured some more coffee.

"Chamberlain is not going to do anything about it. All he'll do is put pressure on the Czechs to accept Hitler's terms, and of course the moment they say yes to one demand, there'll be another on the table. And all we do is tell the Czechs to carry on saying yes until they are left without a country . . . How was the minister, by the way?"

"Which one?"

"Hore-Belisha."

"Fine in private, but in cabinet he just rolls over with the rest. I tell you, I wasted my time there."

"Not entirely," said Halliday, drawing something from an attaché case. "We received the cabled authority for these and I had them printed up for you."

Macrae opened the packet. It was a two-page authorisation to enter the UK, carrying the seal of the Foreign Office and signed and stamped by numerous functionaries in London – in the name of Sara Sternschein.

"God, that was quick. I only saw him yesterday," said Macrae.

"Maybe he doesn't roll over quite as much as you think. But note the date. That pass is only good for two weeks." Halliday smiled and went to the door. "Let me know if you see your chum in the army, will you?"

"Which chum would that be?"

"Just let me know. And you might ask him about Nuremberg."

"I have not had enough coffee to deal with riddles."

"You know all about Nuremberg, don't you?"

"What I read in the papers."

"That's the Rubicon. Hitler will use his speech to bind the military to his war strategy. He will commit the army, and very few officers will challenge him after that. They wouldn't dare defy their overall commanding officer."

"Sure of that?" said Macrae.

"They're Prussian, aren't they? But maybe your chum and his friends have other ideas."

Halliday leant forward, close enough for Macrae to smell the toothpaste on his breath, a minty scent that did not quite cover up last night's stale whisky.

"You've just been to London, haven't you? And you've had a tête-à-tête with the prime minister. That will be in the British papers this morning. What did he tell you in confidence, that wily old bird Chamberlain? That they are going to bring the fleet down from its base in Scotland the week before Nuremberg – right?"

"Wrong."

"So who's to know? Let us suppose that certain elements of the High Command in Berlin believe that the Royal Navy will bring forward its autumn manoeuvres in the North Sea. They would know that the sight of those big battleships close to the German coast would make the ground shake here in Berlin."

"And if that doesn't happen, which it won't?"

"Get a grip, Macrae. You're missing the point. If the army *think* those manoeuvres will take place, if they *think* the British finally mean business, they will strike the day after Nuremberg."

Halliday left, leaving the door open. Macrae could hear him shuffling down the corridor, his unlaced shoes flapping on the carpet. We're talking to the same people, he thought. He wondered if Koenig was a recipient of the sizeable sums that Halliday was alleged to have at his disposal.

He looked back at the documents and smoothed the papers on his desk. Halliday had been right: it expired on 22 September. It was now the 8th. She would be gone in two weeks. Sara Sternschein would soon be in England, a homeless immigrant – but far from the Salon, far from the Gestapo, and safe.

Macrae was embarrassed to find that even though he tried to shield his face beneath his hat, the woman at the entrance of the Salon still recognised him and gave him a friendly "*Guten Abend*" as she pressed the bell. Inside, a young woman dressed in the usual grey dress took his coat and hat.

"*Sind sie allein?*" she asked.

He nodded and she gestured towards a table for two at the back. It was nine o'clock and the club was half full of dark suits worn with tasteless, garish ties. The smoky haze was thicker than usual and, for the first time, Macrae saw swastika armbands worn by two stout middle-aged men at the same table. They were laughing over glasses of beer, an unusual sight at the Salon, which preferred to serve its guests wine or spirits.

He threaded his way to the back, noticing that the guests rarely acknowledged each other with even a glance. It was as if the diners wished to neither see nor be seen. The exception tonight was the two beer-drinkers, who looked at him curiously. They were party members, he guessed, and had probably been directed to the Salon as a reward for a favour given or dangerous task undertaken.

He sat down and ordered a whisky sour from the same woman who had taken his coat. She lingered at the table, suggesting a special dish on the menu and asking if he was comfortable. For the first time, he looked at her properly: young, early twenties perhaps, and flaxen hair with hazel eyes. She was beautiful, with clear skin the colour of apple blossom drawn tightly over high cheekbones. Black eyebrows arched over those light brown eyes. She smiled and bent low as she laid the knives and forks. He caught the familiar scent of lavender, which reminded him immediately of a long-ago aunt.

The old lady had lived just outside the city of Perth, in what she called the Kingdom of Fife. Macrae had been sent to stay with her every summer as a young boy. His parents never explained why he had to waste part of his long holidays in this fashion, merely telling him that at mealtimes he should eat what was put in front of him and never ask for what was not on the table. She was an old lady, Aunt Maeve, and he remembered the lavender smell on the cushions in her sitting room and on his pillows at night. When she died, she left a small amount of money to the local golf club and not, as his mother and father had evidently hoped, to her young nephew.

There was no sign of Sara. He looked at his watch. It was still early. He picked up the menu and glanced over the long list of steaks, chops, venison, calves' liver, bratwurst and the token appearance of a salmon fillet.

The waitress placed his drink in front of him and made a fuss of wiping the table. He asked her name. Erika, she said, from Mannheim. Her English was heavily accented but understandable. Had he changed his mind and decided to have something eat, she asked. He looked at those hazel eyes and apple-blossom cheeks. He shook his head. She suddenly sat down beside him, something he had not seen a waitress do before.

"Can I get you a drink?" he asked.

She smiled. "Not here, but next door, yes, I would like one very much."

She looked at the fanlight door and then back at Macrae, still smiling. She placed a hand on his arm and leant into him, the lavender smell stronger than ever. Aunt Maeve never married but was rumoured to have had a succession of lovers throughout her life, and indeed deep into old age. He had once heard his mother describe her as "godless", and no doubt his parents, as members of the Wee Free Presbyterian Church, would have had little to do with her but for the prospect of an inheritance.

There was still no sign of Sara. Perhaps she was behind the fanlight door that night. Perhaps he would meet her there if he allowed the hazel-eyed Erika to take him through to the Pink Room. He was about to ask about Sara, but stopped.

"No, thank you," he said. "I must go."

He paid and left, seeing Erika frown with disappointment.

He walked fast through the Tiergarten, swinging his arms to get the blood moving.

The bar at the Adlon almost felt like home by now. He seated himself on the leather stool by the spray of flowers with the familiarity of a regular drinker taking a favoured chair by the fire in an English country pub. The barman raised a bottle of Johnnie Walker enquiringly and Macrae nodded, lit a cigarette and looked around. Shirer and the American correspondents were at their usual table.

He tried to catch the American's eye, but the journalists were deep in conversation. The other tables were full, mostly with well-dressed foreigners and their wives or mistresses. It was always easy to tell Berliners at the Adlon. The Nazis wore their uniforms and regalia on the rare occasions they came to the hotel, in order to remind everyone who was in charge. German civil servants and businessmen wore almost identical pinstriped suits, with heavily padded shoulders and turn-ups.

"How was London town – still ringing them bells?"

Shirer had eased onto the stool beside him. Macrae was pleased. He wanted to talk to Shirer; in fact he wanted to talk to anyone. He felt the sudden need to get drunk and talk about anything – the latest Garbo film, the love life of his lavender Aunt Maeve, how to make a good whisky sour, why the Germans so rarely ate fish. He wanted to know why an American ballet company was holding a gala performance of *La bohème* in Hitler's Berlin and what his wife was doing there with her lover. She had known he wouldn't want to go.

He looked at his watch. It would be the interval soon and later, after the final curtain, there would be a gala dinner. They would discreetly leave and make their way to a little restaurant down by the river and there dine by candlelight, drinking white wine from Alsace. Where would he take her on a summer's night – into the Tiergarten? There in the dark, would she kneel and unbutton him just as she had done in the Surrey garden those long years ago? No, Koenig was too smart for that. He would have an apartment somewhere, borrowed from a friend, and there she would undress slowly, twirling around while he lay back on the bed smoking a cigar, watching her, and . . .

"Are you all right?" said Shirer.

"Sorry. What were you saying?"

"London, how was it?"

"What bells?" Macrae said, remembering Shirer's opening remark.

"The bells of St Clements, Shoreditch, you know – the old Cockney song?"

"Oh, those bells. I'm not a Cockney, thank God. Anyway, London was fine. Tell me about Washington. What's Roosevelt going to do about all this?"

Shirer dismissed the question, saying that White House thinking was irrelevant. To Macrae's alarm, he seemed to have picked up news of the disaffection in the ranks of the German army.

"A little birdy tells me that certain elements in the army are getting restless – know what I mean?"

"No, I don't," said Macrae, laughing. "Have another drink."

Shirer leant over, bringing his face within an inch of Macrae's. The barman looked curious but kept his distance. He had learnt that the foreign press swatted him away like a fly if he tried to eavesdrop.

"All right, in plain English: there's something brewing in the army. They don't want to go into Czechoslovakia," he whispered.

Macrae laughed again to cover his concern. If the CBS correspondent had heard rumours of army unrest, the Gestapo would be far ahead of them, with dates, names and numbers. He slid off the bar stool.

"I hope you haven't written that," Macrae said.

"Not yet. I'm working on it. Purely off the record, can you give me a steer on that?"

"No. You're dreaming, Shirer. Wait till you watch the army bow down before their leader at Nuremberg – then talk to me about a coup."

"Ah, Nuremberg," said Shirer. "Now you're talking. All roads lead to Nuremberg – see you there."

• • •

It was raining when he got outside again. There must have been a thunderstorm, because flashes of lightning flickered on the horizon, together with a rumbling that sounded like distant artillery fire. He knew the sound well. They had sat in their trenches, he and his men, and smiled into steaming cups of tea when they heard that echoing thunder; it meant someone else was getting it far down the line in a different sector.

There was a queue of people sheltering under umbrellas waiting for a taxi. There were none to be seen and after ten minutes Macrae was still standing on the pavement behind two middle-aged couples and an old lady. The yellow light of a cab emerged from the rain, its windscreen wipers struggling against the curtain of water. People in the queue moved forward. Suddenly Macrae pushed ahead of them, shoving the couples aside and almost knocking the old lady over. "Take me to the hospital," he shouted at the driver, and turned to the startled line of people as if offering this an excuse. Once in the cab and through the Brandenburg Gate, he directed the driver to take him home.

He instantly felt ashamed. How every un-English, how unlike the behaviour expected of a British diplomat. The house was in darkness but the light was on over the front door. He put the key in the lock and turned to look across the road. He thought he had seen a figure sheltering under the trees when the cab pulled up, and he half expected the person to emerge and flag down the vehicle. There was nothing, nobody, just the night rain and an empty house. He opened the door, slung his dripping raincoat on a hat rack made of old antlers and went up to the drawing room.

The coal fire had been well stocked and was still alight. The coals glowed in the darkness with a warm, comforting light that reminded him of teatime in the nursery during winter nights in Scotland. Liking the effect, he turned on a single standard lamp. He went to the window to draw the curtains. They would be having dinner somewhere now. He looked at his watch. It was almost ten. No, they would be in bed by now, in a strange apartment or maybe a hotel. Well, he was going to have a large drink, turn the light off, sit by the fire and let his mind wander over the glowing coals. He went to the drinks table and picked up a bottle of cognac, but decided on red wine from the decanter.

The doorbell rang. He went to the window but could see no one on the doorstep. He went downstairs and opened the door cautiously. She was standing on the doorstep, hatless, wearing a long black raincoat that reached over leather boots. The rain on her face made her look as if she had been crying. Her dark hair was plastered against her skin.

He quickly looked up and down the street.

"What are you doing here?"

"I don't want to come in."

"Of course you must come in. You're soaking. Quickly."

They spoke at the same time, blurting out the words so that they collided and jumbled into gibberish. He held the door open and closed it quickly as she stepped into the hall. He helped her off with her coat and hung it on the antler stand, where it dripped onto the floor.

"What are you doing here?" he said again.

"I won't stay long. They told me at the club you had been in. I thought you might have my papers. I didn't know when you were coming again. So I came round. I hope you don't mind."

"But you shouldn't be here."

"You're alone, aren't you?"

The grandfather clock chimed ten o'clock. They would have dined well, those two, good food and fine wine no doubt adding to the passion of their encounter. Curiously, the thought made him hungry rather than angry.

"Yes. Come in and have a drink. I'll get us something to eat."

"I'm not staying. I came for the papers."

He placed both hands gently on her shoulders. She was wearing the grey Salon dress this time and not the usual clingy eye-catching outfit. The dress felt damp.

"Come upstairs and dry out. There's a fire in the drawing room. I'll get the documents. You want a drink?"

She said nothing as she took off her shoes and started up the staircase. She paused at the landing and looked down.

"Did you say a drink?"

"Yes. Brandy?"

She nodded. He went into the kitchen, poured a glass of brandy and another of red wine, carved two generous slices from a venison pie in the fridge, placed them on a tray with a jar of pickles and some bread, and walked carefully up the stairs.

She was sitting cross-legged on a rug by the fire, holding her head to the heat, so that her hair fell in a black curtain in front of her face.

He placed the tray on the rug and sat down beside her.

"You shouldn't be here, you know."

"I'll leave if you want me to."

"It's all right, we have time. How did you know where I live?"

"They know at the club; don't ask me how."

Of course they knew at the club, he thought. They know everything. The Gestapo had been watching him since he arrived, and now he had a Gestapo agent sitting on the rug in front of his fire. With a brandy in her hand.

"I know what you're thinking," she said. "Don't worry. I just want the papers and I will go."

"No, stay," he said.

He knew he was being stupid, jumping the taxi queue again, pushing that old lady out of the way in the pouring rain, an irrational, impatient act born of the enveloping madness of his life in Berlin.

"Where is your wife?"

"At the opera."

There was a silence. He raised his glass and looked at the golden tongues of flame dimly visible through the ruby clouds of burgundy. He should never have pushed that lady out of the way. Unforgivable behaviour.

"I have your travel permit, but there is a small problem."

"What?"

"It is only valid for two weeks. You have to leave by the twenty-second of this month."

She laughed. "That's not a problem. I can't wait to get out of here."

"Where will you go?"

"I don't know. Train to the Dutch border, train or bus to Rotterdam, and then a ferry."

"To England?"

She nodded, looking at the fire. "Yes, England."

"You have money?"

"Enough. I have been thinking of this for a long time."

"And in England what will you do? You have family? Friends."

She shook her head. "Don't worry. I will be fine."

"I can give you a number to call. There will be people interested in talking to you."

"Is that a condition for this?"

"No."

"Good, because I have done with all that."

She raised the balloon of brandy, drank and began coughing.

"I must go," she said.

"Back to the club?"

"Where else?"

He leant forward and kissed her lightly, then more firmly. She pulled away.

"Not now, not here."

She got up and smoothed her dress. He pulled the envelope with the documents from the inside pocket of his jacket and handed it to her.

"Thank you," she said, and in the firelight he could see she was crying real tears. She wiped her eyes with the back of her hand, sniffed and smiled. She held up the envelope. "This is my new life. Thank England for me."

They went downstairs. He helped her on with the raincoat and opened the door.

"Come to the club tomorrow night," she said. "Late, about midnight."

Macrae shook his head. "Too dangerous. You said so yourself."

"You will be safe, I promise, and I have something for you."

She kissed him quickly in the hall and pulled away as he tried to draw her towards him again.

"Tell me now."

"I don't have time; your wife will be back soon." She looked at the clock. It was almost eleven. She turned at the door. "Tomorrow, late?"

"I can't."

"You must. General Beck was with me last night. He was very drunk – and very indiscreet."

"Beck? Are you sure?"

"As sure as his medals – and he has a lot of them."

With that, she walked into the night. It had stopped raining. A broken-faced moon glowed above the trees, a pearl strung on the necklace of the night. He watched her cross the road and disappear into the gardens that lay between the house and Charlottenburger Chaussee. It would be a twenty-minute walk back to the Salon. She would start work again and take another man into her arms and into her bed. Sara Sternschein, the woman who had just kissed him, the woman with whom he had lain beneath the bushes of the Tiergarten, the woman who last night had slept with the chief of the General Staff of the German army.

He had no idea when Primrose came to bed, but he woke the next morning to find her setting a cup of his favourite Earl Grey on the bedside table.

"You were sleeping like the dead," she said.

"When did you get in?"

"Oh, I don't know, late. There was a party after the opera."

He remembered that she said she would find a friend to take his place.

"Who did you find to go with?"

"Didn't I tell you? That nice woman Daisy Wellesley. She loves opera. Charming, she is, such good manners. Drink your tea."

She was wearing a bathrobe and went to the bedroom door.

"I'm going to have a bath, so don't rush," she said. "Oh, and I almost forgot. I met your friend Florian at the opera. He had a message for you."

Koenig was there?"

"Yes, with a group of friends, mostly officers and their wives, I think. Now, what was it he wanted me to tell you?" She frowned, thinking. "Oh yes, the cartographic room at the Prussian State Library on Unter den Linden. There are some old maps he wants to show you . . . Can't think why."

Macrae swung his legs out of bed. "Did he say when?"

"Oh, eleven, I think."

"When, for Christ's sake, Primrose? What day?"

He was shouting. He had lost his temper. He had pushed the old lady out of the way again. Primrose gazed at him blankly. That is what she always did when he got angry. She refused to engage, closed up like a clam and walked away.

"Tomorrow," she said, and went into the bathroom.

At the embassy that morning, Macrae was told that his appointment for a private interview with the ambassador had been cancelled. Sir Nevile Henderson had decided to travel to Nuremberg a few days before the National Socialist Party rally in order to "get the lie of the land", as his secretary put it.

"He sends his apologies and hopes to see you there," she said.

He will certainly see me there, thought Macrae.

There was a pile of letters and cables on his desk. He called Daisy in and began the Monday-morning chore of sorting through them together, until they reached that time of morning when coffee, or in his case black tea, was less a luxury than an urgent necessity.

She sat as usual in a corner chair. They gossiped about who was doing what in the mission, what new films were on, harmless trivial conversation. Daisy had a full social life and her famous ancestry seemed to encourage rather than deter German suitors. It was not long before she thanked him for the spare ticket to the opera.

"Your wife and I had such a good time – champagne before and a wonderful first act with that American soprano."

"First act?" said Macrae.

"Well, the second act was brilliant, but Mrs Macrae didn't feel well and left at the interval. I hope she got home all right. I offered to go with her, but she was frightfully decent and said she would manage."

The next day Macrae walked into the map room of the Prussian State Library in a well-lit gallery at the back of the building. Koenig was leaning over a large display case when Macrae entered. He was wearing a grey lounge suit with scuffed suede shoes and holding a magnifying glass to an old map that had been laid out on a raised display desk. The only other person in the room was an elderly attendant in a shiny black suit with a swastika armband. The man's face was a map in itself, a series of deep lines and clefts in skin the colour of old parchment. His clothes hung loosely on a skeletal frame and he was leaning against the wall as if it was the only way of remaining upright.

Macrae wondered whether the display of Nazi insignia at the heart of such a learned institution was a demonstration of personal conviction or merely another example of political camouflage. The attendant certainly did not look like one of the National Socialist Party's "strength through joy" warriors.

Maps going back to the early days of European cartography in the twelfth century hung on the walls, illuminated by spotlights slung from ceiling gantries. The display desks contained the most interesting examples. Leaning over his shoulder, Macrae saw that Koenig was using the magnifying glass to examine an early-seventeenth-century map of the territory that would become known as Germany. At that time it was a collection of kingdoms, all shaded in different colours. In elegant Gothic script the inscription read "The Kingdom of Germany 1648".

Koenig turned, snapped out a straightened arm and said loudly, "*Heil Hitler!*"

Immediately the attendant levered himself away from the wall, straightened up, stood stiffly to attention, raised his arm and gave a loud "*Heil Hitler!*" in return that echoed round the room.

Koenig gave a broad smile and shook Macrae's outstretched hand, placing an arm around his shoulder. Speaking in a whisper, he said, "Everyone's an informer these days – it's the only way to make any money." Then, speaking normally, he went on, "Let me show you something of Germany's great past. Make notes if you wish."

Macrae reached inside his jacket for a notebook and, having searched in vain for a pen, accepted a pencil from Koenig.

"It is 1648 and the Thirty Years War has just ended," said Koenig, "and here you see the medieval city of Nuremberg, a key trading centre and focal point of resistance to the Hapsburg Emperor." He lowered his voice again. "The crisis will be triggered here at the party rally. The speech will be at 6 p.m. and he will fly back to Berlin that night. Then the Potsdam division under Brockdorff will move into the city to make the arrest." He raised his voice. "And here you see in Thuringia a garrison strategically placed to repel invasion from the east." He pointed to a small town on a crossroads. His voice dropped to a whisper again. "This is where General Erich Hoepner commands an armoured division that will block any move by the SS from Munich." Then, in a normal voice, he said, "You are making notes?"

Macrae was writing rapidly in the few remaining pages of his notebook.

"Old maps are like old buildings and old people – they have great stories to tell," said Koenig, moving his finger from one medieval city to another: Hamburg, Munich, Mannheim, Hanover, Frankfurt.

He described the part they played in the First German Reich, the empire that called itself Holy and Roman but was in fact a series of seventeenth-century principalities that would unite to form modern Germany two centuries later. Bismarck would be the emperor of the Second German Reich, waging victorious war against the Balkan states and France.

Koenig rolled up the map and took another scroll from the shelf. He unfurled it and Macrae saw a map of modern Germany. Once again, Koenig's finger moved from city to city, explaining the successful development of industry and tourism in a loud voice but laying bare in whispers the plans for a coup against the Führer of the Third German Reich.

The key factor was the number of generals with operational command of infantry or armoured units who were prepared to back their leaders, prominent but unnamed figures with senior commands in the military. The names of Erwin von Witzleben, commander of the Wehrkreiss 11 Brandenburg Division, based just outside Berlin, and Eric von Brockdorff-Ahlefeldt, commander of the Potsdam garrison, went into Macrae's notebook. In Berlin itself the finger paused and began tapping. Count Helldorf, with overall charge of the police, was another disaffected Nazi who would join the coup.

The plan was to arrest Hitler the moment he gave orders for "Case Green", the invasion of Czechoslovakia. The Führer would not give the order explicitly in his speech to the faithful in Nuremberg, but if his words were unambiguous in that respect, the plotters would move that night. Otherwise, they would wait until Hitler had committed himself to military action and then seize him.

Macrae looked around the room. The attendant had shuffled off, presumably satisfied that the two well-dressed gentlemen in the medieval map room were amateur cartographers.

"What will you do when you have arrested him?" said Macrae in a quiet voice.

"We have decided not to kill him. That is very important. It would just turn him into a martyr. He will be put before a People's Court and tried for treason. The judges have already been assigned. There will also be a panel of psychiatrists under an eminent professor, Karl Bonhoeffer – have you heard of him?"

Macrae had not. He put the name into his notebook.

"I am giving you his name so that you may see that this operation has been well planned. Bonhoeffer is very respected in his field and he has seen the early reports of Hitler's mental condition when he was in a military hospital after the war. He has concluded the man is mad."

Macrae knew that the British foreign secretary, Lord Halifax, had reached the same conclusion, but that had not dissuaded the government from its policy of appeasement.

"You mentioned the leaders of the operation . . .?" Macrae left the question dangling. Koenig smiled.

"You would not expect me to reveal that, would you? Let me ask you a question instead – when will the British and French make their intentions clear?" Koenig looked over Macrae's shoulder and suddenly raised his voice. The attendant had returned and was lounging by the door. "And that concludes my little talk on these medieval maps, which show how our great Third Reich has its roots planted in the history of the First Reich. Thank you for listening."

Koenig walked from the room, pausing to give an exaggerated Hitler salute, which was enthusiastically returned. The scene reminded Macrae of a Charlie Chaplin film, characters creating comedy through the absurdity of unreal and outrageous behaviour. Chaplin had said in Hollywood recently that Hitler seemed to be impersonating him rather than the other way round.

They met an hour later in a coffee shop on the second floor of the KaDeWe, the largest department store in Europe. Koenig had chosen the venue for the anonymity conferred by crowds of women shoppers struggling to find seats in the cafeteria, with bulging bags and small children eager for ice cream and chocolate biscuits.

They ordered coffee and glasses of iced water while waitresses moved past with trays of sandwiches, cakes and glasses containing elaborate ice-cream creations.

"You see, we can still give our people the luxuries of life," said Koenig. "We don't spend *all* our money on arms. You were about to tell me something?"

"I thought you were about to tell me who was going to lead the operation."

Koenig frowned. "There are two commanders who will lead, but they want to know for certain that the British will make their move."

Macrae sipped his water. He looked around as if trying to catch sight of a lost child or a harassed wife; at least, that is what he hoped any casual observer would think. He turned back to Koenig.

"The navy will bring forward their autumn North Sea manoeuvres. The deployment will be unannounced," Macrae said. "The day before the Nuremberg rally, the Home Fleet will leave its base in Scapa Flow. The battle-class cruisers will be in plain sight of your coast the next day, when your Führer is due to speak. This is a clear breach of diplomatic protocol."

"The Royal Navy?" said Koenig. "Yes, of course."

He sipped his drink. He took a guarded look at the crowded tables around them. Take your time, thought Macrae. You have much more to lose than I do.

"Your navy is the one force that Hitler respects." Koenig's voice was once again a whisper. "He has no time for the British soldier, still less for the French, but your navy is different. The sight of those ships off the north coast will enrage him. He'll go mad. He will order counter-manoeuvres, but we have nothing like your heavy cruisers – yet. The papers will be full of it. British provocation. Britannia shows her true colours. There will be an official protest from the Foreign Ministry. Goebbels will have a fit."

Koenig was excited. He was sitting up straight in his chair and Macrae could see his mind was racing ahead to the effect the news would have on the conspirators. Britain had finally nailed her colours to the mast – literally. Her ships had sent the signal they had waited for. At last the oldest European democracy was going to stand up to a maniac who was using bluff and terror to pursue a master plan that could only lead to a new war. Koenig gulped his coffee down and raised the cup for a refill. He reached into his pocket and produced a diary and began making small entries.

Macrae felt deeply ashamed – that he had had to lie to stiffen the sinews of the German resistance, that his own government had no intention of doing anything that might meet with Hitler's disapproval, that he had accepted his wife's infidelity with the man sitting across the café table from him. He had never gone along with that tired old apology for criminality, namely that the end justifies the means. On this occasion, he reluctantly had to admit that Halliday had been right. The lie about the Royal Navy had worked.

"I wouldn't write this down," said Macrae.

"I'm not – just making diary marks. Today is the eighth of September. The closing rally when Hitler speaks is on Monday the twelfth, and then the White Ensign will be flying in sight of our ports. Excellent!"

The waitress arrived with fresh coffee. Koenig paid her, refilled both their cups and drank his quickly. He seemed to be about to leave.

Macrae had planned to confront him quietly and with dignity in the museum. Are you conducting an affair with my wife? *Conducting an affair*. What a ridiculous phrase; it made the lovers seem like principals in an orchestra. In fact, what they were doing was fucking each other in borrowed apartments, in other people's beds, and for all he knew his own bed. This wasn't an affair of the heart; this was just two people turning to each other for the satisfaction they could not find at home. And that was what hurt most of all. It wasn't as if they made much of a secret of it.

There had been no opportunity in the map room. Now he wanted to put the question to Koenig here, in a crowded cafeteria full of mothers with their ice cream-slurping, chocolate-smeared children, the middle-class Berliners enjoying the fruits of National Socialist rule. It would be a simple question, posed with calm to avoid a scene: "I have meant to ask you, Colonel Koenig, are you fucking my wife?" That was reasonable enough, wasn't it? Husbands had a right to ask that question of their wife's lover, didn't they?

"I must go," said Koenig. "This has been very satisfactory. We must stay in touch. I will contact you."

"Thank you," said Macrae, and he rose to follow him from the room.

• • •

There was a singer at the Salon that night, the Marlene Dietrich lookalike, who was so admired by the Nazi High Command. It was close to midnight, but there she was, sitting on a bar stool, wearing black jacket, fishnet stockings and black top hat in a pale caricature of the original. The smoky voice and the famous numbers were a passable imitation of the real thing. Macrae closed his eyes and listened.

An army coup would end all this. The Salon, the girls, the Gestapo that used the place for blackmail, extortion and probably worse – the whole ghastly edifice of terror would crumble into dust. A Germany without Hitler was a pleasant dream, although there were some in London who wondered whether a new regime would be any different. Driven by that aggressive Prussian gene, wouldn't a collection of generals embark on similar plans of conquest in the east? Maybe, but at least the Jews might be spared the fate that any sane person could see awaited them in the Third Reich.

The Jews, they were leaving as fast as they could but already the exodus had been slowed. There were still roughly six hundred thousand in Germany and time was running out. Halliday had picked up hints of new and more ominous plans being drawn up by the Gestapo to deal with what was casually called the Jewish Problem. Heydrich was supposed to be in charge. Heydrich, the man who ran this brothel. Heydrich and his Jewish whore. He opened his eyes and looked around.

Sara was in the corner listening to the singer. She smiled and slowly walked over and sat down. The sight of her next to him, smiling at him, those dark eyes on his, her hand beneath the table taking his, made him suddenly feel happy, a surge of simple pleasure at her presence.

"Can I get you a drink?" she said.

"A whisky would be good. Highland Park, if they have it."

She raised her arm and made a signal with her index and forefinger. Moments later the Highland Park arrived. A good malt spoilt by two large ice cubes. The song that Marlene Dietrich made famous while still unknown herself, "Falling in Love Again", floated across the room.

"You like our new singer?"

"A poor copy of the original."

"Germans like her songs. They close their eyes and dream of the good old days. They're a sentimental people."

"I don't see much evidence of that in Berlin."

"That's because you're not looking."

"Where should I be looking?"

She got up, brushed the creases from her skirt and looked at him, eyebrows raised, as if mocking his question. Then she smiled at him, inclined her head slightly sideways and turned to walk towards the fanlight door at the end of the room. He drank the whisky in one, got up and walked after her.

It was well after midnight when Macrae got to Halliday's apartment, not far from his own house in Charlottenburg. He rang the bell insistently for five minutes before the door opened. Halliday squinted at him from a darkened hallway, his bulk mostly covered by a faded paisley-patterned silk dressing gown.

"I know it's late. I'm sorry," said Macrae.

Halliday stepped aside without a word, waved him in and pointed to a door across the hallway.

The sitting room was sparsely furnished and spotlessly clean. Crowded bookshelves rising from floor to ceiling covered one wall. A desk and a chair had been placed by the window and a sofa and two armchairs were arranged around a coal fire, from whose dark embers a slight warmth emanated.

The only other furniture was a trolley in one corner, which contained bottles of whisky, vodka, gin and brandy, and soda siphons. The floor was of dark polished wood which, without the presence of carpet or rugs, gave the room an institutional feel, that of a headmaster's study perhaps. There was not a painting, photograph or ornament to be seen. For a moment, Macrae found it difficult to imagine the shambolic character of Halliday living in a room stripped down to such spartan essentials. Then he realised that this was where Halliday played the endless game of bluff and counter-bluff, betrayal and deceit, a game that could only be won without distraction – save that of the drinks trolley.

"Do you take water in your malt?" Halliday was pouring generous measures into two crystal tumblers.

Macrae nodded and sat down. He had asked for a large glass of water but Halliday had dismissed this request, saying that anyone who came banging on his door after midnight was going to join him in a large whisky or leave immediately.

It was three in the morning when the two men finished talking. The fire had lost all warmth, the room was cold and the whisky bottle stood empty on the tray.

Halliday had sat in his armchair, eyes closed, legs splayed out in front him, listening as Macrae explained Koenig's detailed analysis of the mechanics of the putsch and the careful planning that had gone into it. Occasionally Halliday raised a hand and, with eyes still closed, said quietly, "Repeat that last bit, please."

At one stage he had risen, gone to the desk, taken out a notebook and scribbled some notes.

Through the blur of fatigue and whisky, Macrae took a certain satisfaction that he was briefing a British intelligence agent with information that would soon be on the desk of Sir Stewart Menzies in London. Usually, it was the other way round.

It was when Bonhoeffer's name came up that Halliday rose from his chair and went to pour the last of the whisky.

"You know Hitler was in a military hospital at a place called Pasewalk at the end of the war?" he said. "Temporarily blinded by mustard gas. That's when he began ranting about defeat and the fall of the monarchy as being the fault of Jews, communists, Marxists, trade unionists – he blamed them all. A lot of people think he went clinically mad in that place and has stayed mad ever since. If a psychiatrist like Bonhoeffer is involved, it means they must have obtained his hospital records. He wasn't classified insane at the time but he was certainly mentally unbalanced. So, they are going to put him in a lunatic asylum? Interesting. Well, we must to bed."

Halliday stretched and yawned.

"There is one more thing," said Macrae quickly. "General Beck is to lead the coup. I think Canaris is involved as well."

Halliday walked to the drinks trolley, picked up the empty whisky bottle, put it down again and bent down to peer at the lower shelf.

"Exactly how do you know that?" he said, pulling out another bottle, unscrewing the top and placing it on the trolley.

Macrae had been thinking of how to explain the source of this information since leaving the Salon. He thought of telling Halliday that he had gone to meet William Shirer for a drink there but the American had not turned up; then the information about Beck had surfaced in conversation with the girls. He knew a professional like Halliday was not going to believe that.

"I can't tell you. Trust me, it's true."

"I like you, Macrae," said Halliday, "but it's late, I'm tired and trust is not something I have a lot of time for right now. See you tomorrow."

He looked at his watch and screwed the top back on the whisky bottle.

"Oh, it is tomorrow. Dear God."

"Suppose I told you my source confirmed that Professor Karl Bonhoeffer has looked over the Pasewalk records and is prepared to declare Hitler insane after his arrest?"

Macrae had him now. Halliday stood quite still for a moment, clasped his hands, looked at the ceiling.

Macrae went on: "And suppose I tell you that General Beck resigned as chief of the General Staff on 18 August, but accepted Hitler's request that the news should not be made public for two months to avoid disaffection within the army?"

"Suppose we have another drink," said Halliday.

13

The National Socialist Party has refined its annual rally in Nuremberg into a ritual that weaves the cult of leader worship and xenophobia into a propaganda extravaganza choreographed with such skill that the vast crowds leave the arena in a state of mass hypnosis.

Macrae folded the newspaper clipping back into his wallet. That was a description of the rally the previous year by the correspondent of the *Manchester Guardian*. This year, 1938, the Nazis promised an even more grandiose spectacle. He had seen newsreel footage of previous rallies, but nothing had prepared him for the scale and ingenuity of the theatrical effects by which Goebbels and Albert Speer projected Hitler to his audience in Nuremberg, to the German people across the nation and to the wider world beyond; here was the messiah, the leader of a Third Reich that would last one thousand years.

The closing rally of the party congress took place as usual that year on a Monday after a weekend of festivities and speeches in and around Nuremberg attended by almost one million people.

On the old airfield built for the Zeppelin airships just outside Nuremberg, Albert Speer had constructed a stadium whose centrepiece was two tiers of white marble seating which rose to the long pillared arcade of the old war memorial honouring the nine thousand soldiers from Nuremberg who had died in the Great War.

A huge white swastika within an alabaster wreath of oak leaves stood atop the arcade, glowing in the sunlight of a late summer afternoon. Traditional Nazi flags, black swastika on a white circle against a red background, had been placed in their hundreds in the recesses of the arcade and at vantage points around the arena.

Macrae had arrived in the city by train on the Monday afternoon and had taken his seat along with senior members of the diplomatic corps in Berlin and a host of German and visiting dignitaries. Unlike the precision with which the various speeches and march-pasts had been organised, the seating for the guests lacked formal arrangement.

Macrae found himself sitting among a group of Italian members of Mussolini's Fascist Party. Several rows in front he could see Sir Nevile Henderson with the other ambassadors. There was no sign of Halliday or anyone else from the British mission in Berlin.

The most senior members of the Nazi Party were seated on a platform that had been built out from the tiered seating and from which speeches were already being made. Macrae could see them all, Göring, Himmler, Goebbels, Speer, Heydrich and Hitler's deputy, Rudolf Hess. Lesser party functionaries occupied privileged seating immediately behind the platform. Gathered at one end of the upper tier were the senior officers in the three services, army, navy and air force, an arrangement designed to remind the military that they were servants of the Nazi Party and not vice versa.

The most astonishing sight of all was the sea of people in the stadium, massed ranks of humanity reaching back to the circle of seating that enclosed the whole arena. They stood there in the sun in their hundreds of thousands, divided into orderly groups identified by flags. Each flag rose above a brass sign denoting the name of a regional Nazi Party or SS unit. Groups of women stood to attention in white short-sleeved blouses and long grey skirts. SS men stood stripped to the waist, strong muscular bodies gleaming with sweat.

It was four in the afternoon and the march-past was about to begin. Macrae knew Hitler would take the salute, make a short speech to the crowd and then retire, before re-emerging for the highlight of the whole weekend extravaganza, his main address in the torch-lit darkness. Then the fate of Czechoslovakia would be announced, a mailed fist would be raised to crush the racially inferior Slavonic peoples who had dared to defy the Reich; the German tanks would roll in the next morning. Macrae knew the armoured units were in position, along with six divisions of infantry within a few miles of the frontier.

Hitler arrived in his custom-built open Mercedes, standing at the front, grasping the windscreen with one arm while raising and lowering the other in repeated salutes to the forest of raised arms around him. Four bodyguards stood on running boards behind him as the car was driven slowly around the stadium, giving the maximum number of people a chance to glimpse their Führer.

A mighty roar erupted from the crowd as Hitler walked onto the podium, raising his right arm in salute to the crowd and then turning to face the dignitaries behind him, arm still raised. It was the first time Macrae had seen him in the flesh. He was smaller than he expected, but the moustache, the plump cheeks and the weak chin were true to every portrait and photograph.

He was wearing his usual military uniform, with the Iron Cross 2nd Class pinned to the jacket. The noise rose as the first planes of the fly-past came into sight. Every head turned skywards as, four abreast, the Dorniers and Focke-Wulf bombers flew low over the stadium. Then came the tanks, towed artillery and armoured cars, rumbling immediately in front of the tiered seating.

Macrae noted the long-barrelled 88 mm artillery weapons, which had been improved since the early version had gone into action in Spain. The British army had nothing with the range and firepower of such weapons. He squinted against the lowering sun, trying to identify the various types of tanks in the parade. The German High Command held nothing back on these occasions. Every new weapon was on display, designed to impress and intimidate foreign observers and send a message to the many enemies that Hitler had already damned in speech after speech: Czechoslovakia, Poland and the communist-Jewish conspiracy that called itself Russia.

Around him, everyone was standing, craning to see the weaponry and openly cheering every new display of military might.

Macrae felt faint. He reached for the hip flask that Daisy Wellesley had placed in his pocket. Daisy had also wrapped sandwiches in greaseproof paper and put them in his briefcase. He noticed other guests were similarly supplied. He didn't feel hungry. He felt as if he had stumbled into an alternate universe, a nightmare that had slipped its moorings in the quiet waters of his unconscious mind and sailed into the real world.

Goebbels had called the annual Nuremberg rally the High Mass of the party, and this was exactly what Macrae was witnessing: a pseudo-religious event at which worshippers were prostrating themselves before their messiah.

It reminded him of the occasion at school when his sixth-form class, boys aged about seventeen, had been taken to see the sun rise at dawn over the Stonehenge ruins in Wiltshire. It had been the summer solstice, when the first light crept over those ancient stones at four thirty in the morning. The boys had stood shivering among a small group of people, including druids in white gowns and other eccentrics, as the first rays of the sun gently brought the stones to life.

Their teacher told them it had been a temple raised by ancient men to their sun god, and it was for this reason that the stones were arranged in such a way as to catch the first light of the longest day. Archaeologists had established from excavations that human sacrifices were made there. In reverence to the sun, he said. And it was reasonable to assume, was it not, that such sacrifices were made on this very day of the year? The boys had drunk tea from thermos flasks and stamped cold feet round the stones, concerned less by the majesty of such early architecture and long-ago human sacrifices than by the cold, and the prospect of a bacon sandwich at a nearby roadside café.

And here he was again at the heart of a temple raised to a new sun god, a small man, rather plumper than his photographs, who was now raising the blood flag of the Nazi Party, so called because it was said to have been dipped in the blood of those party stalwarts who had been killed in the Beer Hall Putsch of 1923.

The Führer had taken this sacred relic and brushed it against other flags around him, thus sanctifying the swastika emblem with the blood of slain martyrs. The thievish mind of Goebbels had invented this ritual, stealing the idea from the Catholic Mass.

Macrae looked across to where the military High Command were sitting. The one senior figure missing was General

Beck. Macrae hoped he knew why he was not there. The Gestapo would have noted his absence but would not have been surprised. They would have known he had resigned and would not expect him to attend.

Koenig would be there somewhere, along with the leaders of the conspiracy. They believed that Hitler would make a fatal mistake that night, propelling Germany into conflict with her eastern neighbour and pointing the way to a wider war in Europe. They believed that the Royal Navy was off the German coast in response, validating the ruthless action they would take.

They were ready to move in the hours after Hitler had spoken, signalling the start of Case Green. The planning for the coup had been completed and the conspirators had even agreed that green was to be the new national colour, replacing the blood-red swastika flags of the Third Reich.

The party congress reached its climax that night, eclipsing the grandeur of the daytime parades with a display of light, fire and the thunderous baying of political slogans rapturously chanted by the massed multitude. An ocean of faces gazed up in adoration at the stone plinth on which their leader would speak. The effect seemed to suck the oxygen out of the stadium, so that the vast crowd would occasionally fall silent, dazed and breathless, before people recovered themselves and returned to chanting "*Ein Volk! Ein Führer!*" and "*Sieg Heil! Sieg Heil!*"

Macrae had been invited to join the ambassador for the grand finale of the rally and, to his surprise, Halliday had also taken his place beside them.

Powerful searchlights were now beamed into the night sky, eclipsing the stars and creating a cocoon of light around the stadium that was said to be visible eighty miles away. On either side of the podium, flames glittered and flickered from fire bowls, while in the stadium itself the thousands of flag-carriers now also held flaming torches, which moved in the darkness like the eyes of a vast assembly of wild creatures.

Sir Nevile Henderson leant over and said to them both, "I spent six years in St Petersburg before the war and saw Russian ballet at its finest, but for sheer grandeur I have never seen anything to match this."

Macrae muttered his interest in this remark, while Halliday grunted, produced a hip flask and took a long swig by way of reply.

Sir Nevile resumed his upright stance. That was the problem with the Secret Service, he thought. They didn't teach their agents how to behave properly on occasions like this. In fact, it was a mystery to Sir Nevile and to most of his peers exactly what such agents were taught to do. Halliday rarely told him anything of interest.

Several rows ahead of the diplomatic guests, Joachim Bonner turned and watched the ambassador. He saw Halliday taking his whisky direct from the flask and smiled. The Gestapo knew all about Halliday. They had watched him for two years. The man might look like a shambolic wreck, and his drinking surprised even those Gestapo agents who spent nights in the bars of Berlin watching him, but he was clever.

They had never identified the agents he ran, men and women prepared to betray their country for English gold; nor had they broken the code by which he communicated with London. Halliday had the ability to vanish on crowded streets and lose his trackers. He was a professional, and Bonner rather admired that. He turned his attention to the man next to Halliday, a thin-lipped Englishman with a long nose. The face was familiar. He flicked through images in his mind and then remembered the file on Colonel Noel Macrae and the smudged photo that went with it.

So that was the British military attaché. Bonner tried to remember why they held a file on him. Macrae's service in the embassy in Vienna had been noted, as had his unguarded comments about the National Socialist government in Berlin. He had been overheard expressing his loathing for everything about the party and its leaders. Bonner remembered that the girl in the Salon, Sara, had been told to get to work on him. Had anything happened; indeed, had the girl even tried? He frowned, drew out his pocket notebook and scribbled something. He looked around.

Heydrich was sitting bolt upright a few feet away, gazing intently at the stand where Hitler would soon make his speech. He had been asked to give his views on a draft of the Führer's message to the world that night. This was a privilege granted to only a few of the inner circle, and the honour was all the greater because it came from the Führer himself and not that clubfooted buffoon Goebbels. Hitler wanted to use barely coded rhetoric to signal the strike against the eastern neighbour. Goebbels had drafted a speech accordingly.

Then there was a change of mind. For the first time in their relationship, Heydrich had seen the Führer fretful and worried. Was he going too far, would such a speech drive the British and French to come to the aid of Czechoslovakia? He had posed the question to Heydrich directly because he knew the man he had promoted to head the Gestapo was a master of detail. Heydrich had taken care to inform himself about the military progress of the armed forces since the rearmament programme had begun in 1935.

Hitler had sat drumming his fingers on the leather arm of the chair in his study at the Reich Chancellery, waiting for the reply. It was one of the difficulties of dealing with the chancellor that while his questions were usually framed with a long perambulation through recent European history, beginning and ending with the iniquities of the Versailles treaty, he expected short, decisive answers.

In this case, it was impossible to give a straight answer. Heydrich knew – they all knew – that the generals were not ready for war. The Czechs had a good army and modern equipment. Their border defences were strong. They were a tough people, and behind them stood Britain and France, and maybe even Russia. A war in the autumn of 1938 was unthinkable. Yet that was exactly what Hitler appeared intent on unleashing in his speech. He wanted to give his generals the signal to begin Case Green.

Heydrich answered the question respectfully, thanking the Führer for asking his opinion while desperately trying to think of an answer that would satisfy his leader's evident desire for an early war. He quoted an old German proverb: "You do not have to climb a tree to pluck the ripest apple."

Hitler beamed. He understood this brilliant young man perfectly. He liked the way he had drawn such wisdom from somewhere deep in Germany's rich cultural past. He had watched with admiration as Heydrich had expanded the range and operations of the secret police. He ran the Gestapo without fear, without forgiveness and without mercy.

Heydrich was also smiling as he left the chancellor. On the spur of the moment he had simply made up the quotation. As he looked around the stadium that night, he caught Goebbels's eye a few seats away and smiled. The propaganda chief would never have dreamt of fooling Hitler in such a fashion.

Bonner shifted in his chair and rather wished he too had bought a hip flask like Halliday. The Führer liked taking risks and he usually judged them well: the march in the Rhineland had been a masterstroke based on the correct assessment that the French were too weak politically to react to anything but a full-scale invasion. The Austrian Anschluss was based on a similar reading of the resolve of the major European powers. No one wanted another war – and after all, Austria was German in all but name, was it not? But Case Green was a move too far.

The Gestapo had reported mutinous talk at senior officer level, but Heydrich had dismissed it, saying soldiers and their officers always complained about everything – especially in peacetime. Bonner was not so sure. Beck had resigned, but Hitler had not dared announce the fact, fearful of reaction from his own party. Beck was popular, a regular career soldier who had won many military honours in the last war. He had agreed to keep quiet, but that might not last.

Above all, Bonner wished to get back to Berlin. There was work to do there, files to read, intelligence to evaluate, interrogation sessions to supervise. And there was that girl Sara. He needed to see her. She had not delivered of late; something was wrong. It was her brother, of course, but he was safe enough. He thought of his own wife and two sons, Franz and Tomas, safely tucked away in that two-storey suburban home with their mother. She was a good woman, Trudi, and an excellent cook. She had made a good home for him and the boys. How old was Franz now? Eleven, and football mad. He would do better at school if he didn't spend all his time reading about Bayern Munich in the sporting magazines. And Tomas, just nine, the quiet one, very much his mother's pet. Bonner would be home from this political orgy – and that was how he thought of it – tomorrow night. He needed to see his boys; they kept him sane. And he needed Trudi too. But he wanted that woman in the Salon. That was the problem.

His thoughts were broken by a roar of "*Sieg Heil!*" as Hitler ascended the steps to the plinth only a few feet away from him and stood at the rostrum. The searchlights that had been beamed into the night now swung down. Some were trained on the plinth, illuminating the Nazi leadership in a glaring white light, while others held the giant swastika above them in a fierce spotlight.

Hitler's deputy, Rudolf Hess, stepped up to the rostrum three times to introduce Hitler, but on each occasion he was forced to step back by the cheers and chants that rose in waves from the stadium.

Finally he managed to bellow out: "*Und jetzt . . . Unser Führer!*"

Hitler positioned himself at the rostrum, placed a sheaf of notes on the slanted lectern and waited for the noise to die down. The cheering and chanting continued until he raised his hands, commanding attention, and the crowd fell silent.

Then came the long pause. They all knew this was the way he began, with a moment of silence while he looked out into the starlit night above him and down at the torchlights bobbing amid an ocean of faces below. Goebbels had taught him this technique, drawing on the work of American specialists in the art of public speaking.

Goebbels had never been to America but had learnt from the work of the big advertising agencies on Madison Avenue in New York. The use of symbols and slogans, the techniques of projecting short messages on billboards that clicked with the hopes and fears in the subconscious mind, these were skills that were constantly being improved in New York, Washington and Los Angeles. Goebbels had ordered all German diplomatic and consular officials in the US to report on the evolving techniques, especially those involving speech therapists used by politicians in Washington and the big stars in Hollywood.

He drummed into Hitler the key lesson: make them wait, make them want you, build the sense of anticipation until the audience almost begs you to begin. After that, Goebbels was fond of quoting the old Hollywood maxim that the way to grab an audience was to give them an earthquake in the first reel and then build to a climax. But Goebbels didn't attribute the quote to its originator, the studio boss Sam Goldwyn. Goldwyn was Jewish.

Hitler had learnt well; he knew that when he finally began it would be with words that would bind his audience and the nation to him and make them recognise what they all knew to be true, that he was their saviour. That night in Nuremberg in 1938, the German chancellor opened with lines that might have been taken from a love letter.

"That you have found me among so many millions is the miracle of our time, and that I have found you means that together we can be sure of Germany's future. You, the German people, can be happy that the chaos of the past is over. We now have a fixed star to guide us."

Bonner could see Goebbels beaming with pleasure as the words echoed over the stadium, just as he knew they would echo throughout the capitals of Europe. The propaganda chief had written the speech and made sure that every major news organisation was in Nuremberg that night to hear it. The correspondents of all the great newspapers were at a long table below the plinth, taking notes and talking into telephones.

Newsreel cameras, whose footage would soon be shown in cinemas around the world, were filming the event from the front row of the crowd. They had come to hear a master orator make war on his enemies, and they were not disappointed.

Hitler quickly set aside the romantic sentiments with which he had opened the speech. He turned to the target for that night, the enemy he intended to crush first with his oratory and then with his army. Waving clenched fists at the crowd and raising his voice in rage at the injustice and humiliation heaped on his fellow Germans across the border, he bellowed his anger at Czechoslovakia and its leader, President Beneš.

The phrases thundered over the stadium, each building in a crescendo of hatred in which Beneš and his nation were pilloried as bloodthirsty tyrants persecuting a helpless German minority.

Hitler paused for dramatic effect every few minutes, allowing the crowd to match his rhetoric with roars of "*Sieg Heil! Sieg Heil!*"

They would fall quiet again as the figure on the rostrum raised both hands, nodding his head in appreciation and looking down at his typewritten notes. Then the hoarse voice, magnified by dozens of speakers around the stadium, would fill the night again.

Bonner could see, as did Macrae a few rows behind him, that the effect on the crowd was hypnotic. Weary after two days of festive propaganda, people were now slipping into a state of narcosis. The torchlights around them, the fierce light on the speaker and above all the simple repeated slogans that were bellowed back and forth from the speaker to the crowd seemed to have left the entire arena in a trancelike state.

Macrae stared at Hitler's back, watching the arms rise and fall like those of a marionette, listening to the crash as clenched fists slammed into the rostrum and seeing the silvery spray of spittle in the glare of the searchlights. He grasped an elemental truth at that moment that he had never heard mentioned before. The mass hypnosis was carefully planned, that was evident, but the man who most notably succumbed to the narcotic effect of the occasion, the man who was himself projected into a hypnotic trance, was Hitler himself. The leader of the Third German Reich had worked himself up into such a state of fury, and had so bewitched himself with his jumbled sloganeering, that he had left the real world and become a mindless creature of his own dark night.

Macrae looked across to Sir Nevile Henderson. The ambassador sat there with a broad smile, gazing at Hitler, it seemed to Macrae, with admiration. The rest of the visiting dignitaries and the Nazi leadership looked spellbound, like children at a Christmas party when Father Christmas has appeared. Only at the far end of the seating did the row after row of military officers look less than impressed. They had heard it all before. But this night they were waiting for the coded command to begin Case Green.

To their surprise and that of everyone present in Nuremberg that night, 12 September 1938, Hitler held back. The menace and the threats were there, as was the undisguised racial hatred of the Slavonic people, who were derided as the Jews of Europe. But as the diplomats, the army and the senior Nazis present noted, Hitler did not commit himself openly to war that night. He demanded justice for the German population in Sudetenland and left it at that.

Later that night, as Macrae joined the crowds streaming from the stadium, he felt two hands descending on his shoulder. He tried to twist around but could not turn against the grip.

He glimpsed an army uniform and heard a low hissed whisper.

"Where are your ships? Where is the British fleet?" The grip was released. Macrae turned to see Koenig walking away from him, pushing through the crowd.

"Friend of yours?" Halliday had fallen in beside him. Both were hoping for a lift to their hotel in Nuremberg with the ambassador, but this was an offer that Sir Nevile must have forgotten, because there was no sign of him.

"No," said Macrae.

"He looked a worried man," said Halliday.

Not for the first time, Macrae wondered just how much Halliday knew and who he was really working for.

"I think we're all worried, aren't we?" he said carefully.

"What worries me is not this lot here," said Halliday, "it's the home team."

"Home team?"

"Number 10. The PM and his merry men will be running around like rabbits after this. Something in my water tells me that they are going to do something really, really stupid."

14

The news that the British prime minister had flown to Germany for a face-to-face meeting with Hitler broke like a bombshell around Europe. It was just three days after the Nuremberg speech and this was Britain's response. Headlines from Moscow to Madrid heralded the initiative as a new era of peace in Europe, while politicians and diplomats scrambled to identify the real significance of what was widely described in the press as a masterstroke of diplomacy.

As he flew to Munich, Chamberlain congratulated himself both on what *The Times* had called a diplomatic bolt of lightning and on the Machiavellian skill with which he had handled his cabinet.

The morning after the Führer's Nuremberg outburst, Chamberlain had summoned an informal meeting of his inner circle of ministers shortly before the full cabinet assembled. Headlines in every paper across the continent had reported Hitler's venomous attacks on Czechoslovakia. As Lord Halifax, Sir John Simon and Sir Samuel Hoare stepped into 10 Downing Street, the BBC was reporting an uprising of the German ethnic minority in Sudetenland. Martial law was declared as the Czech government clamped an iron hand on the riots and demonstrations.

Across Germany, radio stations amplified reports in the morning press with detailed accounts of atrocities committed against German speakers across the border. The reports of rape and pillage were so colourful, and so similar in detail, that it was clear that they had been fabricated within the Propaganda Ministry on Wilhelmstrasse. But Joseph Goebbels, the street-sharp outsider who had been crippled by polio as a child and forced to conceal his disability during years of bullying at school, knew the value of an oft-told lie. The fiction of Czech brutality against helpless German women and children was repeated until it became fact.

Britain's official policy of appeasement lay in ruins; at least, that is the way it appeared to the press and most of the government. Chamberlain took an entirely different view. An untitled brown folder lay before ministers as they took their seats in the Cabinet Room. This was unusual, and Lord Halifax looked sharply at the prime minister. The foreign secretary didn't like changes to the official routine of government business, and he didn't like surprises. He suspected the folder contained both. He opened it, to see a typewritten agenda.

The first eight items concerned routine reports. A number of British warships in Scapa Flow had been brought out of the reserve in which they had effectively been mothballed since the last war. Crews of the 7th Destroyer Flotilla had been summoned from leave and returned to full complement. There was a question about the need to improve cipher facilities at the embassy in Berlin.

Halifax and his ministerial colleagues round the table stiffened as they saw that item nine was described simply as "The Z Plan". Item ten was "Publicity for the Z Plan".

Sir Neville Chamberlain watched as his most loyal ministers scanned the agenda and turned to him with questioning faces. The Z Plan was his initiative, his answer to Herr Hitler, and it carried with it his hopes for preventing a second world war. He alone, Neville Chamberlain, prime minister of Great Britain, would take responsibility for the high risk it entailed. But he could not argue the case for the Z Plan to his full cabinet alone. He needed his most trusted ministers with him when he put the plan to what he suspected would be a sceptical, if not hostile, meeting later that morning.

"May I suggest we take items one to eight as read and approved and move to item nine." The dry tones of Lord Halifax elicited nods around the table.

Chamberlain turned to his new cabinet secretary, Edward Bridges, who had been told of the Z Plan. Bridges was a civil servant whose orderly mind mirrored the workings of the antique clocks on the mantelpiece. The difference was that the clocks told the prime minister the right time. The cabinet secretary merely told him he was right.

"Yes, of course," said Chamberlain. For a man as certain as he was of the righteousness of his political principles, and especially of the inarguable case for his appeasement policy, he felt unusually nervous. Sir Robert Vansittart was in the room. The powerful permanent under-secretary at the Foreign Office had made and unmade more than one foreign secretary in previous governments, and had recently drifted dangerously close to criticising government policy in relation to Germany.

Chamberlain cleared his throat, took hold of his lapels and leant forward in his chair, looking in turn at his ministers as he spoke.

"Gentlemen, I intend to ask our ambassador in Berlin to convey a message this morning to Herr Hitler. I will offer to fly immediately to Germany to conduct face-to-face negotiations, to settle once and for all his territorial claims. I have studied his speech last night at Nuremberg and he has not done anything irrevocable. Herr Hitler has opened the door to peace, gentlemen, and I intend to step through it."

There was a pause as ministers sought to understand what they had just been told. More than one of them thought that this was a premature and undignified reaction to a crisis that had yet to unfold. But they said nothing.

"With cabinet approval, of course?" said Vansittart.

"Of course; that is why we are here. I want to take soundings with you all first. By the way, have we heard from the French?"

Vansittart realised the prime minister had been made aware of the cable that morning from the French premier, Édouard Daladier. The government in Paris had been unable to decide how to act in the event of German aggression against Czechoslovakia, a nation it was bound by treaty to defend. Daladier had appealed to Chamberlain to strike whatever bargain was necessary with Hitler to prevent just such action.

"Yes, Prime Minister," said Vansittart wearily. "The French are out of the game. The ball is in our court."

And that, he reflected, gave Chamberlain a free hand to launch a diplomatic mission that would probably encourage the very war it was designed to prevent. Chamberlain had been clever. The one minister with the weight to oppose him, the secretary of state for war, Sir Leslie Hore-Belisha, had not been asked to attend the informal meeting. Hore-Belisha would speak at the full cabinet but, whatever his criticism, he would find little support. The prime minister would justify his one-man diplomacy in the name of securing a lasting European peace. Few would have the nerve to argue with that.

Vansittart played the only card left in his hand.

"With respect, I suggest you don't send a message to the German chancellor saying you are prepared to fly immediately to meet him. It sends the wrong signal."

"And what signal would you like me to send him?"

"Mobilise the fleet. Send our capital ships into the North Sea. Have them deploy within sight of the German coast. Show Hitler that if he attacks Czechoslovakia he will face, at the very least, a naval blockade."

Those present in the room would remember for a long time the face of the prime minister as he reacted to this statement. The grey pallor that characterised Chamberlain's features suffused into a deep red. Sir John Simon told his wife later that evening that the prime minister's salt-and-pepper moustache seemed to darken and bristle.

The prime minister spoke slowly, chopping his reply into words of almost one syllable, like a headmaster talking to an errant schoolboy.

"Have you not read the reports from our ambassador in Berlin – of whose appointment to that post two years ago I believe you personally approved? Are you aware that Sir Nevile Henderson has advised that any further threats or warnings to Herr Hitler will push him over the edge, if not of madness then of mad action? Are these warnings of no account? Do they mean nothing to you?"

Vansittart had never been spoken to in such a manner in the Cabinet Room, least of all in front of his colleagues. He was framing a suitably curt reply when Sir John Simon spoke.

"Assuming cabinet approval, when would you go?"

Chamberlain smiled benignly on his home secretary. He could see that he and his colleagues were reacting well to his lightning stroke of diplomacy. Vansittart had been neutralised and would not be invited to full cabinet later that day.

"The day after tomorrow. I have never travelled in an aeroplane, but I am told that the flight will take only three hours and that the weather is good."

An hour later, Chamberlain repeated his plans to the full cabinet.

To his slight surprise, he carried his ministers without dissent. It was only when he revealed that he had already sent a message to Sir Nevile Henderson asking him to arrange the meeting with Hitler that there was a rumble of irritation around the table. The prime minister had clearly pre-empted cabinet approval, but these were dangerous times and despite the breach of constitutional protocol and the risks of a humiliating diplomatic disaster, there was unanimous agreement. Their sixty-nine-year-old leader would make his maiden flight in forty-eight hours, flying to Munich for talks with the German chancellor.

In the British embassy in Berlin, the staff were as surprised by the news as anyone. The previous night, Sir Nevile Henderson had left by train for Munich, where he was to meet Chamberlain's plane. He was unaccompanied and had told no one the reason for his journey.

Macrae and Halliday found themselves in the ambassador's outer office with David Buckland and staff from the press-relations section. They were all trying to respond to an avalanche of calls from newspapers and radio stations. The two phones on the secretary's desk in the outer office were ringing furiously and a teleprinter machine in the corner was clattering out reams of copy. The secretary herself was close to tears. All she could tell them was that Sir Nevile

Henderson had left on a late train to Munich the previous evening and he had told her to keep his journey absolutely secret.

Halliday steered Macrae to an empty office. The two men sat down. They had heard the news of Chamberlain's mission to meet Hitler only an hour earlier, on German state radio.

"Well?" said Macrae.

"Man's a genius," said Halliday.

"You're mad!" said Macrae. "Time you went home."

Halliday smiled. "I'm talking about Hitler. He's got the British prime minister on bended knee, desperate to strike any bargain, make any concession, sacrifice any territory, as long as it's not ours, of course; anything as long as he can go home and say . . ." Halliday stood up and raised his arms to the ceiling. "'Peace, my friends! Peace! I have achieved peace!'"

Halliday sat down. "I don't even think the bastard knows how clever he is."

"Go on."

"Because he's put the kibosh on those plans your friends have."

Chamberlain's sudden arrival in Germany had been such a surprise that Macrae had forgotten about Koenig. He would have been trying to get in touch, trying to understand if there was a devilish subplot to the dramatic news of Chamberlain's mission. Halliday was right. Britain had played the peace card, allowing Hitler to play for time. There was no chance the army would move now.

"See you later," Halliday said.

15

Joachim Bonner sat in his office, trying to make sense of the press reports clattering in on the tape machine from Munich. There were Union Jacks flying alongside the swastika on the main road from the airport. The official cars taking Neville Chamberlain and his party to the railway station had been cheered by people along the route. Men old and young had raised their hats to the British party and women had waved scarves and handkerchiefs. The news had seemed so unlikely that Bonner had phoned Gestapo headquarters in Munich asking for confirmation. He had been told that people were overjoyed at the prospect of peace and that in the bars and cafés toasts were being raised both to Hitler and, more significantly, to the British prime minister.

Bonner called Hilde into his office. The woman would have a view on the situation and he was curious to know what it was.

"What do you think of this business of the British prime minister suddenly flying to see the Führer?"

Hilde thought for a moment and said, "I lost my father in the last war. Would you like a coffee?"

He watched her leave, swinging that rounded rear at him as if in invitation. She was clever and probably capable of great cruelty. She never raised an eyebrow when the occasional scream penetrated the office. She had also shown an interest in the reports of the interrogation sessions and had once asked if there were any opportunities for training and a transfer to an operational department. He had turned her down because she was too useful to him; anyway, finding someone you could trust with the intelligence that crossed his desk wasn't easy. But he knew that she was due for training and promotion. Men broke under torture and interrogation more quickly when a woman asked the questions and inflicted the pain. Statistics gathered over the last five years had proved the point, but not many women liked the job. Hilde would. She was tough. And Hilde, like everyone else in Germany, it seemed, wanted peace.

Bonner thought for a while. What would the Gestapo do if there were peace in Europe? Suppose the British, those romantic dreamers in that soggy island of theirs, actually persuaded the Führer to accept the Sudetenland in exchange for a peace treaty? What would the Nazis and their National Socialist Party do? Beat their swords into ploughshares, turn their tanks into cars? Dig up all the mines laid along the border with France? What would happen to the new Me 109 fighter that was supposed to outfly anything the British could put in the air? And that advanced long-range artillery gun that Krupp was bringing into production? Above all, what would happen to people like him, whose whole career had been based on the detection and suppression of opposition to the regime? Where would an outbreak of peace and prosperity leave the communists, the anarchists, the fascist-hating leftists and all those feeble-minded sexually confused critics of National Socialism in the media and the arts? Was it conceivable that the sworn enemies of the Reich would salute a man who had restored German pride, united its people and committed his great nation to peace and prosperity?

Bonner relaxed and reached for a cigarette. Hilde didn't like him smoking in the office, but with luck she had taken her fat arse off to the canteen for coffee. It wasn't going to happen. Peace was unthinkable. Every single step that the Führer had taken since he came to power in 1933 pointed in one direction. You didn't have to be a genius to see that deep in Hitler's gut was a craving for war, a visceral yearning to avenge the humiliation of 1918.

Perhaps if you plumbed the depths of the man, you would find another dark secret, a desire to extinguish memories of a shameful past, when he lived rough on the streets of Vienna in those years when the city was an imperial capital. There, little better off than the beggars crouched outside the opera house pleading for coins, the young Führer had failed at everything he tried to do, especially his pathetic efforts to become an architect. Like most in the Gestapo, Bonner knew the history well, although Goebbels had been careful to destroy the records and sanitise biographies for public consumption.

The fact was that Adolf Hitler was a broken failure of a young man when he joined up in 1914. In the trenches of Flanders, where he ran messages under fire, he suddenly discovered that he could do something useful. That is when a nobody who had done nothing and meant nothing to anyone suddenly became a somebody. He had won an Iron Cross 2nd Class, although no one knew exactly what it was for, and at the end of the war they were dishing the medals out like rations just to keep the troops going. Still, Hitler loved his medal. He was said to keep it in a purple velvet-lined box on his dressing table and prop it up so that he could see it first thing in the morning. He wore it on every occasion, especially when meeting foreign dignitaries.

No, peace wasn't going to happen. In any case, there would always be the communists and the Jews. The reds would never give up the struggle, and as for the Jews, the Gypsies and the Roma, there was going to be no peace for them and plenty of work for a policeman, a secret policeman, of his calibre.

Bonner put out his cigarette, tipped the contents of the ashtray into the waste bin and walked to the window. He wondered what Reinhard Heydrich would make of the Munich talks. Knowing his boss, he would dismiss the whole exercise as a stunt designed to throw dust into the eyes of the British. And Heydrich was probably right. He knew better than anyone that there wasn't going to be peace. All that man wanted was to get on with his work and his womanising. His work was now concentrated on the Jews and their future. Heydrich had a whole department working on ways of speeding up their forced emigration.

Their ill-treatment had intensified, with carefully organised street beatings, confiscation of property, public abuse of their womenfolk. Despite all that, far too many clung to the country they had lived in for centuries. Heydrich had demanded an answer to the problem in meeting after meeting with his senior staff. How are we going to get rid of this scum floating on the clear waters of our Aryan race? Everyone suspected that Heydrich himself had formulated answers but was seeking ideas that might match his own so that he could present the Führer with an agreed Gestapo solution to the problem.

There were vague reports that a number of two-ton commercial lorries capable of carrying thirty to forty people at a time had been fitted with new sides and canopies to make them airtight. Tubes had been designed to clamp over the exhaust pipes and inject the poisonous carbon monoxide into the interior. There were said to have been successful tests on sheep and pigs, which had died within minutes of being gassed. Those were the rumours, but even in Gestapo headquarters few believed that Heydrich would go that far.

The solution to the Jewish Problem was to strip them of their property and valuables and expel them en masse. That seemed to be the consensus among his colleagues, but Bonner was not so sure. When it came to the Jewish question, nothing was beyond the Obergruppenführer of the Gestapo and the SS. Hitler did not call him a man with an iron heart for nothing. Thinking of Heydrich reminded Bonner that he had received no recent reports from the Salon. It was a project in which the Gestapo boss took a close interest. He pressed the bell to call Hilde.

The humiliation of the British prime minister began the moment his plane landed at Munich airport on the morning of 15 September. He was met by the foreign minister, Joachim von Ribbentrop, a man who had openly declared his hostility to Britain and its empire. The limp handshake, the cursory greeting, the lack of any diplomatic nicety told their own story. Chamberlain and his ambassador were driven to the railway station for a three-hour journey to the small town of Berchtesgaden in the Alps. On the journey, the train passed several troop trains full of cheering soldiers – a deliberate reminder of the war that was waiting in the wings of the meeting with the chancellor that day.

The prime minister and a small party of officials were given just thirty minutes at a local hotel before a fleet of cars took them on the short drive up winding roads to the Berghof, Hitler's mountain retreat.

The Führer was waiting at the top of a steep flight of steps. The greeting was carefully orchestrated. Hitler, in uniform and wearing his peaked army hat, leant down with an outstretched arm to shake the hand of the prime minister, who was forced to look up at him from the bottom of the steps. Chamberlain too was smiling, but he looked old and tired, a compliant figure come to beg for peace from a young warlord.

The cameras flashed, capturing the moment on film and photograph. The results were flown to Berlin, where they were shown in cinema newsreels to crowded audiences that night. The next morning's papers across Europe all carried the same photograph of a beaming Führer, the swastika armband prominent on left arm, the Iron Cross glinting, looking down on his elderly guest.

"It's an absolute bloody disaster and, you know something, it's going to get a whole lot worse."

Halliday raised his glass and accepted another generous measure of whisky. He looked around the guests seated in the sitting room of the Shirers' Berlin apartment. Noel Macrae was there with Primrose, Percy Black from the US embassy with his wife Joan. William Shirer was in the kitchen fixing a special dish from Cedar Rapids in Iowa, where he had spent his childhood. Every now and then there was a crash from the kitchen followed by the sound of muffled curses. The dinner had been a long time coming and Theresa Shirer had spent almost an hour pouring drinks, apologising for the delay and darting into the kitchen to help her husband. It was her first dinner party in their new home, and her husband had warned her that their English guests were heavy drinkers.

"Does William want any help?" asked Primrose.

"He's trying to cook a pork dish with apples that his mother used to make and I am afraid he's having trouble remembering the recipe. It shouldn't be long."

"We can always eat out, if that helps," said Halliday. He was hungry and never saw the point in eating late.

"No, no, I am sure he won't be long," said Theresa, leaving the room.

There was a silence during which a whispered argument in the kitchen became embarrassingly audible. The guests resumed their conversation but in rather louder tones to cover the growing volume of argument in the kitchen.

"I don't know why you're all so critical. He's trying to prevent a war; surely that's an honourable thing for a politician to do? Anyway, he's our prime minister – shouldn't we support him?" Primrose looked at Halliday, framing her question with a frown.

"He's prostrating himself before a man who is bent on war. Our prime minister is an embarrassment, frankly."

"That's a bit steep, Roger," said Primrose. She liked Halliday because, like most women who met him, she thought his chaotic clothes, his destructive alcoholism and the brilliant mind of an intelligence agent were masks to conceal a wayward child looking for his mother. She also felt protective towards a man forced by moral convention to conceal his sexuality.

She turned to her husband. "What do you think, Noel?"

Before Macrae could reply there was another crash from the kitchen. Shirer emerged, sweaty-faced and wearing a smeared apron. The strong odour of burnt meat followed him into the room. He ripped off his apron, went to the sideboard, poured himself a drink.

"Every night back home my mother would cook strips of pork layered with apples and surrounded by caramelised onions, carrots and corn. A classic Cedar Rapids dish," he said. "She taught me how to cook it, and damn me if I haven't forgotten. I am sorry, folks, we'll have to eat out."

They were both drunk when they undressed for bed that night. Macrae watched as Primrose struggled out of her clothes, flinging them across the room at a wicker laundry basket before collapsing into bed.

The dinner had been a pointless affair when they had finally found a restaurant with a table for seven. Theresa Shirer kept apologising to no one in particular while trying to explain that her husband should have cooked a deep pan pizza, which would have been easy because she had the pastry bases in the freezer.

No one listened. Shirer had launched into a long conversation with Percy Black about the isolationist movement in America and the New Deal politics of Roosevelt's second administration. Halliday had fallen into a drunken stupor at the table and left before the first course had arrived. Primrose had talked to Joan Black about the Aztec ruins in Mexico, which they had both visited when students.

Mrs Black had said, "Mexico is little more than a bandit country now. Hard to think how they could have produced such beauty – I mean all those pyramids, temples and stepped terraces."

Primrose said, "That's the trouble with genius, it doesn't get passed down – look at Shakespeare."

Mrs Black had seemed puzzled by this remark, and Macrae saw that Primrose herself was surprised by what she had said.

"I don't know much about Shakespeare," said Mrs Black. "Did he have children?"

Primrose laughed and said, "I'm talking rubbish. He had a boy called Hamnet but I think he died when young. Have we ordered, by the way?"

After Halliday's departure Macrae had found himself isolated from these conversations. He sat back, letting his mind drift. He had not heard from Koenig since their brief encounter at Nuremberg earlier in the week. Chamberlain had returned to London after three hours of talks with Hitler, to consult the cabinet. The next meeting was scheduled to take place at Bad Godesberg on the Rhine in a week's time. No one knew what had been discussed or agreed between the leaders, but the peace diplomacy led by Britain and supported by France was gaining momentum. A provocative deployment of the fleet off the German coast was out of the question.

Somewhere in this tangle of diplomacy and deceit, Colonel Florian Koenig and his co-conspirators were making fresh plans – or perhaps they had decided to abandon the whole risky venture. Either way, he knew Koenig would feel betrayed by the British – Perfidious Albion all over again.

Primrose was lying on the bed wearing only a light dressing gown. Her eyes were closed, but he knew she was not asleep.

"I need to talk to Florian," he said. "Have you seen him lately?"

Primrose opened her eyes.

"No, why would I?" she said, staring at the ceiling.

"I thought you two had become quite friendly," said Macrae.

They paused, husband and wife gauging the direction of a conversation that could either lead to another violent exchange or wither into silence. It was late, they had drunk too much as usual and neither wanted to confront a truth evident to both.

"Why would I see him before you do?"

"I don't know. I'm just saying I need to speak to him. It's important."

They left it like that, her infidelity acknowledged but ignored, his the greater deceit. He knew that, for Primrose, Koenig was an adventure, an antidote to the boredom of Berlin, an escape from the tedium of the marriage bed.

He found it extraordinary that his wife should be bored in a city where great issues of war and peace were being decided, where anyone with the faintest interest in human psychology could witness intelligent, ambitious men from decent professional families utterly corrupted by power and drunk on dreams of national redemption from the shame of the past.

Some of the greatest Catholic families of Germany had lost sons to the Nazi Party, young men equipped by school and church with a coat of a moral armour that had been corroded by the ideology of racial nationalism. How could anyone not be interested in seeing this tapestry of evil being woven right in front of them? Yet Primrose clearly yearned to be back home in England, far from the mindless conversational pleasantries of the diplomatic round of drinks and dinners, and far from the swastikas and the jackboots.

How easily we lie to ourselves, Macrae thought; because that wasn't true, was it? His wife yearned not for England but to be with her lover, the colonel who was trying to plot the downfall of the Third Reich. That was where she wanted to be, in his arms, in his bed, her heart thudding, her sweat cooling on his skin, inhaling the exotic scent of a man destined for martyrdom.

16

Bonner asked the driver to drop him off half a mile from the Salon and then walked fast down late-evening streets. He was angry but he didn't want to show it when he reached the club. He wanted to control himself, because that was the only way to be in control. Lose your temper and you lose control – a very old police maxim that he had been taught in training school back in the days after the war, when police work was a straightforward job of tracking down anarchists and communists.

There had certainly been enough of them scurrying around like rats after the war. In those days the job was simple. You were given a name and address and told to make an arrest, then follow through with an interrogation, to make sure the criminal went to court with sufficient evidence against him to secure a conviction. When things went wrong in the interrogation – and they did – you opened the manhole cover in the street behind police headquarters and dropped the body into the sewage system. The system was simple, and it worked because everyone did as they were told. But it wasn't working now.

He pushed past the woman on the Salon's door, eliciting a stern rebuke. Even Gestapo officers were supposed to wait for a moment before the woman nodded approval.

He saw Sara immediately at the bar. She had her back to him and was talking to Kitty Schmidt. He allowed a woman to take his coat and walked over. Kitty turned and smiled. Sara stared ahead.

"Gruppenführer Bonner, we haven't seen you for a long time," said Kitty Schmidt. "What will you have?"

"I need a room," he said, nodding to the fanlight door. "And send me a bottle of whisky."

He took Sara by the arm, swinging her around so that she was forced to face him.

"And you'll join me," he said. "We have business to discuss."

"Are you sure?" she said.

He tightened his grip on her arm, squeezing hard.

"Yes," he hissed. "I am very sure."

Sara looked at Kitty, who nodded and said, "Room fourteen."

They went through the fanlight door and past several girls talking to men in the Pink Room. Sara hurried down the corridor, conscious that Bonner was walking immediately behind her, almost literally breathing down her neck. She knew he was angry and she knew why.

Once in the room, Bonner grabbed her by both shoulders and threw her onto the bed. She bounced back immediately and came at him, swinging tightly clenched fists. He grasped an arm, twisted her round and slammed her against the wall. He leant into her neck.

"Where are the tapes, the recordings, the photographs?"

"I don't know what you're talking about."

He pulled her back and slammed her head into the wall again.

"Yes, you do. The Englishman, he was here. You were with him. In the room. You were talking to him at the bar. I've heard he had his hands all over you. You took him here. I want to know what happened."

"Nothing happened. He wanted to talk about his wife. They all do."

"Why were the tapes turned off?"

"I don't know. Probably a technical problem. It happens all the time."

"You're lying!"

He spun her round, twisted her dress in his fist and slapped her hard with the back of his hand.

"Get your clothes off."

Sara wiped blood and snot from her nose.

"Fuck off."

He pulled her back, ripping the dress again. She tried to knee him in the groin and bite his arm. He slapped her hard twice with the open palm and back of his hand, bringing more blood from her nose and mouth. He stepped back.

"I said, take your clothes off."

She stood up. There were tears in the dark eyes, and beneath streaks of blood her face was the colour of paper. She was shaking as she undressed. Bonner reminded himself that he had intended to keep calm and not lose his temper. Still, a little slapping would hardly harm the girl. She needed it. She was an arrogant bitch. There was something about her he couldn't fathom, a look of contempt in her eyes suggesting that she was his superior. He watched her undress until her clothes were on the floor, then pushed her back on the bed.

"I want to know what happened," he said.

"Fucking bastard," she said. "What have you done to my brother?"

"Your brother is a piece of shit. What happened with the Englishman?"

"He wouldn't take the pills."

"Liar."

"He watched his drink. He's a diplomat. They're trained."

"You had him here in this room and you just talked about his wife? For Christ's sake, what have you got between your legs? You think it's private? It's not. It's mine, ours, it belongs to the party and you use it when we tell you to."

"Is that what I am going to say to Obergruppenführer Reinhard Heydrich? That my cunt is yours, too? I wonder what he'll think of that!"

She sat up on the bed, laid both hands on her pubic mound and smiled at him through the tears, the snot and the blood on her face. Bonner knew he had lost. He had been a fool. Sara Sternschein might bed and betray important foreigners in these rooms, but that was business. When it came to the party, or more specifically the Gestapo, she was Reinhard Heydrich's Jewish whore, and his alone.

There was a knock on the door. Bonner looked through the spyhole and opened it. Someone passed him a tray with a bottle of scotch, two glasses and a jug of water. He poured a large measure for both of them. For a moment, he thought she was going to throw it back in his face.

He got a white fluffy dressing gown from the back of the door and threw it at her. He took out a cigarette case and offered her one. It was forbidden to smoke in the rooms. She got up, put on the dressing gown and used it to wipe blood from her face. She drank the whisky and accepted the cigarette. They were both playing a game, he thought, but she was well ahead of him.

"It is Heydrich who wants the Englishman," he said quietly. "That's why it's important."

"I know my brother is dead. That's what's important."

He wondered who had told her that. An informant in the police, a client here at the salon? Interesting, because it wasn't true.

"Your brother is alive," he said. "He is back in Buchenwald. He tried to escape. He's a smart boy. He almost got over the wire, but they caught him. He's going to cooperate with us. You should be pleased."

In fact, Joseph Sternschein had been badly beaten, put against a wall and shot – but they'd used blanks. It was an old trick. They wanted to break him, turn him and use him as a double.

"You're lying. I don't believe you."

"I don't care what you believe."

"I want to see a letter from him."

"You think I'm a fucking postman? Here, look at this."

He fumbled in his wallet and produced a small photo of good quality taken with a professional camera. There was Joseph, frail, thin, his ribs showing, a scar down one side of his face, cheeks hollowed out, looking like an old man. He was holding a copy of *Der Bild*. She could not see the date, but the front cover was dominated by a picture of Hitler at the Nuremberg rally. That had been only last week.

"When was this taken?" she whispered.

"You're not asking any more questions. Your brother is alive – for the time being. I want the truth about the Englishman."

"And I want the truth about my brother."

"I've told you. What more do you want?"

There was a silence.

"He wouldn't take the pills," she said.

Bonner finished his drink. She sat there on the chair a few feet away, the dressing gown half open so he could see the curve of her breasts and the creamy expanse of her thighs. Her brother was alive, but he wouldn't live long if he didn't cooperate. Neither would she, if Heydrich found out that she had somehow compromised the recording staff in the Salon. And he could guess how she had done that. He got up and left without a word.

At eight the next morning, Sara Sternschein joined the long queue outside the consular offices of the British embassy. The consulate, which occupied premises alongside the main building in Wilhelmstrasse, did not open for another hour. No provision had been made in the way of extra staff to cope with the number of people seeking visas or travel documents allowing entry to the United Kingdom. By nine, the queue stretched well down the street towards Unter den Linden. The German Foreign Ministry had objected to the unsightly scene, as had the Ministry of Propaganda across the road.

Jews were being forcibly encouraged to leave the country, but that did not mean that the authorities wanted foreign newspapers carrying photos and stories of them desperately queuing to acquire the necessary documents. The queue was therefore limited to fifty people. Those arriving after this number had been reached were given tickets and told to return that afternoon. The morning was warm but Sara wore a headscarf to cover the bruises on her face and to conceal her identity from those watching the embassy. They would be in the offices across the street recording all those in the queue. Later they would try to put names to faces.

She carried her British travel document in her bag. She needed more time now and planned to ask for an extension. Ahead of her, the queue was made up mostly of middle-aged women; all of them she judged to be Jewish. Their clothing was worn and stitched with the yellow star on the front. They all clutched large leather handbags that looked as if they had been handed down for generations.

Further down the street, at the main entrance to the embassy, she watched the diplomats, secretaries and other more lowly office staff arriving for the day's work. She knew he would be among them.

It was around eleven o'clock when Sara finally entered the consulate and was ushered into a brightly lit office containing two desks. The walls were lined with grey metal filing cabinets. A large framed photograph of King George VI hung over the door at one end of the room. At the other end, by a small high window, a round-faced clock ticked loudly.

At each desk sat a grey-haired middle-aged woman. One appeared utterly immobile and sat staring at a document. The other had her pen poised over a scatter of documents in front of her. Every few moments the pen descended, moved rapidly to write something and then rose again. There were no other staff in the room. Sara watched for what seemed like several minutes and then coughed loudly.

"Please sit down," said the woman with the pen, without looking up.

There were chairs in front of each desk. Sara sat in front of the woman who had spoken.

"Name and papers," said the woman, again without raising her head.

"Sara Sternschein. I wish to extend my permit to enter the United Kingdom," said Sara, and she pushed her document with the Foreign Office stamp and her German photo identity paper over the desk.

The woman studied her travel document briefly, then looked at her identity card. Her face reshaped itself with a frown that stretched from forehead to chin.

"Wait here," she said. She rose and walked through the door.

Sara looked at her watch. It was eleven thirty. She hadn't got home from the Salon until one in the morning and had risen at six thirty to make sure of a good place in the queue. She was exhausted and hungry. Breakfast had been coffee and some toast and jam. It seemed a long time ago.

She watched the clock on the wall until the hands moved to fifteen minutes before noon. She got up, flexing her arms backwards in a stretch, when a voice said, "Sit down, please."

The second woman had not raised her head and continued to stare intently at a document. The voice seemed to come from the far end of the room. Perhaps King George had commanded her to sit down, or maybe the clock had found a voice. Sara sat down.

Ten minutes later, the door opened and the woman with the pen beckoned Sara. She followed her through an ill-lit grey-painted corridor and then opened a door into the sudden luxury of a large hall overhung with two chandeliers, which illuminated a tiled mosaic floor. A broad, carpeted central staircase rose between portraits of whiskered dignitaries. There were people everywhere, well-dressed men in suits with briefcases, young women clutching files, older women with trays of tea, moving across the floor and vanishing behind various doors around the hall or going up and down the staircase.

Sara had read a translation of *Alice in Wonderland* as a little girl and now felt that she too had fallen down a rabbit hole into a world of mad hatters and March hares. She followed the consulate woman through a door that led into a room furnished with two comfortable armchairs and a sofa arranged around an unlit fireplace. Sara noticed that a pot of coffee and two cups had been placed on a table by the window.

"Miss Sternschein, sir," said the woman, and left.

"Thank you. Please have a seat," said a familiar voice.

Noel Macrae was standing by the fireplace, smiling at her.

She sat down, feeling faint and in need of a strong cup of coffee.

"What are you doing here?" she said.

"I rather thought I might ask you that question. I thought you had left."

"He's still alive."

"Who?"

"Joseph. They've still got him in Buchenwald."

She was sitting with her head in her hands, her voice muffled.

"You'd better have some coffee. Here."

He poured a cup, added two lumps of sugar and passed it to her.

"I came to extend my travel document. I can do that, can't I?"

She looked up at him, trying to reconcile the man in the dark suit, ironed shirt and tie and neatly combed hair with the man in the Tiergarten, the man she had made love to under the winter trees with their leafless branches, the man she had taken to her room at the Salon and watched as he shed his clothes and lay on the bed, the bed provided by the Geheime Staats Polizei for the purpose of blackmail, extortion and murder. But she had not played their game, she had made sure the tapes were turned off. They had made love slowly, awkwardly, then with a fury that flickered like a flame long after their sweating bodies had cooled.

"It could be difficult," he said. "The pass was only for two weeks. You told me you were leaving."

"And we said goodbye. I know. But I've told you, Joseph is alive. I can't leave now."

"Who told you that?"

"It doesn't matter. It's true. He showed me a photograph."

"He?"

"Bonner. In the Salon."

"Bonner – he's Gestapo, isn't he?"

"Yes. Very senior. But that's not the point. Joseph's alive. I can't leave."

"We were given good information that your brother had been shot."

"It was a lie. I was shown a photograph."

A sound louder than the distant hum of voices and feet clacking on the tiled floor beyond the door now filled the room. It was an urgent rattle.

Macrae moved from the mantelpiece and sat beside her. She was shaking, her coffee cup rattling against its saucer.

"You say Bonner showed you a photo?"

"Last night. He was asking about you, wanted to know why there had been no tapes."

He gently slid back her headscarf.

"And he did this?"

"Yes."

Macrae took the document and stood up.

"The photo could be a fake."

"It wasn't. It was him. He looked like a skeleton, but he's alive."

"It could just be a lie to keep you at the Salon."

She stared at the floor, still talking in a whisper.

"We're twins. I know he's alive."

"Because Bonner told you?"

"I think he's telling the truth."

"For God's sake, Sara, he's Gestapo!"

"So am I, if it comes to that."

"They forge documents, fix photographs. They're good at it."

She got up and looked at him. "He's alive. I just know it."

He took a step towards her, but she stepped back.

"I'll do what I can about this permit," he said.

"How long will it take?"

Macrae looked at the document, then up at the clock. It was almost noon.

"It shouldn't take more than a day. But what's the hurry? You're not leaving now, are you?"

Sara shook her head.

"Meet me in the Tiergarten tomorrow, then – well after dark, say nine."

"I'll be at the Salon."

"With those marks on your face?"

She looked at the mirror and touched the vivid bruises on her cheek.

"All right, make it ten."

It had been a good season for grouse shooting on the moors in the north of England and Scotland that year, and by mid-September there was promise of excellent sport in the coming weekends. So there was some grumbling among members of the British cabinet when they were summoned on Saturday following Neville Chamberlain's meeting with Hitler at the Berchtesgaden, to hear his report and decide on the next step. The newspapers had concluded that Chamberlain had been outmanoeuvred by the German leader and forced into more concessions over Czechoslovakia.

However, since the two had met in private with only an interpreter present, the reports were based on briefings by either side and thus contradictory. A private briefing paper circulated by Lord Halifax suggested a very different and more positive outcome. Either way, most cabinet members felt the meeting could well have waited until Tuesday for the usual cabinet session.

The news that a senior delegation of senior French ministers was arriving in London on Sunday to discuss joint guarantees to Czechoslovakia in the event of a German attack did not change this view. The French could wait until Monday as well.

The mood of the twenty ministers at Number 10 on a hot September Saturday was not improved when the prime minister launched into a long description of his wearying journey to meet Hitler in his mountain retreat. The flight had been an enjoyable experience, he said, the reception in Munich a deliberate snub, the following train journey uncomfortable and the final dash up the mountainside in a Mercedes frankly unnerving.

After Chamberlain's account of his talks with a man he described as "the commonest little dog you ever saw", it was Lord Halifax who summed up the British diplomatic position with a clarity that allowed everyone to break for lunch.

"Since one power dominates Europe and that power is Germany, we have no alternative but to surrender the Sudetenland region to the Nazis and submit to humiliation," he said.

This was not a view shared in the British embassy in Berlin, at least not by Sir Nevile Henderson, who had been present, although outside the room, at the first round of talks with Hitler. The ambassador had concluded that peace was not just a possibility but the likely outcome of the diplomatic initiative that he was masterminding with his friend and ally

Lord Halifax in London. The French had frankly given up. The American interest seemed to be to persuade European nations to raise their immigration quota for Jews from Germany without increasing their very own tight limit, and Russia was busy, as usual, purging its armed forces of the officer class.

This left the way clear to persuade President Beneš of Czechoslovakia to cede a large portion of his territory to Germany. It would not be easy, Henderson realised, but it could be done. He would be the man to make the president understand that without such a sacrifice they would all be consumed in the fires of another world war.

Henderson made a note of the phrase. It was not the cool language normally used by a senior diplomat, but that was exactly why it might make those hot-tempered Czechs realise that neither Britain nor France was going to bail them out.

It was exactly a week after Hitler's speech at Nuremberg. Sir Nevile walked the corridor from his private residence to his office, where his secretary briefed him on his diary for the week ahead and he was dismayed to learn that Colonel Macrae had managed to insert a meeting just before the main morning session with all senior staff.

He considered cancelling but rejected the idea. Macrae was a problem, but he had been effectively dealt with by the prime minister and would be transferred when the crisis was over.

The two men exchanged minimal greetings and did not shake hands. Macrae sat on a chair in front the ambassador's desk.

"Am I right in assuming that this conversation is of such a confidential nature that it cannot be raised in the staff meeting?" said Sir Nevile.

"I wish to apprise you of the balance of forces between Czechoslovakia and Germany and the likely outcome of any conflict between them. If you think that is a fit subject for the general staff meeting, I will of course raise the matter then."

"Is this new information?"

"It is up-to-date information of which, I believe, His Majesty's Government is not fully aware."

"You'd better go on then, but briefly, please."

"The Czech army has thirty-eight combat-ready divisions, of which fourteen are armoured and equipped with tanks of variable quality. The old T-21 is no match for what the Germans can put in the field, but the LT-35 light tank is a first-class weapon, especially in the hill country along the German border."

Macrae paused. The ambassador had placed the palms of his hands together as if in prayer and was gazing at the wall behind him.

"The Skoda armaments factory in Sudetenland is the largest in the world and it is turning out high-standard military hardware, from mortars to machine guns and heavy artillery. The Czechs have slipped a little in developing their air force but have numbers of the B-534s, which are the best fighter biplanes in any air force. Morale in all services is high."

"I appreciate the information, but what is your point?" The ambassador had placed his hands palm down on the desk, as if preparing to rise and leave.

"If I may finish, Ambassador. The fortifications along the border with Germany have been well designed in depth and consist of three lines of fixed emplacements and minefields capable of withstanding prolonged artillery barrage."

"Forgive me if I repeat myself, but what is your point, Colonel?"

"My point is that the German High Command knows all this. They will not, indeed dare not, attack Czechoslovakia while Prague controls the Sudetenland. It is crucial to the defence of the whole country, and the generals have already told Hitler they would not be able to penetrate it."

"Well, that is very interesting." Sir Nevile looked at his watch. "We have a meeting in a few minutes."

"A final point, Ambassador. If it is British diplomacy to strip Czechoslovakia of the Sudetenland, we will effectively deny them the ability to resist German invasion. If, however, we stand with the government in Prague, we will engineer a confrontation between Hitler and his army. His generals will never agree to a frontal attack against those defences."

"Ah yes, that is one of your favourite theories, this fantasy of a coup. Product of an overactive imagination, if I may say so."

"It is a fact, not a fantasy. Before I was allowed to address the full cabinet on the subject, I understand you cabled the prime minister saying that senior military sources had denied any disaffection within the High Command. Is that correct?"

"That is correct."

"May I ask who those sources were – between us, of course?"

"My sources remain confidential."

"May I suggest that those sources belong in the very realms of fantasy that you have just mentioned."

"Are you accusing me of lying to the British cabinet?"

"Not at all. I am merely suggesting that certain people might view the information in your cable to the PM as the product of an overactive imagination, that's all."

The ambassador and his attaché stared at one another in an unblinking gaze that to an onlooker might have revealed animosity provoked by a professional disagreement. Both men knew it went much further. They hated each other.

17

Summer refused to give way to autumn in Germany that September. In balmy weather, crowds thronged the pavement cafés in Berlin during the week and streamed out to the lakes around the city at the weekends. Brewers and ice-cream manufacturers reported record sales. Leni Riefenstahl's film *Olympia*, glorifying the 1936 Olympics in Berlin, had been released earlier in the year to critical acclaim and was still playing to packed cinemas across the country. The state-controlled press exulted in reports that the film had been admired in most Western countries for its technical and creative virtuosity.

To Macrae and most of the foreign diplomatic corps, it seemed that the German people would reach for any distraction to deafen themselves to talk of war. In the second week of the month, a hurricane had devastated the east coast of the United States, especially Long Island and southern New England, causing the deaths of six hundred people, many of whom were swept into the sea as huge waves pounded the shorelines.

The disaster eclipsed all other news in the German press and became a talking point for days. Goebbels flew film crews to America to report on the devastation and made sure the disaster was the lead item in cinema newsreels. It was whispered in the corridors of his ministry that he took pleasure in reminding the most powerful nation on earth that it was not immune from the heavy hand of Providence.

In France, Britain and America, public opinion had decided that despite the barrage of threats from Berlin, despite the fact that Czechoslovakia had ordered a partial mobilisation, despite the fact that Poland and Hungary were moving forces to the Czech frontier, anxious for territorial gains if the Germans should attack, there would be no war. It was as if the people of those countries had decided that collective willpower could dictate the course of history. It was a time of illusion, when the truth became whatever anyone chose to believe.

For Gruppenführer Bonner and his Gestapo colleagues in Prinz-Albrechtstrasse, the surrender to illusion became apparent when a major military parade through Berlin was met by sullen crowds who openly turned their backs on the sight of troops, tanks and towed artillery.

Hitler himself witnessed this rare public protest from his reviewing stand on Charlottenburger Chaussee. Crowds that had been bussed in to line the route melted into the trees and slipped away rather than greet the troops with the usual triumphant raised-arm salutes and cries of "*Sieg Heil!*"

To the Gestapo, this was disturbing evidence that the Führer had lost his popular appeal and, worse still, had aroused active hostility among his own supporters. Even the ever loyal Reinhard Heydrich was worried. He ordered teams of agents to sift through photographs and film of the crowds, trying to identify known subversives. There were none to be found, which was hardly a surprise, as Bonner pointed out, because all such troublemakers had long ago been locked up or liquidated.

"Are you telling me this was a spontaneous demonstration by ordinary people against war and against the Führer?" Heydrich demanded. He had called a meeting of his senior staff to review the apparent show of disloyalty.

"Those are your words, not mine," said Bonner, allowing himself a smile.

Heads nodded in agreement around the table. It was not often Heydrich was wrong-footed in this way.

The next day, radio and press coverage reported huge crowds in Berlin applauding the troops and a beaming Hitler was pictured on the front pages returning their salutes with his own.

Macrae had actually watched the parade and seen Hitler frowning as the crowds refused to show any enthusiasm for the military and their hardware. Hitler had turned halfway through the march-past and begun a long, whispered conversation with Goebbels and Göring.

Macrae had observed the three men through field glasses from his balcony. As usual, Goebbels was doing the talking. Hitler, head bent, was listening and Göring impatiently looking around, waiting to give his own views. Macrae had put the field glasses down and tried to measure the distance. About five hundred and fifty yards, he estimated. He had killed men at greater range in the trenches.

He had picked up the glasses again and focused on the trees beyond the broad avenue. There in the darkness she had met him as arranged, punctual to the minute. He had given her the extension to her travel permit. It was valid until the week before Christmas. They had embraced without a word and held each other, listening to the murmur of the night wind in the old elm trees. They had made love with a passion he had never known before, he with his hand clamped over her mouth to stifle her cries, and she arching her back against the hard earth, thrusting upwards as if she wanted to lift herself from the ground and fly away. It was warm and it hadn't rained for weeks. Afterwards, they had lain on a dry bedding of fallen leaves, their heads resting on their bundled clothes, and let their cigarettes glow briefly in the dark.

There would have been others in the park that night, couples seeking precious moments alone and, most dangerous of all, men committing the crime of loving their own sex, risking death in a fast fumbled grapple beneath the bushes. There would also have been listeners moving through the trees, waiting to switch on bright torches and snarl commands at their victims.

They had never discussed the risks, although they were far greater for her than for him. They had talked in whispered murmurs about the extension to her travel pass, about where they might meet when the autumn rains came. Then they had kissed for a long time, their sweat-cooled bodies clamped tightly together, before dressing and parting.

The humiliation of the British prime minister and his government unfolded throughout the month like a macramé paper cut-out that had been tightly folded and then released. For the rapidly diminishing number of those who felt that America might at last turn outwards from the policies of the New Deal and issue a stern warning to the Nazi regime, Franklin Roosevelt had a swift reply.

The American president was already planning a campaign for an unprecedented third term the following year. At a press conference, he stated that it was one hundred per cent certain that the US would not get involved in any hostilities in Europe. When questioned further, he would not even express a view on the behaviour of the Third Reich towards its citizens and neighbours.

In France, Édouard Daladier had repeatedly confided to anyone who would listen that France would not go to war for Czechoslovakia or for any other east European country Germany chose to annex. Goebbels's obedient newspapers and his string of radio stations hailed these announcement as the voices of peace and waited for Britain to fall into line. Neville Chamberlain did so with an alacrity that astonished even Hitler and his confidants.

On 22 September, Chamberlain returned for a second meeting with Hitler, this time at Bad Godesberg on the Rhine. Once again, the Führer positioned himself at the top of steps at the front of the hotel, so that he could be photographed looking down on his visitor as they shook hands.

The British party also found that they had been given rooms on the opposite bank of the Rhine, far from the splendid hotel occupied by the Führer and his officials across the river. This meant they had to be ferried back and forth to meetings. The crude symbolism of these arrangements was hardly necessary. The whole world could see that the elderly Englishman with his wing collar, his watch chain and his waistcoat was about to be given a brutal lesson in power politics.

And so it proved. In the second of their two meetings, the Führer launched into a frenzied diatribe about the persecution of ethnic Germans in Czechoslovakia, renounced all previous agreements on the subject and told his startled visitor that the Sudetenland would fall to the German army by the end of the month, on September 30th – in exactly eight days' time.

Chamberlain returned to London convinced he was dealing with a madman but clinging to the hope that a peace deal might be extracted from the wreckage if Czechoslovakia . . .

If Czechoslovakia – there was the rub. This was the heart of the issue that confronted the British cabinet and that was being examined carefully by the interested parties in Berlin, in Paris, in Moscow and above all in Prague. Was the sacrifice of Czechoslovakia, a nation of fifteen million people, the price that had to be paid for peace in Europe? And if the price was paid, would there be further demands?

Macrae had not been included in the British delegation at the talks on, or rather across, the Rhine. Protocol demanded his presence, since military matters were clearly on the agenda, yet he had not been surprised at his exclusion.

He and Sir Nevile Henderson had not spoken since their last encounter. He remained at the embassy, watching the cable traffic that connected the prime minister to his cabinet in London. The teleprinters clattered from dawn deep into the night, delivering reams of coded reports. Finally, it seemed the British government, if not the blissfully deluded public, were waking from the dream of peace and confronting the reality of war – a war for which the country was woefully ill-equipped.

The War Office in London had cabled Macrae for the latest news of Germany's rearmament programme in light of the 1 October deadline. The reply was the same as it had been for several months: in armour, aircraft and artillery the German military were ahead of anything the British or French could put in the field. The crucial difference was manpower. The German conscription programme had given their generals a pool of several million trained men to draw on. Training programmes were accelerating. In only one area did Britain maintain superiority – naval power.

After the Bad Godesberg talks, the British cabinet agreed that the main battle fleet should leave its Scapa Flow base for manoeuvres in the North Sea. But the orders from Downing Street to the Admiralty were clear. The manoeuvres must not take the big ships within sight of the German coast.

Macrae felt himself a distant observer of these events, much as he had in the trenches with his sniper rifle. The powerful telescopic sights gave him a sense of detachment from the horrors around him. He could look over several hundred yards of cratered mud deep behind enemy lines and see men hurrying from trench to trench, bent double to escape a possible line of fire.

He had once trained his rifle on a man squatting to relieve himself in a shallow depression. The fellow was hunched up and seemed in pain as he defecated. Macrae had held him for a moment in his sights and then swung the rifle away, seeking a less obviously human target. He preferred to be disconnected from the inhumanity of war. The abstraction of a sniper's role was such that a snap shot at a head bobbing up from a distant trench would seem more like target practice than killing a fellow man.

And that was how he felt now, disconnected, a spectator at a theatre of the absurd, wishing to leap onto the stage and warn the actors, but imprisoned in paralysis and unable to do so – a nightmare familiar to psychiatrists.

There were nights when his feet took him where he did not want to go. He would walk from the embassy past the Brandenburg Gate and through the Tiergarten. When he reached his own house just off the avenue he would walk on, telling himself he needed the exercise. When the park gave way to the suburb of Charlottenburg itself, he would keep on walking. There were art galleries whose windows were filled with the kind of wholesome art approved by Joseph Goebbels. There were cafés with amazing cakes and small taverns where a weary diplomat could take a glass of cool white wine without fear of interference. And there was also the Salon. Although he reached the door several times, he never went in.

Primrose continued her life with the other embassy wives on the usual round of dinners, cocktail parties and charitable work. She and Macrae met more often now for supper at home and occasionally for dinner at a neighbouring restaurant. They began to make love, although they did so not as lovers, nor even as a long-married couple who recognised the departure of passion, but rather as strangers seeking mutual solace stripped of emotion. Afterwards they would lie, breathing hard, sweating, saying nothing, not touching, two people bedded in different worlds.

They talked over drinks and meals in the desultory fashion of people whose thoughts were elsewhere. They discussed news from friends and family at home, embassy gossip and whatever entertainment happened to interest them in the city. They never talked of the prospect of war, because Primrose dismissed the idea as a fantasy dreamed up by journalists and politicians. Germany would take Czechoslovakia, expel the Jews and get back to making good cars and running an efficient railway system; that was her view and that would be the end of a middle European melodrama as far as she was concerned.

"And the Jews?" Macrae had asked. "Expelled, stateless, stripped of their homes and possessions after living here for centuries – is that what you want?"

"They can go to Palestine, can't they? They want their own country, don't they? Well, we should give them one – solve the problem for all time."

They never talked of Koenig either. Primrose said she had not heard from him for weeks and Macrae believed her. He had also tried to contact Koenig without success. He had sent carefully worded anonymous notes to the staff headquarters stating the times of the morning service at the Berliner Dom on Sundays. But Koenig never turned up.

Macrae realised he was almost certainly with his unit on the endless manoeuvres being conducted along the eastern border. He also knew that, like his fellow officers, Koenig would be taking care to stay well away from Berlin and any contact with foreigners.

Roger Halliday had disappeared again too. Macrae had not seen his colleague since just before Chamberlain's first meeting with Hitler. Even Daisy Wellesley, a reliable embassy gossip, had no idea where he had gone.

"Better not ask," was her advice. "Those people do things a little differently from the rest of us."

Sir Nevile Henderson had also been absent from the embassy for much of the month of September. He was shuttling back and forth between Berlin and London and now spent most of his time working from 10 Downing Street. Daisy Wellesley was twice summoned to London to work with him, but after the last occasion said only on her return, "They're working on the next step," she said. "God knows what that will be."

Macrae had a good idea what that step would be. As the weather changed and the warmth of September gave way to the autumn rains in the last week of the month, the nations of Europe would prepare for the final act of delusion and deceit. He remembered a story he had heard from a fellow officer in the war. Flying over Normandy as a passenger in an open biplane, the man said he had looked down to see two cars moving fast on separate roads towards a junction. The high hedgerows prevented the drivers seeing each other, and their speed and distance from the crossroads made a collision almost certain. Powerless, he and the pilot had watched for almost a minute as the cars converged, until they collided and burst into flames.

He was gripped by the same feeling of impotence now. The army putsch against Hitler had been forestalled by the British peace diplomacy. Koenig and his conspirators had been denied the strong signal they needed to confront the Nazi regime.

The American military attaché, Percy Black, passed on reliable information that the Luftwaffe was testing a prototype jet engine-powered aircraft. In the naval dockyard at Hamburg, a 42,000-ton battleship named *Bismarck* was being constructed and would be launched the following year. The ship, and its sister the *Tirpitz*, also under construction on the north coast, would be both larger and more powerfully equipped than any vessel in the British fleet.

Macrae could do nothing as he watched a stream of cables revealing that Chamberlain planned a third meeting with Hitler, this time in Munich.

18

William Shirer was by temperament a cheerful optimist who delighted in the regular absurdities of life in the Third Reich. As a radio journalist, he worked hard to attract and hold the interest of an audience that stretched across America. The intellectual elite on the east coast and the wealthy upper class on the west coast were a natural audience for Shirer's narrative of the lawless actions and limitless ambitions of the Nazi regime.

The difficulty that he and CBS faced was how to reach out to a truly national audience and get the struggling farmers and their hard-pressed wives in the Midwestern corn belt and the good old boys in the southern states to tune in to what was happening in Europe.

Descriptions of Hitler's latest denunciation of the Czechs, the punitive treatment of the Jews and the slow-moving machinery of European diplomacy did not interest people struggling to avoid foreclosure and debt. The New Deal had been up and running for five years, but the misery of unemployment and the struggle for a livelihood in the Dust Bowl states remained unchanged for many people.

When Shirer invited Macrae to tea at the Hotel Adlon, he gladly accepted. Shirer was always good company and usually very well informed. He had seemed excited on the phone, claiming to have information that would "really get them talking out there in the West and might even make you Brits sit up".

Macrae had been spending a lot of time at the hotel, finding refuge in the calm of the bar, where the unchanging nature of the staff, the guests, the cocktails, the potted plants and the floral display seemed a bulwark against the world outside. Even the Gestapo informant shaking cocktails at the bar had become an essential feature of this orderly universe. Macrae had never taken tea in the bar, nor had he seen any journalist do so. The sight of the famous American correspondent presiding over a table laid with a large teapot, patterned china cups on saucers and a collection of cakes on small plates was a surprise.

"I have news for you," said Shirer, beckoning him to a seat. "Sit down, sit down."

It was four o'clock in the afternoon and the bar was empty except for a lunch party of German businessmen who were drinking their way towards the cocktail hour. Shirer poured the tea, handed a cup to Macrae and offered him a small cake.

His face was flushed and there was a sheen of sweat on his bald pate. He seemed animated and Macrae wondered whether he had been drinking. He pushed the thought away. Shirer took his job very seriously and he obviously had something to say.

"No thanks," said Macrae. "I'm not a cake person. A toasted scone with jam is about as close as I get."

"Is that a Brit joke?" said Shirer, suspicious that his guest was making fun of him.

"No. I don't have a sweet tooth."

Shirer sat back suddenly, smiling. "You just said it!"

"What?"

"'Sweet tooth'. That's my story – that's what is going to get them talking all over America."

"Really?" Macrae smiled and sipped his tea. Maybe Shirer had been drinking.

"Yeah, and you British might do something with this story, so listen up."

Shirer had been covering the recent rounds of talks between Chamberlain and Hitler in Berchtesgaden and then on the Rhine at Bad Godesberg. But it was during the first session in Hitler's mountain retreat in the Bavarian Alps that he had come across a story that threw new light on the Nazi leader, or so he said.

As the talks had dragged on from morning into late afternoon, Shirer had grown weary of waiting for a meaningless communiqué and had gone for a walk in the town. While taking coffee in a patisserie, he had heard a young woman at the counter talking about an order for a special cake and chocolate biscuits. She was due to pick up the order but said she would wait because she wanted a change in the topping of the cake. It was an apple cake but she had said it needed more nuts and raisins strewn across the cream on top, and the cream had to be thicker.

The pastry shop was empty and Shirer had only half listened to the conversation as he drank his coffee. Then he heard the phrase "Führer cake", and paid attention. The young woman was dressed in the black and white dress of a maid. Outside, Shirer could see a large official car with a chauffeur at the wheel. The engine was running, but when the young woman went out and spoke to the driver, the engine was turned off.

The woman re-entered the shop, at which point Shirer rose from his table, introduced himself as an American tourist and offered her a coffee while she waited. The young woman accepted and said her name was Elizabeth.

"This is where it gets interesting – are you listening, Macrae?" said Shirer.

No one ever called him by his first name, and Macrae preferred it that way. And he was indeed listening.

Shirer and Elizabeth had talked for half an hour while the cake was being altered. Shirer learnt that she came daily to the pastry shop to collect the "Führer cake", Hitler's favourite apple cake. It was specially baked with extra quantities of sugar, but the raisins and nuts were a key ingredient, apparently because as a vegetarian the Führer liked to think it made the confection more healthy. The cake was collected every day, along with a selection of smaller pastries and chocolate treats.

Shirer had told the girl that, as a tourist, he had come to the Berghof hoping for a glimpse of the Führer and planned to ask him for an autograph, if there was a chance. Elizabeth had laughed at the naive optimism of the American and said that no one in the town ever saw the Führer when he was in residence. Even she, a maid who had worked in his household for two years, only saw him once a day at teatime. Her main task was to prepare and serve the afternoon tea and make sure the right amount of cake and biscuits were on the table. And how he loved his tea, she had said. It was served punctually at four o'clock and was the most important meal of the Führer's day.

Shirer hardly had to ask a question. Elizabeth had happily talked of her master and his pleasure in the cakes that she served him every day. He was always joined on these occasions by his consort, Eva Braun, and old friends from the war or the days of struggle in Munich in the twenties. The big names of the Nazi Party were never present. The Führer did not like to talk business at teatime, she said.

Tea would last for an hour while cakes, biscuits and chocolate petits fours would vanish from the table. Hitler simply ate one after the other, reaching out over the cups and saucers and stuffing them into his mouth, so that the tablecloth and his jacket were soon covered in crumbs.

"But you know what the real story is?" Shirer said.

He could see the diplomat's eyes had strayed to the bar, where the early-evening crowd were beginning to assemble.

"Hitler likes cakes?" offered Macrae.

"No, no. You're missing the point. That special apple cake is never served at teatime. No one ever sees it. She told me it is put in a cupboard in the kitchen on Hitler's orders and whenever he wakes up in the middle of the night, which he usually does apparently, he goes in and takes a piece like a guilty schoolboy stealing a cookie. Don't you see? He sets the whole thing up so that he can steal his own cake in the middle of the night! How does that grab you?"

Macrae wondered what the War Office in London would say if he revealed in a confidential cable that sources in the Führer's household had revealed that Hitler's guilty secret was a fetish for stealing his own apple cake.

"Have you done anything with this story yet?" he asked.

"Nope, but I will. See, it will present Hitler as a real person, a midnight muncher, a cake-lover, a man who eats two pounds of chocolate a day."

"Is that what she told you?"

"She told me everything. She just wanted to talk to someone, I guess. The guy lives on a sugar high. Don't tell me that's not interesting."

"It's fascinating," said Macrae. "Let me buy you a drink."

They took their drinks at the table rather than at the bar, to avoid the attention of the barman. Shirer talked of seeing Hitler close up for the first time during the talks on the Rhine and noting the dark rings under his eyes and the pronounced twitch of his left shoulder as he walked. The man was close to a breakdown, he suggested.

It was on the second martini that Shirer returned to the subject of Hitler and the cakes.

"What do you think of the story?" he asked.

"Interesting," said Macrae cautiously.

"You Brits are dumb fuckers sometimes," said Shirer. "It's a good little human-interest story for me, but don't you see what it is for you?"

The American was not laughing. He looked almost angry, the rounded cherubic features suddenly darkened into a scowl.

"Not exactly," said Macrae, wondering whether he was being stupid or Shirer was simply being obtuse.

Shirer finished his drink and picked up his briefcase.

"I have been covering this shit for three years now. I see a train coming down the track real fast and I see no points ahead, no red lights and no buffers."

Shirer looked across the table, waiting for a response.

"And we both know the destination – right?" said Macrae.

"You got it," said Shirer, getting up. "Now, go bake the man a cake."

"Bake a cake – what are you talking about?"

Shirer struck his forehead in a theatrical gesture of frustration.

"Infiltrate the pastry shop! Add a little ingredient to the cakes! Get it now?"

One of the privileges of his rank was that Bonner was picked up by a car every morning from his home in an outer suburb and driven to the office. His wife would always come to the garden gate, fussing over him, straightening his tie and pulling a triangle of white handkerchief from his breast pocket. If the children were not at school, they would be required to wave him off.

Bonner liked this routine because it began his day, as it would end, with the fixed certainty of domestic life. In the hours between, he would be required to enter the world of Reinhard Heydrich and his satanic plans to further the aims of the Führer and the Third Reich.

Bonner travelled with a full set of newspapers in the car but never bothered to read them, because Goebbels's ministry circulated summaries of the main stories the evening before. He took care never to bring official documents home. Firstly, there was the question of security, and secondly because he valued the journey as a chance to think. He would close his eyes and tell the driver not to use his horn and to take his time. It was the only opportunity he had to reflect on the world outside that five-storey building on Prinz-Albrechtstrasse.

There were reports from Canaris's intelligence agency that the British were trying to pull together a four-power conference to meet at Munich. They honestly thought they could cobble together some final deal to avoid a war over Czechoslovakia. Bonner pushed the thought to one side. There was going to be a war sooner rather than later, whatever the British and French did. The diplomacy was a charade, another of the Führer's tricks to buy time for the generals to prepare. That was the trouble with the army. They always wanted more time.

Bonner thought of Franz and Tomas, beautiful sweet kids, all flaxen hair and shining eyes. He wanted the war to be a quick one: smash the Czechs, take Poland and then do the deal with the British. He wanted his boys to grow up tall and strong in a country at peace.

The Gestapo could keep the peace at home – it was the Nazis and their ambitions abroad that worried him. There was whispered talk of a Russian campaign. Bonner looked out of the window as the car drove up the avenue past the Siegessäule column. There was a lesson in history to be learnt from that memorial. Bismarck was a great man, a warrior leader, but look where it had all led – straight to the trenches in Flanders.

The car swept on towards the Brandenburg Gate. People were walking to work through the park, mostly young men enjoying the exercise and saving the U-Bahn or bus fare. Pretty women too, dressed in smart business clothes, long pencil skirts and well-fitting jackets, and with those clip-clop heels that had become fashionable. He thought of Sara siting there on the bed, bruised, bloodied and with that fluffy dressing gown half draped over her body. That had been a mistake. He was surprised at himself. He could have had any woman at the Salon if he wanted – why that girl?

He knew the answer, but again pushed the thought to the back of his mind, along with all those other things he didn't want to think about – a diplomatic charade, a phony peace and then the war. Sara was trouble. She wasn't doing her job. But he should not have beaten her.

As for the British military attaché, entrapment was pointless now. Events were moving too fast. Anyway, the Gestapo's problem was too much information, not too little. They did not have enough people to filter and analyse the reports that came in from all over the Reich every day. The *Blockwarte* were the worst; those snoopers in every apartment block were usually women seeking to earn a little cash by turning in neighbours supposedly hostile to the Reich or the Führer. The reports were almost always baseless and caused more trouble than they were worth.

The real value in this flood-tide of daily reports lay not in the information it contained but in the fact that it showed the agency had broad public support. The Gestapo had not had to recruit this army of informants; they had almost all volunteered – and hardly for the payments, which were very small.

Most policemen expected to be unpopular with the people they try to serve, so it was gratifying to Bonner that the Gestapo functioned efficiently because it had public approval. The great majority of his countrymen felt safer because the secret police were doing their job. The Gestapo was not a top-down tyranny oppressing a terrified population, as the foreign press would have it. The organisation relied on solid public support.

Bonner smiled to think that all those well-intentioned democratic politicians abroad, especially idiots like Chamberlain, could not recognise that fact. The Nazis and their so-called machinery of terror had not appeared out of a clear blue sky as if summoned by a cloven-hoofed Mephistopheles. They were in power under their Führer because that was the will of the German people.

This was what made his job acceptable, thought Bonner; even if there were times when the citizenry of the Reich might collectively have raised their hands in horror at the Gestapo's methods. But that was the lot of a secret policeman. You did the dirty work, you snouted out enemies of the regime like a pig after truffles and you neutralised them.

But someone had to do it, someone had to keep the peace for ordinary, decent people, hard-working families with kids like his own children, like Franz and Tomas.

The car pulled up outside the headquarters. Bonner got out and looked up at his office on the fourth floor. Hilde would be looking down, waiting for his arrival. By the time he entered his office, there would be fresh coffee and a stack of files on his desk. Another day would begin in the service of

Reinhard Heydrich, his boss Heinrich Himmler, and higher still on the shrouded summit of the Nazi hierarchy, Adolf Hitler. But his real master was the German people. Bonner told himself he was a lucky man.

The peace that was declared after the Munich conference at the end of September 1938 brought joyous celebrations in most capitals of Europe, especially London and Berlin. The British prime minister returned to London hailed as a hero who had saved a generation from the horrors of war. Chamberlain had scarcely alighted from his aircraft at Heston aerodrome when he produced a piece of paper and waved it aloft to prove that peace was assured.

The one sheet of foolscap paper carried the scrawled signature "*A. Hitler*" and declared that the agreement reached between Italy, France and Germany in Munich was "symbolic of the desire of our two peoples never to go to war again". Czechoslovakia was not party to the negotiations and was forced to give up the Sudetenland, her armaments industry and her border fortifications or face an immediate invasion. Britain and France sugared this poisonous settlement by promising to guarantee the Prague government against any further territorial demands by Germany.

To his astonishment, the Führer was held up in papers across the world as the arbiter of peaceful diplomacy. On his return to Berlin, a triumphant welcome confirmed the fact. As far as the German public was concerned, the Munich agreement meant an end to the threats of war that had pervaded German radio and press reports all month.

Hitler's surprise at being hailed an angel of peace turned to irritation when he discovered that Neville Chamberlain was as popular as he was on the streets of Berlin. Posters praising the British prime minister appeared in shop windows, and the Union Jack fluttered alongside the swastika on street corners in the centre of the city.

It was not until the second week of October that the regular meeting of senior staff resumed at the British embassy. The stress of the negotiations leading to the Munich talks had taken its toll on the ambassador. Sir Nevile Henderson had been in bed for days under the care of a specialist flown in from London.

As he took his place at the head of the conference table, his staff could see the ambassador had not fully recovered. His skin was yellowish, the cheeks were sunken and he had clearly lost weight. There was a silence as everyone sat down. It was the first time he and Macrae had been in the same room together since their angry confrontation a few weeks earlier. Neither man looked at the other. Roger Halliday had returned without explanation or apology for his long absence. Macrae grabbed him in the corridor before the meeting.

"Where the hell have you been?" he hissed.

"Teaching the Czechs how to cut their own throats," said Halliday, and walked past him into the meeting room.

Sir Nevile looked down at typewritten notes and read a statement summing up the world in which the allies, Britain and France, now found themselves.

It was a recitation of diplomatic triumph snatched from the jaws of disaster. The Munich agreement, which had won popular approval and political support across Europe, would finally check German aggression and bring about a new era of peace. The political compromise and territorial sacrifices had been painful, but they had been necessary to gain a written agreement from the German chancellor.

Sir Neville looked around the table and asked for comments.

Halliday raised his hand. The ambassador nodded. Without a word, Halliday slid a sheet of paper onto the table. Everyone craned their heads. It was a photostat of an official German document stamped with the word "*Geheim*" across the top. The paper was passed to Henderson, who adjusted his glasses and picked it up. He read slowly, then placed the document face down on the table. He closed his eyes and gave a deep sigh.

"Where did you get this?"

"It's genuine, if that's what you're asking."

"How do you know?"

"Does it look like a forgery? You know his signature. After all, he signed that ridiculous piece of paper that the prime minister waved around at the airport."

The careworn face of the ambassador flushed, bringing colour to the pallid cheeks.

"I will ask you for the last time to show some respect when you address these meetings, Mr Halliday," he said. "If this is not a forgery, we must cable London at once. And I have a right to know its provenance."

"May we know what we are talking about?" It was David Buckland, the political attaché.

Halliday and Henderson exchanged glances. The ambassador nodded.

"This is a political directive from the office of the Führer to the supreme commander, General Keitel," said Halliday. "It is dated 21 October and requires the general to prepare for, and I quote, 'the liquidation of the remainder of Czechoslovakia'. The provenance is General Keitel's office. Do you wish me to reveal the name of my informant?"

"I am not going to discuss this any further. Let London

decide what to do," said the ambassador. Those around the table half expected him to get up and walk wordlessly from the room as he normally did when humiliated in this fashion. Instead, he smiled wanly at his staff and said, "I am afraid I will not be able to join you tonight, doctor's orders, but do enjoy yourselves."

The reception that night was one of the embassy's occasional soirées designed to allow diplomats, consular staff and their families to relax, free from the attentions of the police and the Gestapo.

Within the embassy they felt safe and, as Sir Nevile said, it was good for people working under such stressful conditions to be able to let their hair down once in a while. His absence meant that a hundred and twenty embassy personnel, including wives, gathered in the embassy's ballroom for drinks, a buffet supper and dancing to records played on a wind-up gramophone without the benefit of a host.

For much of the evening, Primrose and Macrae talked and danced with different people. It was not that she was avoiding him, he told himself; she was just being social. Finally, when the lights were dimmed and the last dance was announced close to midnight, he asked her to join him on the floor. He tried to hold her close, but she gently pushed back on the embrace. Around them, couples were clinging to each other, barely moving to the music. In the darkened recesses of the room, some junior staff were even kissing.

Macrae moved through the steps of a waltz, his hand on hers and his arm around her waist. Her body felt stiff and although she smiled at him in the low light he could see she was looking over his shoulder. The music finished but the couples around them continued dancing. Primrose stepped back and said she needed a cigarette. They went outside on the small balcony overlooking Wilhelmstrasse.

"Is anything wrong?" he said.

"Why?"

"No reason." There was a silence as they gazed out at the night. Somewhere, midnight chimed from a church clock.

"Have you heard from Koenig?" he said.

She turned her head away and said nothing.

"He's back?"

She nodded, her back to him.

He turned her towards him.

"I need to see him as soon as possible."

"He says he can't come to Berlin. He's in the country. The whole unit was given leave after Munich."

"All right," he said carefully. "Let's see if he will have us to stay. A weekend maybe. It's the hunting season."

"Why do you want to see him so badly?"

"Nothing to do with you, my dearest. I just need to talk to him."

"You really mean that?"

"Yes, I do. It's urgent, very urgent."

Sara knew her brother would never cooperate with the Gestapo. He would play them along, feed them false information, try to gain privileges of better food and maybe a little exercise, try to escape again. Then they would kill him.

She would know the moment it happened. Twins are like that. It had been like that all her life. She had always known when Joseph was in trouble, when he was hurt – and he had known the same about her.

A symbiotic force bound twins, an elemental shared existence that was as strong in life as it had been in the womb.

When the Englishman had told her that Joseph was dead, she had almost wanted to believe him, because at least it would mean his suffering was over. But deep down she had known he was still alive, as she knew now.

When they were children, their favourite game had been hide-and-seek in the big house on the outskirts of Hamburg that her parents had bought when the money began to come in from the export of clothes to the newly-arisen Soviet Union. The twins had grown up in that rambling old place, with its cellars and attics full of family junk from centuries back, and the garden that sprawled down to the river through a wood made up of magnolia trees. Whenever they played with their friends, somehow she was always the seeker – and she always knew where to find her twin. On one occasion he had hidden in the water tank in the attic and totally submersed himself, using a straw to breathe. She had been drawn to the attic, sensing his presence, and had looked everywhere, until she suddenly knew he was in the tank.

Afterwards he had gone downstairs into the kitchen, still dripping wet, and for the first time she had seen her mother lose her temper and try to beat him with a wooden spoon. How old were they then? Ten or twelve maybe, and Joseph was too big and strong for a beating; he had just laughed and run away. Later, when he had got changed, he had come up behind his mother in the kitchen and surprised her with a big hug. He had held her, with his arms tight around her waist and his head buried in her back. She had cried. If only your father were here, she said, but that was what she said all the time, about everything.

Poor Mother. Father had gone to the factory one morning as usual and found it had been requisitioned. They had just moved in and taken it over. There was a party official in his office, a competitor, as it happened. The man had warned him that he would be arrested for economic sabotage if he complained.

Father did complain. He fought back. He said that even in Hitler's Germany in 1936, the year of the Olympics in Berlin, a whole Jewish business could not just be taken away overnight. But he was wrong. He had gone to the party offices in Hamburg and had never come back. He just vanished. At first, they thought he had been taken to a camp, but the authorities denied it.

Then Sara's mother heard he had fled to Russia. Whatever it was that happened in the party offices, he had left there and then. He had little money and no clothes, but he had been right. He knew they would have come for him that evening at home and they would probably have taken them all. As it was, Mother had collapsed when she heard the news and had a stroke shortly after. She lived in a chair in the kitchen, semi-paralysed, unable to speak, and spent her time staring at the magnolia trees in the garden.

They said her mind had gone and that she could not even recognise her own children. But of course she did; there was a flicker in those grey eyes when Sara gave her soup or when Joseph brought her chocolate and kissed her grey head. She would smile then, a smile that began in the eyes and lifted her face until her lips parted. She might have lived for years like that with her children looking after her.

But Joseph had been stupid. Sara tried to remember how old he had been when he began putting those leaflets around and defacing party posters. He must have been just nineteen. He and a few friends, including his girlfriend, had held secret meetings under the magnolia trees planning sabotage. She had told him to stop and warned him about the girl. He had just laughed and told her to look after their mother.

Then it happened, just as she knew it would. A Kommandant from the Gestapo had come to the house with two men when it was still dark and dragged Joseph from his bed. They had beaten him in the hall, kicking him with their boots. Their mother had been upstairs, asleep, and never heard a thing.

Sara had watched it all from the top of the stairs in her dressing gown. She had seen the look the Kommandant gave her as they dragged him away – a murderous look that said, "We're going to come back for you." And six months later they did.

She was arrested not in the morning, as they usually did, but in the late afternoon when she came back from her job as a typist in a brick factory. It was a warm evening in June and the magnolia trees in the garden were still in blossom. They brushed aside her protests and gave her ten minutes to pack a small suitcase and say goodbye to her mother. The poor woman was sitting as usual in the kitchen and did not know what was happening. That was a blessing.

Sara was put in a car and driven straight to Berlin through the night. The next morning, she had found herself in a small room in the Prinz-Albrechtstrasse headquarters, where they showed her a letter from her brother. The offer was simple: collaborate and he will live. Refuse and you will join him in the concentration camp. That's how her life in the Salon had begun.

And that's where she would have to stay as long as he was alive. Joseph wouldn't want that. In fact, she knew very well that he would be furious with her. He would tell her to escape, to risk everything to flee Germany. If he knew she had a travel permit, he would go mad if she didn't use it. But she couldn't, not just yet.

It wasn't sentimental. It was a cold calculation. There was just a chance that she could say something to Heydrich. He had not been near her for weeks now, but he would come back for her. He always did. And after she had done all those dirty little things that he liked, he would smoke and drink and watch her dress and talk. He would talk of music, how his father had given him a violin as a parting gift when he joined the navy. He would talk of his love of Mozart, especially his favourite violin concerto, number six. Then he would move on, his voice edged with anger, to talk of his wife Lina, who was being unfaithful with not just one lover but several.

He could have had them killed, he said, but they were all in the party, and quite senior as well. But he loved his two boys, especially the youngest, Heider, who was now four years old and beginning to show real promise on a small flute. This was always a one-sided conversation, a long monologue from a man who merely required her to listen, smile and nod her head. He would talk like this for an hour or so, as if he had just dropped in for a chat with an old friend. She found the conversation utterly bizarre but understood that her role was to sit and listen to a man who had no one to talk to, no one to trust, no one with whom to share the small confidences of family life and memories of a happier past.

Sara felt that if she timed her approach carefully, she might just find a spark of humanity in the man, a flicker of life on a frozen planet, anything that would allow her to persuade him that her brother was just a stupid boy who did not deserve the death awaiting him in the labour camp. She would beg him, plead, promise to do anything for him.

If there was any consolation to be found in all this, it was that her mother had died. They said it was shock or grief, or whatever it is that kills a mother when her two children have been dragged off by the Gestapo. The neighbours found her in her kitchen chair with her eyes wide open, still staring at the magnolia tree.

19

The invitation to join the shooting party arrived in a formal typewritten letter to the embassy addressed to Colonel and Mrs Macrae. Colonel Florian Koenig invited them for a weekend at the end of the month, it said, but a handwritten addendum at the bottom of the page read, "Bring that antique rifle of yours; there are plenty of deer on the hills above the tree line and boar in the woods below."

Macrae and Primrose arrived at the lodge in time for dinner. Gertrude was the same ethereal presence, looking, as Primrose observed while they changed for dinner, as if she had dressed up as a ghost at a fancy-dress party. Koenig seemed preoccupied and said little at drinks before dinner, offering only a toast to welcome them.

The meal passed with desultory conversation about the weather, and only when the subject of the hunting season arose did Koenig appear interested in the presence of his guests. He talked animatedly of the fine stag to be found on the high ground and the driven boar hunt that had been arranged for the next day.

"And what are we ladies supposed to do while you go slaughtering wildlife?" asked Primrose.

"We are to join them," said Gertrude, who appeared interested in what was going on for the first time. Her ghostly pallor had been replaced by a semblance of colour. She was smiling at last. "We are going to show the men that women can shoot just as well as they can."

"I don't think I know how," said Primrose. "My husband is the marksman, aren't you, darling?"

She reached out across the table, sliding her hand towards him in a gesture of affection he found embarrassing. He placed his hand on hers briefly.

"I am sure Gertrude will lend you her rifle. What is it, by the way?" he said.

"I have a .22 – a lady's gun. It doesn't kick," said Gertrude.

"But no good against boar," said Koenig. "I will lend you something more suitable, a .303."

"Thank you but no. A .22 will do fine. I want to give the boar a chance. This is supposed to be a sport, isn't it?"

She spoke in a tone that suggested to Macrae a history of discord in the house over the ethics of hunting. Koenig shrugged, dropped his napkin and rose from the table.

"It's no sport for the boar if he is left wounded by a pellet from a .22," he said. "But as you wish, my dear."

Macrae had expected Koenig to suggest a nightcap to talk about the folly of Munich. Instead, their host left the dining room with the suggestion that they all go to bed early.

They assembled the next morning in front of the lodge, with sunlight filtering through the trees and the ground glittery with a sharp frost. An open Mercedes truck with seats built into the back was panting outside the front door, puffing exhaust into the cold air. They clambered in and a chauffeur drove them over the hill into a lightly wooded valley.

Koenig explained that the four of them would conceal themselves in two hides about four hundred yards apart on opposite sides of the valley. The hides were camouflaged to look like large bushes and were made up of wooden platforms, to give elevation when aiming. Koenig said that beaters would flush boar and roe deer from their cover in the wood and they would shoot the animals, always taking the boar first, as they ran towards them. Macrae and Gertrude would go in one hide, he said, and he would take Primrose into the other.

"What about the beaters?" asked Primrose. "Aren't they in danger when we start shooting?"

Koenig explained that a horn would sound to signal that the beaters had cleared the wood. This would be just before the quarry broke cover. He repeated the instruction to shoot the boar first. They were faster and infinitely more dangerous than deer. A wounded four-hundred-pound boar with tusks a good eight inches long could easily demolish a hide if it chose to. Then it would turn on the occupants.

"So you see, my dear, there is an element of sport in the hunt."

He was speaking to Gertrude, who tossed her head and shrugged. She was wearing headscarf, gumboots, corduroy trousers and a waterproof jacket. She had slung her .22 rifle over her shoulder like a marching soldier. Macrae realised the gun was less a threat to a boar than a rebuke to her husband.

They heard shouts and ringing bells coming from the far end of the wood. They tramped off to their positions and climbed into the hides. Macrae laid his Lee–Enfield on a narrow wooden plank and eased the barrel through a screen of bushes. He peered through the sight.

The edge of the wood was about a thousand yards away. The boar would come along the valley and swerve up the sloping sides when they realised that there were hunters concealed ahead of them.

A boar travelling at thirty miles an hour showing only his snout and tusks would not be an easy shot. The hide was tough and only a direct hit would kill the animal. Once it had swerved sideways, the boar would be showing its flank and shooting would be easier, but there would be more chance of wounding the beast. Macrae did not want to leave a wounded animal to die a lingering death. He would take the boar head on at the outside range of his rifle, about eight hundred yards. He should be able to get off three or four shots before the animals realised the danger ahead and changed course.

He loaded the gun, slipping the magazine with five bullets into the chamber. Solid .303 rounds, three inches of pointed brass of the kind that had carried death across the trenches. The sniper heard only a crack as he fired. The target would hear a fizzing hum if the bullet missed. Macrae had missed many times, but he had also killed many men with this gun. And that is why he had never used it since. It had accompanied him on his travels in its leather case stamped with his initials "NM", and he had taken it out and cleaned it, but never once had he fired it – until he had taken Koenig's stag. It was a fine British rifle, with superb optical sights that had helped him become a sniper with one of the highest kill records in the British army.

He looked across at Koenig's hide across the valley. The sides were not camouflaged and in the distance he could just make out two figures blurred into one on the platform. He swung his rifle up, looking through the sights. Koenig was showing Primrose how to hold his rifle. He was standing behind her, leaning into her, one arm with hers under the barrel and the other under her right arm around the trigger guard. Koenig's head was on her shoulder and he was talking to her, guiding her through the manly art of aiming and firing a Mauser sporting rifle.

What was he saying to her? *Aim for the forehead just above the eyes, hold the butt tight into your shoulder and squeeze?* Or was it *I've missed you, I want you come to my room tonight when he's asleep, Gertrude never sleeps with me these days*?

"See anything interesting?" said a voice at Macrae's shoulder.

He put the rifle down. Gertrude was holding out her hip flask.

"No, just aligning the sights."

Gertrude smiled. "She isn't the first and she won't be the last. Here, have a bull shot," she said.

She lifted the head of the flask, created a cup, poured a measure and handed it to him. Macrae drank, grateful for a pause in the conversation. He struggled for a response to a statement that invited no reply and decided to give none. He felt the vodka and beef broth burning the back of his throat. He winced and she smiled, taking the flask and drinking straight from the neck. Sounds of shouting and bells grew louder from the wood. They turned to take up their positions.

"You don't like shooting, do you?" she said.

"Why do you say that?"

"Female intuition."

"I haven't used a gun in twenty years – except for that stag," he said.

"So why now?" she asked.

Somewhere in the back of his mind, buried far from rational thought, lay the awkward answer to that question. He pushed it aside. There was an easier response.

"I don't like to disappoint my host," he said.

Macrae looked through his sights again. The hunting horn sounded three times, long wailing notes like the trumpets that had sent men into battle for centuries. He slid his rifle into his shoulder and took up his position. There was a shot beside him. Gertrude stepped back, reaching for the binoculars.

"Too soon," said Macrae, squinting through his sights.

The woman was obviously trying to ruin the shoot. Boar were breaking in numbers from the wood, fast-moving dark creatures, mostly males with tusks. But they were too far off for a clean shot. The boar came up the valley, powerful heads bobbing up and down with each stride. Their speed was surprising. Macrae trained his sights on the lead animal, bringing the cross hairs to bear on a large tusked head. He aimed and fired, feeling the familiar kick against his shoulder. The animal somersaulted and slid along the ground. Boar began breaking right and left across the valley. Macrae could hear shots from Koenig's hide. He looked back through the sights at the boar that had now scattered over the valley floor and up the hillsides. He fired four more shots in quick succession, snapping the bolt back each time to inject a new cartridge into the breech. The boar fell cleanly, shot not through the flank but each time through the head, close to the eye. He pulled out the magazine, slotted in a new one and swept his telescopic sights up the hill.

There they were, fleeing boar heading for the safety of the summit and the far side beyond. He had once shot a German soldier running from a camouflaged forward observation post. The man was an artillery spotter. When he realised he had been seen, he ran madly back to the safety of his lines, ducking and weaving. He had been hindered by a heavy uniform, which was probably why Macrae had missed with his first shot. The man had tried to strip his jacket off while running, which made his movements improbably erratic. He had thrown his jacket and rifle away and was almost at the trench when a bullet struck his head, toppling him forward.

Now he fired five more shots, taking a boar with each one. The range was about five hundred yards, he guessed. He could hear shots from Koenig's hide but had seen no sign of his kills.

He stood up, straightened his back and put his rifle down. His hands were trembling. He felt faint.

"Did you say you had not used a gun for twenty years?" Gertrude was looking at him, frowning and smiling at the same time, the note of incredulity clear in her voice.

"Bit longer, actually," he said. "Anything left in that flask?"

Like every other member of the British embassy, Macrae had walked to work on the morning of 10 November. Most of the pavements were covered in broken glass from smashed shopfronts and apartment windows. The streets were littered with broken furniture and household goods. There were no taxis, buses or cars moving in the city. Only the fire service seemed willing to risk their heavy engines on the rubble of glass in order to hose down smouldering houses close to the scores of synagogues throughout the city.

When dawn broke, there was little left of such places of Jewish worship. As elsewhere in Germany, the larger synagogues had been burnt down completely in the night and left in smoking ruins. Hundreds of smaller synagogues had been torched but not wholly destroyed. Houses and apartments belonging to Jews had been broken into and their contents vandalised or tipped into the street. Crowds had gathered to stare at the piles of broken mirrors, paintings, ornaments and furniture that lay heaped up on pavements. No one dared touch such goods and no one asked what had happened to their owners.

The staff meeting at the embassy had been put back that morning owing to late arrivals and also the need to get as much information as possible about the violent events of the night before. It was noon when Sir Nevile Henderson took his seat in the conference room. He noted that his colleagues looked visibly shocked. That was understandable. He himself felt pained and aggrieved at the reported events of the night. It was a diplomat's job to accept that in certain postings there would be dangers. But this was Berlin, capital of the Third Reich, a proud and powerful nation that lay at the heart of Europe. Mob rule here was unthinkable.

He had been woken at midnight by a call from David Buckland with the news that organised Nazi paramilitaries in all major cities had begun attacking Jewish properties. He had dismissed the reports as exaggerated and reminded himself that Buckland was young and inexperienced. He had gone back to sleep. There had been no news on the German radio that morning, but when he found the locally employed cook crying in the kitchen, he realised something had gone badly wrong. She was a good German girl, since the embassy did not employ Jewish staff if it could help it. The woman said she feared for her Jewish neighbours, who had simply vanished in the night.

That was when Sir Nevile had gone out and walked the streets of the city centre. What he saw disturbed him deeply. The National Socialist Party had evidently lost control of the thuggish elements of its own organisation. On his return, he placed a call to the office of Field Marshal Göring. A message was taken by his secretary, who declined to give any information about the field marshal's whereabouts.

The meeting began with a report by the political attaché, David Buckland. He had been up most of the night and looked ashen-faced. He took a deep breath and read from a typewritten document. Reports of destruction of Jewish property and violence towards Jews all over the country were pouring in all the time, he said. So far, one hundred major synagogues had been destroyed, eight thousand Jewish homes burnt out and Jewish businesses attacked throughout the country, especially those in the centre of cities. More sinister were the beatings and the bestial treatment of elderly Jewish women and children. They had been driven into the streets and attacked by organised gangs. Many had been murdered in their homes.

"Did the police not do anything?" snapped the ambassador.

"No. The mob was made up of Nazi Party members and many were part-time police. They all wore their swastika armbands quite openly. They used official vehicles and carried military weaponry."

"What was the cause of this – who ordered it?"

Sir Nevile looked around the room. Heads were bowed towards their coffee or their notebooks. One or two people sat back and stared at the ceiling. No one seemed to want to answer the question. Halliday at the back was preoccupied with extracting congealed mucus from his left nostril.

"I can hardly believe this was sanctioned at any senior level," said the ambassador. "I have placed a call to Field Marshal Göring and I hope to speak to him very soon. I am sure he will enlighten us."

Halliday drew an old handkerchief from his pocket, blew his nose loudly and raised his hand. The ambassador nodded. At least the man had stopped picking his nose.

"A word of caution, Ambassador. I think you will find that Göring and all those gangsters at the top of the party were well aware of what was to happen to the Jews and their property."

The reference to the government of a major European country with whom the United Kingdom had diplomatic relations as "all those gangsters" was typically provocative. Sir Nevile Henderson had put up with Halliday dressing like a tramp, reeking of alcohol and picking his nose in his meetings. He was not going to accept such a casual insult to a host government to which he was the accredited diplomatic representative.

"I would ask you to justify such a remark," he said. "And I would like to see you afterwards to discuss your use of language in these meetings."

"They were aware of it because they ordered it – all of them. And the Führer himself was made fully aware. I think the excuse was the shooting of a junior German attaché in Paris a couple of days ago, but I am not fully informed on that. The point is that this pogrom has long been planned. With Hitler, timing is everything. We gave him Czechoslovakia at Munich, which saved him going to war for it. Now he can turn on the Jews, because he knows we will do nothing."

"That is the kind of malevolent analysis I would expect to find in the *Manchester Guardian*," said the ambassador. He looked around the room, seeking eye contact with his staff as he spoke. "I understand all of you are deeply shocked by what we have heard of the events last night. But I must ask you to remember that our mission in the Foreign Service is to act dispassionately and to provide London with an analysis of events without exaggeration or emotion. It is particularly important not to place weight on rumour and gossip. It is on those principles that our diplomacy has always been based."

The ambassador sat down. Halliday tilted back on his chair, placing his arms behind his head in a gesture that pulled a length of crumpled shirt from his waistband, revealing an expanse of hairy stomach.

"My source is Goebbels himself. He made a speech on Munich radio immediately after meeting with Hitler, saying that retaliatory action against the Jews had been agreed by the highest authority. That was the signal for the pogrom."

Halliday tipped his chair forward with a thump, rose and moved towards the door, the flapping of his unlaced shoes the only sound to break the silence of the room. He turned at the door, as Macrae knew he would, and faced the table.

"We should remember that we are not dealing with a head of state, nor indeed with the supreme commander of the German army, nor the leader of the National Socialist Party. We are dealing with the author of *Mein Kampf*, and if any of you are surprised by what happened last night, and what will continue to happen to Jews in this country, I suggest you reread that very enlightening book."

He closed the door behind him. The meeting had effectively ended.

They called it Kristallnacht, and even in the Salon the next night Sara caught whispered conversations expressing shock at the savagery and degradation inflicted on the Jewish community. She heard the word again and again – Kristallnacht, the night of crystal – as if the orgy of violence could be covered up with a pretty name. It wasn't just the foreigners who appeared troubled by the violence.

Military officers, mostly army but some from the Luftwaffe, were in there that night, along with plump party members wearing swastika armbands over their expensive French suits. They all seemed worried. The conversational hum in the room was muted. The girls too were having trouble finding business. The Pink Room was almost empty. People seemed to want to drink and talk, and then drink some more.

It was Kitty Schmidt who told Sara the full extent of the atrocities. As befitted a woman who was running a brothel for the Gestapo, and who made sure that its senior officers were well entertained, Kitty was very well informed.

She took Sara aside and whispered terrible news: over the next week twenty thousand Jews would be arrested on charges of economic sabotage and sent to one of three camps – Dachau, Sachsenhausen or Buchenwald. The aim was to so traumatise the Jewish community that the remainder would abandon their homes and possessions and flee the country.

"You have family?" said Kitty.

She had never asked Sara about her family, her friends or her life outside the Salon. Kitty Schmidt was a professional madam just trying to survive, like everyone else caught in the Nazi net. She accepted a Jewish woman at the Salon because that is what Heydrich and Bonner wanted. She did not question their orders. She knew the reason and accepted it. A Jewish whore was the ultimate carnal pleasure for a drunken Nazi.

"My mother died last year, thank God. I have a brother in one of the camps."

"I am sorry."

Kitty laid a hand on her cheek and smoothed it.

"This will end one day," she said. "Be patient."

Sara nodded but thought, be patient for what? For a Jew in Germany, there was no future worth waiting for. The future had been cancelled.

That night, Sara entertained a client described as a special guest of Reinhard Heydrich. He was a well-dressed Russian in his middle fifties and told Sara he was a businessman, although Sara knew that was a lie. Businessmen had great folds of fat hanging over their waistline, the result of too much eating and drinking at other people's expense. This man's body was lean, toned and muscular. He was military or intelligence, maybe both. It would not normally have bothered Sara, but she was curious that the Gestapo should send a Russian to the Salon at a time when Goebbels and his Propaganda Ministry were vilifying Moscow as the capital of a Bolshevik-Jewish global conspiracy.

The man was polite and said very little after she had taken him to the best room in the house. They walked down the corridor, past the numbered doors with their spyholes and up a short flight of stairs, to what Kitty laughingly called the honeymoon suite.

The room had mirrors on three of its four walls and a large mirror on the ceiling over the double bed. On the far side of the room, there was a bathroom behind a mirrored door. The colour scheme was crimson. A small fountain was playing in a corner and a cluster of flowering orchid plants had been placed on a table by the door. There was a bar, behind which two glass shelves were lined with bottles of vodka, whisky, rum and gin. Bottles of German champagne had been placed in ice buckets on the counter. A tray of plated cold meats, pâté, soused herrings and sliced fruit sat alongside dark rye bread and a slab of butter on a small candlelit table laid for two.

Sara had been told to stay with the Russian until the next morning, her first overnight booking at the Salon. She had protested, but Kitty Schmidt had insisted. The order came from the top, she said. The Russian was to be given the finest hospitality the Salon could provide. That was why the best room had been reserved for the night. A sign had been placed on the door saying "Do Not Disturb."

The Russian had spoken not a word but had thrown his jacket on the bed and sat down to eat. Sara, who was feeling hungry herself, watched him devour every morsel of food on the table.

Then he had begun to drink – vodka, one shot glass after another. He spoke once, in good German, to ask her to take her clothes off, and continued drinking, looking at her reflected image in the mirrors while she sat on the bed. He drank an entire bottle, then stood up, stretched, belched and walked over to the bathroom.

When he returned, he began to undress but tripped while taking his trousers off, collapsed on the bed and fell asleep. The cameras and microphones recorded no more than the sight and sound of a snoring guest of the Third Reich and his very bored courtesan companion. Around midnight, Sara heard the faint click that told her the equipment had been turned off.

When she awoke the next morning, she thought at first that the Russian had died in the night. He was lying on his back, not making a sound. His face was grey and his limbs felt cold. She tried to shake him awake but there was no response.

She was suddenly frightened. Bonner was bound to blame her. After a few minutes of vigorous shaking, the man had coughed and opened his eyes. He sat up and began talking a language she assumed was Russian. She made him some coffee, kissed him sweetly on the cheek, whispered "*Heil Hitler*" in his ear and left.

When she walked out that autumn morning to return to her room, she knew she had found her future. The certainty of what she had to do almost made her skip with joy. It was as if she had been walking blindly through a thick fog, which had suddenly lifted to reveal the path ahead.

20

In Berlin that Christmas, the weather was colder and the festivities more extravagant than anyone could remember. The mercury at Tempelhof airport dipped to minus twenty in mid-December. Record-breaking snowfall swept in from the north and blanketed the city for days.

This did nothing to deter the citizens of Berlin from enjoying what many believed would be their last Christmas at peace for a long time. They whispered this thought among themselves at home, but never in bars or restaurants. They were going to enjoy the winter carnival of 1938, because it might be their last.

Military conscription had already taken most young men for a compulsory eighteen months' service, unless they could show they were employed in a reserved occupation. Throughout Germany, families desperately sought jobs for their sons in armaments factories or in the power and telephone companies. The number of young men applying to become medical students in major universities or hospitals rose dramatically.

All military conscripts and many regular soldiers and airmen were given ten days' leave to join their families for the holiday. Those returning to Berlin from their units were amazed at the extravagance of the seasonal decorations and the lights on Christmas trees on all main streets and in the big department stores. The newspapers remarked that Berlin looked more than ever like a winter wonderland as the festive lights assumed strange shapes and colours in the swirling snow showers. On the streets, carol singers competed with the collectors for the Nazi Party winter-relief programme, an unsubtle method of extorting money in the name of the poor but actually for party funds. Everyone gave something, to avoid being reported for antisocial behaviour.

As he walked down Wilhelmstrasse on his way back to his office, Bonner counted fourteen Christmas trees in the windows of the British embassy, the Propaganda Ministry and the Reich Chancellery. Except for those at the embassy, all had swastikas instead of stars at the top. Bonner considered himself a good Nazi, but the party's attempt to take religion out of Christmas and turn the whole celebration into a pagan feast to mark the winter solstice was ridiculous. Germans had always loved their Weihnachten and, back in the Middle Ages, had been the first in Europe to invent Santa Claus, the Christmas tree and all that went with it.

Goebbels had been given the task of reinventing Christmas when the Nazis came to power back in 1933. A Christian celebration to mark the birth of a Jewish messiah was hardly going to chime with the ideology of the National Socialist Party. The mental gymnastics that followed had been the subject of much bar-room humour throughout the country, until it had become dangerous to make such jokes.

Saint Nicholas, better known to German children as Father Christmas, became the Norse God Odin, carols and hymns like "Silent Night" were rewritten to remove all reference to Christ the Saviour, and so it went on.

Most people simply ignored the ideological interference with their midwinter festival and carried on with their celebrations as usual. The Gestapo were well aware of popular feeling and chose to do nothing. Bonner despised Heydrich as an unbalanced fanatic, but in this case he was right. Tradition trumped ideology at Christmastime. The churches, on the other hand, were very much the business of the secret police, which is why no senior religious figure had spoken out against the Nazification of Christmas. Nor, indeed, had a single senior churchman condemned the atrocities of Kristallnacht. They were all frightened, which is just as it should be, thought Bonner.

As he trudged through the frozen slush on the steps of the Gestapo headquarters, Bonner noted that the festive season had left no mark on the building. The blinds were drawn tightly on all windows as usual, and hardly a glimmer of light escaped from the building.

Heydrich had permitted one tree in each of the two canteens, with the swastika at the top and black Iron Crosses hanging from the branches – nothing else. He had said that any office decorations would be inappropriate at a time when the country was facing enemies on all sides.

Bonner placed his shopping on the floor of his office and congratulated himself. It was 17 December and he had bought presents for all the family, including his elderly father and mother in Heidelberg. He had even bought something for Hilde. He was particularly proud of the gift. It showed real imagination. Even that ox of a Bavarian girl might just appreciate the thought that had gone into it.

He unwrapped the present and looked at it. An hourglass filled with coloured layers of sand that filtered through from top to bottom with such precision that in exactly sixty minutes the top layers lay in their separate colours in the lower chamber.

It was a fragile ornament made of fine blown glass that stood on its own base. Bonner had been fascinated while watching it in the shop, where an assistant had turned it upside down for him. Here was a metaphor for the ultimate absurdity of life, the shifting sands of time trickling to eternity before one's very eyes.

He wrapped the hourglass carefully and put it in his desk drawer. It was far too good for Hilde. She would just break it. He would give her a decent bottle of schnapps instead. She could swill that with the new boyfriend she had met in one of the interrogation teams. He got the bottle out of one of the shopping bags, placed it in its wrapping paper on his desk and pressed the buzzer. He heard her clumping across the floor in the office next door.

"Happy Christmas," he said as she entered, and he presented her with the bottle.

Her response surprised him. She carefully took off the wrapping paper and placed the bottle on the desk. She gave him a little bow and said, "Thank you, sir. Will you join me in a glass?"

They drank schnapps and water for half an hour, talking of family, the weather and the surprisingly high quality of the food in the canteen. As the conversation petered out, Hilde smoothed her skirt, straightened her back against the chair, looked him in the eye and said, "I was wondering whether . . ."

The words choked off in a spluttering cough.

"You want to join your boyfriend in the interrogation section – is that it?" Bonner asked.

"I am a quick learner," she said. "I would be good."

The schnapps had beaded her face with sweat. Her dress seemed drawn more tightly than usual over her plump figure.

"What makes you say that?"

"Because the art of interrogation is knowing when to stop, knowing when they are going to talk. If you go too far, they either lose consciousness or they find some inner strength to resist you."

"Or they die," he said.

"Exactly. It's all a question of timing."

She had learnt a lot from her new boyfriend. He would have to let her go.

"Very well," he said. "I will see what I can do after the holiday."

He watched her leave, that fat bottom of hers swaying through the door, as if beckoning him to follow. He wondered if she did that deliberately.

They had drunk half the bottle, which meant that one more wouldn't hurt. He poured himself a glass, mixed it with a generous splash of water, leant back and lit a cigarette. He heard Hilde leave the office next door.

He had not given her much of a Christmas present; they had drunk half of it already. He would get her something else. He wondered if she would give him a present, indeed if anyone would. All he ever got from his wife and kids were silk handkerchiefs, aromatic candles and knitwear. No doubt his wife had knitted yet another cardigan for this Christmas.

Bonner tried and failed to blow a smoke ring at the ceiling. He was fifty-one years old and had worked hard ever since he left school at fifteen. His first job had been as a butcher's boy, back in Heidelberg. He had come a long way and done a lot for his country since then.

This year, he would give himself a present. He deserved it. He had worked his team hard. The Jewish Problem was well on the way to solution; tens of thousands were crossing the borders seeking sanctuary in Europe or Palestine. The major organs of state in Czechoslovakia had been infiltrated, with a little help from Canaris's military intelligence agency. Heydrich didn't trust Canaris and neither did Bonner. When they wanted information from the Abwehr they paid their own informants in the agency. On the home front, all was quiet. The Mauthausen camp that had opened in the summer in Austria was full to overflowing already and the new extension to the Sachsenhausen camp outside Berlin was filling up nicely.

At their last staff meeting, Heydrich had actually praised him in front of all senior members of the team. He had made a little joke about not wanting to formalise Bonner's role as deputy, in case Himmler gave him the top job. Except it wasn't really a joke, was it? Heydrich was always on the lookout for any threat to his authority.

The Obergruppenführer was in a good mood that Christmas and had given six of his senior staff the new Walther P38 pistol. It was not in production yet, although the army had placed a large order.

Heydrich had been very excited when he handed out the weapons and kept talking about the merits of the Walther against the older and heavier Luger. In fact, Bonner noticed at once that the P38 was too big for a shoulder holster and could only be worn on a belt holster beneath a jacket. Even then, it was bulky and uncomfortable, but Heydrich insisted his officers carry side weapons at all times – even at Christmas. The magazines were to be removed in official buildings. That was Heydrich all over: detail, detail, detail.

Christmas, thought Bonner; yes, he deserved a treat, a real treat. He thought for a while. A new suit? He could certainly do with one. A lobster dinner at the Adlon? Nice idea, but there was no point taking his wife; she would just complain about the extravagance. So what, then?

He knew what he really wanted, but was it worth the risk? Put it another way, who would ever know? Not Heydrich; he had gone south that morning for Christmas with that harridan of a wife and those ghastly kids with their scrubbed faces and brilliantined hair. No one would dare tell him, and even if they did, would he really care? That was the problem. He would.

He made up his mind. A night with her would be his Christmas present to himself. She would whine on about her brother, of course, but so what? He had kept the miserable little bastard alive, hadn't he? She should be grateful. Anyway, he would give her the beautiful hourglass as a present. She would like that. He would say it was a reward for her good work, and it was true. The Russian had praised her and talked of her elegant manners and demeanour, as if a brothel was a bloody modelling school.

The man from Moscow had been very important and claimed to have enjoyed his time at the Salon, even though the tapes had showed he was asleep most of the night. There were strange dealings going on between Berlin and the Kremlin. Even Heydrich didn't seem to know why the Russian was so important. Bonner thought it wise not to ask too much about that for the time being. Best to enjoy a night at the Salon – all night for once. He would call Kitty Schmidt and arrange it – tomorrow night. It was a Sunday, but the Salon would be open for business. The run-up to Christmas was the busiest time for Kitty Schmidt and her girls. Bonner drained his schnapps and picked up the phone.

The embassy began to empty the week before Christmas as staff headed home to Britain for the holiday. Sir Nevile had left earlier in the month for treatment in a London clinic.

The rumour was that he had cancer, but Halliday said it was a nervous breakdown as the man realised the extent of his misjudgement of those in power in Berlin.

Primrose Macrae had wanted to go home and spend the time with her family, but her husband had persuaded her to stay. They would invite William Shirer and Theresa for lunch on Christmas Day, he said, and then they would all go for a walk in the Tiergarten afterwards, if it was not snowing. Maybe Halliday would join them. Primrose had put her foot down. She liked the man, but she would not have him as a lunch guest. It was not so much the way he dressed and the amount he drank, but that he never took a bath.

"He also breaks wind regularly in a room full of people; have you noticed that?"

Macrae had indeed noticed how Halliday would shift in his chair during meetings and lift his haunches in a usually unsuccessful effort to fart silently. People tried not to sit next to him. Sir Nevile Henderson was aware of the problem and had added it to the long list of reasons to lobby for his transfer.

"Ask him round for drinks on Christmas Eve instead," said Primrose. "He'll be lonely, and anyway he's great fun if you sit upwind."

As they made their Christmas plans, Macrae waited for the excuse that would cover his wife's meeting with her lover. It would be a night out with the embassy wives or an afternoon shopping for family presents before the last post to England on the 19th. He didn't mind; in fact, he welcomed the idea.

It would allow him the same latitude. He had seen the gift he wished to give Sara, a bracelet made of small amethysts in the jeweller's shop in the Adlon. He had bought it and left it there to be picked up the day he would drop in on the Salon.

A quick Christmas visit. Her travel permit expired on the 22nd. He would have to meet her before then.

Roger Halliday knew that Christmas in Berlin that year would be a busy time, but even he was surprised by all the intelligence requests descending on him from that discreet office in Broadway, London. Actually, Sir Stewart Menzies, the famed "C" of the Secret Intelligence Service, did most of his work from White's Club in St James's Street, which is where Halliday had been recruited, fresh from Balliol College, Oxford, over a long lunch that had ended with coffee, brandy and the offer of "a job on the dark side of life, dear boy. Bloody good fun."

Menzies always said he did his best thinking in the calm of his club, far from teleprinters and telephones. Clearly, he had been spending a lot of time in the elegant morning room of White's in the days before Christmas. The list of requests to his man in Berlin was a long one. The prime minister's office wanted to know where and with whom the Nazi leadership was spending Christmas. The War Office passed on a request from the Royal Air Force about the new German Me 109 fighter plane that had been exhibited at the Paris Air Show the previous week. Someone had heard that the four machine guns on each wing had been of a smaller calibre than would actually be used in production. Was this a deliberate deception? Then there was the question from C himself. Was Hitler sleeping with Eva Braun, his purported mistress? If so, where and when did the two have sexual relations?

Halliday knew the answer to that. He had already sent London the name of the pharmacy in Munich where Braun had purchased her diaphragm and to which she returned regularly to buy supplies of lubricant. He also knew why

C wanted to know. Eva Braun's sister was in a relationship in Munich with a man of Jewish descent. Hitler did not know and Eva Braun was desperate for her sister to break the relationship before he found out. There was a propaganda windfall for the British if they could expose that juicy scandal.

But the big questions that came from the Foreign Office, and again from C himself, concerned the conspirators: General Beck and his successor as chief of staff, Franz Halder; Admiral Canaris, head of military intelligence; and Colonel Hans Oster, his deputy commander at the Abwehr. Then there was the former mayor of Leipzig, Carl Goerdeler, the most senior civil servant in the regime and the man who had reportedly, and at great risk, agreed to form a civil administration after a coup. What were they planning, what were they thinking, and were they still a coherent group?

Halliday groaned at these questions. The truth was he did not know. In all likelihood, the conspirators were lying low, disgusted with the pusillanimous attitude of the British and French towards their monstrous leader and terrified that the Gestapo would hear of their treachery.

He decided to drop in on the Salon one night to see if any of the big names were around. That would at least tell him that they still felt able to show their faces. The dark and dangerous side of the Salon rather appealed to Halliday. The women didn't interest him but he liked watching the men drawn by lust and alcohol into those rooms at the back, struggling against temptation like flies in a web feeling the approach of the spider.

Halliday had planned to spend Christmas Day, as he always did, in the luxury of his own company. He would rise late, breakfast on bacon and eggs, then attend a service at the nearest Protestant church. He would return for a glass of champagne at noon, light the coal fire that he had laid the night before and open a bottle of burgundy, which would be placed to breathe beside the fireplace. He would then sit down with a second glass and a bowl of olives, to read a Dickens novel. He knew them all almost by heart now, and that year he had decided to return to *Great Expectations*.

At three o'clock he would stoke the fire, carve the cooked turkey that had been delivered the day before from the food hall in Wertheim's department store and pour a glass of wine. He would then serve himself a plate of cold, thinly carved white meat, sliced tomatoes, rice and plenty of chutney. He would sleep after lunch and rise around six o'clock to finish the champagne while listening to one of the Beethoven symphonies, probably the ninth, on his wind-up gramophone. A perfect day, alone and at peace with the world.

Except this Christmas he would not be at peace. The office had decided to send over a young man to assist him. He was a fluent German-speaker who had already served in the embassy in Vienna and was presently stationed in Moscow. He came recommended by Menzies himself. Undoubtedly, he could do with some help, but it was a damnable nuisance. He would have to entertain the man on Christmas Day.

He usually refused all invitations on Christmas Eve but on this occasion he had accepted drinks with the Macraes. He liked Noel Macrae, although he thought him naive. He found Primrose arrogant and possessed of a social intolerance bred into English women of her class. But there was something different about her, a rebellious streak beneath the pale painted face, that appealed to him. She was edgy, a risk-taker, someone who indulged rather than suppressed her sexuality.

Since William Shirer had joined CBS the previous spring as a radio journalist, his distinctive high-pitched voice had become famous in America. Ed Murrow, the network's European manager, had hired him to bolster coverage of the continent and told him the audience would not worry about his voice as long as they got the news.

Shirer was supposed to be based in Vienna, but the news unfolded from Germany that year in a rolling series of headline stories that kept him at the microphone in the Berlin studio almost every day. From the Austrian Anschluss to Kristallnacht, the CBS correspondent riveted his listeners with broadcasts detailing Hitler's tightening grip on Germany and his threat to make war on his neighbours. He was careful to give only the news and present the facts rather than his own opinions. He told his listeners they could make up their own minds about the news he brought them.

At Christmas that year, Shirer decided to relax this rule and give his audience a feel for how ordinary people were spending Christmas in Berlin. His producer liked the idea. Paint us a picture in words, he said, and Shirer did, describing a snowbound city with black swastikas edged in silver glittering on candlelit festive trees. Christmas Eve was the time Germans celebrated the festival, he told his listeners, rather than the following day. On 25 December, the big stores in all major cities in Germany would be open until lunchtime so that people could exchange presents, buy gifts for those they had overlooked and maybe even get a last-minute Christmas tree.

He described Berlin as a city ablaze with lights, and at its centre was the Brandenburg Gate, where searchlights illuminated the great chariot drawn by four horses atop the monument – an observation that allowed Shirer to remind his audience that the charioteer was deemed by the National Socialist government to be Victoria, the Roman goddess of victory. When the triumphal archway had been completed in

1791, however, it was known as the Peace Gate and the charioteer was said to be Pax, the goddess of peace.

Throughout the city, curtains had been drawn back in most homes so that other people could look in and admire their neighbours' decorations. Seeking to show his audience the difference in the way the two countries celebrated the holiday, Shirer noted that Germans placed real candles on their trees rather than the electric ones favoured in America. They ate goose rather than turkey and did not leave stockings full of presents to be opened by children on Christmas morning.

However, the broadcaster confessed to his audience that the real mystery of Christmas in Germany that year was one he was unable to resolve. In Washington, President Roosevelt, his wife, Eleanor, and their family would spend Christmas Day in the White House. A press release would describe their activities and the guests that joined them for a drinks party in the evening.

In Berlin, the Propaganda Ministry refused to divulge any details of where, how and with whom Adolf Hitler would spend his Christmas. Shirer had enquired among his German contacts but no one knew where the Führer spent 25 December, or whether he celebrated it at all.

His best guess, Shirer said, was that the German chancellor had gone to the Berghof, his mountain retreat in Bavaria, to plan for the year ahead. However he chose to celebrate Christmas, or whether he did at all, was not important. This was a man whose actions in the coming year were likely to determine the future of Europe. Would 1939 bring peace to the continent – or war?

Shirer finished the address and returned to his rented apartment, happy that his wife Theresa had finally agreed to join him from Vienna. They would lunch with the Macraes on Christmas Day.

• • •

Gertrude Koenig could not interest her husband in the usual round of parties in the Mecklenburg district or even in the plans for Christmas Day itself at the hunting lodge. Large numbers of relatives from both of their families expected to be invited for the traditional Christmas Eve dinner and to stay on for a few days. Such invitations were highly desirable, and not just because Florian and Gertrude's Christmas Eve party always ended with a dance.

Many wealthy Berliners owned houses in the lakes around Mecklenburg and Christmas guests would find themselves in an uproarious cavalcade of lunches, dinners and dances as house parties exchanged visits. Romances among the young would bloom beneath the mistletoe, while the older generation drank too much, gossiped about the old days of the Kaiser before the war and made sly comments about the behaviour of the new generation.

Koenig would usually arrange the family festivities with the skill of a staff officer. He had often told Gertrude that the military science required to plan the movement of armies of men and materiel to the front line was child's play compared with the planning and diplomacy required to organise his family Christmas. He would immerse himself for weeks beforehand sorting out which relatives could comfortably be accommodated for the Christmas week and who should be politely put off with the promise of an invitation at Easter.

This year, he told Gertrude, the happiest Christmas he could imagine would be one without friends or family. There was no reason for any celebration, and instead they should have a quiet Christmas on their own, with only their dogs for company.

There had been a row. It was at the end of November, when Gertrude had walked into Koenig's study one evening. She noted the half-empty whisky bottle on his desk. He was drunk again. She brandished the sheaf of letters from uncles, aunts, nephews, nieces, brothers and sisters virtually inviting themselves for Christmas. He had taken them and thrown them into the fire. She had burst into tears. He had finished his whisky, thrown the dregs into the fire so that the flames leaped over the burning letters and taken her into his arms. He told her she could have whatever Christmas she wanted, providing he had nothing to do with the arrangements.

She knew the reason. Every weekend Koenig came home from Berlin there had been long meetings in the study with military friends and colleagues. She knew most of them, but they came dressed in civilian clothes and barely acknowledged her. Koenig's mood darkened with every visit. There were times that autumn when he did not come home at weekends at all.

When she called his office the following week, she was told he was away – on manoeuvres or on a staff training course. She suspected these were lies, a cover for something else. He was having an affair, probably with the English bitch. They had hardly made it a secret the last time she came to stay with that strange husband of hers. She had accepted it because there was little she could do about it.

But there was something else going on, something that frightened her. Munich had brought peace to the country and yet Koenig had damned the negotiations as a farce. That was why she wanted family around her at Christmas, a warm and comforting blanket of people to remind her that there was some normality in life. They would have Christmas with as much of the family as they could squeeze into the eight rooms of the hunting lodge.

21

Bonner arrived at the Salon laden with several bulging shopping bags. He was in civilian clothes as usual on such nights. Only Heydrich chose to wear full Gestapo uniform when calling on Kitty Schmidt. He was greeted at the door and escorted to the bar, where a seat had been reserved. He unpacked several boxes of chocolates and miniature cognac bottles – gifts for the girls, he explained.

He placed a wooden box on the bar, ordered a vodka martini and looked around. The tables were full and the bar was thronged two or three deep. Every girl in the house seemed to be on duty that night, but there was no sign of Sara.

There was the usual mix of uniformed military, mostly army, and civilians. Among them he spotted Carl Goerdeler, sitting at a table with other civil servants, Bonner supposed. Goerdeler was a former big city mayor and a noted economist. He had never appeared on any list of regime officials who used the Salon. He was said to be a financial wizard and a member of the party, but not political. Interesting, thought Bonner. He would check on the man tomorrow.

He scanned the room again and saw a familiar face at the back by the window, sitting alone on a table for two – white-haired, shaggy locks tumbling over his collar, dressed like a tramp. Even across a crowded room, Bonner could see the British agent was drunk. He had been seen there before, and Bonner wondered what a man of his tastes was doing in the Salon. He would hardly be there for pleasure.

Several people slapped Bonner heartily on the back, wishing him seasonal greetings. They were mostly from the army but one or two were Abwehr intelligence who seemed to know him. He returned the greetings and watched them shoulder their way through the crowd. They were sitting on Goerdeler's table, he noted.

Bonner slipped a hand under his jacket to adjust the belt holster. All the back-slapping had shifted his new Walther. He wondered whether he should unpack his gift for Sara and let it stand on the bar, then thought the better of it. Some oaf would knock it over.

And there she was beside him, moving into a seat that had been vacated by a drunken colonel in the artillery at Kitty's orders. She had a glass of white wine and raised it to him.

"Merry Christmas," she said.

"And to you." He pushed over the wooden box.

Sara untied the ribbons, flipped the latch on the box and took out the hourglass. She gave a little gasp as she set it down.

"This is for me?"

"Yes. Turn it upside down."

Sara turned the glass and watched as the coloured sands began to trickle through the narrow glass neck. On either side, drinkers at the bar craned their heads to watch.

Halliday stood up at his table, peering over the crowd at the bar. He had seen Goerdeler and the Canaris crowd, and that was all he needed to know. The conspirators were still talking to each other. Meeting so openly in a Gestapo brothel was probably a smart move. Good camouflage.

He saw the coloured hourglass on the bar and recognised Bonner from photographs on file. The Gestapo officer seemed to have given one of the house girls an hourglass. She was the dark-haired one he had seen in the Salon before. Very odd, but stranger things had happened in the place. He headed for the door. He had to be at the railway station to meet his new colleague early the next morning.

Sara held the hourglass carefully in her hands as she and Bonner edged through the crowd to the fanlight door. She had wanted to stop the sand clock and start it again so that she could watch it properly, but Bonner had been in a hurry as usual. The Pink Room was crowded and there were few carnations left in the bowl. They walked down the corridor to the staircase at the end and up to the best room in the house.

It was only a week since she had entertained the Russian there. Now she had to do the same for a senior Gestapo officer: Bonner, the man who had ruled her life for two years, the man who had beaten her. Bonner, the man who had given her a Christmas present, and for whom she was now to be a festive gift for the night.

The hourglass was beautiful; she had never seen anything like it. Sara turned it upside down and carefully placed it on the table by the bed. She watched the sand begin its sixty-minute journey and looked around the room. Kitty Schmidt had excelled herself. On a table, there was caviar, champagne on ice and plates of cold lobster. They hadn't given caviar or lobster to the Russian, she remembered. Poor man. He must have had a terrible hangover the next morning.

She watched the sand as Bonner threw off his clothes. First red, then yellow, then green flowed through the neck – rainbow colours to track the thin thread of time.

Bonner sat down on the bed and looked around with approval. This was going to be a night to remember. He could see Sara was happy to be with him. She had liked her present. She was a professional, as he was. This was what he wanted and she was happy to provide it. Both would make sure that Heydrich never found out. She certainly wouldn't tell him. He would probably have her killed. In fact, there was no probability about it. He would definitely have her killed. That was Heydrich's way. That psychotic violin player saw the world as a spider sees its web. She would just be another fly caught in the silky gossamer threads that he wove to trap his victims. That was the insane thing about Heydrich. He regarded a whore like Sara as his personal property, yet he ran a brothel where she was reserved for very important people. Well, he was one of those now, and to hell with Heydrich.

Bonner had been asleep for several hours when Sara woke him. He was lying on his front and felt her hands gently massage his neck and shoulders. He squinted at his watch. It was six in the morning. He turned his head and saw she was naked. He tried to remember the night before. It had been quite a performance. Now she was starting again, the hands moving down his back, stroking, kneading, bringing him slowly to life. His head ached and he felt thirsty, but he wouldn't tell her to stop, not just yet. This was his Christmas present.

Something cold and hard pressed against his neck. The first in a crowded jumble of thoughts told him she was using an ice pack to wake him. No, it was the cold barrel of a gun. His gun. His new Walther P38. He began to turn, levering himself upright. There was a click and then another. He flung himself around, grabbing for the gun. She was staring at him with a wild look in those blue eyes, pulling the trigger again and again. His new P38 was aimed at his chest. The little bitch was trying to kill him. With an unloaded gun. He had taken the magazine out. Thank God for Heydrich's attention to detail.

She threw the weapon at him. He instinctively ducked. The gun thudded into the bedhead. Now he was going to kill her. Heydrich should have done it long ago. Jewish traitress, assassin, whore. She thought she could give him the fuck of a lifetime and then turn his own gun on him. She would die slowly. He would do it himself in one of the execution rooms. He would get Hilde to watch. She would learn new ways of making a human die slowly and in agony. The thought warmed him as he clambered from the bed. He didn't see the hourglass scything towards him. It slashed into his face and neck. He dimly saw her face twisted in hatred and felt a terrible pain as he slumped back, blood spurting over his body in shiny red arcs.

Sara stood over him, heard his last gargled words, watched as he clutched his neck with one hand while the other flailed at her. She picked up the jagged remnants of the hourglass and rammed it into his neck, twisting hard. More blood spurted out, choking a last scream. She saw his eyes rise into his head and watched the body shake violently in its death throes, then slump back. Blood and coloured sand smeared his face and ran in rivulets down his chest.

She stepped back, looking down at the blood that covered her arms and stomach. She had anticipated that and had remained naked for the final act in the drama she had so carefully plotted. True, she had not counted on an unloaded gun – but everything else had gone as planned. She had worked through the timetable with a precision that would have impressed the man she had just murdered.

Sara showered and, fifteen minutes later, closed and locked the door of the Salon's honeymoon suite. She made sure the "Do Not Disturb" sign was in place. No one would dare enter that room and interrupt a senior Gestapo officer at play. Not for hours. Not even Kitty.

She walked through the empty main room and let herself out. She knew there would be nobody around. The cleaners did not start until nine. It was still dark, but there was plenty of traffic on the street. Her heart was pounding, yet she felt calm. The amount of blood had been a surprise. There had been so much of it. And the gun. The bastard hadn't put the magazine in. It hadn't mattered. She had done what she had to do. He had made a terrible noise with that final choking scream, but the rooms were totally soundproof. All she had to do now was follow the plan. She would catch a tram and go straight the Ostbahnhof. She would take no luggage to the station, only her handbag, with make-up, a comb, a bar of chocolate, money and the British travel permit.

The first train to Duisburg left at seven fifteen. It was an express and would take three hours. She would change for the cross-border train to Rotterdam. Then a bus ride to the Hook of Holland, a bus that stopped everywhere and took hours. That didn't matter. She would be much safer on that bus than hanging around the ferry terminal waiting to board the night boat to Harwich in England.

She told herself that her travel permit would allow her to leave the country without a problem. They would see she was a Jew from her name, but that would not matter. She was travelling on an official English temporary passport valid until 22 December. Anyway, she reflected, official policy was to expel Jews, not keep them in the country.

Then again, that might not apply to a woman who had just murdered a Gestapo officer. Sara smiled at her grim little joke. When would they find out? He had probably told his wife he was away at a conference. His office would not worry unduly for several hours. It was Christmastime and even Gestapo officers were not expected to keep office hours.

She had worked it all out so carefully. She would be across the border and into Holland by noon. She would still not be safe. She had heard many conversations in the Salon about German agents operating in Holland. She would only feel safe when she boarded the evening ferry from the Hook of Holland. She had deliberately chosen a complicated route to make pursuit much more difficult. No one would think she was going to the Hook of Holland. Ferries from that port crossed the North Sea to Harwich, on the east coast of England. A train to Rotterdam and a ferry across the Channel to Dover would be a much more obvious choice. Her ferry to Harwich would leave at nine thirty in the evening and arrive the next morning at six-thirty. It was a Dutch ship, the SS *Batavia*. She knew what she would do when the ship cleared the international three-mile limit. She would sit down and cry.

Sara reached the Ostbahnhof at just after seven. There were uniformed police on the station concourse, but no more than usual, she told herself. At the barrier, she handed the inspector her one-way ticket. He punched a hole in it and handed it back without a word. She boarded the train, choosing a compartment that was already almost full. As the train pulled out, she watched Berlin slipping away, the city centre sliding into the suburbs, the suburbs into industrial wasteland. She would never see the city again. She leant back and breathed a long sigh. Duisburg was the next stop, a station that was the hub for all long-distance rail traffic in northern Germany. There would be a forty-five-minute wait for the connecting train to Rotterdam.

If they were looking for her, that is where they would be. Customs officials would examine the luggage of passengers on the cross-border train at Duisburg and there would be passport checks at the border itself. They would ask her why she was leaving the country and where she was going. She had her story carefully prepared. She was a student returning to London, where she lived with her parents. She had been at the world-famous language school in Berlin learning German. Where had she stayed? In a hostel near the Gendarmenmarkt. Why did she want to learn German? Because it was the most cultured language in Europe and she wished to teach that language to students in England. She had worked out the answers to every question they might ask her. She had planned for this day ever since that night with the Russian.

As the train cleared the city and picked up speed in open country, Sara looked around at her fellow passengers. It was early in the morning and most seemed asleep. For some reason, she felt she was being watched, but she told herself this was understandable paranoia. She had just murdered a man; not just anybody but a senior Gestapo officer. With that thought in her head, she began to tremble uncontrollably. She felt sick and hurried to the lavatory. She was violently ill. She threw water in her face and looked in the mirror. A haggard, sleepless face looked back. She was in shock, she told herself. She slapped her face hard on both cheeks. She stopped shaking.

At Duisburg, Sara and other passengers joining the Rotterdam train were directed to a reserved waiting room. Customs officials entered and asked if anyone had anything to declare. It was a cursory visit, but they were followed by several police officers.

Kitty Schmidt arrived at the Salon at ten thirty that morning, slightly later than usual. She had done some Christmas shopping and went straight to her office, put the bags down and began to check the takings of the night before. There was thirty thousand marks in notes of various denominations in the safe, their best night of the festive season. She was counting the money when a woman cleaner appeared in the door and muttered something about the best room in the house. She appeared frightened.

Kitty took the master key and followed the cleaner. On the carpet below the door to the room was a fresh red stain that appeared to have oozed out of the room itself. Kitty bent and touched the stain with her finger. It was not wine, as she had thought; it was blood, wet, red blood. Kitty told the cleaner to tidy another room and opened the door of the honeymoon suite.

She stepped inside and closed the door quickly behind her. There was a sickly smell in the room. Bonner was lying with bedsheets covering his lower body and congealed blood and sand across much of his torso. His face was frozen in a grotesque parody of a medieval gargoyle, mouth open and blood-smeared teeth in a rictus grin. The sight and smell of the dead man made her retch.

Kitty Schmidt knew at once what had happened and what she had to do. The Jewish girl had murdered a senior Gestapo officer. And she, Kitty Schmidt, mistress of the most infamous brothel in Europe, had to leave the country. Now. She went straight back to the office, scooped up the cash and told the cleaner to go home. She knew her life and that of anyone who worked at the Salon would be very short once the Gestapo found out what had happened.

The railway crossing at the Dutch border with Germany was only a few hundred yards from the main road between the two countries. Convoys of vehicles, lorries, buses and horse-drawn carts were waiting at the frontier in lines that stretched back along the road as far as Sara could see.

The train had stopped to allow the frontier police to board and examine all passports. Sara could hear them moving down the carriage, flipping open documents, asking questions. She concentrated on the chaos of traffic at the road frontier.

A woman beside her followed her gaze and said, "The Dutch government closed the frontier to all road traffic yesterday."

"Why?"

"Too many Jews wanting to get out. Many leave their transport and try walking through the woods at night. The Germans shoot a lot of them, apparently."

Sara turned away to find a passport-control officer looking down at her. His uniform was new and he was young, hardly more than a schoolboy. He had a pistol in a holster on his belt. Sara tried not to look at it. Hanging from a lanyard around his neck was a stamp. In one hand he held a clipboard file.

She handed him the travel permit. He opened it carefully, spread it on his clipboard and examined it. He said nothing, but she watched his eyes moving back and forth across the document. She thought of time trickling through the hourglass in coloured sand. She wondered if they had found him yet.

"English?" the official said.

"Yes. Going home."

• • •

It was only later, when the train was well on its way to Rotterdam, that Sara realised that the parents of that youth must have arranged his job with the frontier police, to avoid conscription. It was a reserved occupation and they were probably a decent family living close to the border who knew what strings to pull to keep their son out of the army.

He had placed that precious piece of paper on his clipboard and stamped it vigorously, then returned it to her with a smile. She had been lucky, just as she had been with that beautiful hourglass Bonner had given her. She began shaking again and clutched her arms around herself to control the trembling. It was almost one o'clock and she had eaten only an apple all day. She would get a sandwich at Rotterdam and some coffee. She was free, almost safe, and soon she would be a long way from Berlin.

The feeling persisted that someone was following her. She got up and walked the length of the carriage. Seats were two abreast on either side of the corridor. She recognised no one. People glanced at her and turned back to their newspapers or the window. She told herself not to be silly.

It was four o'clock in the afternoon when the train reached Rotterdam. The passengers flooded onto the platform, only to be shepherded into a long hall with queues leading up to two desks manned by Dutch frontier police. Here passports were stamped after lengthy enquiries about the final destination. Her temporary passport carried no Jewish identification, but the name was enough. Where had she been born, what was her occupation, where was she going, why had she left?

The questions went on for almost an hour. Several officers examined her English documentation in turn, each muttering something to the other as the document was handed over. She could see they were frightened. They have closed their borders to fleeing Jews because they do not want to provoke Germany, she thought. Hitler wants to expel an entire race of his own people and no one wants to take them, for fear of harbouring opposition to the mighty Third Reich. And now the Dutch are helping the Germans shoot anyone trying to cross the closed frontier at night.

It was dark when they returned her travel document and let her go. She caught the bus to the Hook of Holland with only minutes to spare. She still had not eaten. They had given her nothing more than a glass of water in that little back room in the passport office where all those frightened men tried to decide whether to put a German Jewess with English papers back on the train across the border to Germany.

She had a meal at last at a harbourside café. The SS *Batavia* loomed over the quayside, its black-painted bow, white superstructure and single funnel illuminated by floodlights. The hull was rusty, paint flaked from the deck housing and the portholes were smeared with encrusted salt. It was the most beautiful sight she had ever seen.

Sara forked a dish of pasta and tomato sauce into her mouth, refusing to take her eyes off this wondrous vessel. It was eight o'clock and they would board in an hour. She ordered a bottle of Heineken beer and drank thirstily.

The sailors told her the crossing was a good one for a night in midwinter, but to Sara it seemed that the ship and its passengers were unlikely to survive to reach the English coast. The *Batavia* heaved and groaned, sliding down one huge wave before wearily clambering up the next. Every now and then, the ship rolled sideways, the twin masts dipping perilously close to the waves. Sara sat in the upper lounge, wrapped in a blanket, miserably waiting for seasickness to drive her yet again to the lavatory.

Even then, feeling as close to death as a perfectly healthy human being can do, she knew she was being watched. Someone was following her. She had seen the dark blue hat with the feather of a game bird on the train from Berlin, hadn't she? And the woman with the crocodile-skin handbag, had she been on the bus from Rotterdam? Then there was the man with polished shoes and an umbrella – had he been on the Rotterdam train, or had he got on at the Ostbahnhof? She had no evidence and had seen nothing to support her paranoia beyond her intuition. But she just knew.

The *Batavia* docked at six the next morning in Harwich. A salty rain slanted in from the sea, driven by a wind that whipped spume from the wave tops. The dockside cranes, wharves and terminal sheds were shrouded in a thick grey mist that defied daylight.

Everywhere she looked she saw the same dark grey, only a shade lighter than black. Even the faces of the porters, the dockers and the passport officials looked grey. God must have created a special hue of grey in his celestial paintbox for this island nation, she thought. She looked back at the ship that had carried her to freedom. It was no longer the glamorous vessel she had seen the night before. The *Batavia* looked like an old dog that had come in from the rain and was about to shake itself dry.

She bought a copy of *The Times* at the station. "Tuesday, December 20th 1938, price 2d," it said on the front. She was going to read every word, from the advertisements on the front page to the sports news at the back. She was going to learn everything she could about her new homeland. England was going to be her refuge, her harbour, her haven. She said a silent prayer to thank her father for his foresight in making his children learn the language of Shakespeare, Milton and Dickens. That is how he described it. No other nation on earth ever had such cultural heroes, he said, not even the Greeks. She would find a job and start again.

On the train to Liverpool Street Station in London, she sipped a cup of weak milky tea and repeated her destination to herself: Liverpool Street Station, Liverpool Street Station, Liverpool Street Station. The wheels on the track picked up the refrain and whispered it back to her. She was safe, she was free, she was going to Liverpool Street Station in London. She began to read *The Times*. There was a full page of personal advertisements on the front. A widow, through great misfortune, was forced to ask for a loan of £300. She offered references as to her good character. The Hon. Mrs F. Gore wished to make it clear that the photograph of herself in the window of a shop in Bond Street had been used without permission.

She turned inside to find that the classified advertisements continued over two further pages. Turning page after page of dense text, she came to Imperial and Foreign News on page 13. Sara half expected to see a report from Berlin of a grisly nightclub murder. Instead, a correspondent reported in a single column that Field Marshal Göring was holding talks with wealthier members of the Jewish community in Germany to speed Jewish emigration. The story said that the government hoped to complete its anti-Jewish policy by persuading Western nations to take the remaining six hundred thousand Jews in Germany over the next two years.

Over the page, Sara read that there was no sign of any change in the severe cold that had brought widespread snow to eastern and central England. The temperature at Kew Gardens in London had fallen to 26 degrees Fahrenheit. Frozen points meant delays to many rail services, especially on east-coast routes to Liverpool Street.

She began to feel better. Now at last she could tell herself she was free. She had escaped. She wondered about Kitty and the other girls in the Salon, then pushed the thought away. Finally, she allowed herself to confront the guilt that had followed her every step of the way from the Salon to that rust-bucket port in England. Her brother Joseph. What would they do to him in vengeance? She knew he would have urged her to escape; she could almost hear him pleading with her to flee, to escape any way she could. She had told herself there was nothing more they could do to him, even if he was alive.

She took comfort in the thought that he had been killed long ago, that Bonner had merely been lying, as Macrae had said. She hoped that was true, although the voice of intuition told her it was not so. Her guilt was still there. Maybe that was why she had felt followed and watched. Maybe it was her conscience that had dogged her steps all the way from Berlin.

Liverpool Street Station looked rather like the cargo port she had left two hours earlier. The same fortress-grey colour everywhere. The same grey faces, only here they were hurrying to buses, taxis, and down into the tube station. It was very cold and it was snowing. The pavements outside were awash with slush. She suddenly felt famished. What little she had eaten in the last twenty-four hours had vanished over the rail of the *Batavia*.

Across the road, she saw a welcoming splash of colour in the murk. The word "Café" was spelt out in large letters illuminated in yellow lights. A tropical palm tree formed the letter "C". Inside, in a thick fug of smoke, she saw people eating, drinking tea and smoking. She found a seat in the corner. Yes, she would have a proper English breakfast – bacon, eggs, sausage, tomato and fried bread.

She looked up at the counter to signal a waitress. A middle-aged man in a white raincoat smiled at her. He was carrying two cups of tea on a tray. He walked over and sat down at her table without saying a word. The bulbous veined nose and the locks of white greasy hair that fell over his collar were vaguely familiar.

Before she could say anything, he said, "Welcome to England. I have some friends who would like to talk to you."

22

Sara was exhausted and hardly able to move when they picked her up from the café and drove her away. She had developed a hacking cough on the boat that made her chest ache. She felt filthy, unwashed, and wanted nothing more than a hot bath, some clean pyjamas and to be allowed to sleep for days. Later, they said, later. First, we want to talk to you. They took her to a large house somewhere near Big Ben. She knew that, because she could hear the booming bongs of the hourly chimes very clearly. She was taken to an airy room at the top of the house, with a basin, a narrow metal frame bed and a view over the trees of a garden square. A matronly middle-aged woman ran her a hot bath, then gave her some clean underwear and a mug of tea while the men waited in the car outside. They drove her to an anonymous building in Westminster and led her to a small office, where she remained until they took her to the hospital.

The man and the woman were kind, polite, but very insistent. They wanted to know every detail of her life and especially her time at the Salon. When she begged and pleaded for information about her brother, they said that would come later. They wanted to know about Reinhard Heydrich, Joachim Bonner and the Salon's other customers, as they politely called them. She was careful not to mention Macrae, although they never asked whether any of the Salon's guests were English. They seemed obsessed with Heydrich, his personal habits, what he asked her to do in the rooms, how he ran the brothel and what happened to the films and the tapes.

The interrogators showed no emotion as they probed every detail of her life. She gave them a full account of her time growing up in Hamburg and how her brother had been drawn into the resistance. Their only interest in Joseph was how he had been used to blackmail her into working at the Salon. When questions arose about the sexual practices she had been required to perform, the man left the room and the woman wrote down the details. Sara noticed her hand shook slightly as she did so.

When she casually mentioned the Russian special guest at the Salon, they became particularly interested. They took details of his appearance and later asked her to look at a series of grainy, badly focused photographs. They showed a succession of Russian military men, bulky figures in ill-fitting uniforms with peaked caps, all facing the camera in rows. She quickly picked him out, and they seemed happy. She had asked them who he was but was told not to worry about it.

It was not until late on the first day that she told them she had murdered Bonner. That surprised them. They looked at each other in shock. She liked that. It gave her back a semblance of the control that she had lost when they took her away from the café. They asked endless questions about the murder and could not understand how she had used an hourglass to kill him.

• • •

It was on the second day of questioning that Sara heard someone else in the room answering for her. The voice was clear and the answers absolutely accurate. She looked around but there was no one there. She felt as if she was looking into a goldfish bowl and seeing herself swimming inside. She turned to her interrogators and asked who else had been in the room. They told her gently that the voice had been her own.

She began to cry and shake, and did not stop until a nurse in the hospital gave her an injection. Her nightmares collided with each other, each one replacing the last, until they merged into a kaleidoscope of fearful images: Joseph spread-eagled against the barbed wire of a camp fence, his head garlanded with a crown of thorns; Bonner smiling at her, then vomiting sand from his mouth; Joseph and Bonner together; and then Heydrich, thin lips twisted into a smile, the whip in his hand, beckoning to her.

They told her later that she had screamed in her sleep. She had slept for thirty-six hours.

They took her from the hospital to the house by the river and there she discovered what had been denied her all her life – the kindness of strangers. The same woman who had first looked after her turned out to be the mother of two teenage children. Her husband was a government official. Christmas was only a few days away and the house was decorated with coloured paper chains and balls of fluffy cotton wool stuck to every window. She ate with the family and quickly got to know the two children, a boy and girl of thirteen and fourteen.

Their mother took Sara shopping for clothes and personal items at a large department store in Sloane Square on her first

Saturday morning. That afternoon, she was taken to see some of the sights of London: Trafalgar Square, Tower Bridge, Buckingham Palace. It was Christmas Eve and the tour ended with lunch at a tearoom called Lyons Corner House. Sara wrote the name down, just as she recorded everything she saw and did, in a diary. It wasn't a real diary, just a notebook in which she used a page a day to describe her life in London. She was given books and magazines to read and treats like bars of chocolate. The kindness of these people felt like a warm bed on a cold night.

There were eight for drinks but only seven for dinner at the Macraes' house on Christmas Eve. Halliday had arrived first, apologising for the fact that he could not stay for dinner but knowing perfectly well that his invitation had been couched in such a way as to make it clear he was not expected do so. He didn't mind. He was tired. He had arrived back from London that morning and wanted nothing more than the comfort of his own apartment, a decent coal fire and a bottle of whisky. The brim of his hat was thick with snow and the white raincoat looked soaked through. Macrae took him to the drawing room, deliberately not asking about the sudden trip to London.

David and Amanda Buckland arrived next with a babble of Christmas greetings and remarks about the terrible weather and the snow and the lack of taxis and how they missed Christmas at home. Macrae guided them upstairs, where Halliday was standing in front of the fire with a balloon of brandy in his hand.

No sooner had he given the Bucklands flutes of champagne than the doorbell rang again. Primrose shouted something from the kitchen. Macrae went down to open the door to William and Theresa Shirer.

They were all standing around the fire when Primrose appeared, wearing a white apron and carrying plates of olives and crackers spread generously with pâté. She took off her apron and greeted everyone with little kisses on the cheek.

"Sorry, dinner is going to be late – what have you all been talking about?" she said.

"The weather," said Buckland.

"They say it is going to snow for another week," said his wife.

"It is worse in Vienna," said Theresa. "Twelve inches at the airport."

Primrose took a glass of champagne and laughed.

"Well, there's a surprise. It's snowing at Christmas in Berlin." She turned to Shirer. "William, you know everything; tell us what's really happening; not the boring old stuff in the papers. Rumour, intrigue dark secrets – something to make us draw closer to the fire."

Shirer sipped his champagne and looked at Halliday, who looked back and smiled. He would know, thought Shirer.

"I hear, and this is only a rumour but my sources are confident of the information, that a senior Gestapo officer has been found murdered in the Salon," he said.

There was a pause as everyone looked at the American.

"What is the Salon?" asked Primrose.

"A Venus trap," said Halliday, "run by the Nazis for the pleasure of their High Command and unwary foreigners."

"I thought a Venus trap was a nasty flower that caught insects?" said Primrose, her eyebrows arching.

"A perfect description of the establishment," said Halliday. "The Salon is a brothel masquerading as a high-class bar and restaurant. And you say there has been a murder there?"

Halliday had turned to Shirer. Yes, he definitely knows, thought the American. It would be strange if he didn't.

"Apparently. A few days ago. The place is closed."

"What's happened to the girls there?" Macrae said. "I mean, was one of them involved?"

He had recovered himself, but only just. Halliday saw Primrose glance at her husband with a slight frown. He had decided not to tell Macrae, but it was going to be very difficult.

"I am told the girls vanished, as you might expect," he said. "It was a Gestapo brothel and they would not have looked kindly on the murder of one of their own there."

"You know the whole story, then?" asked Shirer.

"I have heard what you have, and probably from the same source. But it seems to be true."

"It hardly matters. I can't touch it. I'd never get it past the censor," said Shirer.

"Who was he, do we know?" asked Amanda Buckland.

"Very senior. One of Reinhard Heydrich's top men," said Halliday.

Shirer looked at him admiringly. He knew the whole story and probably had the name of the victim. That was what you paid spooks for.

"You haven't got his name, have you?" asked Shirer.

"He is right at the top. Or was."

"And?" said Shirer.

"And it's Christmas. I think I can allow myself another glass of whisky," said Halliday.

"So what will they do, the Gestapo, I mean?" asked Macrae.

"They won't do anything," said Halliday. "Goebbels is involved and he is going to hush the whole thing up. They are not even going to announce the death. It is a huge embarrassment. But Goebbels loves it because he can get one up on Heydrich. They hate each other."

Primrose came over to Halliday and put her arm through his.

"You are a very clever man, Mr Halliday, and I don't think you have anywhere half as entertaining to go tonight. Won't you stay for dinner – please?"

Later that night, when the guests had left and Primrose had gone to bed, Macrae poured Halliday a nightcap. His colleague walked to the French windows and opened them, stepping onto the balcony. It had stopped snowing. Macrae joined him.

"It's warmer by the fire," he said.

"Safer out here," said Halliday.

They looked out at the lights of the city filtering through the leafless branches of the trees.

"It's her, isn't it?" said Macrae.

"Yes," said Halliday.

Halliday told him how he had been at the Ostbahnhof early in the morning to meet a colleague arriving on an overnight Moscow train. He had seen a woman hurrying to catch a train. She only had a handbag and no luggage, which he thought odd for a passenger on a long-distance train. Then he remembered that he had seen her the night before with Bonner in the Salon. He had given her a strange gift, a coloured hourglass. It was just a hunch that made him follow her. He had no idea that she was trying to leave the country until they reached Duisburg, when he realised that she must be the woman with the temporary British travel permit.

He was intrigued and had stayed on her all the way to the Hook of Holland. He had almost given up there, because there was little point following a runaway whore across the North Sea to England. But something about her, the way she kept looking around, the fact that she was obviously terrified of pursuit, made him buy a boat ticket.

Once in London, in a greasy station café, she had told him the whole story. She was obviously telling the truth; Halliday could see that. She was now in a safe house under interrogation.

"The whole story?" asked Macrae.

"Yes," said Halliday. "For an intelligent man, you've been remarkably stupid. It's freezing out here. Shall we go in?"

23

Sir Nevile Henderson returned to Berlin in mid-February after treatment for what he told Daisy Wellesley had been diagnosed as throat cancer. She was surprised that such a reserved figure had revealed this personal information. It was because he was lonely, she decided. A single middle-aged man had no one to talk to about a diagnosis that probably meant early death. So he had turned to her and told her in that casual, stiff-upper-lip manner that had probably been beaten into him at one of those appalling English public schools.

He had not wanted to talk to her further about his illness and he asked her not to tell the staff. It was as if he had mentioned an item for his official diary.

At the first staff meeting, it was noticed that he looked much older than his fifty-six years and that his voice had become hoarse and husky. The doctors in London had been cautious about his illness, telling him that with the right treatment its progress could be delayed, maybe for years.

Sir Nevile had chosen to believe them. It was not a difficult choice, since he had been convinced that his posting to Berlin as ambassador in 1937 was an act of Providence. It was recognised as the most difficult job in the Foreign Service. He had accepted the posting because he told himself that he had been selected with the divine mission of preserving the peace of the world.

He had talked at length with the prime minister in London, and Neville Chamberlain had agreed with him that despite the despicable treatment of the Jews and Germany's rapid rearmament programme, the mission remained to secure a peace deal with Hitler. The prime minister had admiringly quoted Sir Nevile's own words, which he had sent to the Foreign Office in a cable a few days earlier: "'If we handle Hitler right, my belief is that he will become gradually more pacific, but if we treat him like a pariah or mad dog, we shall turn him finally and irrevocably into one.'"

Chamberlain agreed with this analysis wholeheartedly and the two men had got down to the practicalities of drawing Hitler into fresh negotiations. The tactic was to call a European disarmament conference that would embrace Italy, France, Poland and Britain in a pact to reduce arms production every year over the forthcoming five years. The stick was international supervision by the League of Nations, but the carrot was increased economic productivity and growth.

This was the major initiative that Sir Nevile intended to discuss first with Göring, with whom he had established a good friendship. Hitler would listen to Göring. The military would accept, both because they were far ahead in terms of their military inventory and also because they did not want war.

This logic had looked very credible in London, and Chamberlain had had little difficulty in convincing the foreign secretary to go along with the plan. Back in Berlin, however, the idea of trying to explain the initiative to his own staff on yet another bleak morning did not look quite so appealing.

For a start, Halliday had decided to attend and the man was bound to make trouble. Henderson had done his best to persuade the prime minister to sack the agent but he had been turned down. Even the British prime minister did not interfere with the Secret Intelligence Service at that level.

Then there was Macrae. In his absence, the military attaché had become totally unreliable. Henderson had read his cables to the War Office. Macrae had argued that not only was war inevitable but the sooner it happened the better. With every passing month, the German military was increasing its superiority in manpower and weaponry over the combined forces of Britain and France. The navy was the only area in which the British could still hope for superiority. In terms of airpower, the RAF was outnumbered by the Luftwaffe's combat aircraft. However, the early prototypes of the Spitfire fighter plane had proved successful in trial flights and showed that, in time, the plane might outfly the German Me 109 in combat.

"Welcome back, Ambassador!"

It was David Buckland who led the chorus of greetings that morning. Sir Nevile rubbed his hands and smiled. They all seemed pleased to see him, most of them anyway. Halliday was lounging at the back as usual, with his lower shirtfront buttons undone.

The meeting lasted for almost three hours, and by the time it ended just before lunch, Sir Nevile Henderson realised that Providence had overlooked the presence of Satan in Berlin.

Henderson might have discounted the news he received that morning from Halliday had it not been comprehensively endorsed by Macrae and received general nods of assent around the table.

Halliday had revealed in his usual insolent manner that he had what he called "22 carat" information that Hitler planned to march into Prague and annex the rest of Czechoslovakia on 1 March, in exactly ten days' time. The Munich agreement would be publicly torn up, to the humiliation of Great Britain and its prime minister. Further, he said, the Germans were negotiating a secret deal with Romania to gain access to all her oil fields – an essential prerequisite for war.

Finally, and most alarming of all, a senior officer in the Russian NKVD intelligence service had been in Berlin just before Christmas. Secret talks were under way for a military pact between the two countries. At a stroke, this would remove the nightmare that had always troubled the sleep of the German High Command – the prospect of a two-front war.

Sir Nevile flatly refused to believe the last piece of information. He grudgingly accepted the force of Halliday's argument that Hitler was accelerating his military plans. The idea of a disarmament conference, Halliday had said, was a very bad joke, especially since the House of Commons had at last come to its senses and had just voted £150 million for rearmament.

The two men then clashed in a manner with which their colleagues were now wearily familiar. Britain's decision to rearm was designed to pressurise all nations in Europe into accepting a disarmament conference because who, in the dying days of the Great Depression, would wish, or could afford, to enter an arms race? It was a forcing move by the government – and would everyone please note that conscription had not been introduced?

Thus the ambassador confronted the man who headed British secret intelligence operations in Germany. The logic was clear, unarguable, and was the product of the finest minds in the Foreign Office and Downing Street.

But as Halliday pointed out, such theory crafted in the calm waters of Whitehall and London's clubland hardly stood a chance in the stormy seas of Europe. Logic did not apply to Hitler. He did not operate by conventional norms of behaviour. He was a barbarous opportunist seeking an excuse to take Germany to war.

At which point, Sir Nevile had risen to his feet, the pallor and creased lines on his face more obvious than usual. He said there were enough prophets of evil in the world without the British embassy adding to their number. He stalked from the room. As someone remarked, that was how most staff meetings at the embassy seemed to end in those days.

Noel Macrae never knew what finally made his mind up. Perhaps it was the sight of Hitler triumphantly saluting his troops in Prague after his army had seized the rump of a Czechoslovakian state that had been broken up by British diplomacy at Munich. Perhaps it was the extravagant plans for Hitler's fiftieth birthday celebrations on 20 April. Since the turn of the year, Goebbels and his Propaganda Ministry had been priming the press with details of the largest military parade in the history of Europe, which would mark the day in Berlin.

Forty thousand soldiers from all units would march past the reviewing stand on Charlottenburger Chaussee, now renamed the East–West Axis. Two hundred aircraft would fly overhead at a height of only four hundred feet. On the main reviewing stand, twenty thousand guests would gather, both to acknowledge the power of the Third Reich and to pay homage to the man who had lifted his nation from the wreckage of war and bankruptcy to become the foremost power on the continent. Hitler would stand alone, to take the salute on a plinth projecting from the main stand decked with oak leaves and laurel branches.

The celebrations would be nationwide. There would be a new luxury edition of *Mein Kampf*, with blue and red boards embossed with a gold sword. There was to be a major feature film about the life of the Führer and there was even talk of an opera.

There was no end to the madness. In a private coded cable to Sir Leslie Hore-Belisha in London, Macrae wrote, "The bitter truth that has to be faced is that Hitler has risen above politics and is now deified as a god by most of his countrymen and especially the young men and women in the Hitler Youth movement."

Looking back on it, Macrae realised that he had long known that the fiftieth-birthday festivities would provide the opportunity. What he had always lacked was the lavalike flow of anger that would turn motive into action, sweep aside reason and drive him to an act of damnation and salvation.

He would be damned whatever the outcome, no question about that. The salvation, if he succeeded, would be for a generation alive at that moment and for unborn future generations.

The moment arose one morning in March when he came across a Jewish woman in Unter den Linden. It was mid-morning and it was snowing again. She was wearing only a shawl over a threadbare, patched woollen jacket and long skirt. On her feet she wore clogs that were too big and must have belonged to a man, maybe her husband. She wore a large full-brimmed hat that looked as if it had been squashed down onto her head, because the brim was only just above her eyes. The yellow Star of David, prominently sewn onto the jacket, was the only splash of colour on her clothes. She carried a baby no more than eighteen months old on one hip while pushing a wooden cart with another young child with her free hand.

She was being jostled and prodded by two policemen walking behind her. The woman was obviously exhausted and could hardly stand. She kept slipping in the snow and slush, and every time she did so there would be another vicious jab from a truncheon. A small crowd followed the policemen, while a stream of shoppers eddied around the spectacle, heads down, eyes averted.

Macrae had stepped in front of the policemen, waving his diplomatic pass and demanding in a voice of outraged authority to know what was going on. The policemen, robotically trained to respect authority, had stopped and barked some order at the woman. When she turned, her face was that of a ghost. Imprinted on the pallid features was the pleading look of a mother who had accepted her own fate but still clung to the faint hope that she might save her children.

Macrae had demanded to know the reason for her treatment. The police looked at Macrae's diplomatic card and whispered to each other. One spat into the snow. They said she was a thief who had been caught selling stolen butter. They were taking her to the police station on Alexanderplatz. Would the Englishman move out of the way, please? This was Berlin not London, and they had a job to do.

To his shame, that is what Macrae had done. He stepped back and watched as the woman staggered up the avenue with her children towards the main square by the Brandenburg Gate. The crowd had followed, anxious to see justice meted out to a Jewish thief. Once inside the largest police station in the city, the woman would very quickly appear before a single junior judge. Sentence would be passed after a cursory hearing of a few minutes. She and the children would be on the train to a camp the next day. The children would die first in that camp and she would follow. Macrae had seen death in that ghost face. He knew she would stay alive to protect her children, whatever the horrors that awaited them all. But they would all die, because that is what the camps were for.

It had been early March when Macrae saw this. He had done nothing after the initial protest, because there was nothing he could do beyond get himself arrested, detained and then released in a few hours. At least, that is what he told himself. But that day he felt a sense of shame and helplessness that quickly turned to rage. Because there *was* something he could do.

He had taken his rifle out of its case that night, removed the protective oilcloths and laid it on the kitchen table. The telescopic sights had been wrapped separately in fine silk, and this too he laid on the table. Finally, he drew a small velvet pouch from the case and laid it alongside the rifle.

He oiled the mechanism of the rifle, first the bolt and breech, and then the magazine clip. He oiled the spring within the magazine and pushed it gently up and down, so that it slid smoothly back and forth within the casing of the magazine. He pulled the drawstring of the pouch open and shook out five rounds of .303 copper-headed bullets.

The infantry used a different version of the Lee–Enfield, with a ten-round magazine, but snipers preferred the five-round version. A sniper rarely got a second chance after the first couple of shots. He slipped the magazine into the gun, released the safety catch and snapped the bolt up and forward to chamber the first round. He raised the gun to his shoulder, swung the barrel to the window and peered through open sights into the darkness outside.

He tried to remember how many boar he had shot that day on Koenig's estate. Maybe a dozen; he couldn't be exact, because his memory dragged him back years earlier, recalling every shot he had fired. He knew precisely how many men he had killed. Fifteen young Germans, front-line troops, artillery observers, runners and even a sniper like himself, had fallen to this weapon. Their lives had ended, darkening those of their families and friends for ever.

They had all met clean, sudden deaths, a blessing for trench soldiers more likely to live out their lives maimed in hospitals or as gibbering wrecks in lunatic asylums. Their names would be inscribed on a marble memorial somewhere, and flowers would be laid at the base on their birthdays by grieving mothers, fathers, wives and children.

"What on earth are you doing?"

Primrose was standing in the kitchen door, elegantly dressed as if for a cocktail party, which is exactly where he thought she was.

"I thought you were out."

"I was, and I got bored. What are you doing with that thing?"

"Just checking, giving it a little service."

"It's time you got rid of it."

"Why? It's a beautiful piece."

"A piece of your past, I know. That's why you should get rid of it. Give it to a museum or something."

He clicked the bolt back and ejected the bullet from the chamber. It fell onto the table. Primrose shuddered and walked to the fridge, pulling the door open.

"For God's sake, put it away. I can't stand the sight of it."

"You didn't seem to mind guns when we were shooting with Florian. I seem to remember you had quite a few shots."

He was wrapping up the gun and putting the bullets back into the pouch. She swung round from the fridge, a glass of white wine in her hand.

"That was different. That was a country shoot. This is my kitchen, and I come back to find you waving that bloody thing around."

"I didn't know you were coming back. I'll put it away."

She sat down suddenly and slumped in her chair.

"I'm sorry. I just can't stand this anymore."

"What, you mean me?"

"No, it's not you. It's everything. All anyone talks about is war. It's dark all day and it never stops snowing. I need to get away, see some sun, get some light."

He had sat down opposite her. Her eyes were filmed with tears. She sniffed loudly, rubbed her nose with the back of her hand, got up and brought him a glass of wine.

"I want to go skiing up in the Alps. There's sun up there all day long. The air is like champagne, they say. I know you can't get away. You're busy with this bloody crisis. It just goes on and on. But I need to get out."

"Of course, I quite understand."

He reached a hand across the table and she took it, smiling through the tears that were falling gently down her cheeks. She sniffed again and drank her wine.

"I am sure the embassy will help arrange it," he said.

She smiled again.

"No need. I have done all that. There's a little place up in the mountains near Munich called Lenggries. You can ski all day, apparently. The snow is wonderful. Evenings are all glühwein and old folk music."

"But who will you go with? You can't go on your own."

"Of course not. Some friends want to come."

Some friends, or one particular friend, he wondered. It didn't matter. He got up and slid the rifle back into its leather case.

"I am pleased for you," he said. "You need a break, we all do, but you're right, I can't get away."

He leant over to kiss her. She raised her mouth, pursing her lips to meet his. He felt the taste of wine on her lips. She put her arms around him and gave him a quick hug. He felt her cheek against his, wet with tears.

24

No one in the British embassy had ever seen Roger Halliday smile. He would return morning greetings with a nod and sombrely thank people for the occasional courtesies bestowed upon him by way of a chocolate biscuit with his morning coffee or a gift of flowers on his birthday.

In spite of his dour manner, Halliday was generally liked, especially by the secretarial and junior staff, who admired the nonconformist manner in which he dressed, his inevitably late appearances at important meetings and his ill-disguised contempt for diplomatic protocol in general.

The shabby dress and the lack of personal hygiene were dismissed as the eccentricities of an *homme sérieux* and it was generally accepted that Halliday had much to be *sérieux* about in the Berlin of March 1939.

So Macrae was surprised to see his colleague smile broadly as he paced the drawing room in his Charlottenburg house one evening in late March. A nearby church had just struck six o'clock. It was still light outside and there was a lingering warmth at the close of the day that gave a hint of the spring to come.

"Do you mind if I have another glass of that fine Alsace wine?" said Halliday. He spoke in the manner of someone who had thought of a good joke and was waiting for the right moment to tell it.

Macrae poured the wine and followed Halliday onto the balcony. Together they looked silently out through the trees to the broad avenue. To the east, the soaring Siegessäule was being hung with long white streamers edged in red and carrying symbols of the imperial eagle and the swastika.

It was three weeks before the Führer's birthday celebration, but Goebbels had ordered a long and lavish build-up to the event. Workmen were already constructing the stands and seating for thousands of important guests.

The Victory Column, a reminder of the iron fist with which Bismarck had crushed France, was to be a focal point of the march-past. The column carried intricate carvings showing the triumph of German arms as they dictated peace terms to the French at Versailles in 1871. Searchlights were to illuminate these frescoes on the night of the celebrations while fireworks arced overhead. It was known to be Hitler's favourite monument in Berlin, which is why Albert Speer had ordered the whole edifice to be transported stone by stone so that it now faced that other monument to past German glory, the Brandenburg Gate, along the Charlottenburger Chaussee.

"See that reviewing stand through the trees?" he asked Halliday.

"Yes."

"It is almost exactly five hundred and fifty yards," said Macrae. He had paced the distance only that morning.

Halliday stepped back into the room. He was definitely smiling now. He put a finger to his lips.

"Not another word," he said.

Halliday closed the window, still smiling. Macrae was irritated. Perhaps he was being mocked.

"Why are you smiling?"

"Because I've watched you these last few months, Macrae. Anyone who knew your record in the war, knew where you lived in Berlin, knew your views on these gangsters here and above all knew what you thought of the policy of appeasement would know what was going through your mind. My only worry was that the Gestapo might work it out as well, but they don't seem to have done."

"What are you talking about?"

"I'm talking about what you plan to do with that old army rifle of yours – the one you used when you shot all those boar."

Macrae sat down, hoping to give the appearance of calm he certainly did not feel. Halliday had been talking to Koenig. The German colonel had been bypassing him and giving secret information to British intelligence. And now Halliday had guessed what he planned to do. He felt a fool, no he *was* a fool, but it didn't matter, did it?

Halliday watched him, saying nothing while the minutes passed.

"You approve?" said Macrae finally.

And then Halliday laughed, a long laugh that ended with a choking splutter. He sipped his wine, still smiling.

"That's not my job. But I know a man in London who would be very interested. Whatever you do, don't tell the ambassador."

"What should I do?"

"There's a flight tomorrow morning. Tell Primrose it is an urgent recall from the War Office."

"She's skiing."

"Ah, yes. By the way . . ."

"Yes?"

"I'm coming with you."

Sir Stewart Menzies spent his weekends on the country estates of ennobled and wealthy landowners in Gloucestershire, where fox hunting was more a presiding passion than an occasional sport. Every Thursday or Friday evening, he would take the express train from London to Bath. By special arrangement, the train would stop at a private railway station owned by the Duke of Beaufort, where Menzies would alight, often to be personally welcomed by the duke himself. It was with the Beaufort hunt, the most famous in the country, that Menzies took to his horse and followed the master and his hounds every weekend in the season. When the season ended, in May, the duke and his friends would spend their evenings recounting the glories of past hunts and eagerly looking forward to the start of the next season.

It was a curious convenience for Sir Stewart Menzies and his friends that interest in the sport was not confined to their social class. Fox hunting had a wide following among country people of all classes. The young would trail boisterously after the hounds on foot across field, stream and hill every weekend, while their elders gathered to admire the spectacle of the weekly meet, when riders, horses and hounds gathered under the direction of the master. Scarlet-jacketed men with white riding breeches mingled with ladies riding side-saddle, wearing bowler hats and skirts flowing down to their stirrups. They would be handed small glasses of cherry brandy to stiffen their resolve for the hard riding ahead while the onlookers mingled with the hounds and drank glasses of beer served from a local pub.

Menzies liked to think of this weekly pageant as the quintessence of England – a coming together of grandees and yeomen, rich and poor, men and women, all gathered to pursue and celebrate a sport that was born when the great forests of England were cleared in the medieval ages.

Menzies was well aware of the critics of the "mink and manure" set. He knew that the outdated lifestyle of the privileged few on their country estates presented easy propaganda victories for socialists and their communist allies. The fact that fox hunting was a popular country sport that created jobs where few were to be found cut no ice with the metropolitan intelligentsia.

His own answer to such critics came every week on the Monday-morning train back to London. Once in his office on the narrow street off Parliament Square quaintly named Broadway, he liked to think of himself as the mastermind of a piratical enterprise organising deception, theft, blackmail, kidnapping and the occasional murder.

The object was not money but information – secret information held by enemies of the United Kingdom. Menzies enjoyed this double life as a fox-hunting grandee and a swashbuckling pirate, because the first gave him very good cover for the second and both gave him immense pleasure and power.

That Monday morning in March he was due to meet his own highly regarded man in Berlin and the military attaché at the embassy there. The day had begun well. He had been gratified by finally being confirmed as C, the chief of the Secret Intelligence Service. His predecessor Sinclair had died after a long illness the previous November and it had taken the intervening months for the prime minister's office to agree to appoint a fox-hunting friend of the Duke of Beaufort as head of the British Secret Intelligence Service.

There had been those who doubted the wisdom of the appointment. That political outcast and troublemaker Winston Churchill had been fiercely opposed, for one thing. Menzies had been told that any doubts in the cabinet committee overseeing the Secret Service were immediately removed with the remark "When has Churchill been right about anything?"

Macrae and Halliday were ushered into C's office, where a coal fire burnt brightly and a tray of coffee and biscuits had been placed on a low table. Their plane had arrived that morning and they were due to return early the following day. They had just twenty-four hours to win sanction for the plan.

Menzies listened to both men carefully as in turn they explained their proposal. The SIS did not balk at the occasional killing of enemy agents or, on rare occasions, its own traitors, but never before had C been presented with a plan to murder a head of state. And Hitler was not just any head of state. The assassination of the Führer of the Third Reich on his fiftieth birthday was a plan so bold, so freighted with risk, so utterly unimaginable, so terrifying in its possible consequences yet so rich in potential reward, that it immediately appealed to Menzies.

He knew that critics such as Churchill had claimed that a London clubman who spent his time fox-hunting at weekends lacked the ruthless capacity for dirty work required of a spymaster. This would be his answer.

Roger Halliday's advocacy of the plan was a brilliant analysis of the consequences of doing nothing. Hitler was bent on a war for which the British and French were unprepared. The United States would stay out of a European conflict unless directly attacked herself. There were alarming reports that Germany and Russia were seeking a rapprochement that would give Stalin a large portion of Poland and allow the Nazi generals to fight a one-front war in the west.

As for the disaffected generals in the German High Command, all hopes of a coup against the regime had turned to dust. They collectively despised Hitler but lacked strong leadership. They would only act against the regime, Halliday claimed, if Hitler was somehow removed from power. Menzies admired Halliday. He was a highly effective agent and someone who stood up to that recklessly pro-appeasement ambassador in Berlin.

The doubts in Menzies's mind lay not in the assassination itself. If Colonel Macrae was the excellent shot he was said to be, and if his firing position was indeed between five hundred and six hundred yards of Hitler's reviewing stand, he could see that, technically, the killing could easily be accomplished.

There were two problems. Both were political. There was a good chance the assassination would be traced to Macrae and thus to the embassy. Dismissing Macrae as a lunatic extremist who acted on his own would lack credibility. Britain would stand before the world as an exemplar of murderous hypocrisy, a supposedly civilised Christian nation that carried out the extrajudicial murder of its political enemies abroad.

Against that, the concentration camps would be opened and the ghastly apparatus of Hitler's tyranny would be exposed. The generals would reveal secret military plans for an invasion of Poland and probably Russia as well. Europe and the world would see that Britain had acted to free mankind from a monster and to prevent a second European war.

Menzies was confident that, with a cooperative British press and the worldwide reach of the BBC, this view would win international acceptance, not least because it was true. The facts would speak for themselves.

The real political problem lay in Downing Street and the Foreign Office: how to persuade Sir Neville Chamberlain and Lord Halifax, both men of high Christian principles, that there was a moral as well as a strategic case for Hitler's assassination?

As on the hunting field, Menzies deemed that the best tactic was to tackle the problem head on. A high stone wall or a stream in flood were best crossed at the fastest gallop a well-whipped horse could muster.

He thanked the two men and told them their journey from Berlin had been well worthwhile. However, he neither sanctioned their plan nor committed himself to its merits, beyond saying that their proposal required further discussion.

He told them to await confirmation of an appointment with the foreign secretary, maybe as soon as that afternoon. There was no time to lose, Menzies said. If, as he hoped, the plan was approved, much secret work would have to begin on how best to deal with a Germany without Hitler.

The appointment was made for 3 p.m. and switched from the Foreign Office to 10 Downing Street. The prime minister had been briefed on the mission of the men from Berlin and wished to hear their plans first-hand. Roger Halliday was not included in the meeting because, much as Menzies admired his man in Berlin, he did not think it wise to expose a prime minister who was all class and starch to a man who despised social convention. Halliday was a mustard man, thought Menzies, an unconventional outsider without the manners or background of a gentleman. That is what made him such a good agent in the field.

Before the meeting at Number 10, Halliday gave Macrae a final piece of advice. "Don't criticise the appeasement policy, don't even hint that it has failed or that Hitler has pulled the wool over everyone's eyes. Just remind them that we once executed our king in the name of freedom, and surely we can do the same to free the Germans from their tyrant."

They arranged to meet later that day at 6 p.m. on the bridge over the lake in St James's Park, just four hundred yards from Downing Street.

"Don't be late. I'm going to give you a decent dinner," Halliday said, and was gone.

"Colonel Macrae and Sir Stewart Menzies," said the usher, opening the door to the Cabinet Room. Sir Neville Chamberlain and Lord Halifax rose from their seats and welcomed the two men. Macrae was nervous and tripped on the carpet before taking his seat, while Menzies acted as if he was reclining in an armchair at his club and was about to discuss the afternoon's racing with a couple of fellow members.

Macrae looked out of the window and noticed that the view had changed since he had last been in this room. It had been August and the trees in the park were in full leaf. Now, the branches were bare but speckled with green buds. Spring was coming and so was Hitler's birthday. He craned his head, trying to see the bridge over the lake where he would meet Halliday that evening. They would get drunk tonight whatever happened, deliriously drunk.

"We have met before," said a voice, and Macrae turned to see a long hand extended over the table. Mr Edward Bridges, the cabinet secretary, had taken his place and the same stenographer as before had also joined them. Macrae shook the hand and nodded.

"Shall we begin?" said the prime minister. He was looking at a paper that Menzies must have prepared. It was just one side of foolscap and, turning his head to read the upside-down script, Macrae could see the title was suitably vague: "Closing the Road to War."

Menzies began by revealing what he termed new information that showed how decisively the balance of power was tipping against Britain in Europe. Every move made by the Third Reich pointed to war in September. The latest rumours of a German invasion of Holland and a sudden air attack on London launched by the Luftwaffe from Dutch airfields was fanciful nonsense, said Menzies. What he could say with confidence was that a German attack on Poland had been planned in detail and that it would be carried out in connivance with Russia no later than September. That was *not* a rumour, he said firmly. The information was based on hard, verifiable facts.

Lord Halifax sat quite still, arms crossed, his beak-like face showing no signs of interest. Rimless reading glasses hung from a loop around his neck. From the corner of the room came slight tapping sounds as the stenographer's fingers flew over her keyboard. The prime minister merely looked down at the document before him and said nothing.

He raised his head as Menzies finished and looked at Halifax.

"Well, Arthur?" he said.

Lord Halifax uncrossed his arms and picked up the paper. He adjusted his spectacles and looked at it for several moments. He too was a countryman at heart, finding the greatest pleasure in walking the moors of his native Yorkshire at weekends. As a fellow Old Etonian and member of White's, he had supported Menzies's appointment as C.

"If I understand you correctly, Sir Stewart, you're telling us this in order to justify the assassination of Hitler," he said.

"Exactly."

"And Colonel Macrae here is the man who will carry out the killing."

The word "killing" seemed to galvanise the prime minister, who looked at his intelligence chief.

"Are you serious, C?"

"Deadly serious, Prime Minister."

"What would the world say if it were revealed that we had actively carried out the assassination of a legally elected European head of state?"

"By the time the world finds out, if they ever do, Germany will be in the hands of the generals, the Nazis will have been driven from power and the world will be a safer and better place," said Menzies.

"Well, I have heard of many strange things in this room, but I think this paper takes the biscuit. Arthur, what do you think?"

The reply was well prepared and calculated to end the meeting. The prime minister and his foreign secretary had planned this response, Macrae realised.

"We have not yet reached a point in our diplomacy where we can substitute assassination for negotiation," said Lord Halifax.

"I agree absolutely. We can't go round killing foreign leaders because they behave badly, besides . . ."

Here the prime minister got to his feet, drew a pen from his inside pocket and wrote something in the margin of the briefing paper. He handed it across the table to Menzies.

"I thank you both for coming and I apologise, Colonel Macrae, that you have had a wasted journey."

At six that evening, Macrae stood on the bridge in St James's Park looking towards Buckingham Palace. It was dusk but the Royal Standard was clearly visible above the building, which meant that King George and Queen Elizabeth were in residence. They would be preparing for the evening ahead: drinks perhaps with foreign dignitaries and then a formal dinner. They would talk about their regular Easter visit to the royal lodge in Balmoral and maybe the forthcoming summer tour of the United States. They would be as insulated from the world around them as an Egyptian mummy in the British Museum.

He had not been able to remind Chamberlain that a much earlier monarch had met a bloody end on a scaffold in Whitehall for the crime of defying parliament. In fact, he had not been asked to say anything at all at the meeting. It had been an ambush carefully organised by Lord Halifax, and the fox-hunting C had ridden straight into it. Chamberlain's final scrawled comment on the paper outlining the case for the assassination had been one of utter contempt for the whole idea: "This would not be sportsmanlike behaviour," he had written.

Macrae looked left and right, hoping to see the familiar dirty white raincoat flapping around the portly figure of a man who must be as disappointed as he was. Halliday was always late.

He watched a line of ducks ripple up the lake – drake, hen and three smaller birds from last year's brood. There was a flash of coloured feathers as they lifted from the ruffled water and rose like flowers in flight, their petalled wings beating against the darkening sky.

"Beautiful, aren't they?" she said.

He turned, gripping the railing tightly, knowing the voice so well yet feeling the shock of a surprise so total that for a moment he thought he must have imagined the words.

She was standing there beside him, looking older and thinner, smiling, dressed in a smart brown woollen coat with mother-of-pearl buttons.

"What are you doing here? How did you know? When did you . . .?"

His words trailed away as she leant up, gave him a kiss on the cheek and slipped an arm through his.

"The pubs are open; let's get a drink," she said.

"Hold on. My colleague is meeting me here." He wasn't thinking clearly; he couldn't think. Where was Halliday?

"*I'm* meeting you here. It's all been arranged. Come on."

"No, let's walk," he said.

He took her arm and steered her across the bridge towards Birdcage Walk. They swung left on the path around the park. He gripped her arm tightly. She didn't seem to mind. He needed the cold air of a darkening spring evening to clear his head. He needed to understand and work out what had happened. Halliday had fixed this. It was always Halliday. Where was the bastard? Why hadn't he told him?

She began talking in a low voice, as if the plane trees branching over the path were listening. They walked three times around the lake in the gathering dark before she finished. Twice he had tried to interrupt, but she had shushed him. When she had finished her story, they stopped on the bridge, looking back at the lights of Whitehall and across to the gas lamps casting a golden glow along the Mall. There were too many questions to ask, too much more to talk about. It was dark now and getting chilly.

"Let's go to that pub," he said. He put his arm around her waist and drew her to him as they left the park. He felt her arm around him as they walked through streets churning with commuters heading for the nearby Victoria Station. They went into the first pub they came to.

She unbuttoned her coat, placed it over the back of her chair and smoothed her skirt. She was wearing an office-style suit, he noticed. She must have a job somewhere. He wondered if Halliday had arranged that as well.

He went to the bar. She wanted a large gin and tonic with lots of ice. He asked for half a pint of bitter. When the gin was placed alongside the beer on the counter, the bubbles fizzing up through the ice and a slice of lemon, he changed his mind. He would have a large gin as well, he said. The barman sighed.

They raised their glasses and clinked them.

"I never thought I would see you again," he said.

"You saved my life. That's why I am here," she said.

"I think *you* did that," he said.

"Without that permit I would have been in Sachsenhausen by now – or more likely dead."

"Even so, you were lucky. I am amazed you did it."

"What, kill him?"

"Yes. I mean no. I'm not surprised. You had to. I'm just amazed you managed to get away."

"I worked out that they wouldn't find the body until late in the day, or maybe not until the night. I knew Kitty wouldn't say anything – she would just take the money and run. So I had time."

"And Halliday followed you all the way? I can hardly believe that."

She laughed then, an exhilarating laugh with her head back.

"He told me he had a hunch when he saw me that morning at the Ostbahnhof. He's a crazy man."

"And he introduced you to his people?"

"Yes. I have told my story many times, too many times."

"And now?"

"They offered me a job using my language skills in some research."

"What, secret stuff?"

She nodded. "I said no. I want to be a teacher."

They drank their drinks in silence for a while.

"I'm going back to Berlin tomorrow," he said.

"I know."

"Shall we eat somewhere?"

"That would be nice," she said, and she reached across the table and took his hand, squeezing it hard. Her eyes were on his. She raised her glass, drained her gin, still looking at him. In those eyes he saw two figures in the Tiergarten that night, their urgent bodies colliding and coiling on the damp earth under the trees, hearing only whispered words of love and the quiet conversation of the leaves above them. But it was a lie, he quickly told himself. She was surely using him – and why not? Her body, those whispered words, her urgent gasps as she clawed her nails into his back, they were all part of the unspoken arrangement, were they not? My body and a fleeting moment of passion for a laisser passer, a ticket to freedom, that was the deal, wasn't it? There was nothing cynical about that, it was a question of her survival. After all she had murdered a senior Gestapo to make her escape – what would a tryst in the woods with a British diplomat mean to her when her life was at stake? And for him, what had he found as he held her half naked in his arms on those frozen nights in the Tiergarten? A little solace for a wounded heart, comfort denied him at home, was that it?

She released his hand. She was smiling now. "Let's get another drink," she said. Then he knew it was more, much more.

25

Macrae took the gun case from the cupboard under the stairs. He had pushed it as far back as he could behind the brooms, buckets and mops used by the cleaning lady. It was the one place in the house he knew Primrose would not look.

He took it into the kitchen, blowing dust off the initialled leather case, and undid the buckles on the straps. He placed the rifle on the table, took it out of the oilcloths, drew up a chair and sat down to begin the delicate job of attaching the telescopic sights to the barrel. He had bought those sights from Holland & Holland in London twenty-four years ago. Every sniper on both sides of the war had their own favourite make of sights, and the best were custom-made to conform to the optical measurements of the owner's eyes.

Macrae had gone to Holland & Holland because he knew they made first-class sporting rifles. He reckoned that the gun sights that enabled a stalker to drop a stag in the Scottish Highlands at a range of eight hundred yards would be good enough for the trenches. So it proved.

He paused, hearing a sound somewhere in the house. The fridge was whirring quietly behind him. A door creaked somewhere upstairs. Maybe a window had been left open. He knew there was no one else in the house. Primrose had gone off with the other wives from the embassy to take her seat in the stand for distinguished guests.

The civilian parade of local bands and children from every school in Berlin would begin to file past the reviewing stand at 10 a.m. An hour later, the military march-past would begin and it would last for three hours. The climax would come with a fly-past of every type of military aircraft in the Luftwaffe, and especially the new Me 109 fighter, the aircraft that would streak over the city in tight formation only a few hundred feet from the ground with a thunderous roar.

During this time, Hitler and his senior ministers, Göring, Goebbels, Himmler, Hess and Speer, would not leave the reviewing stand except for brief calls of nature. Their arms would rise and fall in salute to the tributes being paid to the Führer on his fiftieth birthday. Their arms would ache, their smiles would freeze into rictus grins and their ears would be deafened by the clamour. It was going to be a very noisy day on the avenue. The rumble and clatter of military vehicles, the cheers of the crowds, the music of the military bands, the planes overhead – all would create a continuous wall of sound. That is what Macrae was counting on. He could already hear the rising tide of sound from the avenue as people gathered and the bands began to tune their instruments.

He stopped fitting the telescopic sight and listened. It was not the cleaner's day. There was a window banging somewhere upstairs. He was not nervous, just curious. He walked upstairs to make sure. In the drawing room, a small side window had been left unlatched and was swinging slowly in the breeze. He closed it and went to the French windows.

Through the trees he could see crowds milling in their thousands, jostling for position. He could also see the reviewing stand very clearly. A lectern had been set up for the big speech that afternoon. There was a table beside it with water bottles and glasses. But no chairs. The Nazi leadership was never to be seen sitting down in public. That was the rule. But Sir Nevile Henderson would be sitting down with all the other heads of mission. He was probably there somewhere already. He would not want to miss a minute of this.

Macrae looked down at his hands. His knuckles were white. He unclenched his fists. The last meeting with the ambassador had been a shock. Primrose still had not recovered from the news – or forgiven him. Because naturally it was his fault. Worst of all, Henderson actually seemed to enjoy telling him.

It had happened a week after he got back from London. He had been asked to stay behind after another tense staff meeting. The ambassador had remained seated at the conference table and gestured Macrae to do likewise. There were two official white envelopes in front of him. Macrae could see his name typewritten on both. Sir Nevile Henderson came to the point with uncharacteristic speed.

"It has been decided that you have fulfilled your duties here with, how shall I put this, with vigour. It is now time for a new posting. I have here a letter from the War Office in which you will see you have been gazetted as full colonel. Congratulations. Here is a second letter from the Foreign Office in which you are designated as HMG's military attaché in Lourenço Marques."

"Where?"

"Lourenço Marques. Capital of Portuguese East Africa. Pearl of the Indian Ocean. An important listening post, given

German submarine traffic in the Mozambique Channel. SIS has a man there. The Abwehr and the Italians are also pretty thick on the ground."

"I don't understand."

"I think you understand very well, Colonel. You are being transferred. I am sure you will have an interesting time."

"When is this to be effective?"

"Immediately, but we understand you will need a week or two to make your arrangements. Your replacement has been told to be in post at the end of April."

"This is outrageous."

"No more so than your recent conduct. You seem to have forgotten that we are a civilised, Christian nation. Good luck in your new post."

And that is how his career in Berlin had ended. There was no appeal and no point in protest. The letter from the War Office had been signed by Hore-Belisha. When he had got the atlas out that night and showed Primrose where Lourenço Marques was, at the tip of the African continent, she had taken the book and flung it out of the window.

She had shouted at him, screamed and yelled, and finally walked out. She didn't come back that night. He had called Halliday, but there was no reply. He had gone to the Adlon for a few drinks and tried to think clearly. Maybe getting out of Berlin at that moment, the last peaceful springtime in Europe for many a long year, was no bad thing.

Maybe he and Primrose could consider themselves lucky to be able to sit out the coming war in the tropical splendour of Lourenço Marques, wherever that was. Maybe he would ask for a divorce. Maybe he should resign from the army and join Sara in London. Maybe he would ask Sara to come to Portuguese East Africa, because Primrose had made it clear she was not going. What had Sara said? She was going to train as a teacher? Well, there should be plenty of teaching to do at the far end of Africa.

The maybes piled up in an untidy heap on the bar like olive stones. He chewed the thoughts over and spat them out one by one. He finished his drink and swept the maybes out of his mind. He knew what he was going to do. Whatever happened, it would not take him to the Pearl of the Indian Ocean.

He looked at his watch. It was almost ten-thirty. The civilian parades were well under way, but he knew Hitler would not appear until the military march-past began just before eleven. Göring and Goebbels would be vying for the attention of the spectators, each trying to stand slightly in front of the other on the platform as they saluted the parading schoolchildren and workers' organisations. Hitler would bide his time. He was a master showman who chose his entrance with care.

Macrae shook the bullets from the pouch and slid five rounds into the magazine. He would need only one or two at the most. Five rounds was a precaution in case anything went terribly wrong. But nothing would go wrong. He slid the magazine into the rifle, flipped the bolt up and moved it forward, injecting the first round into the firing chamber. The first and only round, he told himself.

The rifle felt better once loaded. It was ready to fulfil the purpose for which it had been designed by an American armourer called James Lee, whose gun was first mass-produced in a north London suburb called Enfield. A strange combination that had given its name to a great infantry weapon.

He took the rifle upstairs, walked into the drawing room and looked out of the French windows. He pushed a window open but did not step onto the balcony. There was just a chance that they would be watching windows, balconies and roofs that provided a good line of sight onto the reviewing stand. Possible but highly unlikely. Heydrich and his Gestapo gang thought they had caught, tortured and killed or imprisoned every dissident in the country, and they were very nearly right.

Placing one foot on the low wooden sill of the window, he raised the gun and looked through the sights. There was a clear view of the lectern. He swung the weapon slightly to one side and saw Göring. The field marshal of the Luftwaffe had recently lost three stone at a health farm in the Swiss Alps but looked as absurd as ever in a light grey uniform that sagged under the weight of rows of medals.

Maybe he could take the field marshal out with a second bullet. No, he told himself, don't be greedy. It would be better if Göring were alive after Hitler had fallen. He would make a power grab using the forces of the Luftwaffe. Goebbels and Himmler would fight back with their own special forces. While the Nazis descended into murderous disarray, the army would move in.

And that was what the plan depended on. The more he thought about it, the more he was sure. The conspirators were still there waiting for the opportunity. The assassination would be their chance. They would arrest the leadership, declare martial law and install an interim military government. The whole Nazi house of cards would come tumbling down once the ace in the pack had been removed. Then there would be a bloody settling of accounts.

He put the gun down and looked at his watch. It was ten fifty. Time for a coffee. His hands were trembling slightly. He placed a finger under his wrist, feeling for the pulse. His resting heart rate was fast at eighty-six a minute. He would still have the coffee. Adrenalin was good. He wasn't nervous. What he was about to do was morally right, an imperative that the gods of any religion would recognise. Macrae was neither religious nor superstitious, but that morning he felt the hand of history on his shoulder.

He swung the rifle up again and focused the sights on the spectators. Through the leaf cover he could see the ambassador wearing his usual red carnation. The rest of the embassy staff were obscured.

He went to the kitchen, put the kettle on and looked at his watch. It was ten fifty-three. Seven minutes to go. The coffee would not cool in time. He would burn his mouth trying to drink it. That would be a distraction. He turned the kettle off and took deep breaths.

Keep calm, he told himself. You will do this. There will be bloody chaos for a day or two. The embassy will sit tight. Primrose might even go to London as she planned the following morning, if the trains were running. He would follow when the fuss had died down. As for Sir Nevile Henderson and the prime minister – well, it didn't matter what they thought. They could go to hell.

He walked back up the stairs. There was a groundswell of expectant cheering outside. He swung the rifle up. There was no sign of the Führer. Any minute now. The noise became a roar, a wave of sound that broke over the centre of the city and swept out to the suburbs. The first of the tanks appeared, moving quite swiftly down the avenue, and began rolling towards the reviewing stand; brand new Panzer III tanks, better than anything in the British army.

Macrae stepped onto the balcony and raised his rifle. The noise became a crescendo as Hitler walked onto the reviewing stand and took his position at the lectern. He was wearing his usual army uniform with the peaked cap and Iron Cross 2nd Class. He raised his arm in greeting to the crowds lining the avenue.

The first tanks moved slowly past the stand, while behind lay a long ribbon of camouflaged armour and transport vehicles stretching into the outer suburbs. The intention was as clear as the message it conveyed. This was Hitler's birthday present to himself: an army that he, the Führer of the Third Reich, had forged out of the chaos of the Weimar Republic. It was an army that no one should doubt he intended to use.

Macrae tucked the butt of the rifle into his shoulder, leaning against the door jamb, and peered through the sights. He had Hitler in plain view now, his head and shoulders neatly bisected by the cross hairs. The Führer's stance on the platform meant he was presenting the rear and right side of his body to the rifle. Macrae shifted slightly, focusing the cross hairs on a point just behind Hitler's right ear.

A clean shot would spatter blood and brain over the lectern. Hitler would slump sideways, arms flailing instinctively for the lectern, and then fall to the floor. Death would be instant.

Macrae began to squeeze the trigger slowly, remembering the lesson that was drummed into every sniper: *Rush your shot and lose your target*. He felt the trigger stiffening against his forefinger. He shifted the aim slightly as Hitler moved a pace sideways, waving his arms, working himself into the paroxysm of oratorical triumphalism that characterised all his speeches.

The scream, the blow on his head and the whip-crack of the rifle shot came together with such force and shock that at first he thought he had somehow fallen from the balcony.

He was on his knees, the gun still in his hands, desperately scrambling to his feet. She was screaming obscenities at him. Primrose. She was standing over him, her red-lipsticked mouth opening like a bleeding wound, shouting terrible words he could not understand. She was kicking him, lashing out with her feet so furiously that her shoes flew off and over the balcony. She was swinging wild punches that pounded on his chest as he tried to get up. He felt dizzy and sick as he forced himself up, reached for the rifle and swung the butt into her face, hearing the thud as it connected.

She fell back and he saw the spurt of blood from her mouth. She was lying there, her hands reaching for her mouth, dabbing at the blood, looking at it and still shouting at him. Had he fired the shot? He pulled back the bolt and a spent cartridge case flew out.

He stepped back onto the balcony, raised the rifle and looked through the sights. Hitler was still there on the reviewing stand, his right arm rising and falling. The shot had gone wide or high. No one had heard it. Behind him, Primrose was clambering to her feet, blood on her dress and face. He swung round and pointed the rifle at her.

It would be easy. An accident while he was cleaning the weapon. No one had heard the first shot; why should anyone hear the second? She had stopped screaming. She was talking quickly, taking huge deep breaths. He had been the only one missing at the parade. People had asked where he was. Then she had suddenly realised why. She had known what he planned to do. And she had come back to stop him, stop an act of insanity that would have had them both hanging from hooks in a Gestapo cellar, their lives slowly tortured out of them with cattle prods.

"They would have killed us all, don't you see? Every man, woman and child in the embassy."

Fury robbed him of words. For a fraction of a moment, he wanted to tear her dress off and throw her body over the balcony. Blood was still coming from her mouth. She began to cry, sobbing violently. She walked unsteadily backwards, still looking at him, and collapsed on a sofa. He threw the rifle to one side and sat beside her, his arm around her, holding her tightly, seeing the blood seep into his shirt and trousers.

26

Hitler's birthday parade and the speech he made that afternoon dominated the British papers the next day. The coverage led on the awesome display of firepower and new weaponry on show. There were colourful sidebar stories about the Nazi leadership gathered behind the Führer on the reviewing stand, each trying to outdo each other with medals, ribbons and other insignia.

There were also lengthy analyses of Hitler's speech, which amounted to a brutal warning to the Western powers – meaning Britain, France and Holland – not to meddle in eastern Europe. Newsreels of the display that afternoon played in cinemas around the world, to emphasise the message.

Sara Sternschein cut out every story in *The Times* about the events in Germany and pasted them into a scrapbook, which she kept under her bed in her lodgings in a London suburb. She read the paper from cover to cover every day. It was part of her plan to understand the country that had offered her refuge, and to become English. One day she would show her son or daughter, whichever the baby was to be, the cowardice and complacency of civilised nations like Britain when faced with such barbarism.

The Times, which had been her guide and mentor since arriving in London four months earlier, almost seemed to sanction the Nazi land grab in Europe. Again and again, the leading articles in that newspaper argued that Hitler was no more than a nationalist leader with a legitimate desire to return Germany to its former status as a major power in central Europe. As for the Jews, *The Times*, like every other paper in Britain, scarcely mentioned their plight.

She didn't mind; she had cause to be very grateful. When the long conversations in that room had ended and she had told them everything about the Salon and its customers, they had asked her what she wanted to do. She had said she would like to train as a teacher.

They suggested that she might work in a unit translating German documents and tape recordings of broadcasts. She thanked them but declined. Her mind was made up. She wanted to be a teacher, to make a life and a contribution to the country that had saved her life.

It was Halliday, flitting in and out of London from Berlin, who had helped her. He was always there when she needed him. It seemed that he had never stopped following her from that time he saw her at the Ostbahnhof.

He told her he had been to school in a leafy suburb of London, a famous place that had once produced the well-known writer P. G. Wodehouse. He had made enquiries and there was a position for an assistant helping the modern languages teacher. She would be required to hold conversational classes in German with the boys and help the marking of written work. He would find her a room in the area, he said; it was not far from central London.

She had told him then what she should have told him

before. She would need more than one room. He had not understood at first, and then looked at her and became embarrassed. When, he had asked.

"I am due in five months," she said.

She saw that he was trying to work it out. She could tell him the exact date. It was near midnight in the Tiergarten two weeks before Christmas. They had not even taken their clothes off, not properly anyway. Brandy and the warmth of lust had prompted what she thought would be a last meeting on a freezing night in the Tiergarten. Macrae had given her a Christmas present that night – the amethyst necklace. She had hardly had time to look at it before they parted but now she wore it all the time, the violet translucent stones a reminder of a time and place she could not forget.

It was at school one morning in the tea break that her usual cover-to-cover reading of *The Times* took her to a page listing the service appointments. This was tucked away behind the obituaries and before the weather news. The words made her sit back and grasp her cup of milky tea more tightly. Under "Recent Appointments" she read:

> *Colonel Noel Macrae has been appointed Defence Attaché representing His Majesty's Government in Portuguese East Africa. Colonel and Mrs Macrae will take up their appointment in Lourenço Marques with immediate effect.*

She looked out of the window of the common room. Halliday was walking across the gravelled car park, the same shambolic figure who had walked into her life in the station café that afternoon before Christmas.

In the months since, he had become a friend, the only friend she had in London really. The other teachers at the school were nice, kind people, but they led quiet family lives in small houses with washing lines in the back garden, a couple of kids and a dog or a cat. On Fridays they would invite each other to dinner parties and on Sundays there would be a family roast, with uncles and aunts invited for company. A young Jewish refugee from Nazi Germany did not fit into this suburban world.

She didn't mind. Halliday came to Dulwich on the train almost every week "just to make sure you're not missing Berlin", which was his little joke. Strangely, she did miss Berlin. The excitement, the danger, the sense of a whole continent breaking up like an ice floe beneath her feet – these were unforgettable moments that had turned every minute of life into a razor-sharp memory.

At their weekly suppers at a local pub she would bombard him with questions. First and always there was Joseph. Each time the answer was the same. Her twin was almost certainly dead. There was no definite information, but they would have killed him after her escape. She accepted that truth and was glad, because she instinctively knew now that it was true. His suffering was over.

She learnt that no mention had ever been made of Bonner's murder. The Gestapo had removed all records of his service and told enquiring callers that he had gone abroad for health reasons. Everyone who worked in the Salon, including the cleaners and the kitchen staff, had been arrested and sent to the camps. Heydrich had ordered the Salon to be reopened and the place was back in business with new girls and a new madam. Kitty Schmidt had vanished and was rumoured to have gone to Portugal.

She had not asked him about Macrae, nor told him of their nights in the Tiergarten. Halliday probably knew anyway.

He seemed to know everything. She thought one day he might come back, the man who had given her not just his love, but her life.

Halliday had almost reached the front door and waved to her through the window. She was crying now and waved back through her tears. She was going to have a boy, she was sure of that, a child made of love, close to the midnight hour, in Berlin.

Historical Note

This book is a work of fiction based closely on the events in Berlin during the crucial months of 1938–39. Several of the characters who shaped those events appear in the narrative very much as they did in history. After their stories end in this novel, I think it only fair to let the reader know what happened to them in real life. I should add that as I have researched that period in Berlin carefully, my fictional characters very much reflect the lives of those who lived and died in that traumatic time.

Reinhard Heydrich was badly wounded in an assassination attempt in Prague on 27 May 1942 and died of his wounds a week later. He was given a state funeral in Berlin. Hitler ordered reprisals for the killing. The entire population of the village of Lidice, which was close to the scene of the assassination attempt, was massacred by SS troops or murdered later in concentration camps. Approximately eight hundred men, women and children died in the atrocity. Many thousands more civilians in the area were killed in follow-up operations by SS death squads.

Sir Nevile Henderson, the British ambassador in Berlin, returned to England at the outbreak of war in 1939. His request for a further diplomatic posting was turned down. He wrote a book entitled *Failure of a Mission* and died of cancer in 1942, aged sixty.

Sir Neville Chamberlain resigned as prime minister in May 1940, to be replaced by Winston Churchill. He died of cancer in November that year.

Sir Stewart Menzies, who was chief of the British Secret Intelligence Service at the time of these events, remained as Winston Churchill's spymaster during World War Two. He retired in 1952 and died in 1968.

Lord Hore-Belisha, who was secretary of state for war from 1937 to 1940, refused further office after being sacked by Neville Chamberlain. He died in 1957.

Kitty Schmidt, the madam of the Salon, survived the war and died in Germany in 1954.

William L. Shirer wrote an award-winning account of the Nazi period, *The Rise and Fall of the Third Reich*, and became a well-known author and broadcast journalist after the war. He died in 1993.

Colonel (later General) Mason-Macfarlane was the British military attaché in Berlin from 1938 to 1939, and he did indeed plan the assassination of Hitler from the balcony of his apartment. In March 1939 he put the plan to Neville Chamberlain's government in London, where it was turned down after consideration at a senior level. Shortly afterwards Mason-Macfarlane was ordered back from Berlin and "promoted" to brigadier at a Royal Artillery base. He spent the war as Governor of Gibraltar and to the surprise of his friends won a Labour seat in the general election in 1945. He died in 1953 aged sixty-three.

Acknowledgements

There is a vast library of works covering the drift to war in the 1930s and the failure of the Western democracies to appreciate the true nature of Hitler's Third Reich. I list only those that were especially helpful to me: *Failure of a Mission* by Sir Nevile Henderson (Hodder and Stoughton, 1940); *The Chamberlain Cabinet* by Ian Colvin (Gollancz, 1971); *Hitler*, vols I and II, by Ian Kershaw (Penguin Press, 2000); *The Third Reich in Power* by Richard J. Evans (Penguin, 2006); *This is Berlin* by William L. Shirer (Hutchinson, 1999); *Hitler* by Norman Stone (Hodder and Stoughton, 1980); *Evil Genius: The Story of Joseph Goebbels* by Erich Ebermayer and Hans-Otto Meissner (Allan Wingate, 1953); *The Drift to War* by Richard Lamb (W. H. Allen, 1989); *The Nemesis of Power* by Sir John Wheeler-Bennett (Palgrave, 2005); *A Social History of the Third Reich* by Richard Grunberger (Weidenfeld and Nicolson, 1971); *Hitler's Hangman* by Robert Gerwarth (Yale, 2011); *The History of the German Resistance 1933–45* by Peter Hoffmann, translated by Richard Barry (MIT Press, 1979); *The Gestapo: Power and Terror in the Third Reich* by Carsten Dams and Michael Stolle, translated by Charlotte Ryland (Oxford University Press, 2014).

I wish to thank first my publishers, Thomas Dunne in the US and Peter Mayer in the UK, for their support and faith in this book. In New York, Peter Joseph proved a fine editor and ally, as did Andrew Lockett in London. In New York I also benefited from the forensic attention to the text of Melanie Fried. In Berlin, I was greatly helped by the research into the geography of the city and the Mecklenburg district of Janet Anderson and Oliver Briese. Gavin Stamp was kind enough to unearth maps from the 1938 edition of Baedeker's guide to Berlin. My brother, Stephen MacManus, helped find long-out-of-print books relating to the period in the London Library. My sister-in-law, Susanne MacManus, who was born and raised in Vienna, helped me understand what that city looked like in 1938.

To Mrs Deborah Keegan I owe thanks for helping me achieve some sort of balance between being an author and a part-time media executive. I am also grateful, as ever, to Sophie Hicks, my then agent, for steering this book into print, and to Mrs Kate Kee for her invaluable comments on the text.